R0061571949

2/2012

D0564261

SWITCHBLADE

switch·blade (swĭch′blād′) n.
*a different slice of hardboiled fiction where the dreamers and the schemers, the dispossessed
and the damned, and the hobos and the rebels tango at the edge of society.*

THE JOOK
GARY PHILLIPS

I-5: A NOVEL OF CRIME, TRANSPORT, AND SEX
SUMMER BRENNER

PIKE
BENJAMIN WHITMER

THE CHIEU HOI SALOON
MICHAEL HARRIS

THE WRONG THING
BARRY GRAHAM

SEND MY LOVE AND A MOLOTOV COCKTAIL!
STORIES OF CRIME, LOVE AND REBELLION
EDITED BY GARY PHILLIPS AND ANDREA GIBBONS

PRUDENCE COULDN'T SWIM
JAMES KILGORE

NEARLY NOWHERE
SUMMER BRENNER

PALM BEACH COUNTY
LIBRARY SYSTEM
3650 Summit Boulevard
West Palm Beach, FL 33406-4198

SEND MY LOVE AND A MOLOTOV COCKTAIL!

STORIES OF CRIME, LOVE AND REBELLION

FEATURING STORIES BY:
KIM STANLEY ROBINSON
PACO IGNACIO TAIBO II
MICHAEL MOORCOCK
LUIS RODRIGUEZ
SARA PARETSKY
AND OTHERS

EDITED BY GARY PHILLIPS
AND ANDREA GIBBONS

"Introduction" copyright © 2011 by Gary Phillips and Andrea Gibbons. "Bizco's Memories" copyright © 2011 by Paco Ignacio Taibo II, English translation copyright © 2011 by Andrea Gibbons. "Don't Ask, Don't Tell" and "Darkness Drops" copyright © 2011 by Larry Fondation. "Nickels and Dimes" copyright © 2011 by S John Daniels. "The El Rey Bar" copyright © by Andrea Gibbons. "Poster Child" copyright © 2011 by Sara Paretsky. "The Lunatics" copyright © 2011 by Kim Stanley Robinson. "Murder . . . Then and Now" copyright © 2011 by Penny Mickelbury. "Piece Work" copyright © by Kenneth Wishnia. "Gold Diggers of 1977 (Ten Claims that Won Our Hearts)" was first published by Virgin Books, 1980, as *The Great Rock 'n' Roll Swindle*, and was revised in 1989 © 1989 by Michael & Linda Moorcock. "Cincinnati Lou" copyright © 2011 by Benjamin Whitmer. "Berlin: Two Days in June" copyright © 2011 by Rick Dakan. "Orange Alert" copyright © 2011 by Summer Brenner. "Masai's Back in Town" copyright © 2011 by Gary Phillips. "I Love Paree" originally published in *Asimov's*, December 2000, copyright © 2011 by Cory Doctorow and Michael Skeet. "A Good Start" copyright © 2011 by Barry Graham. "One Dark Berkeley Night" copyright © 2011 by Tim Wohlforth. "Look Both Ways" copyright © 2011 by Luis Rodriguez.

This edition © 2011 PM Press

Published by:
PM Press
PO Box 23912
Oakland, CA 94623
www.pmpress.org

Cover designed by Brian Bowes
Interior design by Courtney Utt/briandesign

ISBN: 978-1-60486-096-2
Library of Congress Control Number: 2010916479
10 9 8 7 6 5 4 3 2 1

Printed in the USA on recycled paper, by the Employee Owners of Thomson-Shore in Dexter, Michigan.
www.thomsonshore.com

ACKNOWLEDGMENTS

A big thanks to all of the authors who submitted their work for this collection, and PM Press for making it possible. Thanks also to Allan Kausch, David Cooper, and Shael Love for their help with "Gold Diggers of 1977 (Ten Claims that Won Our Hearts)" by Michael Moorcock, and Gregory Nipper for his splendid copyediting.

Contents

Introduction

Get your grind on: From the streets of Athens to Watts '65; the Velvet Revolution; sit-in strikes in Flint, Chicago and beyond; the MPLA taking Luanda to the attack on the barracks at Moncada; the Bolsheviks; the Poll Tax Revolt; Stonewall; the Mothers of the Disappeared; the Black Panthers; the Gray Panthers; the Yippies and on and on . . . the fight for a better world has involved various ways to challenge the status quo and change up the relationships of power.

The foregoing was the opening grabber in the solicitation we sent to our potential contributors concerning the anthology you now hold in your hand. It's a bit fuzzy today as to the exact origins of *Send My Love and a Molotov Cocktail!* though the title came from a punk song by the UK band The Flys that PM Press's publisher Ramsey Kanaan suggested. We knew we wanted an eclectic mix of contributors to this collection, and the two of us are quite pleased with the results we believe you'll enjoy in this edition. Most of the pieces are original. A few are out of print or being made available for the first time in a U.S. publication.

We have tales set in the past (or where the past haunts the present), to stories ranging from the tumult of now to futures where uncertainty and the iron heel reign. Herein you'll find renditions of lust and ideals, avarice and altruism, ruthlessness and hope, the left and the right and points in between, the fantastic and the crushing banality of bureaucracies. Yet shot through all of the stories, stories where politics big and personal play a role, is the contradictory and often surprisingly resilient nature of the human animal.

Certainly one of the aspects that made putting this collection together so cool for us as editors and contributors was our respective backgrounds in activism and community organizing. The lessons we took away from those experiences were not only about the need for a incisive power analysis and being aware that goals and objectives have to be constantly readjusted, but just how indomitable are the spirits of everyday working people, be they dealing with faceless slumlords, police abuse, rights on the shop floor or simply banding together to get a stop light erected at a street corner for their kids.

Stuart Hanlon, one of the attorneys who helped overturn the framed-up conviction the FBI orchestrated against former Black Panther leader Elmer Geronimo Ji Jaga Pratt, stated in regards to the $4 million or so in damages his client and friend received post his release, "If you didn't have anything or want anything, they couldn't take anything from you." But that was of course only about material things. As a freedom fighter, the late Ji Jaga long ago learned in all those years on the streets and in prison to keep going forward, to not let the system beat you down. The interesting characters you'll find in these pages are in some respects in the mold of what Ji Jaga, Septima Clark, Emma Goldman and so many others stood for in their pursuit of certain freedoms and truths—maybe not on a world-shattering scale, but for stakes that meant something to them . . . and us. Mind you, some of the other folks you'll encounter in these pages you wouldn't want to meet in a well-lighted alley under any circumstances.

We know though you'll find the stories in this collection entertaining, insightful and damn good reads.

The struggle, as always, continues.

Gary Phillips & Andrea Gibbons

Bizco's Memories[1]

Paco Ignacio Taibo II

Bizco Padilla became a soccer player in prison, so he saw the game in a unique fashion, like a war where anything went. Nothing could've been further from the supposedly British spirit of honorable competition or the prescribed Olympic ethos. His was a warlike soccer, country or death, the kind from which no one was exempted: not mothers, refs, busybodies, spectators nor the cities, nations, or races involved.

We got into the habit of watching the Pumas' games every Sunday on TV. We were the ideal companions: me because I had a thirty-five-inch color television inherited from a stale marriage, and him because he acted as commentator for the match, filling in for the sound that had long ago died in the appliance and that I had never bothered getting fixed.

El Bizco would arrive half an hour before the match to wake me up. Without much consideration he'd kick out my casual ladyfriend from Saturday night's sad fever and start to smoke, pacing around the bedroom while we talked politics.

Once the game started, his squinty eyes would fixate on the TV and the ashes from his little cigar would start to fall all over the place, most substantially around the curve of the kitchen stool he sat on.

Bizco's rules did not include off-sides, a pansy charge by the refs to disallow goals and make themselves hated. He considered infantile any punishment that didn't involve the guilty party eating dirt and getting trampled on. He permitted pulling the goalkeeper's pants down as the goalkeeper jumped up, and said that hand balls were only a foul if they saw you. For a good game there had to be at least

---

1 *Bizco* here is being used as a nickname; it means cross-eyed in Spanish. Translated by Andrea Gibbons.

11

two or three beatings and the red liquid had to flow. A broken leg and bleeding from the nose seemed to fall within the parameters of what he considered normal.

Bizco possessed a clairvoyant sense of the players' psychology. After having seen them touch the ball three times he could anticipate both their movements and their motivations. Bizco knew a lot about egos, manias, and displays of manliness. Above all, he knew a lot about fears.

"Now López is going to make a run along the edge of the field, looking to get behind Guadalajara's defense."

"Look at that prick, complaining for nothing. The guy barely pushed him! If he doesn't like it he can go home, stupid-ass."

Curiously our dominical meetings were teetotal. Prison had made Bizco a ferocious militant for Alcoholics Anonymous. My nonexistent author royalties at the time had condemned me to lemonade with a little sugar. Coffee sometimes—when the Pumas trashed the other team.

We had promised ourselves that when our economic situation improved we would go to the stadium instead of this ritual gathering in front of a mute TV. Bizco agreed to it then, even knowing that part of the enchantment was in the remoteness, the distance, the world that remained outside. The sensation of being prisoner that protected him.

Bizco was so cross-eyed that it was the same to him whether he looked at you face-to-face or sideways, and his scar filled you with fear, crossing his right cheek from his ear to his lip. Just another of the footprints left by prison. They'd thrown him in the joint at the end of the '60s, almost into '70, the last day of the year. All because when he was seventeen he was a messenger for a guerilla force that never took action, and that had been so heavily infiltrated it was the police making decisions on the national committee by a simple majority. Having committed no crime didn't save him from two weeks of torture and a month of preventative imprisonment that was so bad it would've been better if it had ceased to exist in his memories. Later he was sent to Oblatos prison in Jalisco, in those days the highest-security prison the *federales* had.

That's where he became a great soccer player, not through kicking around a ball in the *barrio* or on interscholastic teams. It never had anything to do with sport: just the fucked-up soccer of prison. Gangbangers from *crujía siete*, rapists, sexual predators, and parricides all against the "P," what they called the political prisoners. Guards against inmates. An average of seven wounded, and two or three goals by Bizco per game.

"A header, forcing the goalkeeper to dive to the ground so there's no chance he'll get the rebound."

And then to celebrate you get close to the fallen goalkeeper, spit on him, and say:

"I fucked you, bro."

That's how it went until things began to get bad. Bizco wasn't used to talking about that either. He wasn't used to talking about a lot of things, like where he was born for instance. He didn't talk about his personal life. From what I remember he didn't have any family. To the question of where he was living he would answer with nonspecifics.

"Over there Fierro, in an apartment like a closet."

And then he'd return to the central theme: "Kill him already, asshole, what do you have elbows for? You see that, Fierro? That kid'll go far, he's slick, a true athlete."

One Sunday he disappeared. When I had just started to get worried, he reappeared the next, and from the doorway he told me in a whisper: "If I tell you, you will probably write it down, and if you write it down, then probably I will stop seeing it at night."

It seemed to be the prologue to everything, to the long-hoped-for history surging from the past. I asked him: "Do you have nightmares, Bizco?"

"I have everything," he said, sitting in front of the television that he hurried me to turn on.

As the Pumas came out onto the field in their gala uniforms, the gold and the black, in the less-than-full stands the capricious fans carried off half a wave.

"Who knows why the authorities wanted to screw us and told the director to throw us in with the common population. In the "P" zone we were maybe 150 political prisoners, and there were six thousand inmates. There wasn't a day or a night that they didn't fuck with us.

13

They took hold of a dude from Saltillo and they raped him in the middle of the yard, forced us to watch with their knives in their hands.

"Pure law of the jungle. Punishments at all hours, months without letters, not even permission to go to the library, no visits, cells turned upside down, regular beatings, torture, and so we went with no sleep, our balls shriveled up from living with pure fear. The one who ran the whole operation and passed his time inventing ways to fuck us was ·a real skinny dude, Flaco, who was in the tank for having killed his mother to steal from her. He's the one who got the green light from the director and started arranging things here and there, handing out money and permissions and packets and favors, and they let him traffic coke and marijuana."

"And then?"

"We organized. We started a mutiny and took over the guardroom. The way things were it was better to die of a bullet than die of fear. The whole of the inside perimeter was in our hands. We got hold of like fifteen shotguns. The rebellion lasted three days until we negotiated with the *federales.*"

Another silence, the Pumas had scored an early goal and Bizco had let it pass unnoticed.

"And then?"

"Well, it was a question of pounding some fear into the bodies of those assholes, but we couldn't start killing all of them because that wouldn't have put an end to it, one of them dead and they'd just be back for revenge . . . And so we organized a football game. Just us, political prisoners against political prisoners, without a fucking ref, with only one goal, just kicking the ball around, all 150 of us, even the ones who didn't know how to play. And we were playing it hard for half an hour there in the main yard with all the rest of the inmates watching. I scored a goal."

"With your head?"

"How could I? The only head that counted was Flaco's, that's what we were using for a ball, Fierro."

That's where he left it. Then he returned to narrating the Pumas game with the same flavor as always.

Don't Ask, Don't Tell

Larry Fondation

We sit in a café.
   The coffee is strong.
   You are unarmed.
   The wind blows hard and the waiter closes the door.
   "Hercules," you say.
   I raise my eyebrows, silent.
   You understand me.
   "The wind is strong, the waiter is stronger," you say.
   I understand you.
   "I must," you say.
   "I know," I say.
   "Do you?" she asks.
   I try to hide that her remark has hurt me.
   She starts to speak again.
   I put my finger to my lips.
   Unmistaken, she draws her body across the table, and—unveiled—she kisses my lips.
   Sand straddles our table. The waiter was not quick enough.
   I return her kiss.
   She leaves and I order another coffee. I linger a while and I read a thick book by Felipe Fernández-Armesto, a history of the world. Night crashes quickly, crescendos to darkness, like the clap and bang of a falling bomb. I return to my barracks.
   The Wagner morning comes suddenly. Neither night nor day can last. Despite the dust, I can see clearly from the compound window. In the mile or so that separates us, the uprooted air lifts matter, dark and real, dead and alive, heavenward like the Ascension. The dawn is punctuated. I make the sign of the cross and I speak aloud in Latin:

"In nomine Patris, et Filii, et Spiritus Sancti." I fall silent as the base alarm sounds full alert. I fall to my knees. I rise again within seconds as I am called, with my company, to the scene.

Nickels and Dimes

John A Imani

"Fuck it. I ain't been arrested lately."

UCLA—May 11, 1972

It was a beautiful day that no one noticed. Least of all me.

The knot in my midsection was churning. Burning. Bubbling. Bursting. Turning itself inside-over like a pack of sharks threshing and slashing their way through what used to be calm shallow waters now chummed and become bleeding foam. But, as I stood there watching, the bloodletting going on inside me wasn't because of the impending menace of the row after row of armed and armored cops heading towards them.

The pigs were John Wayneing their way slowly—sashaying down Main Street at High Noon in their minds—savoring their own swagger, licking their own (pork)chops, greedily but patiently anticipating the thuds of their truncheons, the slash, the crash, the crush of flesh, skull and bones. The "bad guys," a pack of tied-dyed long hairs, sat grouped about "King Bruin" himself, the latest and perhaps star of UCLA's high-flying perennial National Championship basketball teams, all yelling today's favored slogan, "Fuck Chuck." They were camp squatted sitting in the street fifty feet to the left of me right in front of the school's administration building.

Inside the chancellor, Charles Young of "Fuck Chuck" fame, surrounded by and sheltered with a beefed-up security, peeped out a second-level window to watch the carnage he'd ordered up unfold. The front line of the cops was another fifty yards beyond these student "leaders." Stretching to my right—looking like lambs looking for Jesus—sat the rest of the crowd of demonstrators, perhaps two hundred weak. It was gonna be the usual pig-fest with a few more

17

busted hippy heads, a few more notches carved into nightsticks well worn. And that bothered me. But that wasn't what was bothering me. Not at all.

And it wasn't from any sense of outrage at the outrageous continuously recurring nightmares such as the mining of Haiphong Harbor, the by-now daily "incidental" or "accidental" incursions into Laos, the carpet bombings in Cambodia, the multiple My Lai–type massacres in Vietnam. Or even at the war in Southeast Asia as a whole. Or even at war itself in general. And what was eating me alive from inside out wasn't twenty-four years of being black in America, fifteen years of which having grown up a Nigger in the South, sired up out of the loins of Nigger ancestors who with their present-day Nigger descendents had totaled up some 246 years of human bondage in chattel slavery followed by 107 years of third-class/third-rate citizenship all the way to this very fucking day. Eight years ago, Bob Dylan had electrified our movement and set it to verse singing "The Times They Are A-Changin'" but all about me, all around me, as far as I could see and all that I could see was nothing but the "same ole, same ole": Niggahs takin' a foot up they ass. Yeah, that pissed me off. That pissed me off big time and had been pissing me off for a long long time. But today, and for a while now it seems, that wasn't what had me pissed.

～

And, as an aside, naw . . . it wasn't from burning the candle at both ends and putting the platinum-white hot jet of a blowtorch to its middle. Wasn't from the women I was using who used me. Fair exchange ain't no robbery. And, naw, it wasn't from doing dope, lots of dope, as I was selling more. With a positive cash flow being *de riguer*, as real Niggahs don't get to deficit spend, a steady flow of five- and ten-dollar bags, "nickels" and "dimes," flew out of my hands more than compensating—economically that is—for the masses of the dopes that I imbibed, that I smoked, that I snorted, that I shot . . . I was teetering . . . teetering on the very verge of slip-sliding onto the rain-slicked highway lanes of an ever-tightening spiral that pointed only one way. Down.

But before a dope fiend can reach the bottom-level of his fiendishness he has first to run out of dough; but the hippies and the hipsters, the flower-children and the militants, I sold my dope to keep my coffers topped. They visited so often that it got around that it was my crib was what was meant when someone made mention of going to cop at the five-and-dime store. A dime was three fingers-full of a wax paper sandwich bag of unspectacular Mexican weed. A nickel less than half that. Rule of thumb: rule of thumb. Occasionally, the spectaculars did come in: Acapulco gold, Panamanian red, the lush green leaves of Oaxacan or the smoky deeply satisfying buds of Michoacán and the ante went up or the fingers went down. Either way the monies came and continued to come. But now even the dough provided no salve. How much healing can be bought and lumped-smeared across a gaping festering gash? How much good could it do?

That knot in my stomach—doubling me over as if in the midst of a thousand story elevator free-fall—wasn't from anything. Or anybody. Or any reason at all. It was from nothing. Nothing. Nothingness. Nihilism. Negativity. A wide open wound had acid-burned its way into and through the lining of my guts. I was burnt out, spent out, used up, about to give up. So . . . "*Fuck it. I ain't been arrested lately.*"

Twenty-five yards from the students the slowly advancing cops presented their arms, raising their truncheons and grasping them in both haunches of their pig-feet hands in a "ready-to-chuck" position across their chests. Just behind them a big black pigsty of a bus with windows barred and blackened. I looked at the star athlete and saw his minions leaned in and milling about him. Saw them looking nervously to him. Saw him looking nervously at the oncoming slow dark-blue tide. Saw two minutes into the future and saw the same damn thing I had seen two days past: they were gonna run.

The words of the great Rahid rang out their echoes in the caverns of my mind: "Resistance *must* be given whenever the state attacks us. Resist! 'Resist!' as Bunchy Carter said, 'Even if all you can do is spit.' Comrades, listen up . . . If the state intimidates the revolution with just the threat of its violence then the revolution is dead; if, however, the state does not intimidate us even with its use of its unmatched violence then the revolution, dear Comrades, emerges stronger than it was before the battle it has just lost."

I looked at them . . . and they were gonna run. They were gonna get up and give up, slinking back like a pack of Pomeranians, whose high-pitched snappy yaps immediately morph themselves into a stirred and mixed-up mélange of whined whimpers and hapless yelps with but the first throaty growl of the irritated Big Dog. *"They gon' run. Yeah . . . them m'f'ers gon' run like dogs. Jis' liken two days ago they ran scatterin', whoopin' and yelpin' they way down Wilshire Bl from in front of tha Federal Building . . .*

Them m'f'ers gon' run."

Yeah, I wanted them to get hit. I wanted them to get hit. I wanted them to really get a taste of what it was like. A taste. A taste of what it was like to run up against the cops, these same cops, who Niggahs in South Central—and ghettoes around the world—faced off with every day. *"Fake playin'-at-revolution-wannabes."* Hippies. Hippies with leather headbands around their noodles protecting such enlightened thoughts as the idea that not taking regular baths was one of the forks along the garden road leading to a purification of one's soul. *"Or some silly-assed shit like that."* Hippies. Raising Cain on campus until summer break came and they cut their hair, jumped on planes and became white again. Hippies. The son of Doctor such and such or Attorney so and so. One of them pretend-to-be hippies, who bought plenty of dope from me, was the son of a Washington big-wig privy to one of the President's ears.

Another's father, I knew, did physics at Lawrence Livermore where plutonium triggers for thermonuclear weapons were designed, tested and refined. Many of them knew—much better than I can tell you, pal—the obvious and the subtle, the prima facie and the idiosyncratic, the degrees of separation and interconnections . . . the webs by which their parents and their fore-parents—and themselves in their later years—were wedded to the very system, making them part of its fabric, that they purported to attack. And better than ninety percent of them, to this day, not knowing that less than half a mile and three years away, through a series of—on the surface, only vaguely linked—yet underneath tightly interwoven and interconnected events—Panthers Bunchy Carter and John Huggins had been killed for their and their fathers' and their father's fathers' sins. It was a web woven of so many degrees of closely connected separations that when it unraveled it would have to unravel in a rage and a vengeance. And now, this vengeance was to be mine.

The pigs were close now. And I saw some students starting to edge their weight back on the hinds of their legs and their butts. The next thing would be for them to turn tail. "*Naw . . . fuck, naw . . .*" Amidst and through the tie-dies, fades and pastels of the rag-tag oleo of hippies, flower children and revolutionary-wannabes I strode towards the line of cops. I saw a pig point his paw at me as I sat down at the front of the line, arms folded rested as if a strange sensation of long-missing satisfaction was washing over me. From ten yards away the cops suddenly broke from their slow advance into an out-and-out charge.

As I was hustled roughly onto the bus, I turned against the cops who were holding me against my will and saw and heard the clash and smash of blows, the crush and crunch of dirty-blonde long-haired skulls now matting themselves into clumps of strands with the red red flow of the streamings of blood. Curious. I thought I caught a glimpse of one figure standing erect amongst the huddled and hunkering-down mass as the maze of swine—as if a plague of man-sized locusts—swept in on them.

M'f'ers, thank god, had been so anxious to get my high-yellow "Black-assed-coming-to-the-front-and-sitting-down-smart-assed-Nigger-m'f'ing"-self that two of them, one on each arm, had bodily lifted me as they snatched my 135 lb. (soaking wet) wanna-be-soldier-in-the-people's-army-dope-dealing-and-dope-using-ass from off the pavement of Ackerman Way that they forgot something. My legs touched down with my feet hitting the ground in a scrape. I don't know if at the pig-sty academy they had practiced "Two-man Body Carrying" or what but I swear I could feel a breeze rushing past my face as they hustled me towards and onto the bus. In a last heave they landed me face first into and onto the bus's steps. That was to be the last brush of fresh air that I had for three days. Literally. Meanwhile the pigs were laying into and laying it onto the ones who were either inspired to stand their ground by my walking to the front or were too late to run away as the riot squad's saunter had hastened into a stampede with their blows meshing blood with blonde. I almost felt sorry for the m'f'ers.

The star athlete was second or third on the bus with his captors prizing and showing him off to the others pigs who paused just for the moment, but only for a moment to savor their companions' capture. Then they went back to cracking heads. They had cuffed the star athlete and then shoved him onto the bus. Again, they made a mistake. Fifty others were soon on the bus handcuffed from behind—some so tightly that their wrists began to change color and swell—then they were shoved onto the bus-cum-paddy wagon. Each of the prisoners, almost to a (wo)man when she or he alight from the vehicle's stairs and found a seat gave a bit of bravado in a yelled curse at the cops that failed to penetrate plate glass windows.

After that, it got quieter than a m'f'er on that bus.

SNAP! went something and I turned and saw the star athlete had broken the strap that linked the hard plastic wrist-cuffs. An awed HUSH . . . that for a moment accompanied then quickly transformed itself into a CHEER! He must have thought he was back in Pauley Pavilion for he gave a fist pump in response to their dotes. The cops had been so busy "shining and showing off for the white folks" (themselves) that they had cuffed him in front and with the wrists and strength of a seven footer he had, with a GRUNT!, snapped the cuffs in two. "*Cuffs! Cuffs!*" I had no cuffs!

I hadn't even noticed so great was the forbearing of bail, court, time and fine-money dollar signs that had been bouncing around and bouncing off of the gray matter in my head inflicting their own meta-level hematoma. "*No cuffs! I ain't got no cuffs.*" I had no cuffs . . . and a pair of nail clippers! I snipped at the cuffs of the imprisoned next to me. Snipped at it at its weakest thinnest point. Snipped at it until with a final SNAP! it gave way and my seatmate's hands came free from behind his back. I handed him the clippers and he went to work on the wristlocks that were turning his hands blue. The star athlete also had a tool. Other implements were soon forthcoming from the pockets of those who had been arrested but, critically, not searched. By the time the bus had made the climb up and over into the Valley and had arrived at the Van Nuys jail on board there were fifty-two people with fifty-one pairs of plastic handcuffs littering it's aisles. A CHEER! had gone up with the rending of the last pair. Then the silence of imprisonment reigned.

"Well, what are you gonna do?"

Leaning back against the dank of the cell wall, my eyes rose up from the feet that had materialized in front of me and kept climbing. Outlined against the steel gray backdrop drab of concrete, bar and cell she leapt out from its background as if life—up until that second—had been a scratchy black and white silent movie with not even a tin-pan score that had just jump-cut itself Technicolor 3D with a hi-fi stereo soundtrack. Dark auburn hair crested a forehead framing fire-green eyes and then cascaded down and across her shoulders. She looked just like Lauren Bacall. Sculpted in bronze. She was built like Bacall, all 5'10 of her looming directly over me, complete with Bacall's high cheekbones and wide-for-a-woman's shoulders. No wonder Bogie fell for that dame. This one . . . like her. She was a touch elongated but elegantly so almost like her figure had leapt from an Ernie Barnes painting. She was what down South they call "A long drink of water." Just as easily she could have been gangly as she ended up graceful. But the bones thrown in the dice game of life had rolled out of her palm, banged themselves on the table of life, and chanced up a natural seven.

"Well, what are you gonna do?" she repeated herself.

"*Everything!*" I wanted to yell. I had been hit by the same thunderbolt that had transfixed Michael Corleone when he first saw Appolonia. "*Everything*," my mind Bogied to her, "*Everything . . . Schreetart, I wanna do everything ta ya', wit' ya', because of ya'.*" I fell for her like an apple on Newton . . . I caught myself. I must have been tripping cause I was taking so much time with these thoughts in my mind that she repeated herself. Again.

"Well, what are you gonna do?"

I sat up straight.

"Do about what?"

"About. What. Do. You. Think!"

She spoke down literally and figuratively to me. The cadence was fifth grade teacher to soon-to-be-repeating-fifth-grade student. I drew myself up from the wall reaching up to a full two inches below meeting her eye-to-eye. *"Naw . . . she's 5'11."* And growing.

"Huh," I managed.

"About continuing to take a stand and not copping a plea to the trumped up charges that they're going to file. You led folks into this. I saw you go to the front."

"So what? I saw you standin' up ta tha cops liken you was playin' tha lead role in *Joan of Arc* or somethin'." Yeah, it was her that I had caught glimpse of. "You wanna lead somebody go 'head. I ain' tryin' ta lead nobody nowhere. I've had enough of leadin'."

And in truth I had. Had had my fill. Had had it up to here. Had had it. Time spent before UCLA at LACC organizing and then guiding City College's Black Student Union through a series of encounters with the administration, the police and right-wing students had drained every bit of desire to quote unquote "lead." Anybody. Anywhere. For any reason. Even for Rahid.

"You know that if someone doesn't take a stand," she gestured at the sad sacks cringing around the holding tank, "then all of these 'mopes,'"—*"mopes,"* she called them—"will end up copping pleas. As if we did something wrong and not the cops."

"Lady, you don't . . ."

"Louisa. My name is Louisa."

Louisa. *"Yeah, yeah, Louisa."* The *au francais* of the handle fit her like an all dolled up Orange County trophy wife wrapped and ready to be ravaged in a plunged-neck thousand-dollar Gucci gown—commando underneath.

"Well then, Louisa, what I was gonna say was that you don't need to convince me that it was the cops who was wrong . . ."

"But you're going to cop-out and cop a plea."

"Hey, I ain't got no money for an attorney. And what do you think a public defender will do but plead me out? And you?"

"I will defend myself."

"You know the one about the lawyer who has himself for his client, I take it?"

"Are you trying to be funny?"

"Never mind."

"How could they convict us when we just sitting in the street?"

I could have said "*You weren't,*" but I let it pass.

"'Sitting in the strect' in violation of a direct order to move."

"And you're the prosecutor now?"

"No, ma'am. Just the facts."

"Well, Joe Friday," she disdained, "haven't you got any backbone?"

"Last time I checked I did. It's sitting right above my black ass. You know, the black ass that has had a number of foots stuck up in it."

"Don't cry the racial blues."

"Don't hide behind the baby blues."

"My eyes are green . . . "

BOI-ING! "*Don't I know it?*"

". . . and I'm not hiding behind anything. I want to fight their bullshit charges."

"Then go ahead."

"And you won't?"

"Why should I?"

She gestured at the "mopes," "Because of them."

"Huh?"

"Them."

"Them who, the 'mopes'?"

"Yes. The 'mopes' who right now are being bailed out by Mommy and Daddy who will get them a lawyer, pay their fines and get their records expunged."

"Right on," I admitted, "Now what could we do and why should I do anything to help them?"

She answered both questions at once.

"We could shame them."

"*Damn!*" She had a point. I didn't notice it then. Frankly, now that I look back upon it, I couldn't tell you just when it had happened but the torque in that knot in my craw, that proto-bleeding-ulcer, that open sore bottomless-pit of nothingness had loosened, disgorging a bit of its bile.

To make a long story short, we both went to court and we both went to jail. It's just that I took the long way around to it. Initially, along with all the other "mopes," I had taken the plea. "No contest" was effectually the same as "Guilty." 'Sides they were talking six months if you went to court. That's the way justice, rather Just-us, is effectuated in the People's (that's a laugh) Court: plead guilty to something you didn't do and you can get "Probation." Fight the frame-up, lose and do six months. It's like confessing to witchcraft while they burn you at the stake. I guess the notion is that at least your eternal soul won't have to keep on sizzling while your mortal body's being seared.

I couldn't do six months. I didn't have the time. Not for principle. Not to shame them. Not for the "mopes." Not even for long, lean and luscious Louisa. I went before the bench, copped a plea and got off with a fifty-dollar fine. And . . . probation. Not her. I heard she got the six months. I say heard 'cause I didn't go to her trial. Though I wanted to. She didn't want me to and told me so in no ways about it. Six months. Okay, so it ain't a "dime-to-death" stretch in a state penitentiary but it can seem so when you're young. I did go and see her once a week in the county. Put some dough on her books.

At first she gave me the cold-shoulder and turned and walked right back out of the visiting room when she saw who sat behind the wire. I couldn't blame her. Her jailhouse conversion of herself to the path of martyrdom had been complete. And hell hath no fury like that of the convert. The second time I came, she walked to the bars and whispered through the wire, eyes down and head nodding as she spoke "Thank you for the money. Came in handy."

Then abruptly, she spun on her axle and left. The third time she sat down and I talked. The fourth time she talked. After the fifth time I was due to drop payment three of the ten dollars a month I had agreed to. I didn't. They did. A month and a half later when I got in from a summer class a black-and-white was waiting.

"Why didn't you make the agreed-upon payment of your fine?"

"I'm a student . . . and besides it was too much money . . ."

On that phrase the judge looked down at the case and quickly interjected:

"Fifty isn't too much for participating in a riot."

My backbone stiffened and the Niggah in me came out:

"It wasn't a riot, it was a political demonstration. It only became a riot when the cops started beating people on the head."

The cracker slammed down his gavel, peered down at me over the bench and with a glance to his left reminded me of the frowning armed pig bailiff whose private fancying about sugar-frosted doughnuts I had so rudely interrupted with my challenge.

"Are you going to pay the fine?"

"Nope."

"Then I'm going to give you thirty days in the county jail."

"You're only sending me to jail 'cause I'm poor."

"*And a Nigger, Nigger, Nigger . . .*" echoed the judger's thoughts bouncing around in the judge's mind. Oh, yeah. *How could I have forgotten that?* But I kept that thought to myself and my mouth shut as he again slammed down the gavel and the pig came with the cuffs to hustle me off to the big pig-pen. Aww . . . it weren't about the money. The lettuce in my garden was green and growing. Nickels and dimes rang up, rang down and rang again and again the cash registers in my mind and in my pocket. Naw. This weren't about the money at all. Not at all. It was about right. And she was right. She had a point. She had made her point. She had pointed her middle finger at the system and told it to go fuck itself. And, to its credit, it had made her pay. But it had collected no interest out of her ass. It had passed a tax that it couldn't collect.

In spite of the nature of my nature, the thirty days was a piece of cake. I say "in spite of the nature of my nature" cause I take to confinement, be in a cell or even a room with closed windows or within the smothers of a serious love affair, like the tiniest bit of being on just this side of the particle/wave continuum, subject to some smart-assed m'f'ing sociopathologically deviant particle physicist seeking to knock down Heisenberg's barrier and confine the bit to this particular place at that particular time. A confinement that means that its velocity equals zero and therefore does not exist. Now, existence is very very very difficult to deny. Absent speed, the necessitated complement of location, the entrapped attempts to flee its confinement by smearing itself out, canceling out the very existence of any concept of location until all that the scientist has left on his hands—in a manner, complementing the self-inflicted come-stain perpetually darkening the groin of his pants—is naught but an enigma smeared out and into the ether and the firmaments denying the scientist, bedeviling even the laws of God it/our/sel(f)ves. Quantum jitters. And just like such a quantum bit, I don't take well to being locked up. I jitter.

Yet the time was a piece of cake. It turned out like a turnover, an icy-rich chocolate moussey confection done up in whipped cream and sprinkled dark chocolate chips topped off with a maraschino cherry. Dreams as yet to be deferred, have a way of taking and making the best out of bad and the better out of worst. Dreams that can metamorphose an ocean oasis out of mere mirage. At night, that helped. It also helped that I got lucky. Inspired by something or the other, drugs or TV, maybe even some wacky woman, I had been on a basically vegetarian diet for a few weeks prior and when I went to jail the job they assigned me was in the kitchen. It was with only a bit of jailhouse diplomacy that I landed a gig in the salad-making section.

I mean I had lettuce, tomatoes, cabbage, etc up the gazoo. I ate so much of the shit that even the dump I took was green. I had scarfed so many veggies that the first thing I did when they let me out was to walk straight down Macy Street to Phillipe's and order up a lamb sandwich. Double-dipped. The meat tasted swell and I snapped it up, the grease feeling good as it glided down my gullet. The knot in my stomach . . . gone. Long . . . gone.

Louisa had one more month to do when I got out. When she called on Wed I told her that I would pick her up when they let her out that Monday morning at 7 a.m. The alarm woke me out of a bad-assed dream that I would have loved to have finished. In it, leaning over me, a mass of auburn hair framing flaming cat-green eyes that slowly came closer and closer falling with me as I fell. I fought to stay asleep but the persistence of time overcame that of memory. I fought my way out of the sack, brushed my teeth and jumped in the shower to get some water on my ass.

I twisted a joint, took six or seven hits, pulled on some rags and hit the door just as the sun was coming up. The tail end of the night's gray-black itself was turning tail to run, fleeing before the coming brilliance of the oncoming rays. Within myself I was mind-synch-singing the Beatles' "Here Comes the Sun" and everything under it seemed right under it. For a long awaited change.

~

The ride I pushed was a jet black '56 Mercedes 180D which actually wasn't. Someone had swapped out the diesel for a gas engine before I got it as part of a long and complicated dope deal. It had a four-speed manual transmission with the stick on the steering column. It came equipped with a Blaupunkt AM/FM radio that I had amped up and connected to one of the new Sony cassette stereo decks. To handle the load I had two 18"x12"x4" house speakers under the front seats on 30' length speaker wire so that when I left UCLA—headed towards my favorite "get-high" spot located on a bluff near the beach, overlooking the vast and wide expanse of the Pacific—and turned left out of Royce Dr and cruised to the beach down Sunset Bl's slope— "slip-sliding away" all the way down and around its date palm tree-clad curves—oblivious to the motorcars piloted by top-of-the-line self-anointed "captains of industry and finance" with their upscale bleached blonde Beverly Hills and Bel Air bimbos sitting beside them, the cars sometimes in front of, sometimes an oncoming glittering golden blur, sometimes but a fainter and fainter sparkle of an apparition glistening in the rear-view mirror.

And when I drove by blasting, maybe, John Fogarty howling "Fortunate Son," the neighbors in their street-lining mansions knew that I had been there. A couple of years before, I recall Rahid recalling Bunchy, the Panther had admonished Niggahs to "Do something . . . Do something even if you just spit." Well, the sonic blast let loose as I passed million-dollar pads was my hawk-too-ee: "*Fuck you rich mother-fuckas. I hope I woke up yo' babies and yo' ol' day-nappin'-assed mommas up.*" Laughing at the recollections, I slid a tape into the Sony.

"Something happening here . . . What it is ain't exactly clear," Buffalo Springfield throbbed out of the speakers under-seat and into my body and bones, "There's a man with a gun over there . . . Telling me I've got to beware , , ," "*Ummhoo,*" I thought, "*This is tha jam that shoulda been played on a loudspeaker hung from a buzzing-overhead pig helicopter when tha cops had snatched me up off of my ass on Ackerman and slammed me into their 'fuzzmobile.' Yeah, it shoulda been playing as tha star athlete and his cronies, flunkeys and tout men, et cetera, et al and et cie were snatched up off they white asses too. Ummhoo, it shoulda been playing when Louisa, standing unintimidated, refused to bow before the state and its power; shoulda been playin' when that beautiful dame had been rushed and roughed, subjected to the "incidental" probings and diggings of pig paws, onto the waiting bus . . . Standing. She was standing! Standing like a signal, a symbol, a portent, a portrait-that-ought-to-have-been memorialized in pure and blended oils bit-by-heroic-bit on top-grade canvas already stretched and aged with a half-chalk ground emulsion of gesso and virgin linseed oil. All tha babe needed was a torch in one hand, a book in the other and a crown across her brow. Lady Liberty. Democracy's Dame. Freedom's Femme. My comrade and my friend. And my-lover-I-hope-to-be."*

"What the hell is this?"

She pointed at my "ride" after we'd walked the two blocks to where I had parked.

"That's my 'ride,'" I meeked like a "mope."

"It's totally petit-bourgeois."

"*Petit bourgeois?*" Weren't nothing petty about my ride. I mean did she know how many nickels and dimes I'd slung for this bad-assed m'f'er?

"Awww . . . That's cold," I told her waving her off but stung by her air. Being this close to her after six long months of waiting and this is what I got? "*Damn.*" Inside the ride, I side-long glanced at the delicate golden hairs asleep on her long olive arms; paused upon the grace of her Nefertiti neck; examined—almost-tasting—the Grecian *entasis* that was her lips; sighed at the curves of her wide hips; and, lusted after the rise of her swelling tits lurking but a millimeter beneath fabric denying my kiss. And all the time, somewhere in the background of the foreground she continued her berate. All of this inside of me was building up the pressure as she let off six months of steam. My motor idling but inside I was all but stripping my gears.

I shifted the car into first and we drove straight out the freeways

and on towards the beach. On PCH as I neared my spot a white-robed hippie looking a little like Jesus with a sick-assed self-satisfied wan of a smile held up a sign:
"When the power of love overcomes the love of power/
The world will know peace."
—Jimi Hendrix
"Isn't that what we're about—the love of the people?" I wanned in simple harmonic resonance with the now-passed "Christ."
"It isn't love of the people but hatred of the people's oppression, that makes one a revolutionary. "Love . . . Love," she all but spat out the word, "Love is a hippie's pipe dream. Hatred is the fuse of the soldier's pipe bomb . . ."
"Yeah. Yeah. Yeah." As I drove on the words *love* and *pipe* and *fuse*, *bomb* and *dream* arranged themselves into circumstantial text in the back of my mind: I would love to be laying some pipe and blow off the bomb this dreamboat had lit the fuse to on the day we had first met. Instead, I lit the roach I had in the ashtray. After hitting it I caught a glance of her glare as I held it out to her.
"Are you kidding me?"
No, I wanted to answer. "*Sheesh. I'm just kidding myself.*"

The sex wasn't good, it was great.
Yet all the while as we fucked the sneaking suspicion arose and loomed that while I was enjoying her body, she was too. I mean she was enjoying herself. Only herself. Hell. I couldn't blame her. I mean "*With all of those toys*". And when she came, she came deeply from within emitting a long slow selfly-satisfied sigh.
You know, it's amazing how sex clears the mind. How after things that had been said and had just passed by like a leaf blown in a breeze come back into razor-sharp focus. The love/hate thing I mean. *She was right.* As usual, she was right. As always, she was right. Naw, these punks, these would-bes, these wanna-bes, these 'mopes' couldn't handle it. Couldn't wouldn't take it upon themselves to make a real strike at the system. Direct action was what was needed. Naww . . . they couldn't do it . . . but "The Union" could.
"The Union." Our union. "The Union" I had been avoiding. "The

Union" I'd shirked because of all of the internal debates—squabbles born, commenced and continued—the clash and clang of contending ideologies fashioned of blood and iron. There were Black Muslims with their melanin and Mother Ships. U.S. Niggers with their Swahili and bubas. There were Panthers howling their coronation of the lumpen as the "vanguard of the revolution." Reds and their working class. And a few hairy, patchouli-smelling, peace-sign-waving, black Hippies and their "freedom" whatever the fuck that meant. It was an amalgam, an oleo, a conglomeration, a cornucopia and a mish-mash. But this was a non-homogenous mixture that had been molded, fired, cured and hardened into an iron fist. A fist composed of these intra-contending separate fingers that had folded themselves into an inter-dynamic weapon ready, willing and able to strike.

The Union. The Union with its secret codes and secret handshakes. The Union with its passwords and co-signs. The Union with its many-layered and thereby almost-impenetrable barriers to entry, its multiple levels of security. The Union that had held itself together in spite of the contentiousness of its constituents; it had been stitched together in the wake of Bunchy and John Huggins killings. None. I mean *none* of the Panther/U.S. violence and contentiousness raging its way through Lost Angeles made its way past the parameters, the purviews and the prerogatives bounded within "The Union's" hori-zon: "Abandon All Bullshit All Ye Who Would Enter Here." Nothing else. Nothing more. "The Union." Held together and forged into "The Sword of The People" by the vision, the foresight, the courage, the cunning, the presence and the strength of one man—a man still yet amongst us yet in the process becoming legend—"The Chairman," Rahid. Rahid who, after consultations with the Central Committee, made all decisions. Rahid, "The Chairman," who had anointed me as his replacement when the time came, as surely the time would come, when he would be taken away from us.

Me.

The "First Comrade" cradled the device, eyeing it intently as if he were a Hassid examining an altogether rare uncut stone. Yet it was simple. A basic Molotov cocktail. A bottle of incendiary with a wick of torn fabric. Nothing but a basic Molotov cocktail . . . with a twist. Within each of the sawed-off-at-the-neck wine bottles was an elongated metal cylinder itself coated with a gray plastic goo. Studded in the goo were eight to ten balls of .00 buckshot. Simple, at the same time, ingenious. Simple . . . and deadly effective.

"Where did you get it?" Rahid began his interrogation.

"What the hell do you mean 'Where'd I get it?' I made them."

"You made them?"

She turned to me, ignoring Rahid and the others grilling her with their eyes, "Is this m'f'er deaf?"

"Look, woman," "The Chairman" exploded. "This ain't no god-damned game!"

"Right on!" howled Secretary of Cultural Affairs Umoja.

Another brother, Usamu, the Chief Propagandist who edited and ran The Union's paper, *The Black Nation*, co-signed the sentiment.

"Gimme five, my Brother."

The slap of the palms morphed into the beginnings of the Union's secret shake as knuckles collided knuckles and then each grasped the others thumbs in a twirl that before it ended with another clash of knuckles-to-knuckles included a subtle slide of the pinky finger across the bottom of each other's palm. The cross-examination continued:

"I asked you," Rahid bored in hefting one of the devices, "if you made this?'"

"Of course I made it," she snapped back.

"What's that thing for?" he said indicating the cylinder within.

"Technically, it's a delayed demolition device."

"A what?"

Field Marshal Raymond, the Panther, jumped in. "Bitch talk like the po-lice."

"Right on," co-signed William 5X.

But curiosity was melting suspicion in "The Chairman's" mind.

"A delayed . . . "

"Demolition device. A 'DDD.'"

With military precision she ticked off the attributes of the contents:

"Take an empty CO2 canister from a compressed air BB gun, fill it

33

with black powder. You can get it at any gun store. Coat the canister with double-ought shot from a 12 gauge stuck in a composition of silica sand—what's called 'fire clay,'" she asided. "Mixed with zinc oxide and using thermoplastic resin as a binding agent and you have a device capable of withstanding the heat of gasoline flames for approximately ten to fifteen minutes . . ." The pause was electric. ". . . just about long enough for the cops to arrive."

"BAM!!" went The Leader.

"BAM!" went the dame.

"Inshallah!" breathed William 5X.

The realization echoed in the awed silenced room: "*We could finally make them motherfuckers pay.*"

"How did you . . ."

"I have a degree in chemistry from Berkeley."

The awed silence in the room continued because we were listening to the whistle our minds had blown.

"Berkeley," it came from Rahid, more awed statement than query.

"Berkeley. While I was there I joined SDS. Kids . . ." she disgusted. "Yet there I hooked up with one of them, I won't tell you who, but he was 'Weatherman.'"

Another wolf-whistle bounced and ricocheted off the gray-mattered canyons of our brains. "Yeah . . ." the pause hung like all our animation had been suspended, ". . . yeah, I'm 'Weather Underground,' she looked around, "And there's money in it for you . . . A lot of money. And all you got to do is pick up a phone and dial 9-1-1."

"Hey! But you went to jail," interjected the Panther. Pointing at me he added, "'Second Comrade' told us you went to jail with him."

"Under the name you—and the police—know me as."

She reached in her purse and pulled out a flannel sack. In it were several driver licenses and a fistful of credit cards. She took a breath.

"Okay . . . So now you know. So just what are you going to do about it?"

"Oh, sister, you cool," "The Chairman" ruled. "Shit . . . All we was doing was trying to make sure . . ."

"I don't mean about me," she cut him off.

Silenced again.

"I mean . . . Are you serious or are you playing games like the rest of those New Age hippies that I got busted with?"

She was right. We were more serious, more committed, more dedicated, more . . . revolutionary.

~

It was a movie. It had to be a movie. I watched in slow-motion sepia-tone as the bitch slunk back from the scene, a sly smirk on her mug, and melded indistinguishably into the ranks of the pigs. Vanishing back into the murk and muck, the mud and the mire, from which all such snitches, informants and deep deep-cover agents-provocateurs slink back into only to pop back up again, like a bad penny, at some other time, in some other place, on some other campus, in some other state, to position herself in some other protests of some other movement so as to attract, seduce, allow into her draws and then set up some other sad-sack "mope" seeing in her eyes new visions and new horizons. Seeing not the treason residing in them just past the glint of their gleam. The last words of our conversation banged themselves off walls in the theater that was my mind:

"But I came and I saw you in jail."

"Yeah, and I was there on the days you were there."

"You tha mother-fucking LAPD."

"Nawwww," she hissed, her husky voice the same level, the same tone, the same slow dripping pace as when she had come, "I'm the mammy-fuckin' FBI."

The wrench of the knot returned and made itself at home.

The El Rey Bar

Andrea Gibbons

*The sun fell from the sky today, about fucking time too. Weeks it had
been loose, wavering, drunkenly unsteady across the sky. I watched its
thread snap, though no one else saw. It hit the city, bounced once and
disappeared to sink into the ocean's swallowing. It gave itself without
struggle.*

    *I wondered about that in the sudden darkness and the mad falling
of stars.*

    *We were all strangers then, all strangers, though my fingers still ach-
ingly sought the warmth of a hand that had never known mine. They
found rubble's chill weight and I sat my eyes stone, dark and unbeliev-
ing, from nothing to nothing they turned as the earth slowly slowed its
spinning. Everything collapsed to its center and I collapsed to mine. I
was not afraid of death but of struggling with no one to hear me. I was
not afraid of life but of living with no one to love me. I was not afraid
of my fears but their small nature shamed me, and their unmastered
strength left a trail of ashes in my stomach that I pursued, fury in hand.
Fury in shards of hope ripped from a broken bottle, demanding account-
ability. Was it Isaac who wrestled with god in the darkness and held?
Jacob? I could not remember, but I sought god out even as Los Angeles
unforgivably opened her legs one last time with a no and a whimper,
and screaming came in through the windows.*

I was at the bar. It was not on my list of things to do, and I had so
many things to do. There was just too much; everything was fucking breaking. It forced you to realize you couldn't do all of it. And
then relief came, because some things just weren't going to get done.
Fact. And you just had to say fuck it, and figure out your priorities. I
looked with pity on the people still running around squeaking over

the wrong things, wringing their hands. And then felt ashamed of myself, but you can always tell those driven by love and fury from those running on six cylinders of guilt. Of course, most of the guilty ones had already run to the places they commuted from and now counted on to keep them safe, so I couldn't talk shit about anyone still here. But my *comadres* were still out hunting down supplies or dealing with today's emergencies, and they were the only ones I wanted to talk to when I got back to our office turned community center turned emergency shelter, muscles aching from the weight of the food and the water.

I washed the soot and grime off my face, cleaned the blood from the new and jagged scratch down my arm. Stared at it between all the bruises and thought it was a good thing I wouldn't be dressing to impress anytime soon. If ever. My throat hurt, my eyes hurt, my heart fucking hurt. My nostrils were still full of burning.

Children were screaming, laughing, fighting. I just couldn't handle the noise, the people, the stress and the smell. So I texted Caro and Evie, and then headed towards a quiet beer. I spent the trip wondering how much longer our cell phones would actually keep working. But then I stopped thinking at all, just sat there in the El Rey with exhausted content as that first cold swallow went down smooth. Thanked fucking Christ this spot was still open for business, a little room to breathe. Glad they had the right protection. One of my favorite dives, more full up, more nervous, serving more tequila than usual. But the hipsters had cleared out, maybe for good, and Chente was on the jukebox. Some of us sang. Only then did I think about my priorities. I rolled the word around in my mouth stretching out its syllables, wanting to spit out the anger and sweat, the futility of it. Or let the beer wash it down. But half the world was on fire; we had to do something, no? Something. Priorities had to be set. I wondered one more time who in fuck had blown up the first bank and most of the mall with it. I wondered if there would ever be a time again when the causes of this thing would matter, not just the survival of their effects.

I was watching the door, expecting my girls any minute. So I saw him as he walked in with a bunch of *pelones* I didn't know. I hadn't seen him in years, and sure hadn't been missing anything either. If

I could have gotten the hell out of there without him seeing me, I would have run. Fast. I hunched down onto my stool and stared into the bar instead, but it didn't work. I heard his voice behind me.

"God damn, Gloria?"

I stood up and gave that smile that says anything but happy to see you. Especially cuz his eyes were running me up and down. You wanna see me angry? Just try that if you're not my man. Just fucking try.

"Damn, girl," he said, "you're looking good. How the hell are you?" He held that "good" too long, that hug too long; left his hand round my waist until I removed it. I should've said something. But I didn't know what to say to someone who'd been family, some kid I'd known such a long time. Long story. Sad story. I knew more sad was coming, and fuck if I wanted to hear it. I came here to wash sad away.

"I'm good, I'm good. And you?"

"It's my first night out since I got stabbed. Three times, check it."

He lifted up his shirt and I saw the bandages, other marks almost healed, bruises on his skin. First night out; kicked out of an over-whelmed hospital early I was sure. Amazed he even got into a hospital, must be the baby-face good looks still helping him through the mess he made of his life. Now here he was, already drunk, high. My heart broke a little more.

"Damn, girl, it's good to see you."

"Good to see you too, Angel." And silence then, it wasn't good to see him, and I hate lying. His face was puffy, all that was fine in it steadily disappearing into whatever shit he was doing to himself now. He looked at me again, had trouble concentrating, uppers and down-ers together I thought. I'd seen all the variations, hoped he wouldn't crash while I was there.

"So what the hell happened to you?" I asked. "Is it cuz of all this?" I gestured at the television.

"Nah, same old thing. You know how it is." A couple walked in even as he said it, and he broke off to stare at the girl. Always a girl with Angel, he was a fucking predator. She was pretty, knew it too, all falling out of that red halter-top. She didn't look away either. Not until they were passed us and settled into the back corner.

38

Same old thing, I thought? Same old fucking thing when L.A. was burning and they were parking tanks on the corners? Ninety-two was a hell of a riot, but this? They'd blown up a fucking bank. To start with. And whoever had started it, terrorist cell or not, shit was homegrown now. This was more like a war, and it wasn't just the ghetto now. It was everywhere. I looked up at the TV; saw the flames in Santa Monica and down Wilshire. Can't say I was sad it wasn't just my neighborhood on fire. Angel looked up too.

"This is some crazy fucking shit, ey?" He snapped into excited. He reached into his pocket and pulled out a handful of watches. "Girl, check these out. Rolexes." His shiny eyes were hot on my face. "You believe it? Goddamn gold fucking RO-lexes. Thought I'd missed all the action." He laughed and lightly patted the shirt over his stab wounds, still looking at me like he wanted me to be proud of him, like I should be. He'd never figured out what would have made me proud of him, even after I told him. "You know what I can sell these for?"

"Shit," I said. "You think anyone's buying watches right now?"

"Huh." He paused a minute, smiled that still charming smile. "They will. These're the real thing. Might be a while though, huh." He kept thinking. "Hey, Gloria." I already knew what was coming. "You got a place now, right? You think you could do me a favor? You think you could hold them for me? I'm with my mom but you know how it is."

I laughed. "You know I can't do that, Angel. How many years you known me?"

"Same old Gloria, you haven't changed at all." He laughed too, playing it like he didn't care. "Girl, it's good to see you. You know I love you like family. But goddamn you used to piss me off back in the old days, always in the house and I couldn't smoke out, couldn't sell my crystal. Damn, girl, you were fucking annoying. But you know I always loved you, right?"

"Right," I said, and drank some more of my beer. More silence.

"Girl, you want some Vicodin? They gave me a whole bottle, you fucking believe that?" He pulled the prescription bottle out of his shirt pocket and shook it.

"Nah. You know I only ever took that shit after my surgery." I had another drink.

39

"What about jewelry, cuz Roman knows all the spots, we're going back out tomorrow. You want rings? A necklace? A bracelet?"

"Nah, Angel, you know I don't want any of that shit. It's too fucking dangerous to go out there. You got enough water, enough food? That's the only reason to go out. You should be looking after your mom and your little brothers."

"Same old Gloria, always taking care of other people, huh." He had his hand on my shoulder and was getting all misty-eyed. Fuck. "You know I got your back, right?"

"Right," I said.

"You with me, girl? You family to me? Three gangs got your back." He listed them. "They all got your back. You need anything, just let me know, we all got you." He listed them again, counting them off on his fingers. "You're safe, you don't have to worry about any of this shit." He waved at the TV.

"Thanks." I didn't ask him where they'd all been when he was stabbed.

"I love you, girl," he said, hugging me again. I hated him drunk, he'd always get soft like this, then head straight to depression. I'd never forgiven him for what he said last time I'd been around for that. Took me a while to realize he wasn't actually sorry for anything he'd done, just for himself cuz it had turned people against him. Told me all kinds of shit I didn't even know about, shit that he'd done way back when, when things were damn hard. Actually wanted me to make him feel better about his fucking me over, fucking his family over. I couldn't handle it again, especially not after the day I'd had. Not now.

But that's when Caro and Evie showed up. I breathed a sigh of relief, made my excuses. "Don't leave without saying goodbye!" he said hugging me again. Goddamn, I thought, enough with the hugs. I lied and said I wouldn't without blinking, and finished off my Red Stripe.

"Cougering again?" Evie elbowed me into the booth.

"Shut up," I said, grinning in spite of myself. "I'm nowhere near forty. Still a fox, baby, still a fox. Besides, I've known that kid fucking forever."

"Never stopped anyone before," she laughed. "And he ain't no kid. What the hell's he on?"

"Besides the Vicodin and the booze? No fucking idea."

We ordered drinks all round. Talked some shit to help get rid of the stress, made jokes about how fucked-up everything was. It was working too. But we got quiet after Caro pointed at the TV.

They were building a wall.

It had been almost two weeks since the bombing and the madness started. It had entered a holding pattern in the hood but the edges were rippling through Los Angeles now. There had been a lot of arrests, blame bounced back and forth between rioters and terrorists. Of course, we knew round here they'd always seen us as pretty much the same damn thing.

"Why don't they turn the goddamn sound up?" Caro asked. I looked around and shrugged, no one was really watching but us. The news hadn't been anything but twenty-four-hour speculation for the past week, that and lame excuses from the government. Mainly people watched it now to see how many of the "rioters" they could recognize, or to watch the cops getting rocks thrown at them. You didn't need sound for that. But now a manicured news presenter showed plans, computer-generated approximations. No maps, of course. It was a fucking huge-ass wall, a TJ–San Ysidro border kind of wall. Ticker tape claimed it would be temporary. And looked like they were building it just east of La Brea, to curve round where soldiers lined up to protect Hancock Park. At least that bit of it. You couldn't tell where the wall was supposed to stop. They're the kind of walls that don't stop. Just grow, meet up with other walls.

And then they cut to commercials. I still couldn't believe they were showing commercials. Telling you the very latest thing for looting, not buying.

"*Tu creas?*" said Evie, "They're building a fucking wall?"

"When have they ever had to deal with this kind of shit? When did we ever get it together enough to take all that rage to the rich folks?" I leaned back against fake red leather. Thought about what a wall might mean. "What do you think? They planning to keep us in, or keep us out?"

Caro was hell of pissed. "Keep us in where? Keep us out of what? What they going to do? Airlift all the white people from Silverlake?

41

Evacuate the downtown lofts to the West Side? Clean their own damn houses and watch their own fucked-up kids? USC gonna move to the coast? It's not like we're not there too. *Pendejos*. What the fuck."

We all took another drink.

"Shit, it's not like the wall hasn't been there all along though," I said, "we all know where L.A.'s color walls run. Now they're just finally building them."

"Chicken-shit thing to do."

"What you expect?"

"Racist, greedy . . ."

"But what will it mean?" interrupted Evie. "A real wall. What does that mean for jobs, food, school, getting to my *abuela's* house, what?"

"Who knows," Caro said, "we gotta figure that shit out. Where it is. How it works. Whether we tear it down. Or what we build on our side of it. Fuck it, I say we let them wall themselves in, who wants them around anyway?"

We were ready to take all of them on, right then. Build a new world. Damn straight the beer had been flowing. We clinked bottles at that, and that's when all hell broke loose.

Angel. Of course. And I couldn't help it; I jumped up. Saw at once it was all about that girl in red. She was crying and trying to talk her man down, more by hanging onto him than anything. It was always about a stupid girl, and it was always too late for talking down. They were all in it now, that stupid mindless bar-brawl surge back and forth. I fucking hate bar fights. I turned to leave when a fist landed and Angel came flying out of the crowd towards me. I grabbed him, tried to shake him. He stayed still a minute, eyes all glazed over; he couldn't even hear me. Fucking mad-dogging that other guy and ignoring me like I wasn't even there. Except I was there, and holding onto him and yelling too, and I'm strong but that *pendejo* was stronger, and he pushed me hard into the pillar at the end of the bar without saying anything or even looking at me and flung himself back into the fight. I said fuck it and fuck you and went to where Evie and Caro were waiting at the door.

Then the gun went off and a girl started screaming. The fight was over and people were scattering, there was a cluster of people in the back and I craned my neck to see and then there was just a body there on the floor. I could see the blue shirt in glimpses through the crowd. Angel. Just some dead kid I once knew. Drunk and high, shot over some stupid girl in some stupid dive while the city itself was at war. The *placas*? They were all busy defending someone or other's property; they were sure as hell staying away from these neighborhoods. Maybe there would be an ambulance, but I didn't think they'd be coming either. Some girl had her cell phone. Kept dialing 911 but didn't look like they were picking up. We could all forget about emergency services.

We stepped aside to let the panicked crowd rush the door, the white-faced kid with his gun and his screaming *ruca* ran past us with us the rest. I barely saw them, couldn't stop looking at the body on the floor, the shattered head and the blood and just the fucking horror of a dead body that was once someone I knew. If only we'd left earlier, that's what I was thinking. Stupid selfish son of a bitch, even the way he died. My eyes hurt, my skin stretched tight across the bones of my face, my legs didn't feel like they were working. Caro and Evie put their arms around me, goddamn but I was glad they were there.

I looked around, the girl pleading on her cell phone in the corner, just one of Angel's so-called friends still remaining, staring down at the body. Someone had fucked up his eye and it was starting to swell up. One waitress had backed up against the bar, held the other one crying into her shoulder. The owner shut the door on the staring faces outside, locked it. Started pacing up and down and watching the girl with the cell. We were all watching her now as she lowered it.

"They're not coming," she said with wonder, not even angry. "They can't send anyone tonight. They said not to touch anything, it's a homicide scene. They'll try to send someone in the morning."

"Try?" asked the owner. The girl looked at him helplessly.

"Oh hell no, that body can't stay here all night, all day tomorrow, fuck knows till when that body going to stay here. It's fucking July. You think they actually sending someone?"

The girl didn't respond, just stared at Angel wide-eyed. She was in shock I thought, she might lose it in a second. Evie went over to talk to her and led her to the door. Who needed three gangs when Evie had your back?

"You know him?" the owner's chin jutted out at Angel's friend. "You know him?" chin jutting at me. "You get him the hell out of here or I put him in the dumpster, you get me? They're not coming for him."

Fuck. I wished again we had left just a little bit earlier, walked off into the night free of just one more impossible problem. I didn't even feel guilty about it. Felt like I hadn't slept since the first bomb went off. I'd been working so damn hard for the living; I didn't want to work for the dead.

I stood up, pissed off, felt like I'd been in that fucking bar fight. My stomach hurt. I walked over to his friend.

"What's your name?" He started, stared at me without seeing for a second.

"Junior."

"I'm Gloria." We shook hands like it was any old nice to meet you. "You know his mom?"

He nodded, rolled his eyes. "She's fucking crazy."

"I know. You got her number anyway? Angel's home phone?"

He shook his head. "We never call him there."

"Fuck. His dad's in Michoacán I think. And I don't have his number either. Or his sister's."

"Maybe his cell phone's in his pocket?" said Caro. Junior and I looked at each other. He was still shaking his head. I took a deep breath, stepped up to Angel, stepped into his blood. Nowhere else to step. I shivered. There was nothing in his pockets, no wallet, phone, Rolexes, nothing. I don't know why, but I checked for the Vicodin too, gone. Stupid, but that's what made me blink back tears for the first time. Felt like I might not be able to keep shit together after all. Who the fuck robs a kid with no head. I took another deep breath as I stepped back.

"I need another beer," was all I said.

"Anyone else? They're on the house," said the owner as he handed a cold one to me. "You got half an hour. I gotta clean up and get home."

Junior took off his long-sleeved shirt and covered the mess of Angel's head; he was all tatted up under the wife-beater, *sureño* big and gothic across the back of his neck. Little soldier boy, way the fuck out of Angel's league. If Junior told me three gangs had my

44

back I'd fucking believe him. I sat down. "Someone's gotta go to his mom's."

Junior sat next to me, "She hates my ass. And you know she'll fucking jump anyone bringing that news. Then be after them with her *pinche brujerias*."

"You don't believe in that crap, do you?" Evie sure as fuck didn't.

He looked at her. "Me? I don't fuck around with that shit. And she believes it. I don't need Angel's crazy *vieja* trying to kill me with a kitchen knife, and then spending the rest of her life sticking pins into a little Junior doll."

"She will too." I shivered. "She scares the shit out of me." I took a long drink. Evie lit up a cigarette and gave it to me. Passed the pack around to the others after taking one for herself.

"Hey, no smoking in here!" said the owner.

"Call the fucking cops," Evie laughed back. I smiled in spite of myself. I stuffed the giggles down. Way down. They scared me. I focused on logistics.

"We move him," I said after a second. "We can't take him to his pad, but we move him somewhere safe. We write a note to his mom and let her know where he is. Put it under her door. And then go home. What else can we do?"

"Yeah, but where's safe?" Good fucking question from Caro. She always asks the good questions.

"Fuck if I know. We sure as hell ain't going to get him far on our bikes. We could call Reese maybe. Maybe Carlos." Tired. I was so goddamn tired angry nauseous tired.

"Let me see what I can do first," said Junior, "our ride fucking bounced. His ass is gonna be sorry."

He moved to one side and started making calls. The rest of us just sat there. The waitresses started cleaning up the bar, one of them was still crying. I picked at the label of my beer to the sound of broken glass and sweeping, the clinking of bottles. I tried to think. Failed. Just sat there stupid and tired staring at the bloody footprint I'd left on the floor right in front of me.

"They're coming, they have a car. And blankets." Junior sat back down next to me. We smoked another *frajo*.

"We should break into the church then I think, no? The Catholic one down the road, it's nice." My voice broke but we all ignored that. Caro and Evie nodded.

They rolled up ten minutes later, banged on the door even as Junior's phone went off. He nodded at the owner who unbolted the door to let the five *pelones* inside. They crossed themselves when they saw Angel. Stood there quiet and clustered together, trying to look brave. One of them just looked like he was going to throw up. All of them looked very young.

"Who the fuck did this?" demanded the short one. Junior shrugged and jerked his head towards us. They'd save retaliation for later. They unfolded the blankets and started to roll him up.

I looked down at it, and there was so much left, so much that couldn't be rolled up.

"Can we use the broom?" I asked the owner.

He was staring at the floor. "I would have to throw it away then . . ." he said. I hoped he fucking remembered those words as long as he lived. The cost of a broom.

One of the waitresses came up, handed me a roll of paper towels. I unwound them slowly, used them to shovel up the pieces of Angelito. So many pieces, tears rolling down my face, *asco* crackling down my spine. I scraped up what I could and threw it into the blanket, stared at my fingers. Stared at the wandering trails I had left in the blood on the floor, almost like fingerpaint. I wanted to throw up. I went to the bathroom and did, then cleaned up in the sink, watched the blood and bits roll down the drain until the water ran clear and got so hot it was burning my hands.

When I came out it was just Evie and Caro waiting for me, the others had left. It already reeked of bleach.

"You wanna go to the church?" Evie asked. I nodded. "Let's walk the bikes then, I don't feel like riding." We pushed bikes through an almost empty night, the streetlights all broken but the reflected red-orange of fire lit up the darkness and the angry breathing of a burning city. We passed broken glass and locked grates; everything was crusty black. The air stung my throat and my eyes. I couldn't even tell if it was the smoke or if I was crying again. I fucking hated Los Angeles.

When we got to the church they were already in, the wire had been cut and forced jaggedly upwards, some of the shattered glass of the window it protected lay on the pavement beside the open door. It was cool and very dark inside, smelled like wax and incense. They'd laid him on the ground in front of the altar, Junior's bloody shirt back covering the place where his face should've been. Angel's hands lay peacefully at his sides. He was still wearing his hospital bracelet. They were lighting votive candles, surrounding him in a circle of light. It was strangely beautiful, silent tears that I couldn't stop rolled down my cheeks, collected along my nose and chin. They lit candles in front of the *virgen* too, the light flickered across her calm face and I felt like praying for the first time in years. We all stood quiet then, a moment of silence.

We filed outside, closing the door behind us, wedging it shut with stones.

Junior hugged me. "You going to be all right?" I nodded, though I couldn't stop the tears. I couldn't stop them. I never fucking cry. He gave me a folded up piece of paper. "I'll go to his mom's. Here's my cell, call me later, okay? Let me know you're all right." I shoved it into my pocket.

"You guys okay to get her home?" he asked Caro and Evie.

"*Claro*," said Evie, putting her arm around my shoulders. "We should take her to Maria's, no? That's close, we can walk there, stay the night."

"Good idea," Caro replied. Then stared at Junior a minute before we left. "Thanks, man. You're way too good for this gangster shit, you know? Everything's changed now. Come help us, we need all the help we can get."

He shrugged. I couldn't tell what he was thinking, but he smiled at me.

When we got to Maria's I unwrapped the paper. A couple of large pills fell out. He had written his number, and then in sloppy letters underneath: "vicodin, feel better."

I was asleep, half asleep, dreaming perhaps. And then yet another thought caught me on its hook, yanked me from my own depths with horrifying suddenness. I came up into awareness, gasping.

My thoughts prey on me.

I don't know when they started to have teeth, I don't know what they want from me, I don't know what more they can take after landing me curled around my stomach on the floor, tasting my own blood. I suppose these are not times for sleeping. But I ache for it. I feel the tiredness calcify my face, bruise my eyes, carve itself into my forehead.

There is so much I have to do. A harvest of tragedies in the lives of the ones I love. The things I can't answer about how people get by in this world. The fucking wall. On my eyelids I see pieces of Angel, in a silhouette surrounded by candles.

Poster Child

Sara Paretsky

Joggers and cyclists passed the body for almost an hour before anyone stopped. The fog was thick along the lakefront that morning. Through the ghostly layers of cotton, the man looked like a drunk who had passed out in a gush of his own vomit—not something passersby wanted to get close to.

It wasn't until a woman tried to yank her dog away from the pile of litter around the bench that anyone knew the man was dead. He'd been hit in the face hard enough to destroy his eyes, and what was coming from his mouth wasn't vomit but a wad of anti-abortion fliers, sticking out so that it looked as though he was eating a dismembered child.

The woman's legs gave way. She wanted to scream but she couldn't make a sound. The dog stood in the middle of the lake path, barking madly, and a cyclist, going too fast in the fog, collided with it and fell over in a heap of bike, grass and goose shit. He started upbraiding the woman, but she pointed dumbly at the bench; the cyclist finally called 911, but yelled at the woman for not controlling her dog while he righted his bike and took off again into the fog.

The woman thought she heard a child crying, but her legs were too unsteady for her to investigate. After a moment, she decided it was just a gull screaming.

~

Larry Pacheco took the 911 call because he was already near the scene. The baby killers were holding a fundraiser on a boat anchored near Randolph Street. That meant that abortion protestors arrived in force to protest. Some lined Lake Shore Drive, holding up posters that showed slaughtered babies. Another group heckled people attending the fundraiser as they got out of cars and taxis near the mouth of the harbor.

Pacheco was one of some half dozen officers assigned to make sure protestors and baby killers didn't get physical with each other. How any woman could kill her own helpless little baby while it was inside her, Pacheco couldn't understand for one minute. When he found out his older sister had had an abortion, he'd beaten her so hard he'd had to take her to the emergency room afterward to get her eye and her lip attended to. But she needed to understand, murder was murder, and if the law wouldn't punish her, she still had to face the consequences.

Even so, something about these baby savers, lovers, whatever they were, Pacheco couldn't explain it, but they didn't seem quite right to him, either. What kind of job was it for a grown man, like this Arnold Culver—forty-seven years old, eight children—was that a real job, going around the country attacking doctors, holding up posters covered with bloody body parts?

The fundraiser had been going for a couple of hours when Pacheco got the 911 call. His legs hurt from standing around the harbor mouth for hours. He plodded slowly through the cold, damp air to the body.

Like the woman with the dog, Pacheco blenched at the flier dribbling from the dead man's mouth, but he texted his sergeant, told what he'd found: murdered man, probably blunt force trauma, send for detectives.

~

If Lieutenant Finchley, the Area Six watch commander, had realized how high-profile the victim would prove to be, he would have summoned an experienced pair of detectives from the field. When the desk sergeant relayed Pacheco's message, though, the report sounded as though the victim were a homeless man. Finchley sent the two detectives who were in the squad room, Oliver Billings, who Finchley thought was lazy, and Billings' partner, rookie detective Liz Marchek.

When Marchek and Billings reached the lakefront, they found the body easily, despite the fog: at least five patrol cars were flashing their blue-and-whites near the Monroe Street intersection. When one patrol sees something interesting, most nearby units join in, partly to protect their buddies, in case a situation turns ugly, partly for something to do.

Oliver, sticking a hand into the victim's jacket pockets, found the wallet with his ID. Arnold Culver.

"Culver?" Pacheco blurted. "I just saw him outside the harbor where the baby killers are meeting. He had a bunch of kids, and some lady attacked him there, but he was alive."

"Baby killers?" Liz asked. "We've got baby killers meeting openly on the lakefront and we're just letting them go about their business?"

"He means abortionists, rookie," Oliver said. "Some kind of fund-raiser—the boss mentioned it at roll call."

Liz batted her eyes at her partner. "Thanks, Ollie, the technical language confuses me some times."

The evidence team joined them, and Liz went back to the body with the criminalists. "Blows look like they came from above," one of the techs said. "The ME may be able to say how tall the assailant was, but looks like anyone could have done it—they wouldn't have to be big, just damned angry."

Anyone who followed the abortion controversy in America knew that Culver had made plenty of people angry. Depending on your perspective he was either an innovator in ways to stop abortions, or a perverse maniac who didn't respect boundaries of person or property. At any time he faced dozens of lawsuits, but he also had the deep pockets of the nation's anti-abortion churches behind him, so he continued to do things like drop explosives from helicopters onto freestanding clinics, stalk the children of clinic workers, or egg his followers into shooting doctors.

Liz went back to her partner, who was stepping Pacheco through the attack on Culver he'd witnessed earlier.

The mist had been so heavy earlier that you could hardly see cars until they were on top of you, Pacheco said. "Me and Mueller, we were standing outside the harbor, and suddenly one of those holes opened in the fog, and I saw Culver. He had four kids with him, two maybe were teenagers, the other two probably seven, eight, something like that."

Culver had been giving fliers to the kids, and seemed to be giving them instructions. When a white-haired woman in a dark rain coat got out of a cab, Culver sent one of the smaller children toward her with a flier.

Over the noise of traffic and water, Pacheco couldn't hear what the woman said. "But she was plenty mad, detective, the way she moved—she grabbed the paper, rolled it up, threw it at Culver as hard as she could."

"Doesn't sound like much of an attack," Liz objected. "He hit her or anything?"

"The fog covered them up. I walked over, to see if they needed, you know, separating, but the woman was already on the gangway to the boat."

Culver had vanished in the mist with two of the children; the other two, one of the teens with one of the little ones, remained at the mouth of the drive with a stack of fliers. Every time a car stopped, they chanted in shrill unison, "Thank you for not murdering us!"

Pacheco told Oliver he was pretty sure he'd know the lady if he saw her, so they walked on up to the yacht. The last speech was just ending when they got into the dining room.

The cops circled the room and Pacheco found the woman sitting near the podium. Liz recognized her at once: Dr. Nina Adari, who performed abortions at a Loop clinic.

Dr. Adari was so stunned when Oliver and Pacheco bent over her, asking what she knew about Arnie Culver, that she didn't look at Liz.

"What do I know about him? He's a bully and a thug. Why? Has he attacked someone?"

"Other way around, ma'am," Oliver said. "We need to ask you a few questions about the fight you had with him this morning."

"Fight?" Adari repeated as if it were a foreign word she'd never heard. "I don't fight with people. If Culver is claiming that, then you can be sure he's lying."

"Not what we heard, ma'am. We heard you were the last person seen with him. And that you attacked him."

"Do you mean he's dead?" Adari said sharply.

"Why would you think that?" Oliver said.

"Has he disappeared then? I certainly did not attack him. He used one of his children to hand me a disgusting flier, which I threw in Arnie's face, but I don't think that constitutes an attack. Not compared to his assaults on my clinic and on my staff, which the police have paid no attention to."

One of Adari's tablemates put a hand on the doctor's arm. "Take it easy, Nina. Wait until you know what they want before you tell them what you know."

The buzz started through the dining room at once—Arnie, Jr. was dead. He'd been murdered. He'd been run over by a car. No, the police had found him floating in the harbor. It was amazing how fast a room full of people could turn a single fact into a labyrinth of conspiracy. Liz heard someone at a nearby table ask, with a nervous snigger, how late-term was a forty-seven-year-old abortion?

When the people near Adari realized the police were taking her with them, they crowded around her, protesting about Adari's rights, and her innocence.

"She's not under arrest, just coming with us to answer some questions, right, ma'am?" Oliver said.

The group pulled back, murmuring uncertainly. One advantage to picking up older white women at fundraisers instead of gang-bangers in drug houses, Liz thought—they and their friends weren't usually combative. On the other hand, the room was lousy with lawyers, and three of them, a man and two women, were at Adari's side when the cops walked from the room with her.

"Are you charging her?" one of the women lawyers asked.

Liz squinted to read her name badge: Leydon Ashford. Only the hyper-privileged walk around with two last names. Liz tried not to get her hackles up, but she really did not want some snot of a lawyer in the interrogation room with her.

"Not right now. We want to talk to her," Oliver answered, his easy smile in place. He used his smile like a cook with a sugar sifter, knowing just how much he needed to sweeten the pastry.

The three lawyers rode down the escalator with Adari and the cops. They all offered to come to the station with her.

"She doesn't need a lawyer," Liz said. "We just want to ask her a few questions."

"Everyone needs an attorney," Leydon Ashford responded. "I'll just ride over with you, Nina. See that they dot all their 'i's and so on."

⁓

The crowds began to gather outside the station long before the detectives arrived with their "person of interest." Adults with rosaries and angry signs—*Abort the Baby Murderers; Stop America's Holocaust/ Protect the Unborn* and the ubiquitous blow-ups of bloody body parts—were kneeling on the walks right up to the edge of the driveway. They'd brought children with them, children who should be in school, Liz thought, not camped in front of a police station to hear their parents scream curses at a squad car.

"Drive around to the back," Oliver said. "We don't want them attacking the car."

Liz drove past the front gates without slowing. "What are they thinking, involving their children in something like this? This isn't a TV set."

"Yes, it is," Oliver Billings peered in the wing mirror as Liz whipped around the corner. "The camera crews are setting up."

Liz called the desk sergeant on her radio to let him know they were coming in through the back. "You know there's a crowd out front, don't you, Tommy? Oliver says the networks are all there. He says the Christian Broadcast truck was behind us on Roosevelt Road."

"Been watching them on the monitor," the desk sergeant said. "If I'd wanted to work in a circus I'd a learned how to swing from a trapeze. I'll let the looey know you're here."

When the detectives reached the back of the station, fog shrouded the heads of the small group of protestors kneeling by the rear gates, making them look like guillotined corpses.

The protestors didn't try to block the car when the desk sergeant released the gates, but they pounded on the windows and spat as Liz drove past.

"If these are the Christians, the lions don't stand a chance," she muttered to Oliver.

"Their leader's dead; they're angry," he said. "And they know we've got a suspect in the car."

When they finally got through the back entrance and into Lieutenant Finchley's office, the lawyer who'd ridden over with Adari asked Finchley how the abortion foes knew the cops were bringing the doctor in for questioning. "Did you tell them that Dr. Adari was coming to the station?"

"Nothing we do is very secret," Finchley said. "People listen in to police scanners, they video our cops coming and going and put it on the Net. You know that as well as I do, ma'am. And you and Dr. Adari also know how high tempers are going to be riding over Mr. Culver's death, so let's try to keep the rhetoric at a manageable temperature, okay?"

Finchley had a uniformed officer escort Adari and the lawyer to an interview room before pulling Liz and Oliver into his office. "Okay, you two, everything you know. Now. Why did you bring the doctor in?"

"Pacheco—the uniform who found Culver's body—he saw her assault Culver outside the boat where the fundraiser was taking place," Oliver said.

"How'd he know who it was? He study this abortion rights group?" Finchley said.

"No, sir," Liz explained why Pacheco had ID'd Dr. Adari. "We looked up her history online—Culver's been harassing her, she's got a couple of lawsuits against him personally and against his organization."

"Even so," Finchley said, "she's not very big, and she must be twenty years older than Culver on top of it. It's hard to believe she could have attacked him, let alone killed him."

"Element of surprise in the fog, Looey," Oliver suggested. "And whoever killed him was furious—dude had been hit on the head so many times the eye-sockets were destroyed."

Finchley grunted. "Any priors on the Adari woman?"

Oliver hunched a shoulder. "Not since her student days. She dates back to the Vietnam War, got arrested three times in the seventies, once for pouring blood over an Army recruiter."

"Marchek, anything more recent than thirty years ago?"

Liz saw the pulse throbbing in Finchley's left temple. "Uh, well, sir, she seemed to be investigating Culver, trying to dig up some kind of dirt on him, maybe, to stop him targeting her clinic."

"She find anything?"

"We'll ask her that when we talk to her, sir."

"You two need to tread very carefully here. The cardinal has already been on the phone to me, as has the mayor, and the head of the local ACLU, and I can guarantee that Fox and CNN are going to keep this on a twenty-four-hour loop. Any suspects you talk to, especially here at the station, you follow regs down to the smallest sub-paragraph. Capisce?"

"Yes, sir," Liz said.

"And if either of you talk to the press, even to a ten-year-old blogger, you will be walking night patrol in South Chicago for the rest of your short lives."

"Yes, sir," Liz repeated.

"Yazzuh, boss." Oliver sketched a salute.

The lieutenant frowned, which sent Oliver grumbling into the interview room. Every time Finchley refused to laugh and joke with Oliver Billings, the detective magnified the size of his grievance against the new commander. The fact that Finchley was black and Billings was white only made the relationship more volatile.

Liz pretended sympathy with her partner's complaints about Finchley, because Oliver had proved more than once that he'd blind-side her in the field if he thought she wasn't supporting him. Privately, she was glad the old commander had left. She'd only served under him for two months, but he used jokes as a thin cover over his efforts to put women officers off-balance. When he'd assigned her to Oliver, he'd eyed her with a leer and told Oliver to "shape her up, not that there's anything wrong with the shape she's already in." The late-night, post-shift drinking sessions with his special cronies not only created divisions in the station, but brought his buddies, including Oliver Billings, to work with chronic hangovers.

She and Oliver stopped outside the interview room for a word with the officer who'd been listening to the hidden mikes. Leydon Ashford apparently suspected the police could eavesdrop—the officer said the Dr. Adari and her lawyer had murmured so softly into each other's ears that he hadn't picked up anything.

Oliver pulled a chair away from the table and leaned back in it, legs crossed: the suspect was supposed to be lulled into thinking it was a casual chat. He announced his and Liz's names for the recording equipment, but before he could launch into his first question, the doctor narrowed her eyes at Liz.

"Have we met, detective?"

"I don't think so, ma'am, unless I was on patrol for an event like today's." Liz's tone was wooden.

Oliver cleared his throat, demanding attention. "I understand you and Arnie Culver had a history, doctor."

"Every abortion provider in this country has a history with Mr. Culver. Recently, most doctors who prescribe contraceptives have started having a history with him." Dr. Adari had her hands folded in her lap.

"Is that why you attacked Culver outside the fundraiser this morning?" Oliver asked.

"I can't add to what I told you earlier," the doctor said. "He used one of his children to hand me a flier. I tossed it at him. Is that an attack? Is it similar to the time he lit gasoline-soaked rags and threw them at me?"

"That's what we want to know, doctor," Oliver said. "Did you follow him down the lake path? Have a confrontation that got out of hand?"

"No. I told him not to abuse the children he brought into the world by forcing them into his private anti-abortion army, and then I went into the fundraiser, where any number of people can tell you I spent the entire lunch hour. Is there anything else you want to ask me? I have patients waiting."

"To abort their babies?" Oliver asked.

The doctor said, "My patients' privacy is sacrosanct, detective. I can't tell you why they consult me. I can only tell you that it's unprofessional of me to make them wait."

The lawyer said, "Right. If you have any further questions for Dr. Adari, you can call me." Ashford put one of her business cards on the interview table. She nodded at Adari and the two women stood.

"What about the private eye you hired to investigate Culver?" Liz asked.

"What about it, indeed?" the lawyer said.

"How did Culver react to the investigation?" Liz persisted.

"I expect someone in his organization could tell you," Adari said.

"He was suing you for invasion of privacy," Oliver said, "so we can assume he wasn't happy about it."

"He knew a lot about invasion of privacy," Adari said.

The lawyer took her firmly by the arm and steered her from the room.

"Good of you to join in the interrogation there at the end," Oliver said to Liz when the women had left. "I thought you'd turned into a deaf-mute on me."

Liz smiled. "I'm the rookie, remember? I'm learning from you."

"You're the big-mouth licking Finchley's ass. Why don't you use your tongue on Culver's kids. It'll give you practice for when you have some of the little darlings yourself."

"And what will you be doing while I'm honing my daycare skills?" Liz demanded.

"Dr. Adari hired someone to investigate Culver. That's worth investigating."

~

Liz rented the third floor of a converted workman's cottage on the city's northwest side, but when she finished interviewing the Culver children, she headed to her grandfather's apartment in Rogers Park, near the lake.

After her mother was killed in a botched police raid when Liz was nine, her grandparents had raised Liz and her brother Elliot. Grandma Judith had been dead for some years now and Grandpapa lived alone in their old apartment. Even though he'd retired from Temple Etz Chaim, he was still the wisest man Liz knew.

She hadn't always felt that way. As a teenager, she'd battled with him furiously over her mother. She had fought with Elliot, who said their mother was asking for trouble by being part of an anarchist cell, and with Grandpapa, who, she said, sided with the police against the poor. She announced she was an anarchist who didn't believe in Gd, hoping to spark rage in Grandpapa, but he only reacted by calling her "My little anarchist," when he gave her his blessing.

When she told him she wanted to join the police, he'd been troubled, and asked her pointed questions about her motives. "Do you imagine yourself as some kind of resistance hero, infiltrating the police so you can read their covert files?"

It was their last serious argument, because she didn't want to admit how close he was to the truth. Grandpapa hadn't believed she could be a happy cop, but she'd actually taken to the work. Seven years on patrol and then she'd passed the exam to become a detective.

"Detective Anarchist!" Grandfather greeted her when she arrived this evening. "Still keeping order in an unorderable world?"

He didn't follow the news; he hadn't heard about Culver's death and she didn't tell him, just asked about his arthritis, about Mrs. Gelinsky and Mrs. Mannheim, who were competing for his attention, and about the cat, Bathsheba, who ruled the house in the absence of a human female.

"You hear from your brother?"

"Every day, Grandpapa. If you would learn to text, you'd hear from him, too." Her brother Elliot was in Denmark, testing and repairing computer security at his firm's Copenhagen headquarters.

She went into the kitchen to make supper, knowing her grandfather wouldn't have bothered to cook a meal just for himself.

"And what's troubling you, little anarchist," he asked when she'd put an omelet in front of him.

"Nothing. Why can't I stop by to make you supper just because I love you?"

He smiled. "I'm grateful, even if you're telling only a portion of the truth."

"Omitting the truth, Grandpapa. How big a sin is that?"

He nodded: she had revealed the real reason for her visit. "The rabbis put a great deal of thought into that, and the answer is, it all depends. If you're protecting someone from harm, versus trying not to embarrass yourself, versus trying not to show off, versus not violating your own privacy—I would need much more information before I could give you an answer. Did you omit the truth in talking to someone? Or did you commit *g'neivat data*, theft of the mind, encourage someone to believe a falsehood?"

His omelet grew cold as he talked. By the end of the evening, Liz thought if she believed in Gd she'd be in even worse trouble than she was already, but she didn't say it out loud. Not that she had to— Grandpapa realized that when he put his hands on her forehead to bless her, before she left him to drive to her own place.

～

Whether Gd was angry with her, Liz couldn't say, but Lieutenant Finchley definitely was. When she arrived at Area Six the next morning, there was a note taped to the desk she shared with two other detectives: *Marchek, see me ASAP.* Cops usually texted each other; a written note sounded ominous.

The lieutenant sent the desk sergeant away and shut his door. "Why didn't you tell me as soon as you brought Adari into the station yesterday, Marchek?"

Liz stood with her hands clasped behind her, feet apart, as if she were at inspection. The pulse above the lieutenant's left eye was throbbing, a danger sign.

"I'm taking you off this case."

"But, sir—"

"There is no 'but, sir,' in this conversation. The victim photographed you going into the suspect's clinic. How did you expect to keep that a secret?"

"I didn't think my medical history was anyone's public business, sir. Not the victim's, and not my co-workers."

"Your medical history is your business, Marchek, which is why I'm not posting this on the World Wide Web, but when any officer in my command has had prior contact with a suspect or a victim in an investigation, I hear about it first from that officer, not from someone in the Evidence Unit sifting through the victim's papers, unless you think you are V.I. Warshawski, able to operate outside standard systems with impunity. If we don't come up with a better lead in the next forty-eight hours, you and every patient Culver ever photographed will be a person of interest in this crime. Do I make myself clear?"

"Yes, sir." Liz dug her fingernails into her palms to keep her voice from shaking.

"You will assist Sergeant Wrexall at the front desk and catch up on your paperwork backlog until I decide you're ready for the street again. Send Detective Billings in to see me when he arrives. You're dismissed."

Liz wanted to know what the lieutenant was going to say to Oliver, but his manner was too forbidding for her to ask. She kept her head up, her shoulders back, as she walked to the front desk. *G'neivat daat*, theft of the mind, wasn't in the Illinois Criminal Code, but Lieutenant Finchley knew the punishment for it, anyway.

Fortunately, Sergeant Wrexall acted as though it was an ordinary event, detectives to be put on desk duty.

At nine-thirty, when her partner arrived, Wrexall said, "Billings, the looey wants to see you. Whatever you do, don't complain about hemorrhoids—he decided mine were hurting my job performance so he took your partner to help me out here."

After five minutes with Finchley, Billings stalked to the front desk, his lips thin. "What did you tell Finchley about our investigation?"

"Nothing. He called me in this morning and told me I was riding a desk for now—what did *you* tell him about me?"

"That you're a useless rookie. He's putting Clevenger and Cormack in charge of Culver and asking me to assist—to be a third wheel! Oliver held out his thumb and forefinger a quarter inch apart, "I was this close to handing in my badge."

Liz and Wrexall nodded sympathetically. Oliver's father, two uncles and grandfather had all been Chicago cops. He would never resign. Liz felt a flood of gratitude to the lieutenant wash through her. He'd protected her privacy; he hadn't outed her to Oliver Billings.

"Who is V.I. Warshawski, anyway?" she asked Wrexall when they were alone again. "The looey asked if I thought I was like her."

"She's a PI. Gets on a lot of cops nerves because she takes risks and cuts corners we can't—and also because she has an annoying habit of popping up in high-profile cases and solving them."

"Maybe she'll pop up and solve Culver's death," Liz suggested.

~

Thirty-six hours passed with no viable leads, and no sign that V.I. Warshawski was going to pop up. In twelve hours, Lieutenant

Finchley would turn the photographs from the Evidence Unit over to the investigating detectives. Liz would become a person of interest—one among however many thousand Culver had photographed at abortion clinics, but the one whose private history would become part of her partner's arsenal when he wanted to tear her down. Maybe even end her police career just as it was getting going.

If Liz had known Culver was taking her picture when she went into Adari's clinic, she might have killed him on the spot. If the looey hadn't threatened to make her private business public, Liz would have been happy to see Culver's murderer walk free, even if the Sixth Commandment didn't give you the option to choose who you did or didn't murder.

When Wrexall's shift ended, Finchley was still in the station. Liz went to her own desk, pretending to busy herself with cold-case files. Liz kept on working through the shift change. Finchley finally left for the day, with a grunt at Liz to let her know she was still on probation, but holding up well. Liz waited until she was sure the lieutenant had pulled out of the parking lot before going over to Oliver's desk and logging on to his computer. She could have accessed the Culver case from her own machine but she didn't want a trail following behind her.

Culver's password was easy—his star number plus the jersey numbers of his two favorite athletes. Liz loaded the case notes onto a flash drive, logged off, and was in her car before third shift roll call started.

She drove to an Internet café in one of the busy student neighborhoods. She even paid to park—no point in some meter maid reading her plates and noting that a cop had parked here. I'm a thief, she imagined herself telling Grandpapa, a thief of information who knows my guilt so thoroughly I'm trying to hide my tracks in someone else's computer. Even as she squirmed, she paid cash for time on a machine.

The Culver murder was important enough that plenty of people had written notes into the case file. The report from the crime lab: Culver had been killed by one of the sticks used in the posters the protestors had carried along Lake Shore Drive. Someone searching the crime scene had found the shattered pieces of wood covered with Culver's brains and blood, but they hadn't found usable prints or any DNA besides the victim's.

Oliver had entered his notes on the investigation Dr. Adari had started into Culver's life and finances. Adari hadn't discovered anything criminal, although Culver had been taking home close to a million dollars a year from his organization. Oliver had written, "Major motive here," in the margin. Liz shook her head—that was a motive for Culver to kill Adari, not the other way around.

She trolled through blogs and social networks for a bit—sometimes killers made coy comments on websites, eager for recognition of how clever they'd been. The anti-abortion vitriol was so extreme across the Net—directed at Dr. Adari, who deserved to be in everyone's gun sights, according to many posts—that Liz stopped reading it.

She did find a number of photos of Culver, taken at the protest by his adoring supporters, and now posted as precious icons of his martyrdom. Some of the shots showed him with the four children who'd accompanied him to the march. The two boys were dressed in identical pale-blue blazers and ties, the girls in frilly white dresses with blue ribbons, despite the chilly weather.

When Liz had gone to the house two days ago, before Finchley took her off the case, the girls still had on the frilly dresses they'd worn to the march and the younger boy, Jimmy, was wearing his pale-blue blazer and a tie. Only the oldest boy had shed his formal clothes for a sweatshirt and jeans. Maybe that was the one place where he could vent a rebellious adolescent spirit. Liz thought of all her teenaged fights with Grandpapa—maybe it would have been better if her only rebellion had been to wear a sweatshirt to Temple.

The house had been spilling over with children—Arnie's eight, augmented by a dozen more belonging to the neighbors and in-laws who'd gathered to console the widow.

Liz had mouthed the conventional phrases to Culver's widow: sorry to disturb you, but if I could talk to the children who were with your husband this morning? She tried not to flinch from the crucifixes on the walls.

"I thought you'd made an arrest," one of the neighbors said. "One of the baby killers."

Liz shook her head. "We're just gathering information. That's why anything the kids saw or heard could help."

The women reluctantly brought forward the four who'd been with Arnie. Lucy, the oldest of the Culver children, sixteen, followed by Paul, fifteen, and Veronica and Jimmy, seven and eight.

"We take turns going with Dad," Lucy said, when Liz asked why they'd been at the fundraiser with Arnie. "It was Paul's and my turn, and we're training the little ones, how to talk to ladies when they're about to go into death chambers, how to tell them not to kill their unborn babies." Her voice was soft, matter-of-fact.

"Your teachers are okay with you missing school?" Liz asked.

"We're home-schooled, so the atheists can't force us to deny Christ crucified the way they do in school."

The words seemed to be spoken by rote, auto-pilot. Liz wondered why the parents didn't send the children to Catholic school—there were more than enough to choose from—but she knew she shouldn't get into an argument with the children, or the mother.

"So two of you stayed at the harbor to hand out literature, and two of you went with your dad?"

"Jimmy and I, we were at the harbor. Paul and Nicki, Veronica, they went on down the path with Daddy. Daddy was checking on the pickets—our people get discouraged sometimes standing all alone. You can't believe the horrid things Christ haters shout out of their cars. One of our ladies was even crying. Nicki cheered her up, didn't you?"

The eight-year-old nodded without speaking. Paul and Jimmy were silent, too. When Liz asked what they'd seen or heard on the lake path, they just shook their heads.

"The lady you gave the flier to, the one who threw it at your daddy, did you see her on the lake path?"

Nicki and Paul shook their heads again.

"Were you together the whole time?" Liz asked idly.

Nicki gasped, as if Liz had guessed a secret, but Lucy said, "Of course they were together the whole time."

"I thought you stayed up by the yacht where the fundraiser was," Liz said. "What did you see, Nicki?"

"I didn't see, I couldn't see, there was a fog," the younger girl said, breathlessly. "I thought I lost Paul but he was right next to me the whole time. I started to cry, I mean, I almost started to cry."

"That's right. You're a big girl and only babies cry," Lucy said.

Liz tried to probe, gently, sure she'd seen something that frightened her, but Lucy kept answering for her sister, until one of the adults said the children had been through enough. No more questions.

Now, in the Internet café, Liz tried to think it through. The child had seen something, but what? Had she run away from her brother, the way children do—geese, seagulls, boats, all more interesting than one more abortion protest in a life that had clearly been filled with them—and been scolded? Or had she seen her father's assailant?

It was eleven p.m. now. Liz tried to fight down her panic. Think, think, there's a clue in here someplace. Her own notes—the woman who'd discovered the body had said she thought she heard a child crying.

Nicki, Liz thought. The little Culver girl who thought she'd lost her brother in the fog. She'd started to cry when she was supposed to be cheerful. What an abominable way to treat a small child!

Panic, and now anger. Two bad companions for a detective. Liz unplugged the flash drive and went back into the night.

She drove back to the crime scene, but it was too dark to see anything. Liz's brother owned an apartment downtown; he'd given Liz a key when he left for Denmark. She crossed the park and let herself in, slept a few hours in his guest bed, but as soon as the sky began to lighten, she went back to the bench where Culver's body had been found.

The wind had shifted in the night; the fog that had shrouded the city for the last week was finally gone. Liz paced restlessly around the lakefront and the harbor. The benches were filled with the homeless, their possessions carefully laid beneath them to avoid midnight predators. Liz checked each man she came to for a sign of life, but she didn't try to waken them, not until she'd covered a quarter of a mile and found one of them with a pale-blue blazer folded under his head.

⁓

Finchley himself drove out to La Grange with his detectives and the jacket. He let Liz join the team, but told her she was still on probation; she was not to say anything.

When Mrs. Culver came to the door, Finchley showed her the jacket. "We think your son, Paul, lost this in all the confusion on Monday, ma'am, but we want to make sure it's his before we send it to the lab for tests."

In the background, he could hear the children, the oldest girl, Lucy, explaining an arithmetic problem to a small child just out of his sight; a Spanish lesson streaming over the Internet in a corner of the living room. The children were so used to adults coming and going at all hours that they didn't pay attention to the police, until Nicki, passing by with a peanut butter sandwich, screamed, "Paul, they got your jacket."

The doorway was suddenly filled with children; as in *Peter Pan*, they seemed to tumble from every doorway, every piece of furniture. Mrs. Culver looked around her in bewilderment.

"Paul, is this your jacket? Did you lose it at the protest on Monday?"

The boy's face was very white. He stared at it for a minute without speaking, then his face contorted into sobs.

His mother frowned at him. "We don't cry in public, Paul, we control ourselves for the sake of Jesus, who died for us without crying."

"I'm tired of Jesus!" Paul shouted.

His brothers and sisters gave a collective gasp and shrank from him.

"I don't want to be a show child, I don't want to be in court so everyone can see you had a million children and never used birth control, I don't want to go to marches and clinics, I want to play football and have a life like other guys my age! I told you this a million times, I told Dad, but neither of you ever gave a damn about any of us! We were just props to you, props you could show off in public. He sat there on that bench starting to lecture me on my duty to the unborn and I said, 'What about your duty to the born, to us, your children,' and he hit me! He hit me one time too many.

"I picked up that sign, that stupid picture of all those bleeding babies. He worshipped those bleeding babies but it didn't matter how many times he made us bleed! And you, you just said, amen, praise Jesus to whatever he said, so I hit him, I wanted him to see how it felt, and I just kept hitting him and hitting him and hitting him.

Then Nicki started to cry because there was blood on my jacket. So I dropped it in the harbor and took her for an ice cream, and the rest of you can go kneel down and say your rosaries but my only prayer is, 'Thank God that bully can't hit any of us again.'"

~

Back at the station, Liz asked Finchley what would happen to Paul.

"He's still a minor. There's a lot of psychological stress. If they get him a good lawyer he might have a chance."

"Whoa, that mother!" Billings said. "She'll skin him and fry him herself if the state doesn't do it."

"Yeah, that was my impression, too," Finchley agreed. "Marchek—what were you doing at the crime scene this morning, when I'd given you a direct order to stay away from the case."

"Uh, sir, I couldn't sleep, I was taking a walk." What did the Torah say about an incomplete truth that resulted in a lie? Liz couldn't remember.

"Marchek, if I was Mrs. Culver, I'd hand you over for disciplinary action. I am even less merciful than she is—I'm putting you back on the street with Billings. But if you ever again have private contact with a witness to a crime, whether you run into them sleep-walking or meet them in your synagogue, and you tell me about it first. Or you give me your badge. Got it?"

"Yes, sir." Liz saluted and left the room.

"What was that about?" Oliver demanded.

"I was showing off," she said to Oliver. "He didn't like it."

G'neivat daat, that was it. Theft of the mind. She'd just told another half-truth. Maybe quarter truth. She'd tell Grandpapa the whole story tonight and see whether he thought the Torah gave her any wiggle room.

The Lunatics

Kim Stanley Robinson

They were very near the center of the moon, Jakob told them. He was the newest member of the bullpen, but already their leader.

"How do you know?" Solly challenged him. It was stifling, the hot air thick with the reek of their sweat, and a pungent stink from the waste bucket in the corner. In the pure black, under the blanket of the rock's basalt silence, their shifting and snuffling loomed large, defined the size of the pen. "I suppose you see it with your third eye."

Jakob had a laugh as big as his hands. He was a big man, never a doubt of that. "Of course not, Solly. The third eye is for seeing in the black. It's a natural sense just like the others. It takes all the data from the rest of the senses, and processes them into a visual image transmitted by the third optic nerve, which runs from the forehead to the sight centers at the back of the brain. But you can only focus it by an act of the will—same as with all the other senses. It's not magic. We just never needed it till now."

"So how do you know?"

"It's a problem in spherical geometry, and I solved it. Oliver and I solved it. This big vein of blue runs right down into the core, I believe, down into the moon's molten heart where we can never go. But we'll follow it as far as we can. Note how light we're getting. There's less gravity near the center of things."

"I feel heavier than ever."

"You are heavy, Solly. Heavy with disbelief."

"Where's Freeman?" Hester said in her crow's rasp.

No one replied.

Oliver stirred uneasily over the rough basalt of the pen's floor. First Naomi, then mute Elijah, now Freeman. Somewhere out in the shafts and caverns, tunnels and corridors—somewhere in the dark maze of

68

mines, people were disappearing. Their pen was emptying, it seemed. And the other pens?

"Free at last," Jakob murmured.

"There's something out there," Hester said, fear edging her harsh voice, so that it scraped Oliver's nerves like the screech of an ore car's wheels over a too-sharp bend in the tracks. "Something out there!"

The rumor had spread through the bullpens already, whispered mouth to ear or in huddled groups of bodies. There were thousands of shafts bored through the rock, hundreds of chambers and caverns. Lots of these were closed off, but many more were left open, and there was room to hide—miles and miles of it. First some of their cows had disappeared. Now it was people too. And Oliver had heard a miner jabbering at the low edge of hysteria, about a giant foreman gone mad after an accident took both his arms at the shoulder—the arms had been replaced by prostheses, and the foreman had escaped into the black, where he preyed on miners off by themselves, ripping them up, feeding on them—

They all heard the steely squeak of a car's wheel. Up the mother shaft, past cross tunnel Forty; had to be foremen at this time of shift. Would the car turn at the fork to their concourse? Their hypersensitive ears focused on the distant sound; no one breathed. The wheels squeaked, turned their way. Oliver, who was already shivering, began to shake hard.

The car stopped before their pen. The door opened, all in darkness. Not a sound from the quaking miners.

Fierce white light blasted them and they cried out, leaped back against the cage bars vainly. Blinded, Oliver cringed at the clawing of a foreman's hands, searching under his shirt and pants. Through pupils like pinholes he glimpsed brief black-and-white snapshots of gaunt bodies undergoing similar searches, then blows. Shouts, cries of pain, smack of flesh on flesh, an electric buzzing. Shaving their heads, could it be that time again already? He was struck in the stomach, choked around the neck. Hester's long wiry brown arms, wrapped around her head. Scalp burned, *buzzz* all chopped up. Thrown to the rock.

"Where's the twelfth?" In the foremen's staccato language. No one answered.

The foremen left, light receding with them until it was black again, the pure dense black that was their own. Except now it was swimming with bright red bars, washing around in painful tears. Oliver's third eye opened a little, which calmed him, because it was still a new experience; he could make out his companions, dim redblack shapes in the black, huddled over themselves, gasping.

Jakob moved among them, checking for hurts, comforting. He cupped Oliver's forehead and Oliver said, "It's seeing already."

"Good work." On his knees Jakob clumped to their shit bucket, took off the lid, reached in. He pulled something out. Oliver marveled at how clearly he was able to see all this. Before, floating blobs of color had drifted in the black; but he had always assumed they were afterimages, or hallucinations. Only with Jakob's instruction had he been able to perceive the patterns they made, the vision that they constituted. It was an act of will. That was the key.

Now, as Jakob cleaned the object with his urine and spit, Oliver found that the eye in his forehead saw even more, in sharp blood etchings. Jakob held the lump overhead, and it seemed it was a little lamp, pouring light over them in a wavelength they had always been able to see, but had never needed before. By its faint ghostly radiance the whole pen was made clear, a structure etched in blood, redblack on black. "Promethium," Jakob breathed. The miners crowded around him, faces lifted to it. Solly had a little pug nose, and squinched his face terribly in the effort to focus. Hester had a face to go with her voice, stark bones under skin scored with lines. "The most precious element. On Earth our masters rule by it. All their civilization is based on it, on the movement inside it, electrons escaping their shells and crashing into neutrons, giving off heat and more blue as well. So they condemn us to a life of pulling it out of the moon for them."

He chipped at the chunk with a thumbnail. They all knew precisely its clayey texture, its heaviness, the dull silvery gray of it, which pulsed green under some lasers, blue under others. Jakob gave each of them a sliver of it. "Take it between two molars and crush hard. Then swallow."

"It's poison, isn't it?" said Solly.

"After years and years." The big laugh, filling the black. "We don't have years and years, you know that. And in the short run it helps your vision in the black. It strengthens the will."

Oliver put the soft heavy sliver between his teeth, chomped down, felt the metallic jolt, swallowed. It throbbed in him. He could see the others' faces, the mesh of the pen walls, the pens farther down the concourse, the robot tracks—all in the lightless black.

"Promethium is the moon's living substance," Jakob said quietly. "We walk in the nerves of the moon, tearing them out under the lash of the foremen. The shafts are a map of where the neurons used to be. As they drag the moon's mind out by its roots, to take it back to Earth and use it for their own enrichment, the lunar consciousness fills us and we become its mind ourselves, to save it from extinction."

They joined hands: Solly, Hester, Jakob and Oliver. The surge of energy passed through them, leaving a sweet afterglow. Then they lay down on their rock bed, and Jakob told them tales of his home, of the Pacific dockyards, of the cliffs and wind and waves, and the way the sun's light lay on it all. Of the jazz in the bars, and how trumpet and clarinet could cross each other. "How do you remember?" Solly asked plaintively. "They turned me blank."

Jakob laughed hard. "I fell on my mother's knitting needles when I was a boy, and one went right up my nose. Chopped the hippocampus in two. So all my life my brain has been storing what memories it can somewhere else. They burned a dead part of me, and left the living memory intact."

"Did it hurt?" Hester croaked.

"The needles? You bet. A flash like the foremen's prods, right there in the center of me. I suppose the moon feels the same pain, when we mine her. But I'm grateful now, because it opened my third eye right at that moment. Ever since then I've seen with it. And down here, without our third eye it's nothing but the black."

Oliver nodded, remembering.

"And something out there," croaked Hester.

Next shift start Oliver was keyed by a foreman, then made his way through the dark to the end of the long, slender vein of blue he was working. Oliver was a tall youth, and some of the shaft was low; no time had been wasted smoothing out the vein's irregular shape. He

71

had to crawl between the narrow tracks bolted to the rocky uneven floor, scraping through some gaps as if working through a great twisted intestine.

At the shaft head he turned on the robot, a long low-slung metal box on wheels. He activated the laser drill, which faintly lit the exposed surface of the blue, blinding him for some time. When he regained a certain visual equilibrium—mostly by ignoring the weird illumination of the drill beam—he typed instructions into the robot, and went to work drilling into the face, then guiding the robot's scoop and hoist to the broken pieces of blue. When the big chunks were in the ore cars behind the robot, he jackhammered loose any fragments of the ore that adhered to the basalt walls, and added them to the cars before sending them off.

This vein was tapering down, becoming a mere tendril in the lunar body, and there was less and less room to work in. Soon the robot would be too big for the shaft, and they would have to bore through basalt; they would follow the tendril to its very end, hoping for a bole or a fan.

At first Oliver didn't much mind the shift's work. But IR-directed cameras on the robot surveyed him as well as the shaft face, and occasional shocks from its prod reminded him to keep hustling. And in the heat and bad air, as he grew ever more famished, it soon enough became the usual desperate, painful struggle to keep to the required pace.

Time disappeared into that zone of endless agony that was the latter part of a shift. Then he heard the distant klaxon of shift's end, echoing down the shaft like a cry in a dream. He turned the key in the robot and was plunged into noiseless black, the pure absolute of Nonbeing. Too tired to try opening his third eye, Oliver started back up the shaft by feel, following the last ore car of the shift. It rolled quickly ahead of him and was gone.

In the new silence distant mechanical noises were like creaks in the rock. He measured out the shift's work, having marked its beginning on the shaft floor: eighty-nine lengths of his body. Average.

It took a long time to get back to the junction with the shaft above his. Here there was a confluence of veins and the room opened out, into an odd chamber some seven feet high, but wider than Oliver could determine in every direction. When he snapped his fingers there was no rebound at all. The usual light at the far end of the low chamber was absent. Feeling sandwiched between two endless rough planes of rock, Oliver experienced a sudden claustrophobia; there was a whole world overhead, he was buried alive . . . He crouched and every few steps tapped one rail with his ankle, navigating blindly, a hand held forward to discover any dips in the ceiling.

He was somewhere in the middle of this space when he heard a noise behind him. He froze. Air pushed at his face. It was completely dark, completely silent. The noise squeaked behind him again: a sound like a fingernail, brushed along the banded metal of piano wire. It ran right up his spine, and he felt the hair on his forearms pull away from the dried sweat and stick straight out. He was holding his breath. Very slow footsteps were placed softly behind him, perhaps forty feet away . . . an airy snuffle, like a big nostril sniffing. For the footsteps to be so spaced out it would have to be . . .

Oliver loosened his joints, held one arm out and the other forward, tiptoed away from the rail, at right angles to it, for twelve feathery steps. In the lunar gravity he felt he might even float. Then he sank to his knees, breathed through his nose as slowly as he could stand to. His heart knocked at the back of his throat, he was sure it was louder than his breath by far. Over that noise and the roar of blood in his ears he concentrated his hearing to the utmost pitch. Now he could hear the faint sounds of ore cars and perhaps miners and foremen, far down the tunnel that led from the far side of this chamber back to the pens. Even as faint as they were, they obscured further his chances of hearing whatever it was in the cavern with him.

The footsteps had stopped. Then came another metallic *scrick* over the rail, heard against a light sniff. Oliver cowered, held his arms hard against his sides, knowing he smelled of sweat and fear. Far down the distant shaft a foreman spoke sharply. If he could reach that voice . . . He resisted the urge to run for it, feeling sure somehow that whatever was in there with him was fast.

Another *scrick*. Oliver cringed, trying to reduce his echo profile. There was a chip of rock under his hand. He fingered it, hand shaking.

His forehead throbbed and he understood it was his third eye, straining to pierce the black silence and *see* . . .

A shape with pillar-thick legs, all in blocks of redblack. It was some sort of . . .

Scrick. Sniff. It was turning his way. A flick of the wrist, the chip of rock skittered, hitting ceiling and then floor, back in the direction he had come from.

Very slow soft footsteps, as if the legs were somehow . . . they were coming in his direction.

He straightened and reached above him, hands scrabbling over the rough basalt. He felt a deep groove in the rock, and next to it a vertical hole. He jammed a hand in the hole, made a fist; put the fingers of the other hand along the side of the groove, and pulled himself up. The toes of his boot fit the groove, and he flattened up against the ceiling. In the lunar gravity he could stay there forever. Holding his breath.

Step . . . step . . . snuffle, fairly near the floor, which had given him the idea for this move. He couldn't turn to look. He felt something scrape the hip pocket of his pants and thought he was dead, but fear kept him frozen; and the sounds moved off into the distance of the vast chamber, without a pause.

He dropped to the ground and bolted doubled over for the far tunnel, which loomed before him redblack in the black, exuding air and faint noise. He plunged right in it, feeling one wall nick a knuckle. He took the sharp right he knew was there and threw himself down to the intersection of floor and wall. Footsteps padded by him, apparently running on the rails.

When he couldn't hold his breath any longer he breathed. Three or four minutes passed and he couldn't bear to stay still. He hurried to the intersection, turned left and slunk to the bullpen. At the checkpoint the monitor's horn squawked and a foreman blasted him with a searchlight, pawed him roughly. "Hey!" The foreman held a big chunk of blue, taken from Oliver's hip pocket. What was this?

"Sorry boss," Oliver said jerkily, trying to see it properly, remembering the thing brushing him as it passed under. "Must've fallen in." He ignored the foreman's curse and blow, and fell into the pen tearful with the pain of the light, with relief at being back among the others. Every muscle in him was shaking.

But Hester never came back from that shift.

Sometime later the foremen came back into their bullpen, wielding the lights and the prods to line them up against one mesh wall. Through pinprick pupils Oliver saw just the grossest slabs of shapes, all grainy black-and-gray: Jakob was a big stout man, with a short black beard under the shaved head, and eyes that popped out, glittering even in Oliver's silhouette world.

"Miners are disappearing from your pen," the foreman said, in the miners' language. His voice was like the quartz they tunneled through occasionally: hard, and sparkly with cracks and stresses, as if it might break at any moment into a laugh or a scream.

No one answered.

Finally Jakob said, "We know."

The foreman stood before him. "They started disappearing when you arrived."

Jakob shrugged. "Not what I hear."

The foreman's searchlight was right on Jakob's face, which stood out brilliantly, as if two of the searchlights were pointed at each other. Oliver's third eye suddenly opened and gave the face substance: brown skin, heavy brows, scarred scalp. Not at all the white cutout blazing from the black shadows. "You'd better be careful, miner."

Loudly enough to be heard from neighboring pens, Jakob said, "Not my fault if something out there is eating us, boss."

The foreman struck him. Lights bounced and they all dropped to the floor for protection, presenting their backs to the boots. Rain of blows, pain of blows. Still, several pens had to have heard him.

Foremen gone. White blindness returned to black blindness, to the death velvet of their pure darkness. For a long time they lay in their own private worlds, hugging the warm rock of the floor, feeling the bruises blush. Then Jakob crawled around and squatted by each of them, placing his hands on their foreheads. "Oh yeah," he would say. "You're okay. Wake up now. Look around you." And in the after-black they stretched and stretched, quivering like dogs on a scent. The bulks in the black, the shapes they made as they moved and groaned . . . yes, it came to Oliver again, and he rubbed his face and looked around, eyes shut to help him see. "I ran into it on the way back in," he said.

They all went still. He told them what had happened. "The blue in your pocket?"

They considered his story in silence. No one understood it.

No one spoke of Hester. Oliver found he couldn't. She had been his friend. To live without that gaunt crow's voice . . .

Sometime later the side door slid up, and they hurried into the barn to eat. The chickens squawked as they took the eggs, the cows mooed as they milked them. The stove plates turned the slightest bit luminous—redblack, again—and by their light his three eyes saw all. Solly cracked and fried eggs. Oliver went to work on his vats of cheese, pulled out a round of it that was ready. Jakob sat at the rear of one cow and laughed as it turned to butt his knee. *Splish splish! Splish splish!* When he was done he picked up the cow and put it down in front of its hay, where it chomped happily. Animal stink of them all, the many fine smells of food cutting through it. Jakob laughed at his cow, which butted his knee again as if objecting to the ridicule. "Little pig of a cow, little piglet. Mexican cows. They bred for this size, you know. On Earth the ordinary cow is as tall as Oliver, and about as big as this whole pen."

They laughed at the idea, not believing him. The buzzer cut them off, and the meal was over. Back into their pen, to lay their bodies down.

Still no talk of Hester, and Oliver found his skin crawling again as he recalled his encounter with whatever it was that sniffed through the mines. Jakob came over and asked him about it, sounding puzzled. Then he handed Oliver a rock. "Imagine this is a perfect sphere, like a baseball."

"Baseball?"

"Like a ball bearing, perfectly round and smooth you know."

Ah yes. Spherical geometry again. Trigonometry too. Oliver groaned, resisting the work. Then Jakob got him interested despite himself, in the intricacy of it all, the way it all fell together in a complex but comprehensible pattern. Sine and cosine, so clear! And the clearer it got the more he could see: the mesh of the bullpen, the network of shafts and tunnels and caverns piercing the jumbled fabric of the moon's body . . . all clear lines of redblack on black, like the metal of the stove plate as it just came visible, and all from Jakob's clear, patiently fingered, perfectly balanced equations. He could see through rock.

"Good work," Jakob said when Oliver got tired. They lay there among the others, shifting around to find hollows for their hips.

Silence of the off-shift. Muffled clanks downshaft, floor trembling at a detonation miles of rock away; ears popped as air smashed into the dead end of their tunnel, compressed to something nearly liquid for just an instant. Must have been a Boesman. Ringing silence again.

"So what is it, Jakob?" Solly asked when they could hear each other again.

"It's an element," Jakob said sleepily. "A strange kind of element, nothing else like it. Promethium. Number sixty-one on the periodic table. A rare earth, a lanthanide, an inner transition metal. We're finding it in veins of an ore called monazite, and in pure grains and nuggets scattered in the ore."

Impatient, almost pleading: "But what makes it so special?"

For a long time Jakob didn't answer. They could hear him thinking. Then he said, "Atoms have a nucleus, made of protons and neutrons bound together. Around this nucleus shells of electrons spin, and each shell is either full or trying to get full, to balance with the number of protons—to balance the positive and negative charges. An atom is like a human heart, you see.

"Now promethium is radioactive, which means it's out of balance, and parts of it are breaking free. But promethium never reaches its balance, because it radiates in a manner that increases its instability rather than the reverse. Promethium atoms release energy in the form of positrons, flying free when neutrons are hit by electrons. But during that impact more neutrons appear in the nucleus. Seems they're coming from nowhere. So each atom of the blue is a power loop in itself, giving off energy perpetually. Some people say that they're little white holes, every single atom of them. Burning forever at 940 curies per gram. Bringing energy into our universe from somewhere else. Little gateways."

Solly's sigh filled the black, expressing incomprehension for all of them. "So it's poisonous?"

"It's dangerous, sure, because the positrons breaking away from it fly right through flesh like ours. Mostly they never touch a thing in us, because that's how close to phantoms we are—mostly blood, which is almost light. That's why we can see each other so well. But sometimes a beta particle will hit something small on its way through. Could mean nothing or it could kill you on the spot. Eventually it'll get us all."

Oliver fell asleep dreaming of threads of light like concentrations of the foremen's fierce flashes, passing right through him. Shifts passed in their timeless round. They ached when they woke on the warm basalt floor, they ached when they finished the long work shifts. They were hungry and often injured. None of them could say how long they had been there. None of them could say how old they were. Sometimes they lived without light other than the robots' lasers and the stove plates. Sometimes the foremen visited with their scorching lighthouse beams every off-shift, shouting questions and beating them. Apparently cows were disappearing, cylinders of air and oxygen, supplies of all sorts. None of it mattered to Oliver but the spherical geometry. He knew where he was, he could see it. The three-dimensional map in his head grew more extensive every shift. But everything else was fading away . . .

"So it's the most powerful substance in the world," Solly said. "But why us? Why are we here?"

"You don't know?" Jakob said.

"They blanked us, remember? All that's gone."

But because of Jakob, they knew what was up there: the domed palaces on the lunar surface, the fantastic luxuries of Earth . . . when he spoke of it, in fact, a lot of Earth came back to them, and they babbled and chattered at the unexpected upwellings. Memories that deep couldn't be blanked without killing, Jakob said. And so they prevailed after all, in a way.

But there was much that had been burnt forever. And so Jakob sighed. "Yeah yeah, I remember. I just thought—well. We're here for different reasons. Some were criminals. Some complained."

"Like Hester!" They laughed.

"Yeah, I suppose that's what got her here. But a lot of us were just in the wrong place at the wrong time. Wrong politics or skin or whatever. Wrong look on your face."

"That was me, I bet," Solly said, and the others laughed at him. "Well I got a funny face, I know I do! I can feel it."

Jakob was silent for a long time. "What about you?" Oliver asked. More silence. The rumble of a distant detonation, like muted thunder.

"I wish I knew. But I'm like you in that. I don't remember the actual arrest. They must have hit me on the head. Given me a concussion. I must have said something against the mines, I guess. And the wrong people heard me."

"Bad luck."

"Yeah. Bad luck."

More shifts passed. Oliver rigged a timepiece with two rocks, a length of detonation cord and a set of pulleys, and confirmed over time what he had come to suspect; the work shifts were getting longer. It was more and more difficult to get all the way through one, harder to stay awake for the meals and the geometry lessons during the off-shifts. The foremen came every off-shift now, blasting in with their searchlights and shouts and kicks, leaving in a swirl of afterimages and pain. Solly went out one shift cursing them under his breath, and never came back. Disappeared. The foremen beat them for it and Oliver shouted with rage. "It's not our fault! There's something out there, I saw it! It's killing us!"

Then next shift his little tendril of a vein bloomed, he couldn't find any rock around the blue: a big bole. He would have to tell the foremen, start working in a crew. He dismantled his clock.

On the way back he heard the footsteps again, shuffling along slowly behind him. This time he was at the entrance to the last tunnel, the pens close behind him. He turned to stare into the darkness with his third eye, willing himself to see the thing. Whoosh of air, a sniff, a footfall on the rail . . . Far across the thin wedge of air a beam of light flashed, making a long narrow cone of white talc. Steel tracks gleamed where the wheels of the car burnished them. Pupils shrinking like a snail's antennae, he stared back at the footsteps, saw nothing. Then, just barely, two points of red: retinas, reflecting the distant lance of light. They blinked. He bolted and ran again, reached the foremen at the checkpoint in seconds. They blinded him as he panted, passed him through and into the bullpen.

After the meal on that shift Oliver lay trembling on the floor of the bullpen and told Jakob about it. "I'm scared, Jakob. Solly, Hester, Freeman, Mute Lije, Naomi—they're all gone. Everyone I know here is gone but us."

"Free at last," Jakob said shortly. "Here, let's do your problems for tonight."

"I don't care about them."

"You have to care about them. Nothing matters unless you do. That blue is the mind of the moon being torn away, and the moon knows it. If we learn what the network says in its shapes, then the moon knows that too, and we're suffered to live."

"Not if that thing finds us!"

"You don't know. Anyway nothing to be done about it. Come on, let's do the lesson. We need it."

So they worked on equations in the dark. Both were distracted and the work went slowly; they fell asleep in the middle of it, right there on their faces.

Shifts passed. Oliver pulled a muscle in his back, and excavating the bole he had found was an agony of discomfort. When the bole was cleared it left a space like the interior of an egg, ivory and black and quite smooth, punctuated only by the bluish spots of other tendrils of monazite extending away through the basalt. They left a catwalk across the central space, with decks cut into the rock on each side, and ramps leading to each of the veins of blue; and began drilling on their own again, one man and robot team to each vein. At each shift's end Oliver rushed to get to the egg-chamber at the same time as all the others, so that he could return the rest of the way to the bullpen in a crowd. This worked well until one shift came to an end with the hoist chock-full of the ore. It took him some time to dump it into the ore car and shut down.

So he had to cross the catwalk alone, and he would be alone all the way back to the pens. Surely it was past time to move the pens closer to the shaft heads! He didn't want to do this . . .

Halfway across the catwalk he heard a faint noise ahead of him. *Scrick, scriiiiiik.* He jerked to a stop, held the rail hard. Couldn't reach the ceiling here. Back stabbing its protest, he started to climb over the chest high railing. He could hang from the underside.

He was up on the railing when he was seized up by a number of strong cold hands. He opened his mouth to scream and his mouth was filled with wet clay. The blue. His head was held steady and his ears filled with the same stuff, so that the sounds of his own terrified sharp nasal exhalations were suddenly cut off. Promethium; it would kill him. It hurt his back to struggle on. He was being carried horizontally, ankles whipped, arms tied against his body. Then plugs of the clay were shoved up his nose and in the middle of a final paroxysm of resistance his mind fell away into the black.

The lowest whisper in the world said, "Oliver Pen Twelve." He heard the voice with his stomach. He was astonished to be alive.

"You will never be given anything again. Do you accept the charge?"

He struggled to nod. I never wanted anything! he tried to say. I only wanted a life like anyone else.

"You will have to fight for every scrap of food, every swallow of water, every breath of air. Do you accept the charge?"

I accept the charge. I welcome it.

"In the eternal night you will steal from the foremen, kill the foremen, oppose their work in every way. Do you accept the charge?" I welcome it.

"You will live free in the mind of the moon. Will you take up this charge?"

He sat up. His mouth was clear, filled only with the sharp electric aftertaste of the blue. He saw the shapes around him: there were five of them, five people there. And suddenly he understood. Joy ballooned in him and he said, "I will. Oh, I will!"

A light appeared. Accustomed as he was either to no light or to intense blasts of it, Oliver at first didn't comprehend. He thought his third eye was rapidly gaining power. As perhaps it was. But there was also a laser drill from one of the A robots, shot at low power through a cylindrical ceramic electronic element, in a way that made the cylinder glow yellow. Blind like a fish, open-mouthed, weak eyes gaping and watering floods, he saw around him Solly, Hester, Freeman, mute Elijah, Naomi. "Yes," he said, and tried to embrace them all at once. "Oh, yes."

They were in one of the long-abandoned caverns, a flat-bottomed bole with only three tendrils extending away from it. The chamber was filled with objects Oliver was more used to identifying by feel or sound or smell: pens of cows and hens, a stack of air cylinders and suits, three ore cars, two B robots, an A robot, a pile of tracks and miscellaneous gear. He walked through it all slowly, Hester at his side. She was gaunt as ever, her skin as dark as the shadows; it sucked up the weak light from the ceramic tube and gave it back only in little points and lines. "Why didn't you tell me?"

"It was the same for all of us. This is the way."

"And Naomi?"

"The same for her too; but when she agreed to it, she found herself alone."

Then it was Jakob, he thought suddenly. "Where's Jakob?" Rasped: "He's coming, we think."

Oliver nodded, thought about it. "Was it you, then, following me those times? Why didn't you speak?"

"That wasn't us," Hester said when he explained what had happened. She cawed a laugh. "That was something else, still out there . . ."

Then Jakob stood before them, making them both jump. They shouted and the others all came running, pressed into a mass together. Jakob laughed. "All here now," he said. "Turn that light off. We don't need it."

And they didn't. Laser shut down, ceramic cooled, they could still see: they could see right into each other, red shapes in the black, radiating joy. Everything in the little chamber was quite distinct, quite *visible*.

"We are the mind of the moon."

Without shifts to mark the passage of time Oliver found he could not judge it at all. They worked hard, and they were constantly on the move: always up, through level after level of the mine. "Like shells of the atom, and we're that particle, busted loose and on its way out." They ate when they were famished, slept when they had to. Most of the time they worked, either bringing down shafts behind them, or dismantling depots and stealing everything Jakob designated theirs. A few times they ambushed gangs of foremen, killing them with laser cutters and stripping them of valuables; but on Jakob's orders they avoided contact with foremen when they could. He wanted only material. After a long time—twenty sleeps at least—they had six ore cars of it, all trailing an A robot up long-abandoned and empty shafts, where they had to lay the track ahead of them and pull it out behind, as fast as they could move. Among other items Jakob had an insatiable hunger for explosives; he couldn't get enough of them.

It got harder to avoid the foremen, who were now heavily armed, and on their guard. Perhaps even searching for them, it was hard to tell. But they searched with their lighthouse beams on full power, to stay out of ambush: it was easy to see them at a distance, draw them off, lose them in dead ends, detonate mines under them. All the while the little band moved up, rising by infinitely long detours toward the front side of the moon. The rock around them cooled. The air circulated more strongly, until it was a constant wind. Through the seismometers they could hear from far below the rumbling of cars, heavy machinery, detonations. "Oh, they're after us all right," Jakob said. "They're running scared."

He was happy with the booty they had accumulated, which included a great number of cylinders of compressed air and pure oxygen. Also vacuum suits for all of them, and a lot more explosives, including ten Boesmans, which were much too big for any ordinary mining. "We're getting close," Jakob said as they ate and drank, then tended the cows and hens. As they lay down to sleep by the cars he would talk to them about their work. Each of them had various jobs: mute Elijah was in charge of their supplies, Solly of the robot, Hester of the seismography. Naomi and Freeman were learning demolition, and were in some undefined sense Jakob's lieutenants. Oliver kept working at his navigation. They had found charts of the tunnel systems in their area, and Oliver was memorizing them, so that he would know at each moment exactly where they were. He found he could do it remarkably well; each time they ventured on he knew where the forks would come, where they would lead. Always upward.

But the pursuit was getting hotter. It seemed there were foremen everywhere, patrolling the shafts in search of them. "Soon they'll mine some passages and try to drive us into them," Jakob said. "It's about time we left."

"Left?" Oliver repeated.

"Left the system. Struck out on our own."

"Dig our own tunnel," Naomi said happily.

"Yes."

"To where?" Hester croaked.

Then they were rocked by an explosion that almost broke their eardrums, and the air rushed away. The rock around them trembled, creaked, groaned, cracked, and down the tunnel the ceiling collapsed, shoving dust toward them in a roaring *whoosh!* "A Boesman!" Solly cried.

Jakob laughed out loud. They were all scrambling into their vacuum suits as fast as they could. "Time to leave!" he cried, maneuvering their A robot against the side of the chamber. He put one of their Boesmans against the wall and set the timer. "Okay," he said over the suit's intercom. "Now we got to mine like we never mined before. To the surface!"

The first task was to get far enough away from the Boesman that they wouldn't be killed when it went off. They were now drilling a narrow tunnel and moving the loosened rock behind them to fill up the hole as they passed through it; this loose fill would fly like bullets down a rifle barrel when the Boesman went off. So they made three abrupt turns at acute angles to stop the fill's movement, and then drilled away from the area as fast as they could. Naomi and Jakob were confident that the explosion of the Boesman would shatter the surrounding rock to such an extent that it would never be possible for anyone to locate the starting point for their tunnel.

"Hopefully they'll think we did ourselves in," Naomi said, "either on purpose or by accident." Oliver enjoyed hearing her light laugh, her clear voice that was so pure and musical compared to Hester's croaking. He had never known Naomi well before, but now he admired her grace and power, her pulsing energy; she worked harder than Jakob, even. Harder than any of them.

A few shifts into their new life Naomi checked the detonator timer she kept on a cord around her neck. "It should be going off soon. Someone go try and keep the cows and chickens calmed down." But Solly had just reached the cows' pen when the Boesman went off. They were all sledgehammered by the blast, which was louder than a mere explosion, something more basic and fundamental: the violent smash of a whole world shutting the door on them. Deafened, bruised, they staggered up and checked each other for serious injuries, then pacified the cows, whose terrified moos they felt in their hands rather than actually heard. The structural integrity of their tunnel seemed okay; they were in an old flow of the mantle's convection current, now cooled to stasis, and it was plastic enough to take such a blast without shattering. Perfect miners' rock, protecting them like a mother. They lifted up the cows and set them upright on the bottom of the ore car that had been made into the barn. Freeman hurried back down the tunnel to see how the rear of it looked. When he came back their hearing was returning, and through the ringing that would persist for several shifts he shouted, "It's walled off good! Fused!"

So they were in a little tunnel of their own. They fell together in a clump, hugging each other and shouting. "Free at last!" Jakob roared, booming out a laugh louder than anything Oliver had ever heard from him. Then they settled down to the task of turning on an air cylinder and recycler, and regulating their gas exchange.

They soon settled into a routine that moved their tunnel forward as quickly and quietly as possible. One of them operated the robot, digging as narrow a shaft as they could possibly work in. This person used only laser drills unless confronted with extremely hard rock, when it was judged worth the risk to set off small explosions, timed by seismometer to follow closely other detonations back in the mines; Jakob and Naomi hoped that the complex interior of the moon would prevent any listeners from noticing that their explosion was anything more than an echo of the mining blast.

Three of them dealt with the rock freed by the robot's drilling, moving it from the front of the tunnel to its rear, and at intervals pulling up the cars' tracks and bringing them forward. The placement of the loose rock was a serious matter, because if it displaced much more volume than it had at the front of the tunnel, they would eventually fill in all the open space they had; this was the classic problem of the "creeping worm" tunnel. It was necessary to pack the blocks into the space at the rear with an absolute minimum of gaps, in exactly the way they had been cut, like pieces of a puzzle; they all got very good at the craft of this, losing only a few inches of open space in every mile they dug. This work was the hardest both physically and mentally, and each shift of it left Oliver more tired than he had ever been while mining. Because the truth was all of them were working at full speed, and for the middle team it meant almost running, back and forth, back and forth, back and forth . . . Their little bit of open tunnel was only some sixty yards long, but after a while on the midshift it seemed like five hundred.

The three people not working on the rock tended the air and the livestock, ate, helped out with large blocks and the like, and snatched some sleep. They rotated one at a time through the three stations, and worked one shift (timed by detonator timer) at each post. It made for a routine so mesmerizing in its exhaustiveness that Oliver found it very hard to do his calculations of their position in his shift off. "You've got to keep at it," Jakob told him as he ran back from the robot to help the calculating. "It's not just anywhere we want to come up, but right under the domed city of Selene, next to the rocket rails. To do that we'll need some good navigation. We get that and we'll come up right in the middle of the masters who have gotten rich from selling the blue to Earth, and that will be a very gratifying thing I assure you."

So Oliver would work on it until he slept. Actually it was relatively easy; he knew where they had been in the moon when they struck out on their own, and Jakob had given him the surface coordinates for Selene: so it was just a matter of dead reckoning.

It was even possible to calculate their average speed, and therefore when they could expect to reach the surface. That could be checked against the rate of depletion of their fixed resources—air, water lost in the recycler, and food for the livestock. It took a few shifts of consultation with mute Elijah to determine all the factors reliably, and after that it was a simple matter of arithmetic.

When Oliver and Elijah completed these calculations they called Jakob over and explained what they had done.

"Good work," Jakob said. "I should have thought of that."

"But look," Oliver said, "we've got enough air and water, and the robot's power pack is ten times what we'll need—same with explo-sives—it's only food is a problem. I don't know if we've got enough hay for the cows."

Jakob nodded as he looked over Oliver's shoulder and examined their figures. "We'll have to kill and eat the cows one by one. That'll feed us and cut down on the amount of hay we need, at the same time."

"Eat the cows?" Oliver was stunned.

"Sure! They're meat! People on Earth eat them all the time!"

"Well . . ." Oliver was doubtful, but under the lash of Hester's bitter laughter he didn't say any more.

Still, Jakob and Freeman and Naomi decided it would be best if they stepped up the pace a little bit, to provide them with more of a margin for error. They shifted two people to the shaft face and supplemented the robot's continuous drilling with hand drill work around the sides of the tunnel, and ate on the run while moving blocks to the back, and slept as little as they could. They were making miles on every shift.

The rock they wormed through began to change in character. The hard, dark, unbroken basalt gave way to lighter rock that was sometimes dangerously fractured. "Anorthosite," Jakob said. "We're reaching the crust." After that every shift brought them through a new zone of rock. Once they tunneled through great layers of calcium feldspar striped with basalt intrusions, so that it looked like badly made brick. Another time they blasted their way through a wall of jaspar as hard as steel. Only once did they pass through a vein of the blue; when they did it occurred to Oliver that his whole conception of the moon's composition had been warped by their mining. He had thought the moon was bursting with promethium, but as they dug across the narrow vein he realized it was uncommon, a loose net of threads in the great lunar body.

As they left the vein behind, Solly picked up a piece of the ore and stared at it curiously, lower eyes shut, face contorted as he struggled

87

to focus his third eye. Suddenly he dashed the chunk to the ground, turned and marched to the head of their tunnel, attacked it with a drill. "I've given my whole life to the blue," he said, voice thick. "And what is it but a Goddamned rock."

Jakob laughed shortly. They tunneled on, away from the precious metal that now represented to them only a softer material to dig through. "Pick up the pace!" Jakob cried, slapping Solly on the back and leaping over the blocks beside the robot. "This rock has melted and melted again, changing over eons to the stones we see. Metamorphosis," he chanted, stretching the word out, lingering on the syllable *mor* until the word became a kind of song. "Meta*mor*phosis. Meta-*mor*-pho-sis." Naomi and Hester took up the chant, and mute Elijah tapped his drill against the robot in double time. Jakob chanted over it. "Soon we will come to the city of the masters, the domes of Xanadu with their glass and fruit and steaming pools, and their vases and sports and their fine aged wines. And then there will be a—"

"Meta*mor*phosis."

And they tunneled ever faster.

Sitting in the sleeping car, chewing on a cheese, Oliver regarded the bulk of Jakob lying beside him. Jakob breathed deeply, very tired, almost asleep. "How do you know about the domes?" Oliver asked him softly. "How do you know all the things that you know?"

"Don't know," Jakob muttered. "Everyone knows. Less they burn your brain. Put you in a hole to live out your life. I don't know much, boy. Make most of it up. Love of a moon. Whatever we need . . ." And he slept.

They came up through a layer of marble—white marble all laced with quartz, so that it gleamed and sparkled in their lightless sight, and made them feel as though they dug through stone made of their cows' good milk, mixed with water like diamonds. This went on for a long time, until it filled them up and they became intoxicated with its smooth muscly texture, with the sparks of light lazing out of it. "I remember once we went to see a jazz band," Jakob said to all of them. Puffing as he ran the white rock along the cars to the rear, stacked it ever so carefully. "It was in Richmond among all the docks and refineries and giant oil tanks and we were so drunk we kept getting lost. But finally we found it—huh!—and it was just this broken-down trumpeter and a back line. He played sitting in a chair and you could just see in his face that his life had been a tough scuffle. His hat covered his whole household. And trumpet is a young man's instrument, too, it tears your lip to tatters. So we sat down to drink not expecting a thing, and they started up the last song of a set. 'Bucket's Got a Hole in It.' Four bar blues, as simple as a song can get."

"Meta*mor*phosis," rasped Hester.

"Yeah! Like that. And this trumpeter started to play it. And they went through it over and over and over. Huh! They must have done it a hundred times. Two hundred times. And sure enough this trumpeter was playing low and half the time in his hat, using all the tricks a broken-down trumpeter uses to save his lip, to hide the fact that it went west thirty years before. But after a while that didn't matter, because he was playing. He was playing! Everything he had learned in all his life, all the music and all the sorry rest of it, all that was jammed into the poor old "Bucket" and by God it was mind over matter time, because that old song began to *roll.* And still on the run he broke into it: "Oh the buck-ets got a hole in it

Yeah the buck-et's got a hole in it.

Say the buck-et's got a hole in it.

Can't buy no beer!"

And over again. Oliver, Solly, Freeman, Hester, Naomi—they couldn't help laughing. What Jakob came up with out of his unburnt past! Mute Elijah banged a car wall happily, then squeezed the udder of a cow between one verse and the next—"Can't buy no beer!—*Moo!*"

They all joined in, breathing or singing it. It fit the pace of their work perfectly: fast but not too fast, regular, repetitive, simple, endless. All the syllables got the same length, a bit syncopated, except "hole," which was stretched out, and "can't buy no beer," which was high and all stretched out, stretched into a great shout of triumph, which was crazy since what it was saying was bad news, or should have been. But the song made it a cry of joy, and every time it rolled around they sang it louder, more stretched out. Jakob scatted up and down and around the tune, and Hester found all kinds of higher harmonics in a voice like a saw cutting steel, and the old tune rocked over and over and over and over and over and over and over and over and over and over, in a great passacaglia, in the crucible where all poverty is wrenched to delight: the blues. Meta*mor*phosis. They sang it continuously for two shifts running, until they were all completely hypnotized by it; and then frequently, for long spells, for the rest of their time together.

It was sheer bad luck that they broke into a shaft from below, and that the shaft was filled with armed foremen; and worse luck that Jakob was working the robot, so that he was the first to leap out firing his hand drill like a weapon, and the only one to get struck by return fire before Naomi threw a knotchopper past him and blew the foremen to shreds. They got him on a car and rolled the robot back and pulled up the track and cut off in a new direction, leaving another Boesman behind to destroy evidence of their passing.

So they were all racing around with the blood and stuff still covering them and the cows mooing in distress and Jakob breathing through clenched teeth in double time, and only Hester and Oliver could sit in the car with him and try to tend him, ripping away the pants from a leg that was all cut up. Hester took a hand drill to cauterize the wounds that were bleeding hard, but Jakob shook his head at her, neck muscles bulging out. "Got the big artery inside of the thigh," he said through his teeth.

Hester hissed. "Come here," she croaked at Solly and the rest. "Stop that and come here!"

They were in a mass of broken quartz, the fractured clear crystals all pink with oxidation. The robot continued drilling away, the air cylinder hissed, the cows mooed. Jakob's breathing was harsh and somehow all of them were also breathing in the same way, irregularly, too fast; so that as his breathing slowed and calmed, theirs did too. He was lying back in the sleeping car, on a bed of hay, staring up at the fractured sparkling quartz ceiling of their tunnel, as if he could see far into it. "All these different kinds of rock," he said, his voice filled with wonder and pain. "You see, the moon itself was the world, once upon a time, and the Earth its moon; but there was an impact, and everything changed."

They cut a small side passage in the quartz and left Jakob there, so that when they filled in their tunnel as they moved on he was left behind, in his own deep crypt. And from then on the moon for them was only his big tomb, rolling through space till the sun itself died, as he had said it someday would.

Oliver got them back on a course, feeling radically uncertain of his navigational calculations now that Jakob was not there to nod over his shoulder to approve them. Dully he gave Naomi and Freeman the coordinates for Selene. "But what will we do when we get there?" Jakob had never actually made that clear. Find the leaders of the city, demand justice for the miners? Kill them? Get to the rockets of the great magnetic rail accelerators, and hijack one to Earth? Try to slip unnoticed into the populace?

"You leave that to us," Naomi said. "Just get us there." And he saw a light in Naomi's and Freeman's eyes that hadn't been there before. It reminded him of the thing that had chased him in the dark, the thing that even Jakob hadn't been able to explain; it frightened him.

So he set the course and they tunneled on as fast as they ever had. They never sang and they rarely talked; they threw themselves at the rock, hurt themselves in the effort, returned to attack it more fiercely than before. When he could not stave off sleep Oliver lay down on Jakob's dried blood, and bitterness filled him like a block of the anorthosite they wrestled with.

They were running out of hay. They killed a cow, ate its roasted flesh. The water recycler's filters were clogging, and their water smelled of urine. Hester listened to the seismometer as often as she could now, and she thought they were being pursued. But she also thought they were approaching Selene's underside.

Naomi laughed, but it wasn't like her old laugh. "You got us there, Oliver. Good work."

Oliver bit back a cry.

"Is it big?" Solly asked.

Hester shook her head. "Doesn't sound like it. Maybe twice the diameter of the Great Bole, not more."

"Good," Freeman said, looking at Naomi.

"But what will we do?" Oliver said.

Hester and Naomi and Freeman and Solly all turned to look at him, eyes blazing like twelve chunks of pure promethium. "We've got eight Boesmans left," Freeman said in a low voice. "All the rest of the explosives add up to a couple more. I'm going to set them just right. It'll be my best work ever, my masterpiece. And we'll blow Selene right off into space."

It took them ten shifts to get all the Boesmans placed to Freeman's and Naomi's satisfaction, and then another three to get far enough down and to one side to be protected from the shock of the blast, which luckily for them was directly upward against something that would give, and therefore would have less recoil.

Finally they were set, and they sat in the sleeping car in a circle of six, around the pile of components that sat under the master detonator. For a long time they just sat there cross-legged, breathing slowly and staring at it. Staring at each other, in the dark, in perfect redblack clarity. Then Naomi put both arms out, placed her hands carefully on the detonator's button. Mute Elijah put his hands on hers—then Freeman, Hester, Solly, finally Oliver—just in the order that Jakob had taken them. Oliver hesitated, feeling the flesh and bone under his hands, the warmth of his companions. He felt they should say something but he didn't know what it was.

"Seven," Hester croaked suddenly.

"Six," Freeman said.

Elijah blew air through his teeth, hard.

"Four," said Naomi.

"Three!" Solly cried.

"Two," Oliver said.

And they all waited a beat, swallowing hard, waiting for the moon and the man in the moon to speak to them. Then they pressed down on the button. They smashed at it with their fists, hit it so violently they scarcely felt the shock of the explosion.

They had put on vacuum suits and were breathing pure oxygen as they came up the last tunnel, clearing it of rubble. A great number of other shafts were revealed as they moved into the huge conical cavity left by the Boesmans; tunnels snaked away from the cavity in all directions, so that they had sudden long vistas of blasted tubes extending off into the depths of the moon they had come out of. And at the top of the cavity, struggling over its broken edge, over the rounded wall of a new crater . . .

It was black. It was not like rock. Spread across it was a spill of white points, some bright, some so faint that they disappeared into the black if you looked straight at them. There were thousands of these white points, scattered over a black dome that was not a dome . . . And there in the middle, almost directly overhead: a blue and white ball. Big, bright, blue, distant, rounded; half of it bright as a foreman's flash, the other half just a shadow . . . It was clearly round, a big ball in the . . . sky. In the sky.

Wordlessly they stood on the great pile of rubble ringing the edge of their hole. Half buried in the broken anorthosite were shards of clear plastic, steel struts, patches of green glass, fragments of metal, an arm, broken branches, a bit of orange ceramic. Heads back to stare at the ball in the sky, at the astonishing fact of the void, they scarcely noticed these things.

A long time passed, and none of them moved except to look around. Past the jumble of dark trash that had mostly been thrown off in a single direction, the surface of the moon was an immense expanse of white hills, as strange and glorious as the stars above. The size of it all! Oliver had never dreamed that everything could be so big.

"The blue must be promethium," Solly said, pointing up at the Earth. "They've covered the whole Earth with the blue we mined."

Their mouths hung open as they stared at it. "How far away is it?" Freeman asked. No one answered.

"There they all are," Solly said. He laughed harshly. "I wish I could blow up the Earth too!"

He walked in circles on the rubble of the crater's rim. The rocket rails, Oliver thought suddenly, must have been in the direction Freeman had sent the debris. Bad luck. The final upward sweep of them poked up out of the dark dirt and glass. Solly pointed at them. His voice was loud in Oliver's ears, it strained the intercom: "Too bad we can't fly to the Earth, and blow it up too! I wish we could!"

And mute Elijah took a few steps, leaped off the mound into the sky, took a swipe with one hand at the blue ball. They laughed at him. "Almost got it, didn't you!" Freeman and Solly tried themselves, and then they all did: taking quick runs, leaping, flying slowly up through space, for five or six or seven seconds, making a grab at the sky overhead, floating back down as if in a dream, to land in a tumble, and try it again . . . It felt wonderful to hang up there at the top of the leap, free in the vacuum, free of gravity and everything else, for just that instant.

After a while they sat down on the new crater's rim, covered with white dust and black dirt. Oliver sat on the very edge of the crater, legs over the edge, so that he could see back down into their sublunar world, at the same time that he looked up into the sky. Three eyes were not enough to judge such immensities. His heart pounded, he felt too intoxicated to move anymore. Tired, drunk. The intercom rasped with the sounds of their breathing, which slowly calmed, fell into a rhythm together. Hester buzzed one phrase of "Bucket" and they laughed softly. They lay back on the rubble, all but Oliver, and stared up into the dizzy reaches of the universe, the velvet black of infinity. Oliver sat with elbows on knees, watched the white hills glowing under the black sky. They were lit by earthlight—earthlight and starlight. The white mountains on the horizon were as sharp-edged as the shards of dome glass sticking out of the rock. And all the time the Earth looked down at him. It was all too fantastic to believe. He drank it in like oxygen, felt it filling him up, expanding in his chest.

"What do you think they'll do with us when they get here?" Solly asked.

"Kill us," Hester croaked.

"Or put us back to work," Naomi added.

Oliver laughed. Whatever happened, it was impossible in that moment to care. For above them a milky spill of stars lay thrown across the infinite black sky, lighting a million better worlds; while just over their heads the Earth glowed like a fine blue lamp; and under their feet rolled the white hills of the happy moon, holed like a great cheese.

Murder . . . Then and Now

Penny Mickelbury

THEN

They moved single file through the forest, slowly, one step at a time, the leader stopping occasionally to cock his head to one side or the other, pretending to listen, as if he could discern one night sound from another. He could not. He was a child of the city. His night sounds were sirens and big car engines and tinny juke box noise that escaped from night clubs when the door opened to let someone in or out. He was out here in the woods, in the dark, as part of a mission: Playing his part in the Revolution that would not be televised.

William Rodgers, the leader, stopped because he was tired, he was hungry, and he had a political science paper due on Friday morning that he had to finish writing—and worse—typing. He wished for the umpteenth time that he had not agreed to this mission, but as head of the Black Students Union, he'd had no choice. He was the leader. He had to lead. In truth, though, he was following more than leading. Following the minute pieces of string Eric had taped to tree trunks to mark the way through the unfamiliar wood.

"Damn, it's dark out here!" That made the fourth time that X had stated the obvious. The first two times, Eric and Charlie had co-signed, agreeing that it was, indeed, dark. The third time Tamara had made a sound deep in her throat, but she had not spoken. Now she did.

"Yeah, J.T., it's dark out here. It's eleven o'clock at night and we're out in the woods."

"I told you, don't call me that slave name. My name is X!"

"Your name is John Thomas Anderson."

"William, man, I'm telling you: You need to make your woman shut up! She runs her mouth way too damn much."

"Nobody *makes* me do anything, J.T., especially a nobody like you," Tam snarled at him, and William thought that he could see her eyes flash in the darkness. "Like somebody would mistake you for Malcolm X," she added derisively, and tacked on J.T. for good measure, hitting each letter hard and holding on to it, as if savoring the taste made by its sound, though the exact opposite was true.

"We should be almost there," Charlie Gordon, the youngest of the group, said before J.T. could open his mouth to remonstrate. William had been surprised that he'd even joined them, opposed as he was to this revolutionary manifestation of violence. Charlie was a freshman and everybody genuinely liked him. He was easygoing and surprisingly funny—surprisingly because he was so quiet, much more of a listener than a talker. He hadn't said a word all night until now. William wondered how Charlie knew where they were.

"I think that's right," William answered, and looked back at Eric for confirmation..

"It is," Eric said. Probably the only true revolutionary among them, Eric had come up with the idea and the plan to firebomb the two-story building that was the meeting place of the local KKK chapter. It also was the police department and jail, and the police chief was the head sheet-wearer. Eric Mason, senior political science major, knew this because it was his home town, the chief sheet-wearer his personal nemesis.

Three and a half miles due east of the front gate of the state university they all attended, the town might just as well have been on the other side of the moon. This was true for Eric's home town and all their home towns. In big cities and small towns across America in 1968, no matter how loudly James Brown encouraged being Black and proud, no matter how intently Aretha Franklin demanded Respect, they still were perceived as the niggers they'd always been. When the Klan called for a rally and marched down the middle of the town's main street for the purpose of burning Black Power in effigy, it became the social event of the season: Every white person for miles would be in attendance; every Black person for miles would find somewhere else to be. Eric strongly, almost violently, resented the fact that everybody related to him had already left town, though the KKK event would not happen for another three days, on Saturday.

Eric had thought that firebombing the Klan would be a worthy activity for the BSU since the only activity the group had managed, aside from weekly meetings, was a weekly party. The only person who had disagreed out loud was Charlie, and yet here he was, carrying a five-gallon can of gasoline through the woods to be stashed until the night of the Klan rally.

"They like burning things, we'll give 'em a fire!" Eric had said in the BSU meeting the night he proposed this particular activity, and he raised his fist to the sky and yelled, "Burn, baby, burn!" Tam, J.T. and half a dozen other students had joined in. William had not. He'd been trying to think of a way to avoid having the group give the matter any serious consideration when Eric made it a motion and Tam seconded it. His only choice had been to call for a vote, and the resulting whoops and shouts had left no doubt as to the will of the group. He'd later thought he should have called for a show of hands, because two weeks later the BSU membership had dwindled down to the five of them now sneaking through the woods to hide ten gallons of Esso Regular, thirty glass bottles, and yards of ripped up sheets and tee shirts in a rock pit Eric and Charlie had prepared the previous weekend.

"Let's get this done," William said, moving forward again, and the line followed him: Eric directly behind in case William lost sight of the string; Tamara behind him; J.T. behind her; Charlie bringing up the rear. In the deep darkness, they all looked the same, and any racist would have been forgiven for saying so. Again, it was Eric's idea that they all wear black jeans and turtleneck shirts, black combat boots, and green fatigue jackets. All of them had huge afro hair dos. It was only Tam's petite build that identified her as the sole woman among the men, all of whom were close enough to six feet tall for nobody to argue about an inch or two, and in excellent physical condition.

The wardrobe was camouflage costume, but also a matter of practicality. It was Fall in the northeastern United States, and chilly to cold at night. Each of them was glad for the warmth of the heavy jacket and the thick boots, though only two of them—Eric and Charlie—

were comfortable in the woods. For reasons known only to the two of them, this was Charlie's home town, too, and he'd spent many youthful hours playing hide-and-go-seek, king of the mountain, and can't catch me in these woods. He and Eric knew each other casually, acquainted through their younger sisters who were in the same class at the high school. Within the small town's small Black community, it was well-known that Eric was a genius and always expected that he would attend the university.

It was just as well known that Charlie was not a genius, and his attendance at the university was a surprise to all, including Charlie himself. While he was by no means a stupid young man, the mechanics of learning had never excited him. He'd learned what he was taught, he had behaved himself in school, he'd applied to college because his counselor told him to do it, and he'd been accepted—the first in his family to have achieved such a milestone. His parents had been more bemused than proud at the notion of their son the college student, and Charlie always felt that they were waiting for the letter that would explain that the previous letter of acceptance had been, after all, a mistake.

Charlie attended his classes, took reasonably good notes, did the reading and writing he was assigned. He attended his first Black Student Union meeting because he'd been invited. He attended the second because he welcomed and enjoyed the feeling of belonging. He liked being called Brother, and he liked calling people Brother and Sister, liked feeling that the words had real meaning. He also liked feeling that he wasn't alone on the huge campus. The fact that he lived in the town had no meaning during those long hours of the day when he had to make his way from class to class, always the only Black in that class, often not seeing another Black student until the evening hours when they'd meet to share a meal—and that wasn't a daily occurrence. He was, after all, a freshman.

Little more than a child to the likes of William and Tamara and J.T., Eric treated him like a man, but Eric's head so often was in an esoteric cloud of one kind or another. Charlie wasn't the only one who didn't always understand what Eric was talking about but he was the only one too intimidated to question, to challenge. Except the one time. Except the time he objected to firebombing the police station. He'd expressed his opinion and they'd all sat quietly, listening to him. Respecting him. Some of them even agreeing with him when he'd made the point that only Black men would be in the jail when they burned it. The chief wouldn't be there, or any of the white officers. And for a moment, they'd hesitated. Then they'd voted to burn, baby, burn.

Charlie was on tonight's mission because he felt bad that almost everybody else had abandoned Eric. He thought it cowardly to advocate for a position, then withdraw. He thought it manly to support a friend if not the friend's position, and he knew that Eric appreciated his support. He had accompanied Eric on the scouting mission, had helped dig the hole where the gasoline would be buried and line it with rocks, making certain that the combustible material was far removed from anything that would combust—until it was time.

"Are you sure gasoline will burn down a brick building?" he had asked Eric. And Eric had explained in great detail the history of the Molotov cocktail, and the way it worked. As always, Charlie marveled at Eric's vast store of knowledge. Eric explained in his quiet way that he was a revolutionary.

"We'll toss them on to the roof," Eric told him. "The roof isn't brick. It'll burn. Two dozen incendiary devices thrown simultaneously will set that roof on fire in a matter of seconds. Maybe minutes," he allowed, for his knowledge of the devices was purely intellectual.

"Wouldn't it make more sense to make them first, then carry them into the woods, instead of bringing the gas, the bottles and rags separately?" Charlie had asked, and Eric had agreed, and complimented him on his clear thinking.

"But Tamara and J.T. didn't want to do it that way and I didn't want to rock a boat that already was on the verge of tipping over."

They'd had that conversation less than a week ago and though Charlie couldn't imagine anything other than chaos and disorganization on Saturday as the four of them would hurriedly work to fill the bottles, he did agree that carrying the already filled bottles through the woods would have been extremely uncomfortable if not dangerous. As relieved as he was to be rid of the gas can, he couldn't shake his residual and persistent worry about the men who'd be trapped in the jail, consigned to a fiery death, and he realized it didn't matter to him whether they were Black or white. "Phase One of the Mission: Accomplished," William said, putting his gas can in the pit beside the one Charlie had placed there.

"Good work, everybody, and thanks," Eric said as he spread a tarp over the cans, then began to push and shove dirt into the pit to cover the gas cans while J.T. and Tamara covered the bottles and rags with boughs, tree limbs and branches that Charlie and Eric had gathered for that purpose.

"You sure this is secure?" William asked, for even in the dark it was obvious that something was buried there. "You sure nobody will see it?"

Eric gave a slight shrug, then nodded. "Pretty sure. Black folk don't usually come this far through the woods and white folks almost never go through the woods toward Coontown."

"Toward what?" Tam had shouted, then quickly covered her mouth with her hand and repeated the question in a hoarse whisper: "Toward what?"

Eric almost smiled. "Coontown is what they call the Black side of town."

He had explained to them, when it first became apparent that serious consideration was being given to the plan to firebomb the local police station and jail, that a narrow but dense wood separated the Black and white sections of the city. Might be railroad tracks everyplace else. Here it was woods and, Eric said, for his whole life, Black children had played in the woods up to a specific and delineated point, while white people almost never entered these woods. They had no need. They had their own woods that led to a lake, off-limits to the residents of Coontown.

"You said 'almost never' came into these woods," J.T. said. "Define 'almost never.'"

"When they were up to no good they'd come through," Eric said. "Usually teenaged boys or good ole boys drunked up and feeling mighty." Now he did smile, a thin, chilly thing that likely would have been unnerving in full light. "Saturday night's activities likely would be the kind of thing to draw them into the woods, toward us."

"But won't they know that all the Black people are gone?" Charlie asked.

"Sure. They know," Eric replied softly. "But they'll still be mad when they won't be able to find anybody to intimidate or beat up. That's when they'll want to burn. Only they won't get that far. Unless they put out our fire first," he said, then whispered, "Burn, baby, burn," and it sounded like a prayer.

"Still," J.T. said, "I just can't picture them letting us sneak up on 'em and set fire to their police station, no matter how many *papier-mache* Black Power dolls they're burning." His growl was whispered but it sounded loud.

"You saying they'll know what we've got planned, J.T.?" Tam asked.

"No, I'm not saying that, Tamara . . ."

She cut him off. "Because if you are, J.T., I'd like to know how it happened that they would come to suspect *us*. After all, it's not like we've got a hundred fired-up, bushy-headed, fist-raising Black Power militants on our campus. No need for them to give us a second thought."

William had had enough and for once, that included enough of Tam. "Look, nobody has said anything to anybody about any of this. Eric, if you're sure this is safe here for the next three days, let's go. Let's follow the exit plan to the letter. No detours, no exceptions. We meet back at the Black House in half an hour."

"Hold up a second, Will," Tam said, grabbing his arm. "I need to hear J.T. say it."

"You don't need to hear nothin' from me! I 'bout had enough of you. In fact, why don't you tell us that *you're* not the Uncle Tom in the woodpile. You're way too quick to point the finger at other people. William, man, I don't know how you stand her. Bad enough we're out here in the woods, in the dark, without her mouth."

"It figures you'd be afraid of the dark," Tam said, and William was certain he saw her eyes flash. "Always talking about the Homeland and when you get to Africa this and when you get to Africa that, and you can't even hike a quarter mile in an Upstate woodland. You do know, don't you, 'X,' that there are jungles in the Homeland? Dense, deep jungles and no electricity to speak of. Talk about dark."

J.T. made a grab for her but Charlie caught him and William stepped between them.

"I'm sick of her!" J.T. snarled.

"I'm sick of both of you," Eric said, sounding for the first time like the enormity of what he had concocted was finally sinking in. "We're doing this. *I'm* doing this if the rest of you are getting cold feet. I don't mind going it alone. And for the record, Tam, I trust X."

Ironically enough, it was Eric who'd almost called the whole thing off early in the planning stages. He'd become convinced that there was a traitor among them, an Uncle Tom, somebody who was on the payroll of The Man. About half their members agreed while the other half reminded him that not a single one of them knew anybody white on campus, to say nothing to knowing any law enforcement or government types. Sure, they went to classes and lived in dormitories with white students, but they didn't *know* them. And besides, when would a traitor have had time to betray them?

They spent practically all of their free time with each other, studying, partying and planning the revolution. Those who agreed with Eric pointed out—quite correctly—that almost certainly their betrayer would not be white but Black like them, in addition to which almost every even quasi-radical, pseudo revolutionary had heard the clicks on the telephone line that signaled J. Edgar's goons were listening—or knew somebody who had heard the clicks. If any one of them had aroused suspicion, they'd know they were suspected. The real threat of such provided sufficient reason for most of the BSU membership to have had other things to occupy them on this frosty Wednesday night. This sudden, intense need to study angered everybody but Eric. He understood, he said. It was, he often said, one of the most dangerous times in American history to be Black and fear was a natural response to danger.

"Nice of you to call cowardice fear, Eric," J.T. had said in his customary growl. "We're all afraid. We'd be crazy not to be. But sooner or later, everybody has to take a stand."

Five of them had taken a stand on this Wednesday night. As they disbanded, heading off in four different directions—William and Tamara together, J.T., Charlie and Eric each in a different direction—

they gave each other the Black Power salute, intoned *Power to the People* with reverence, and promised to arrive at the Black House in half an hour bringing food and drink. The adrenaline produced by the trek through the woods needed to be fed.

Only Charlie was looking forward to the midnight rendezvous. He thoroughly enjoyed every moment of the time he spent at the Black House, though BSU meetings had, in the past several months, morphed from a fascinating and fiery mix of the political and the philosophical to the merely polemical, with anger usually trumping all attempts to introduce rationality into the discussions. And while he was unnerved by the force of some of the anger, Charlie knew that he was learning much more than ever would be taught in the university's classrooms, for nobody in the school's administrative hierarchy acknowledged that things were changing in the world.

That Black people were angry was evident to anybody who'd been paying even scant attention to events in the United States of America. What white Americans seemed unable or, worse, unwilling to understand was the reason for the anger. Black anger just made them angry, and the angrier they got, the more powerfully they resisted any notion that there could be any justification for what they were seeing on their television screens on an almost daily basis: The rioting and the burning and the talk of power and revolution. Who did they think they were? Guilt was a mighty motivator. Self-righteousness was a deadly one. For a people whose historical landscape was littered with corpses, the tossing of a few bottles of gasoline at a few sheet-wearing murderers seemed to Charlie not an unreasonable response.

He already was scrunched inside his VW Beetle when the thought floated, fully formed, into his brain: Firebomb the KKK marchers, not the jail. Throw the cocktails over the roof, not on the roof. They'd crash in the street, forcing the KKK and their followers to run like hell away from the flames, which would give them, the flame throwers, time to escape through the woods. The Black men housed in the jail would be spared, the sheets would feel the fire, and Charlie et al. would live to fight another day. Eric would, he thought, approve of this plan. So would J.T. and perhaps even William. And, Charlie thought, a few dozen already assembled Molotov cocktails would be convincing.

He climbed out of the Beetle and hurried back through the woods. He didn't think he'd be missed tonight. William and Tamara, who lived at the Black House, probably would rather be in bed than entertaining them. Eric usually preferred the company of his own thoughts. And if J.T. never spent another moment in Tamara's presence, it would be okay. Charlie would do his work tonight, in secret, and then tell them all on Friday night at their final planning meeting. It would be his surprise gift to them.

But it was Charlie who was surprised on Friday night. He'd stopped his car two blocks from the house. He could get no closer because the police had blocked off the street. He backed up, turned around and drove away, thinking frantically about who he could ask about what was going on, because he was certain that whatever it was, the Black House was involved. He drove around for a while, then went home. His mother ran down the walk and grabbed him before he could haul himself out of the tiny car.

"OhGodOhGodOhGod! I thought you were dead, Charlie!" She held him so tight he couldn't breathe.

"I'm not dead, Mama. Why would you think that?"

"'Cause the rest of 'em are dead! That's what they're saying on the TV!"

Charlie broke away from her and ran into the house. He spent the rest of the evening on the floor before the television, not believing what he was hearing: William Rodgers and John Thomas Anderson, Jr., both twenty-one-year-old seniors at the university, found shot to death in an off-campus residence used by Black students to plot against the school and the government; another senior, twenty-three-year old Michael Eric Mason was being held, charged with the murders. It couldn't be true. Charlie didn't believe it.

He learned the following day that it was true. The gun that killed William and J.T. was found in the leather satchel that Eric used to carry his books and papers. His fingerprints were all over it. He also learned that all the Black students enrolled in the university were to be expelled. Immediately. Acting on a tip from a confidential source, the police uncovered a stash of Molotov cocktails buried behind the police department that the dead and jailed Black Power advocates planned to use to disrupt the weekend plans of the KKK.

The march and rally, with more than five hundred in attendance, went off without a hitch. Three Black Power effigies were hung and burned. Participants were given Molotov cocktails to throw at the effigies. Half a dozen of those participants grabbed a handful of Molotov cocktails and ran through the woods to Coontown where they threw them at the first houses they came to. Nine houses belonging to Black residents burned to the ground before the fire department arrived.

NOW

Boxer Gordon was one of the fastest two-fingered typists on the planet. That wasn't always the case. Until five or six months ago, his hunt-and-peck method of typing resembled that of every other non-typist: Slow and error-filled. Then Peggy Brown, that miracle of a woman who had brought light and life and joy back into his dark old life, showed him a free typing tutorial on the public library's website. He'd been self-appointed king of the two-fingered typists ever since. She opined his years and skill as a boxer in the army accounted for his fast fingers. He didn't agree, but he didn't argue.

He put the spell checker to work, corrected the errors, pushed the print button, sat back in the chair and put his sock feet up on the desk. Soon he was re-reading the final report to the client when the phone rang. He looked at the desk clock over the tops of his reading glasses. Too early to be Peggy calling. He picked up the phone. "Charles Gordon."

"Hello, Charlie."

The soft, slightly mocking voice on the other end of the phone shocked Boxer to his core and, truth be told, frightened him. He swung his feet to the floor and stood, though he didn't know why. He gripped the phone. "Eric? Is that you? Really you?"

"It's really me, Charlie."

Boxer dropped back into his chair and was glad for the extra pillows in the seat, otherwise he'd have hurt himself, he went down so hard. "My God. Eric. Eric Mason."

"How are you, Charlie?"

"Where are you, Eric?"

"I'm here, Charlie. I'm back. I'm home."

Boxer didn't know what else to say. He'd put it all behind him, out of his memory.

"I'd like to see you, Charlie. I know you're a busy man but I'd appreciate a bit of your time. Sooner rather than later."

"Of course, Eric. I'm not that busy." He wished he were, then he could have refused.

Eric produced a dry chuckle. Something new, Boxer thought: A chuckle from Eric. Then he thought to himself, the man probably had quite a few new habits. Forty years in prison could produce a shit load of new habits. "I've read about your exploits, Charlie. You've lead a most interesting life. And a productive one, too, I think."

"I have to deliver a client report in about an hour, Eric, and I'm free after that."

Eric gave the name of a by-the-hour motel a couple of blocks from the bus station and a tsunami-sized wave of sadness washed over Boxer. He almost offered the man his couch but he didn't want to trust what forty years in prison might have done to Eric. He'd been a cop before he became a PI, and was infantry in Vietnam before that. Life experiences changed a man, and prison was one of life's most horrible experiences—worse, maybe, than war. No telling who Eric Mason was now, but whoever he was, he wanted to see Boxer—no, he wanted to see Charlie—and Charlie would see him. But first he'd see his client, get paid, deposit the check in the bank, stop by the hospital where Peggy was the late shift nursing supervisor this month to tell her where he'd be, and finally pick up some food to take to Eric.

Boxer assumed that forty years worth of prison chow had left Eric without any pretensions where food was concerned, that he'd eat almost anything. He bought two whole roasted chickens and several kinds of vegetables, bread, dessert, six packs of beer and soda, and, as an afterthought, stopped at a discount store and bought plates, utensils, glasses, napkins and a tablecloth. Eric had said he was "home" but Boxer knew the man had no living family in town, and no real reason to come back here. Unless he, Boxer—Charlie—was the only one still alive who knew his past, and Boxer thought he had succeeded in forgetting it.

He was surprised at what he saw when Eric opened the door. He had been expecting the worst but that's not what he got. Eric looked fit and trim and when Boxer put the bags down and hugged him, what he felt was a prison-hardened body, hours a day spent in the weight room. Of course, the Black Power afro was gone. Eric's hair, all white now, was cut close to the scalp, but there was no bald spot on top. The tell was in the eyes. His eyes, once calm, gentle, peaceful, inquisitive, now were wild, crazy eyes. He knew how to keep them under control, knew better than to let Boxer see too much. Knew also, though, that Boxer had seen more than enough.

"Thank you for coming, Charlie, and please, before we start down memory lane, I want to apologize to you. I know you tried to see me in prison, and you wrote to me all those years ago. I appreciated it, but I wanted to keep you as far away from all that as possible."

"What happened, Eric? I'll understand if you can't or don't want to talk about it. But if you can, I'd really like to know." Did he? Forty years ago, he hadn't. Not really.

Eric nodded but he was looking at the food. "A feast, Charlie. A veritable feast." He licked his lips and rubbed his hands together. "I want to tell you. But I'd really like to eat first, if that's all right with you."

"Of course it is," Boxer said, and he spread the cloth on the table—it was plastic but its bright pattern immediately improved the ragged ugliness of the cheap room. He set out plates and napkins and opened the packages of utensils and glasses. Then he put all the food containers on the table and told Eric to help himself. "Do you want soda or beer?"

"Both!" Eric exclaimed with child-like exuberance. He approached the business of eating the same way. He didn't talk much while he ate except to thank Boxer several times and to compliment both the food and Boxer's choices. Boxer ate a wing and a leg and Eric ate the rest.

"I'm making a glutton of myself and I apologize. This is such a feast, Charlie, and I thank you. Truly I do."

Eric sighed deeply and popped open a can of soda. He drank it down. Then he popped open a beer, took a small sip, frowned, put it down and opened another soda. He turned his wild eyes on Boxer and paused for a second before speaking, as if he wanted to be certain that Boxer saw what was there. "It was Tamara," he said. "She gave me the gun that killed William and J.T. She said I was the one who should have it because I was the most level-headed."

Boxer looked at him but the wildness was gone from his eyes. Nothing left but the emptiness of forty years in prison. "Are you saying that Tamara killed William and J.T.?"

"I don't know if she killed them or if the cops killed them, but I do know she gave me the gun that killed them on Friday afternoon. She was waiting for me after my last class." He smiled a typical Eric smile then, the Eric-smile from the old days—a little shy and a little wry. "I didn't wonder until I'd been in jail for a while how she knew where to find me late on Friday afternoon. I also didn't wonder then what she meant when she told me I was brilliant for having the Molotovs already filled and ready to throw." Eric stopped talking. He smiled that smile again and it was once more the gentle, philosophical Eric. "You did that, didn't you? I always thought it was you who had done it."

Boxer didn't know what to say. So many times he'd wondered whether that had made a difference, wondered whether, if he'd left things alone, there would have been a different result a different outcome. Now he had his answer. "I thought . . . I didn't want to burn the jail. I wanted to burn the cowards wearing the sheets, to scare the shit out of them."

Eric nodded. "I thought a lot about that, too, why we did what we did the way we did it. But much later, in jail, when all I had to do was think and wonder. That Friday afternoon I had no time at all to think. Tamara walked away from me heading toward the front gate, and all the cops in the world came from the other direction, surrounding me. The police chief grabbed my satchel, opened it, pulled out the gun, told me I was under arrest for murder. That's what happened, Charlie. Did Tamara kill them? I don't know. But she did set me up and I had no way to prove my innocence, so I didn't try."

Boxer remembered. Eric had pled guilty. There was no trial. There were no more Black students at the university for quite a few years— not until he was back from Vietnam and hired as the first Black on the city's police department. The old chief, the sheet-wearer, had died and his replacement had come from the state police and had no knowledge of anybody named Charlie Gordon, William Rodgers, John Thomas Anderson or Eric Mason and a failed Molotov cocktail party. "What happened to her? Tamara?"

"She transferred downstate. She wasn't expelled like you and the other brothers and sisters were. Her record was clean. She was just a transfer from one institution in the state university system to another." Eric drank his soda down in several large gulps and crushed the can. "She's a professor now, Charlie. Right here. Tenured. Literature, I believe."

"I didn't know that. Tamara . . . what was her last name? I didn't have much opportunity in my cop days to run into literature professors." And wouldn't have wanted to see her anyway.

Now Eric laughed. "It was Knowles, but get this: Her name's not Tamara. That was her cover name. Or I suppose I should say her undercover name. Her real name was Sandra Smith. It's Gullatti now. She's married. Dr. Sandra Gullatti." He pulled up his sleeve and looked at a watch that might well have been the same Timex he'd worn all those years ago. "She'll be here in about twenty minutes."

It took a long moment for what Eric said to sink in.

"You lived with the thought for forty years that Tamara's a murderer, is that right?"

"Sandra."

"Whatever. The point is you think she's a killer." Boxer held Eric's crazy eyes with his own, not letting him escape, and he finally nodded. Boxer's brain went into overdrive, went into cop-thought: If Tamara/Sandra had killed once, she'd do it again. She hadn't agreed to come down out of her ivory tower to meet somebody she hadn't seen in forty years in a rat trap motel on the seedy side of her university town out of kindness. Eric had set her up to take a fall—and because Boxer was here, he'd fall, too—just like before. Boxer jumped up and began to clear the table of all evidence that a second person was present. Then he scanned the room, looking for a place to hide. There was no place to hide. The closet was barely that, and he wouldn't have gotten on the floor in this place even if he could have fit under the bed. The bathroom. Maybe if he left the door open and stood behind it . . .

"What are you doing, Charlie?"

"Trying to help you set up Tamara without getting us both killed or locked up."

Eric grinned and it scared Boxer. As it should have, for the man reached inside his jacket and pulled out a revolver. It was a .38 Special. "I'm ready this time, Charlie!"

Taken totally off-guard and by surprise, Boxer did something incredibly stupid: He lunged for Eric and took the gun from him, checking to see if the damn thing was loaded. It was. "Where the hell did you get a gun!"

"On Fort Street."

Of course he did, Boxer thought. Illegal any-and-everything could be had on Fort Street. He examined the gun, the serial number filed off. He wiped the weapon and the shells, reloaded it. "You're lucky you didn't kill yourself. You know nothing about guns, Eric."

"I'm already dead, Charlie. The only thing left alive inside of me is the desire to make her pay for betraying us. Give me the gun. I'll kill her, then I'll call the cops and surrender. No trial, just like before, and back to jail and the life I've come to know." He raised his fist in the Black Power salute. "All power to the people!"

Boxer took his arm, pointed him at a chair and told him to sit down. He did. "I want you to listen to me, Eric. Please. Will you do that?" Eric looked at him and nodded. "I'm going to hide in the bathroom behind the door, which will be open so that I can hear everything. You'll talk to Tamara . . . Sandra . . . just like you'd planned, ask her whatever you want to ask her. If she admits to killing William and J.T., I'll arrest her on the spot. All right, Eric?"

"I'd like some more chicken, Charlie, if I may."

"That's fine, Eric," Boxer said, thinking it would look more natural if he were sitting at the table eating when Tamara arrived, and he fixed him a plate and watched him eat as if he had not just eaten enough food for three people half an hour ago, wondering what he'd do with this man after Tamara, for he clearly could not and should not be left to his own devices. He didn't stop eating when the knock sounded at the door and Boxer, heading for the bathroom, he had to motion to Eric to open the door.

Boxer heard the door open. He was glad he couldn't see Tamara. Feeling her presence was sufficient; it was even stronger now than when she was a young woman. And her tone of voice was just as disdainful.

"Well. Eric. Sorry I can't say it's good to see you. What do you want?"

"You know what I want, Tamara, otherwise you wouldn't have come." Boxer heard Eric resume his place at the table, heard the plastic fork clicking against the plastic plate.

"I'm not going to stand here in this shit hole watching you eat rubber chicken."

"Then tell me what I want to know and leave," Eric said, and Boxer tensed at the tone of voice he'd used. He was provoking her. "Did you kill William and J.T. or did the pigs?"

"Which would you prefer?"

"I think it was you. I think J.T. finally convinced William that you were the Uncle Tom in the woodpile, to use J.T.'s expression. I think William had started to suspect you. I know he was getting ready to cut you loose . . . "

"You don't know anything!"

"Yes, I do. I heard William and J.T. talking that night. You'd gone to bed, didn't want to be bothered with us. They were talking about you . . . "

"You could hear through walls, Eric?"

"They were outside smoking. You wouldn't let them smoke in the house. They didn't trust you . . . oh, I should've guessed! A pistol in your pocket! You gonna shoot me now? Who're you gonna plant the gun on this time?"

"I'll find somebody," she snapped.

"How about on me, Tamara?" Boxer emerged from the bathroom holding Eric's .38 on her and he was glad he was because the look on her face was murderous. "Put the gun down," he said.

She stared at him then laughed. "Well if it isn't little Charlie Gordon all grown up."

"Put the gun down, Tamara."

"Or what?"

He pulled back the hammer and she flinched. He watched her eyes. They flashed. William had been right about that: Her eyes really did do that. And she really was a gorgeous woman. Still. Her expertly styled hair was cut short and dyed some kind of bronze that perfectly complemented her bronze skin. She seemed not to have gained very much weight in forty years, and she was stylishly if not quite expensively dressed, the charcoal gray suit and white blouse with pearls at the neck visible under the boxy black coat with the deep pockets spoke: Solidly, comfortably middle class. She looked like a university professor. She probably was a mother, perhaps a grandmother now. He wouldn't have recognized her if he'd passed her on the street—and he doubted that he ever would have, not in his line of work. Too, he'd steered clear of the University.

Eric read his thoughts. "You married, Tam? Or should I call you Sandy? Bet you married a white dude and live in The Heights, far, far away from Coontown."

She whirled away from Boxer and aimed at Eric. Boxer raised the pillow from the nearby bed in his left hand, jamming the .38's muzzle into it and fired rapidly three times. Tamara/Sandra dropped to the floor like all the bones in her body had melted. Eric looked down at her and sagged in his chair as if something had happened to the bones in his body, too.

"That's what she gets for killing them," Eric said.

Boxer wasn't so sure. "Eric, get all your stuff and get out of here. Come on! Do it!"

"And go where, Charlie? I was going to live here for a while."

He thought for a moment. "Walk over to the bus station and take a taxi to the Black Jack diner on Central Avenue." He fished some bills out of his pocket and gave them to Eric. "The taxi driver will know where it is. I'll meet you there as soon as I can."

Eric packed his belongings. It took about half a minute. He looked longingly at the left over chicken. "This Black Jack diner. Is the food good?"

"Some of the best," Boxer assured him

"Can I eat, Charlie?"

"As much as you want, Eric."

He looked at Boxer without crazy eyes. "The Army. Vietnam. Why, Charlie?"

"I'd been expelled from school. What else was there?"

The weary revolutionary walked out of the door, shoulders hunched up around his ears. Then he stopped, straightened up and lifted his right hand in a fist. "All power to the people."

"Right on," Boxer replied softly and closed the door. He had a big mess to clean up in a very short time. Everything he'd brought into the room, including the chicken bones and empty cartons, he stuffed into the intact pillow case. He got a towel from the bathroom and wiped every surface in the room, everything that he or Eric could have touched. He wiped the .38 again and dropped it beside the late Tamara Knowles, AKA Dr. Sandra Gullatti. She still held the weapon she'd brought with her and Boxer expected that it, like the one she planted on Eric all those years ago, had crimes on it. This time, though, it would point back at her. He looked for a purse, realized that she hadn't brought one with her, and knew then that she'd killed J.T. and William. Because she'd come here to kill Eric.

He grabbed the stuffed pillow case, turned off the lights, and gave one last check of the room. The television was on. He hadn't noticed before. The sound was muted and the picture was as grubby as the room. He looked for a remote. There wasn't one so he used his elbow to shut it off. "The revolution will not be televised," he said, and left the room.

Piece Work

Kenneth Wishnia

Hitler celebrated his forty-seventh birthday the other day with a triumphal procession through the streets of Berlin, and he couldn't wait to unwrap his shiny new presents, mainly field-ready motorized units and heavy artillery. Then in an elaborate state ceremony, Air Force Minister Goering anointed him with the imperial title of *Oberste Kriegsherr*. The starstruck reporter for the *New York Times* couldn't understand why the Führer would accept the title of Supreme Warlord, given his repeated claims that he is thoroughly devoted to working for peace, but none of us had any trouble figuring it out.

"You believe that *mishegas*? Adolph frigging Hitler claims he's a peace-loving Socialist, and they just repeat it without question when anyone who's read a newspaper in the last three years can see that he wants to be the next Kaiser," says Benny, the rising steam forming a gauzy veil around his words.

"*Oyb nisht erger*," I say, smoothing out a cluster of pleats in a blue chiffon dress. If not worse.

We have plenty of so-called Socialists right here in New York who support Wall Street's own brand of imperialism, including the head of our union, but there's no point in mentioning that—it would just set Benny off on another one of his rants, and what good would that do? Even with the shop windows open, it's already hot enough by the pressers' stations to curl the wallpaper.

The business agent came by a couple of hours ago, fussing over the new styles and feeling each piece of material with his grubby fingers, before settling on a lousy $2.75 per piece for a brand new tropic print silk evening dress with a double cut-out strap back that's going to retail for $19.95 at Simon's on Fifth Avenue. I figure that after the cutter, the operator, and the finisher are done with it, my share works out to about forty-five cents, which means it will take a couple of hours of heavy-duty steam pressing to pay for just one of my son Aaron's weekly violin lessons. And our second child is due in about four weeks.

A pair of thick rubber hoses dangle from the overhead rod like a couple of sweaty jitterbuggers shimmying down to supply the irons with steam. The 150-gallon boiler is swaddled with thick layers of insulation, but it still radiates enough heat to make a plain cotton undershirt feel like you're wearing a penitent's hair shirt, and I have to work right next to it grinding out piece after piece because that's how we get paid. None of us are paid by the week, except for the almighty cutters, so Benny stands across from me as we drag the big, heavy irons across the delicate chiffons, crepes, and organdies, smoothing out the wrinkles and getting the dresses ready for shipping.

Summer's almost here and the fabric is getting lighter and harder to work with. Slim waists are in this season, with big poofy shoulders and sleeves echoing the leg-o'mutton styles of the Gilded Age. I think of my own dear wife, who may not be as sleek as this year's models, but unlike them, she's built to last. And I ask Benny how many more dresses he thinks we have to press before we can retire or drop dead from heat exhaustion, whichever comes first.

Abe Weinstein looks up from the buttons he's sewing onto a white silk dress with big black polka dots and a *very* thin waist. "Just hang on another dozen years or so, Reb Mordkhe," he says over the clamor of the Singer machines.

Abe is the only one in the shop who uses my full name, Mordecai. Everyone else calls me Morty. Morty Levy.

"For it is written that the Levites shall retire at age fifty."

"Where is it written?" says Morris Gutbeder, glancing up from his machine. "I didn't see it in the Morning *Freiheit*."

"Maybe it was in the *Forverts*," says Benny, but Gutbeder doesn't take the bait.

Abe lets the thread go slack. "The Midrash says that when the Israelites were wandering in the wilderness of Sinai, only the tribe of Levi did not debase themselves by worshiping the Golden Calf."

"No wonder they all became Communists," Benny says, winking at me.

Abe was a respected scholar back in the old country. A real *talmed-khokhem*. He's got a full beard and everything that goes with it. Now he's a finisher, trimming cuffs and seams and doing a little needle-work as needed, and occasionally sharing traditional wisdom amid the industrial activity like a character from a Sholem Aleichem tale who's fallen into our world and can't find his way back to the *shtetl*. Especially with that beard. I've been shaving since I was sixteen.

"Enough of your fairy tales," says Gutbeder. "Where's Linkel?"

"He'll be here," says Grossman, without missing a stitch.

Gutbeder is a big bear of a man and a war vet who looks as out of place handling silk and lace as a Cossack horseman taking the Seventh Avenue Local.

His pal Ruben Grossman served in the Soviet Navy during the Revolution. He was a Russian Jew, I was Polish Jew, and our respective leaders tried to convince us that we two Jews should be shooting at each other. Good thing we saw it differently.

Benny gives the tropic print dress another blast of steam and a once-over as I pick up the pleated chiffon dress and carry it over to the rack that's headed for Oppenheim Collins on West Thirty-Fourth Street. Any excuse to stretch my legs, which always get stiff when I have to stand for a few hours, especially my left knee, a legacy from the war. Not the Great War. I was too young for that. The war Poland declared on Russia in 1919. A little advice to all would-be conquerors: It is *never* a good idea to invade Russia. You will get your *tukheses* handed to you.

Gutbeder and Grossman keep checking the clock like nervous fathers killing time outside the delivery room. But the piece work continues.

I take my time hanging the dress, which gives me a moment to look out the grimy window that some joker propped open with a baseball bat and check out the traffic on Broadway, eight floors below. The same happy bustle as always. No continuous stream of red pouring spontaneously into the streets and threatening to overrun the banks, as some of my *khaveyrim* have predicted every year since Moses led the Israelites out of slavery.

116

I return to the pressers' station just as Moishe Kaufman bellies up in a sweat-stained undershirt with an oily black cigar clamped between his teeth and shoves the bottom half of a navy blue two-piece in front of me.

"Gotta do the sheams on thish one," he says around the cigar.

This is the part of the job I hate. Now I have to turn the skirt inside out and flatten all the seams so he can keep working on it. All that stitched linen has to have a crisp, clean look when it's done, but the time-consuming task of underpressing just adds to my workload without increasing my piece count. And in this style, the finished piece retails for the bargain price of $6.95 at Saks, so you can imagine what my share of it will be.

The metal door bangs open and we all look up as if we're expecting a personal telegram from Trotsky himself in Mexico. But it's only Hillel Glassman with a sackful of furs to store in the back room. The furriers' bosses must be hiding their assets in case the strike goes through.

We've been pushing for a minimum hourly rate for piece work since the days of the Taft Administration, but when the bosses hired goons from Murder Inc. to attack the Needle Trade Workers headquarters on West Twenty-Eighth Street, sending several delegates to the hospital, the cry went up for a general strike in solidarity with our injured comrades. We're tired of being targets.

"Any word?" Moishe asks.

"The Dodgers are down four-zip," says Hilly. "Dizzy Dean's really got his stuff today."

"That'sh not what I meant you little *putzeleh*," says Moishe, exhaling a cloud of cigar smoke that mixes with the steam in front of my face, forming a lethal combination that makes my eyes water.

Brooklyn's second baseman Lonnie Frey got four hits in a 10–7 win over the Phillies a few days ago, but ever since, "Dem Bums" have been stumbling from one anemic loss to another.

Suddenly one of the Italian operators from the shop two floors above comes flying down the stairs, pops his head in, and announces:

"Hey, all a-you guys, Linky's coming!"

~

The little man with the limpid eyes and pale pink jowls had a quiet way of speaking that made people listen closely to every word. The beefy man with him looked like an ex-prize fighter who'd been hit too many times with a loaded glove. They sat at a small round table under the dim lights sipping strong black coffee with their backs to the kitchen and their eyes on the door to the street.

He was paying half a dozen henchmen to sit around and keep their eyes on the door as well, but the little man had a policy of never taking anything for granted. So his eyes sharpened when the little bell rang and the door swung open.

The floor creaked as the messenger approached, hat in hand, bowing like his predecessors in ancient times, and whispered something in the little man's ear.

The little man nodded once, deliberately, as if the news were unpleasant but not unexpected, like the final notice of an overdue electric bill. He dismissed the messenger, contemplated his coffee cup for a moment, then gestured to two of the men sitting around in the shadows.

A couple of chairs scraped back, and Lefty Shapiro and Big Bill Cohen lined up front and center to receive their orders.

"The locals have voted to strike," the little man informed them. "I want you to meet the others in the garage on Thirty-Seventh."

"Then we'll need a car," said Lefty.

That got blank stares.

"To carry the gear."

"What kinda gear you need?" said the guy with the battle-scarred face.

Lefty actually started to list the various items they would need—lead pipes, brass knuckles, maybe some stink bombs—when the big guy cut him off:

"Whadaya need, a friggin' howitzer? It's just a bunch of wheezy needle-pushers, for shit's sake."

"Besides, parking's a real pain in midtown this hour," said Big Bill, "and we need to blend in."

"So maybe we should drive across the bridge and park downtown," Lefty suggested.

"Just take the subway and walk," said the little man, with a calmness that was almost a threat. And with that, the meeting was over.

Lefty and Big Bill got on the subway with a couple of short lengths of pipe awkwardly concealed under their suits. They took the local to Boro Hall and transferred to the Seventh Avenue Express, but as Lefty trotted up the stairs to catch the train, the heavy brass knuckles in his jacket pocket kept whacking against his hip.

"Damn. We should've taken the car," said Lefty, plopping into the seat as the doors closed.

"What for? Gurrah says it's only a bunch of *shnayders.*"

Lefty grunted and licked the dry skin on the knuckles of his right hand.

"Why the hell you always gotta be doing that?"

"Doing what?" said Lefty, his tongue hanging half-way out of his mouth.

"*That.* Licking your damn knuckles."

"Because they're always dry and chapped, all right? Now leave me alone."

He was about to start on the knuckles of his left hand when a woman sitting across from them leaned forward.

"Pardon me, but I couldn't help overhearing you," she said. She was a shapely blonde in her early thirties, in a powder-blue skirt and matching hat with a royal blue bow. Her lips were a lustrous shade of Chinese Red. "You shouldn't be using—um, saliva for dry, chapped hands. You should try using cold cream, or better yet some petroleum jelly."

Big Bill could almost see the woman's words working their way through Lefty's brain as he tried to make sense of the words "petroleum jelly." Suddenly Lefty's knuckles clenched, and Big Bill put a hand out to stop him. The lady's smile quickly faded.

"She means Vaseline, you moron. Come on, this is our stop," said Big Bill, tipping his hat.

They walked two cars down and got right back on. Lefty grabbed a newspaper someone had left on the seat and buried his face in it.

"What's eating you?" said Big Bill under the noise of the train. A poster on the wall told him that smoking Camel cigarettes was good

119

for the digestion. He wished he could have a Camel cigarette right then.

"They raided Saffer's joint."

"Ah, crap."

Lepke and Gurrah had been using Oscar Saffer's garment shop on Broadway near Thirtieth Street as a payoff drop, funneling at least $150,000 through the place in the past year alone.

"Dewey's boys walked out with nineteen cartons of business records."

"Sounds bad, but the worst they can do is get him on tax evasion."

"Yeah, and what if he starts singing?"

"Saffer's no *feygeleh*. They'll fine him five grand, tops, and maybe give him a year in the can. Time off for good behavior, and he's back on the street for the spring season."

Lefty chewed on that while Big Bill grabbed a piece of the paper.

Right there on page three was a story about some kid named Parker who had kidnapped a disbarred lawyer from New Jersey for some screwy reason using a toy pistol, handcuffs, and a fake beard from a novelty store. The Brooklyn D.A. had put out an eight-state alarm that turned up nothing but a bumbling accomplice hiding out in Youngstown, Ohio, until a woman walked right into the police station and said that Parker had offered said accomplice a job with the new Jersey State Police in exchange for helping pull off the kidnapping job, and now all the fingers were pointing to Parker's dad, who just happens to be the chief of detectives of Burlington County, New Jersey.

"It's always a dame who bring these guys down," said Big Bill.

"Those bent cops bring themselves down. Like the dick in the Drukman murder. Thirty years on the job, they call him in for a few routine questions about the extra money in his bank account, and he goes home to Queens and blows his brains out."

"Guess he figured that was his only option."

"There's always options. Especially for a detective sergeant."

They got out at Thirty-Fourth Street and walked up three blocks to the garage. The place smelled of oil and damp cement, and the smell grew stronger as they descended a narrow flight of stairs to the basement and joined a crew unloading gear from the back of a brand new DeSoto. Lefty felt a surge of confidence when he saw all the familiar faces. The Syndicate had sent a small army. The brass knucks in his pocket didn't chafe against his hip anymore. Their weight and power changed as the hunk of metal molded to fit his hand. He took a few practice punches against his opposite palm and drew great comfort from the feeling.

Some of Mendy Weiss's boys were there, along with guys who worked for Little Farvel Cohen and Greenie Greenberg.

They shook hands and made wisecracks until someone dropped a lead pipe and the sound caromed off the cement walls with an ear-splitting *clang*.

"Jeez, be careful with that, will ya?" said one of Little Farvel's boys.

Word was that the Italians were sending some guys uptown to meet them, and even the Madden gang was pitching in.

"I hear they finally caught Old Creepy," said one of Greenie Greenberg's boys, taking a few practice swings with a three-foot length of pipe.

Alvin Karpis (né Karpavioz), a former member of Ma Barker's gang who rose rapidly through the ranks to become "Public Enemy Number One" after the Feds gunned down Dillinger and Baby Face Nelson, had gotten nabbed in St. Paul after a series of hold-ups that left a trail of dead bodies so wide even the Feds had no trouble following it.

"Wonder who they'll promote to Public Enemy Number One now that there's an opening."

"Maybe Torrio."

"He's small potatoes."

"Try telling that to Inky Silver."

Laughter echoed off the walls.

Louis "Inky" Silver had worked with Torrio, managing a brewery in Brooklyn until someone shot him on the corner of Broadway and Sixty-First Street. He survived, but Mayor La Guardia had given orders for Torrio to be arrested the minute he set foot inside the city limits. You had to take the good with the bad in this racket.

The men armed themselves with blackjacks and a crateful of nightsticks that came straight from the supply room in the Twenty-Third Precinct. Soon it was time to mobilize, and they lined up like a bunch of unruly school kids at recess. Someone took a swing and shattered the driver's side headlight on a rusty old Dodge, and some of the guys laughed at that, too. A few of them even picked up broken bricks from a pile in the corner, and Big Bill spotted Lefty licking his knuckles as they made their way up the stairs to the bright light of day.

~

Everything's pretty peaceful so far, considering the size of the crowd. We raised more of a ruckus when Toscanini gave his farewell performance with the Philharmonic and they had to call out the mounted police to restore order. Garment workers are lining the sidewalks from the southwest corner of Thirty-Eighth down to Herald Square. The blousemakers are represented by two different locals: the Italian girls are demanding an end to piece work in favor of a weekly wage, and the Jewish girls are echoing their calls. Even the kneepants makers local is out in force.

Charlie Zimmerman, manager of the dressmakers' union, is on the picket line side by side with representatives of the Workers Alliance of America and the American Labor Party. Protest signs and banners mark the territory of each group with the standard slogans, like the radical proposal for a forty-hour work week, plus the usual smattering of signs for causes ranging from support for the French and Spanish Leftists and a call to enact Kerr-Coolidge (Stop Deporting German and Russian "Aliens") to the Hosiery Workers' endorsement of FDR in the fall elections. And in the middle of all this, an Italian anarchist is holding up a sign in support of the Scottsboro Boys.

But for now we're all comrades. The bosses want the Jews and Italians to fight each other over the scraps, but most of us aren't buying it. Somehow, we just don't believe that the answer to all our problems is the unfettered expansion of mass production, which will supposedly raise wages and create a veritable worker's paradise on earth.

People keep running up to tell us the latest: in a stunning display of popular strength, masses of jobless men and women have taken over the New Jersey State Assembly in Trenton and are holding a mock legislative session in order to demand relief. Thousands of Brooklyn barbers are planning to walk out of their shops if they don't get a guaranteed wage of twenty-five dollars for a five-day week. And the Building Service Employee Union got a substantial wage increase through an arbitration settlement after Mayor La Guardia personally intervened and averted a strike. Tom Mooney even sent us a note of support from his jail cell in California, and a cheer goes through the crowd when word reaches us that a couple of coal miners in Moose River, Nova Scotia were rescued after being trapped in the mine for ten days, even though they had to "crawl like rats" through a narrow hole the rescue workers chipped in the seam.

This eruption of fervent passions and upraised fists demonstrates our ability to shake the world, or at least a few blocks of the Garment District, and I get elbowed into the street. I take a quick look uptown to make sure I'm not about to get hit by a beer truck, but the cops have blocked off Broadway at Fortieth Street. I don't know yet if that's good or bad.

There's a sudden lull in the sloganeering, and a broadcast of the Dodgers game comes leaking out of one of the storefronts just in time for me to hear Durocher, the Cardinals' shortstop, get his fourth hit of the game. Damn.

The cops spread out to let a sergeant through with a four-man escort, and the taunts are fairly minor as they come marching down the middle of Broadway right towards me. I try to elbow my way back onto the sidewalk, but the sergeant steps forward and points at me:

"You there: Who are you? What group is this? The cloakmakers' union?"

"*Vey iz mir.* The *cloakmakers*? That bunch of no-goodniks? I belong to the dresspressers Local 60 of the ILGWU and Branch 360 of the *Arbeter Ring*—I mean, the Workmen's Circle."

"Oh, a bunch of Reds, eh? Well, what's the big idea here? What are you striking for?"

"Generally or specifically?"

One of the cops breaks ranks to come after me with his nightstick, but the sergeant stops him.

123

"Okay, wise guy," says the sergeant. "Generally."

"We are striking for better wages and conditions, and the right to collective bargaining, and and—" I turn to Benny. "*Vi zokt men gerekhtikayt oyf English?*"

"Justice."

"And justice."

"Well, there's too many of you out here. You can't block the sidewalk like this."

This is met with grumbles and catcalls, so the sergeant raises his megaphone and announces: "I have no argument with your right to picket, but you can't block the sidewalk. I need this crowd reduced to no more than fifty people. Now who are your leaders?"

This starts the inevitable argument between the Socialists and Communists over who should represent the workers. So the sergeant tells his men to select every tenth man and orders the rest of us to disperse. And suddenly there's a great deal of pushing and shoving and it isn't long before they start arresting the "troublemakers." The police thin our ranks to maybe one-third of their former size, and people who didn't have the guts to cross the picket lines before are walking right up to us and spitting at us and calling us goddamn Reds and sheenies and telling us to go back to Russia. And the radio is telling me that I can have a brand new DeSoto for only $695, which is almost what I make in a year, when a window shatters and a wild animal roar goes up as if a band of marauding Huns were charging up Broadway.

A sick feeling claws at my stomach and I curse the bosses for hiring more hooligans instead of simply negotiating with us.

A volley of brickbats and improvised missiles arcs into the air toward us and, as if we've regressed to the Stone Age, instinct takes over for a few seconds as we dodge the bricks thudding to the pavement around us and try to steel ourselves against the onslaught. The thin line of protest signs falls apart like a house of toothpicks as the center collapses and people panic and run for cover, and I feel the impact wave pass through the crowd as the first line of strikebreakers slams into us with their weapons held high like an army of *kulaks* with scythes advancing toward a field of wheat.

Imagine what a shock it must be for the scythes when the wheat fights back! With bare knuckles. With lengths of pipe. With shears and cutting tools.

A gangster breaks through the line and smashes a bottle against an Italian guy's head, and the poor guy starts bleeding as if he's been hit by a hunk of shrapnel and falls to the pavement. His pals grab him by the armpits and haul him out of the way, and the gangster finds himself surrounded by a trio of Italian girls beating him with protest signs. Some of the men are rushing around guiding our girls to the relative safety of the buildings when the next wave of hoodlums reaches us.

Benny lobs some loose bits of plumbing equipment at them, then briefly holds them off with a six-inch awl. He cuts a bit of a comical figure thrusting and parrying with that itty-bitty tailor's awl, but he stands his ground and buys us a few precious seconds before cutting to the rear and leaving the field to us.

I stay close to Gutbeder as he wields a heavy length of steam pipe against a couple of gangsters armed with what sure look like standard-issue Police Department nightsticks. Grossman takes off his vest and offers to fight them bare-knuckled, the lousy scabs.

In a situation like this, I'm more of a blunt instrument kind of guy myself, so I end up swinging a baseball bat at the knobby craniums of smirking men with off-kilter teeth while the cops look on like they're taking in the game at Ebbets Field. All they need are some peanuts and Cracker Jack. And I bet you they'll report that they were too busy protecting honest citizens to intervene in the melee.

A *ganef* in a gray topcoat rushes at me wielding a plumber's wrench like a two-handed broadsword. I swing the bat at his head and brush him back, but he comes at me again raising the wrench to block a head shot, so I step back and aim for the outside corner and whack him in the shins as hard as I can. He crumples to the sidewalk, and Grossman comes out of nowhere and kicks him in the jaw, knocking him backwards into the gutter.

But another *ganef* leapfrogs over the body of his fallen crony and crashes into me before I can set up my next swing. He's got thick brass knuckles on his left hand and it's all I can do to grab his sleeve with

125

both hands to keep him from breaking every bone in my face. He's trying to get in a good punch while I cling to the sleeve of his jacket and fortunately it doesn't occur to him to use his other hand until I hear cloth tearing and his sleeve comes apart in my hands. By some strange reflex we both look at his ruined sleeve, and our eyes meet.

I recognize a face from the old neighborhood.

"Irving Shapiro?" I say. "You're running with the gangsters—and for what? What'd you spend on this? The cloth isn't even that good."

Irving's eyes go blank for a second, until one of his buddies yells, "C'mon Lefty, let's blow!"

"So they call you Lefty now, huh, Mr. Big Shot?"

I can see that he's still trying to figure out where the hell a bunch of small-time operators got the *khutspeh* to fight back like that.

"We survived pogroms and prison camps in Tsarist Russia, you *putz*," says Grossman. "What can America do to us that's worse than that? *Ptui!*" He spits on the sidewalk to show what he thinks of the idea.

The strikebreakers and the rest of the bosses' goons are retreating, and Irving slinks back to whatever hole he crawled out of, where his kind are nurtured like vampire bats on the blood of others.

"We did it!" cries Benny.

The enemy is routed, the strikers are cheering, and I feel the blood of the Maccabees flowing through my veins, urging me to join their rebellion against our idolatrous overlords.

My comrades are making wildly optimistic predictions about how we could smash the rackets in a minute if we could only break their political connections and cut through all those layers of protection, and how we're going to take on Hitler and Fascism next, then bring the fight home, and that *nothing* can stop us if we just stay organized.

I spot Abe the old *beysmedresh* scholar sitting on top of a packing crate, his knees dangling above the fray.

"Is the Lord's hand too short?" I say, just to show him that he's not the only one who can quote from the Torah.

"Look around you," says Abe, gesturing toward the bank on the northeast corner of Thirty-Sixth Street, its indestructible Greek columns dwarfed by the brown brick canyon rising twenty stories on all sides from the street below. Rows and rows of identical windows stare down at us. And yet, just above our heads, our own building is sparingly decorated with carvings of interweaving pomegranate vines, an ancient Jewish symbol of plenty.

"Where do you see the Lord's handiwork?" Abe says. "Look at this place, this *goldene medineh*, where they have learned to share a few crumbs from the table with the middle class, and—*poof!*—there goes any hope of you building your socialist state. People will never fight for socialism when they can be bought off with movies, cheap suits—"

The blast of a car horn makes him jump. Traffic is moving in the streets again, their headlights coming to life as the sky darkens. Somebody's car radio is playing a smooth foxtrot that makes me think of elegant ladies gliding around the floor in clothing we made.

I help my comrades straighten things up and stow our weapons for the night. They've been following the news on the storefront radio, and the news isn't all good. It sounds like the Ethiopian freedom fighters will have to abandon the capital city to the advancing Italian forces. So the Fascists are on the march and it's up to us to stop them.

Benny wants to check the afternoon papers, but the first newsboy coming down the block is hawking the *Evening Journal*, a *farkakteh* Hearst paper that we wouldn't be caught dead with. He spots another newsie and has to settle for the *World-Telegram*, and flips through it looking for coverage of the strike. Even Abe comes over and joins our little circle, craning his neck for a better look.

"Hey, maybe this is why there weren't more cops going after us in the street today," says Benny, pointing to an article. "It says the police were too busy escorting a couple of busloads of Nazi officers and naval cadets on a sightseeing tour of the city." Including a trip to the Barnum & Bailey circus, which happens to be in town this week. We gather around, unable to believe what we're reading.

"It says they needed the escort to protect them from protesters."

Abe lets out a sound that's halfway between a curse and a throat clearing, and sinks to the curb as if his legs just can't take the strain anymore.

I try to put this news in the most positive light: "Which means that our turnout would have been much bigger—a lot of our people were probably over on Fifth Avenue telling those Nazi bastards where to go."

Abe shakes his head at me. "And you say *I* believe in fairy tales . . ."

I'm thinking, *the struggle to build a just society is no fairy tale*—the ILGWU is the fastest-growing union in the country—but instead I just help him to his feet and bid him good day and watch him hobble away. Abe comes from the world of *dybbuks* and Kabbalah and superstition, and they don't have much use for his kind in an era that demands social realism. What other option do we have in this strange new land, where everything is for sale—even the soul of a troubled kid like Irving Shapiro?

I say my goodbyes, slap a few backs, and join the crush of humanity heading for the BMT to Brooklyn. A few stragglers on the corners are still talking politics, and a group of Italian machinists are all excited because the Yankees are going to start a kid named DiMaggio in left field. The Yankees notched their fifth straight win, but the Dodgers lost. Dizzy Dean and the Gashouse Gang shut them out, 12–0, and they dropped to last place. I guess some victories are harder to come by than others. But it's too early to call right now and there are still plenty of games left in the season.

Gold Diggers of 1977
(Ten Claims that Won Our Hearts)

Michael Moorcock

For Glen Matlock,
Siouxsie, Nik Turner
and everyone else who was never reduced to this . . .

INTRODUCTION: ADDING TO THE LEGEND

Gold Diggers of 1977 was originally written and published in about two weeks to coincide with the release of *The Great Rock 'n' Roll Swindle*, a reasonably competent film featuring the Sex Pistols, a rock and roll band which revived a number of fashions in the late seventies, rode high (though maybe not very happily) on a variety of publicity stunts (most of which were banal and most of which, of course, worked) and eventually broke up. A fairly typical set of recriminations and antagonisms between band-members, management, record-companies, culminated in a miserable tragedy in Greenwich Village, New York, when Sid Vicious, accused of knifing his girlfriend to death in The Chelsea Hotel, died of a drug overdose.

A great deal of sentimental publicity followed Sid's death—as it seems to follow the death of any rock figure—and another young martyr was added to contemporary popular mythology.

The music press, feeding on its own fictions, characteristically compounded the myth while at the same time appearing to deny it. Like all mass-circulation periodicals, they first inflate someone to larger-than-life proportions and then attempt, often by the cheapest kind of mockery, to deflate the idols they have helped create. Their ugly criticisms of Elvis Presley just before he died were matched in intensity only by the exaggerated tributes following his death. People seem to need heroes desperately and resent any signs of ordinary humanity in them—to the point, on occasions, of assassinating them if they refuse to conform or respond to the dreams of their loonier fans.

When Virgin asked me to write a book to go with the film I agreed (after I'd watched the film) because it fitted in with one of my own obsessions (see for instance "A Dead Singer") and because I'd always seen Irene Handl as Mrs Cornelius. The third reason was that "Anarchy in the UK" introduced a lot of people to the idea of anarchism and presumably led at least a few to Kropotkin and other anarchist theorists whose work is gaining increasing attention. For me, Nestor Makhno is the spirit of romantic, active anarchism, and although he might have been a trifle naïve in some of his hopes, I have a considerable soft spot for him. He, too, died young, of consumption, in poverty and some despair, in Paris in 1936. This story is as much dedicated to his memory as it is to the memory of Sid Vicious and all those others who have, in one way or another, been destroyed by their own simple dreams.

Ingleton
Yorkshire
June 1982

CLAIM ONE: MAGGIE ALL SET FOR VICTORY

Designed by Huber & Pirsson, The Chelsea Hotel was opened in 1884 as one of the City's earliest cooperative apartment houses. It became a hotel about 1905. The florid cast iron balconies were made by the firm of J. B. & J. M. Cornell. Artists and writers who have lived here include Arthur B. Davies, James T. Farrell, Robert Flaherty, O. Henry, John Sloan, Dylan Thomas, Thomas Wolfe and Sid Vicious.

—*Plaque, The Chelsea Hotel, NY.*

"Well, it's not what I bloody corl a picture." Mrs Cornelius waded across the foyer on old, flat feet and lowered her tray of Lyons Maids and Kia-Oras to the counter. "I mean, in my day it was love an' adventure an' that, wannit."

Lifting a crazed eye from behind the hotdog warmer Sergeant Alvarez opened his disturbed mouth.

"Who . . . ?" he began. But his attention was already wandering.

"Now it's all vomit an' screwin'," she continued. "I wouldn't mind if it was Clark Gable doin' it. *An'* there's no bloody adventure, Sarge. Wot you grinnin' at?"

"Who?"

"Oh, shut up, you pore littel bugger. It's that Mrs Vicious I feel sorry for."

"Killed . . . ?" said Sergeant Alvarez.

"Too right." Mrs C. heaved her tray around. "Oh, well. Back into the effin' fray."

As Time Goes By

On the screen an old robber, desperately clinging to the last vestiges of publicity (which he confused with dignity) pretended to play a guitar and wondered about the money. Something in his eyes showed that he really knew his credibility in South London was going down the drain.

"Then who the hell did get any satisfaction out of it?" Mo Collier felt about in his crotch for the popcorn he'd dropped.

"You got a complaint?" Maggy's voice was muffled.

Mo sighed. "Now's a fine time to start asking."

Robbers cavorted on beaches. Robbers limbered up. Robbers made publishing deals and wondered why their victims went crazy.

Mo looked away front the screen. He sniffed. "There's sulphate in the air-conditioning."

"Is jussa keepa way," said Maggy.

"What?"

She raised her head again, impatiently. "It's just to keep you awake."

"Oh."

The popcorn was running out.

A kilted figure came on screen and began to rationalise his own and others' despair. It was called hindsight.

"I think I'd better try to see what happened to it." Mo hated political movies.

"What? The money?"

"Call it that, if you like. Unless you have a plot, see, you can't have the paranoia."

Maggy rested her head on his thigh. "I don't think it *is* sulphate. It's something else." She tasted the air. "Is this an EMI cinema?"

But Jerry was already backtracking.

New Recruits in the Psychic Wars

"As long as we all believe in the New Jerusalem," said Mitzi Beesley, having trouble with her Knickerbocker Glory, "we stay together. And as long as we stay together, we can all believe the same thing. And if we can all believe the same thing long enough, we can believe for a while that we've made it come true. We all have to be a bit over the top. But when some silly bastard goes well over the top, that rocks the boat. The trouble with Johnny, for instance, was that he wouldn't bloody well stay in uniform. And after Malcolm had gone to all that bother, too."

"I wouldn't know abart any o' that, love." Mrs Cornelius waved away the offer of a bit of jelly and ice cream on a long spoon. "Can't stand the stuff. I 'ave ter carry it arahnd orl bleedin' day, don't I?"

They sat together on red vinyl and chrome stools at the bar. Behind them was a big plate glass window. Behind that was the traffic; the Beautiful People of the Kings Road in their elegant bondagerie. Dandyism always degenerated into fashion.

Little Mitzi was having trouble getting to the bottom of her Glory. Her arms were too short. Mrs C. tilted the glass. "Pore fing. There you go." She laughed. "Didn't mean ter interfere, love." She glanced out of the window.

From the direction of Sloane Square a mob was moving. It was difficult to make out what it consisted of.

"Skinheads," said Mrs C. "Or Mods, is it? Or them Rude Boys? Or is that ther same?"

"Divide and Rule," said Mitzi. "My dad always thinks. And *that's* the first lesson in the management of rock and roll bands."

"Oh, well, they all do that, don't they." Mrs C. squinted up the street. "Blimey, it's a load of effin' actors. Innit?"

The mob was dressed in 17th century costumes. "Pirates?"

"Nostalgia hasn't been such a positive force since the Romantic Revival."

"'Ippies, yer mean?"

"The Past and the Future—they'll get you every time."

"I know wot you mean, love." Mrs C. picked up her handbag. "Stick to ther Present. I orlways said so, an' I bloody orlways will. I've met some funny bastards in me time. Lookin' backwards; lookin' bloody forwards. It's un'ealthy. Nar. Ther future's orl we fuckin' got, innit?"

"And it doesn't do you any harm."

The mob was carrying effigies of four young men. Over loud-speakers came the sound of Malcolm McLaren singing "You Need Hands." The mob began to growl in unison.

"I've seen 'em come an' I've seen 'em go." Mrs C. shook her head. "An' it'll end in tears every time. Wot good does it do?"

"It stops you getting bored," said Mitzi. "Some of the time, anyway."

The effigies were being tossed on a tide of angry shoulders.

"You can get 'em attackin' anyfink, carn't yer." Mrs C. was amused. "Give 'em a slipper ter worry an' they won't bovver *you*."

"The Sex Pistols were the best thing that ever happened for British politics at a very dodgy moment in their career." Mitzi reached her money up to the girl at the till. "Or so we like to think. But no bloody B.O.s or whatever they are for them. Divide and Rule, Mrs C. And up goes your Ego."

"I 'ope this doesn't mean they've stopped ther bloody buses again." Mrs Cornelius looked at the clock over the bar. "I'm due for work at one."

"They still showin' that picture?"

"It's really good business."

"I think Malcolm McLaren is the Sir Robert Boothby of his generation, don't you?" Mitzi got to the exit first and pushed on one of the doors.

"Well, 'e's no bloody Svengali, an' that's for sure."

"He did identify with the product . . ."

"'E should 'ave bought an Alsatian. They're easier ter train."

A youngish man in a trilby and a dark trenchcoat went past them in a hurry.

"That's Jerry." Mitzi pulled on her jacket. "He still thinks there's a solution to all this. Or at least a resolution."

"It's one o' ther nice fings abart 'im." Mrs C. directed a look of tolerant pity at her retreating son.

"The trouble with messed up love affairs," said Mitzi "is that you waste so much time going to the source of the pain and asking it to make you better."

"'E'll learn. You on'y got yerself ter blame in the end." Mrs Cornelius saw that the mob had parted to allow a convoy of No. 11 buses through. "I'd better 'op on one o' these while I've still got ther chance."

"The ultimate business of management is not just to divide your group but to divide their minds. The more you fuck with their judgement, the more you control them. It's like being married, really." Mitzi waved to Mrs C.'s lumbering figure as it launched itself towards the bus.

"Don't let 'em piss on yer, dear." Mrs C. reached the platform. "Just becos yore short."

"You can only manage what you create yourself. The trouble with people is that they will keep breaking out."

The mob was beginning to split up. Fights were starting between different factions. Cocked hats flew.

"After all," said Mitzi shadowing Jerry, "someone has to take the blame. But you can bet your chains we won't have anarchy in the UK in our lifetime. Just the usual bloody chaos."

What Do You Need?

"Role models make Rolls-Royces. Kids pay for heroes. But it doesn't do to let either the audiences or the artists get out of control—or you stand to lose the profit. It's true in all forms of show business, but it's particularly important in the record industry."

Frank Cornelius lay back in his Executive Comfort Mark VI leather swiveller and wondered if it would be going too far if he waved his unlit cigar.

"What can I do for you, Mo?" His eyes, wasted by a thousand indulgences, moved like worms in his skull.

"I was wondering what happened to the money." Mo unbuttoned his trenchcoat, looking around at the images of rock singers in various classic poses, emulating the stars of westerns and war films except they had guitars instead of rifles.

"It hardly existed." Frank put his cigar to his awful lips. "Well, I mean, it's real enough in the *mind*. And I suppose that's the main thing. What are you selling me, Mo? Thinking of going solo? This company's small, but it's keen. We really identify with the kids. Can you play your guitar yet? Don't worry if you can't. It's one of the easiest skills in the world to learn."

"What happened to the money, Frank."

"Don't look at me. Malcolm had it."

"He says you had it."

"I haven't made a penny, personally, in six months. It's all gone on expenses. Do you know how much it costs to keep an act on the road?"

"Where's the money?" Mo was beginning to lose his own thread. Frank's responses were too familiar to keep anyone's attention for long.

"Gone in advances, probably. Ask Malcolm, not me. I only became a director towards the end. For legal reasons."

"Where's Malcolm?"

"Who knows where Malcolm is. Does Malcolm know where Malcolm is? Is he Malcolm? What is Malcolm, anyway?"

Mo frowned. "Give me an address, Frank."

"You're not kipping on my floor again. Not with your habits. Haven't you got a squat to go to?" Frank glared in distaste at his brother's ex-friend.

"Where?"

"You're too heavily into bread. That's your problem. You've really sold out, haven't you? I remember you when you didn't give a shit about money or anything else. What are you really after? Mummy and Daddy, is it? If you don't like the heat, you should stay out of the kitchen. I look after a lot of people, but I can't look after you all the time. It's killing me. I have to deal with the hassles, cool out the managements of the venues, pay for the damage . . ."

He raised a suede arm. "I haven't had more than twelve hours sleep in a week. Profits? Do you think there are any profits in this business? If so, where are they? Show them to me."

"They're up your nose, Frankie."

There came a noise from Frank's throat like the sound of an angry baby. Mo recognised it. It was called The Management Wail. It was time to leave.

Public Image

Identity Manipulation Associates (IMA = Whatever You Want Me To Be) had taken over the old Soho offices. Mo was beginning to feel a little flakey around the edges. He'd started off thinking this was a caper: a time-filler. Now, what with one thing and another, it was beginning to smell like an obsession.

"I've had enough of obsessions." He felt the old call to retreat, to get some air. "On the other hand, this might not be one. It could just be ordinary."

He opened the door and went into the lobby. A young woman looked up at him from threatened brown eyes. "Can I help you?"

"I was wondering about the money. Did Malcolm . . . ?"

"We only do identities here. The money comes later."

"Is there anyone I could see?"

"They're all in meetings. Are you a performer?"

"I . . ."

She became sympathetic and far less wary.

Mo was no-one to be afraid of. She spoke softly. "They won't be back this afternoon, love. What do you play?"

"I think it's Scrabble, but I'm not sure."

"Magic!"

He was plodding off again.

Adapted for the Market: Finally It's the Movie

The permanently depressed tones of Malcolm McLaren, doing his best to make some sense of his impulses, could be heard on the other side of the doors.

Mo pushed his way through. There were no pictures, only a soundtrack. The little room was dark, but somewhere in it lawyers and accountants shuffled and whispered. "Why is everybody so unhappy?"

"Sometimes it's all you've got left of your adolescent enthusiasm," said Mo. He began to giggle.

"Were you ever talented?" Aggressive, self-protecting, attempting condescension, a lawyer spoke.

"Did you deliberately set out to shock?"

"I don't know," said Mo. "I don't read the papers any more."

"Have you just come from Highgate?"

"That's an idea."

"It's the image that's important, isn't it?" This was an upper-class woman's voice. Lady D?

"So they say."

Bodies were coming closer. "Well, ta ta."

"Ta ta."

Swallowing Your Own Bullshit

Mo waded into the mud. He was not quite certain what lay on the other side of the vast building site. He wasn't sure why he was trying to get to South London. A helicopter came in low seeming to be observing him. He looked up. "Mum?"

A voice began to sing "My Way" through a loud hailer.

It was beginning to feel like victimisation, or a haunting. That energy was going. Or maybe it had already gone and that was what he was looking for.

All he'd wanted was a bit of this and that. Some peace and quiet. Some fun. Everybody was going crazy. He hated the lot of them. Why couldn't they leave him alone? Why couldn't he leave them alone?

He was dying for a crap.

He cast about for an anchor. Five feet away the back wheel of a new Honda could be seen, sticking out of the mud, as if the rider had tried to make it across this no-man's-land and failed.

Mo blinked. "Sid?"

What the hell did it matter anyway?

Sulphate Heaven

The room was full of heavy metal. In one corner about fifteen old hippies were wondering where it had all gone, while in the opposite corner fifteen punks were wondering where it was all going.

Mo stood in the middle.

"Anybody want a fight?"

A few eyes flickered, then faded again. Wired faces tried to move. It was a musician's graveyard. They existed as far apart as Streatham and Kensal Rise. They had served their turn. Many of them had even shown a profit.

Mitzi came in. "Blimey." She rattled her box.

"Line-up, lads," said Mo. "The lady's got the blues."

"Been to Highgate yet?" she asked him.

"Is there any point?"

"Not a lot."

"I'm on my way," he said.

CLAIM TWO: WE HAVE A GOOD REASON

Johnny Rotten, the angelically malevolent Scaramouche, is a third-generation son of rock 'n' roll—the galvanic lead singer of the Sex Pistols. His band play at a hard heart-attacking, frantic pace. And they sing anti-love songs, cynical songs about suburbia and songs about repression, hate and aggression. They have shocked many people. But the band's music has always been true to life as they see it. Which is why they are so wildly popular. The fans love the Sex Pistols and identify with their songs because they know they are about their lives too.

—*Virgin Records Publicity, 1977*

"Sex and agro are the best-selling commodities in the world. Everybody's frustrated or angry about something, particularly adolescents."

Frank was having his hair redone to fit in with current trends. "Easy on the Vic, Maggy. We don't want to go too far, do we?"

The phone rang. Maggy picked it up. Her hand stank of camphor. "Popcorn."

She listened for a moment and giggled. She turned back to Frank. "It's your mum."

"Tell her I'm dead."

"You're about the only one who isn't."

Frank took the greasy receiver.

"Hello, mum. How are you? What can I do for you, then?" He was patronising.

He listened for a while, his expression becoming devoutly earnest. "Yeah."

Maggy began to pluck at his locks again, but he stopped her. "Okay, mum."

He frowned.

"Okay, mum. Yes. Yes. Look after yourself." He handed the phone back to Maggy. "Well, well," he said.

From the other side of his office door his dogs, a mixed pack of Irish Wolfhounds and Alsatians, began to scratch and whine. He sometimes felt they were his only real security. Moved by some impulse be couldn't define, he placed a reluctant hand on Maggy's bum.

Sentimental Journeys: The Other Side of the Coin

Mo had managed to reach Tooting. Autumn leaves fell onto the common. In the distance was what looked like a ruined Swimming Baths. He dipped into his tub of Sweet and Sour Pork and Chips. His fingers were already stained bright orange, as was his entire lower face. Over to his right the road was up. Drills were hammering. He was beginning to feel more relaxed. It was when they put you in the real country that you went to pieces.

Jimi was waiting for him behind a large plane tree. "I shouldn't really be talking to you, you bastard."

"Divide and Rule," said Mo. "Aren't we part of the same faction any more?"

"What does Malcolm say?"

"Haven't seen him."

"Or the Record Company."

"They haven't released anything."

"Then it could be okay."

"It could be." Mo offered Jimi the tub. The guitarist began to eat with eager, twitching fingers.

"I've been trying to make this deal with the devil all day," he complained. "Not a whisper. What you up to then, you bastard?"

"Very little, my son."

"Got any money?"

Mo shook his head. "How long you got to stay down here?"

"Another six months. Then I might get remission."

"Play your cards right."

"A bit of spit never hurt anybody. Are you in Tooting just to see me?"

"No. I'm looking for a train robber."

"They're difficult to fence, trains."

"You have to have a buyer set up already."

"Things were simpler in the fifties, you know. The poor were poor and the rich were bloody rich. People knew where they stood. I blame it all on rock and roll. Now we're back where we started."

"It was the only way out. That doesn't work any more. You think it does. But it doesn't."

"The music goes round and round." Jimi farted. "And it comes out here."

Rock Around the Clock

Mrs Cornelius flashed her torch around the cinema. "It's filthy in 'ere. You fink they'd do somefing abart it."

Customers began to complain at her. She switched off the torch. "Please yerselves."

She went back into the foyer.

With intense concentration, Alvarez was dissecting a hot dog.

"Found anyfink?" she asked.

"Not a sausage."

"Anybody ring fer me?"

"Ring?"

"Never mind."

She'd done her best to warn Frank. Now it was up to him. Three guardsmen in heavy khaki and caps whose visors hid their eyes marched into the cinema and bought tickets. "This had better be good," said one of them threateningly to Alvarez.

"You can't go wrong with sex and pistols." His mate began to guffaw. They had that smell of stale sweat and over-controlled violence common to most soldiers and policemen. It was probably something in the uniform.

Sonic Attack

"A little vomit is a dangerous thing." Miss Brunner tried to smooth a lump in her satin trousers. Her thin hands were agitated, irritable. "There's no point in going for that. Not unless you mean to do it properly. Vomit has to have some meaning, you know."

"What about gobbing," said her eager assistant, Clive. "Should that stay?"

"Well, it is associated with the band, after all." She sniggered. "Disgusting, really."

"But we have to get into disgust, don't we? Disgust equals the Pistols. Ugly times. You know? But will people be disgusted enough?" This was the constant worry of the publicity department at the moment. "I mean, it's important to associate Sex Pistols with nastiness. They should be synonymous in the public's view."

"True." Miss Brunner touched a finger to a blackened lid. "Should we emphasise the urine angle?"

"Piss-stools." Clive laughed a high-pitched, artificial laugh. "Rebels with bladder problems?"

"Now you're being facetious. It won't do, Clive. This is serious. We want the name in every paper by Thursday."

"But the record isn't mixed yet."

"The record, dear, is the least of our problems. We want the front page of *The Sun* And the rest of them, if possible."

Clive put a pencil to his post-office lips. "Well, we'd better get busy, eh."

"Our first problem." said Miss Brunner, "is to find a nicer word for gob."

And Now, the Sex Pistols Controversy

Mo came out of Balham station and walked into the High Street. DIY shops and take-aways stretched in both directions.

"Nobody ever really hates you," said Mitzi. "It's more that they enjoy being threatened. You know, like throwing a baby up to the ceiling.

You couldn't lose. It's just that you expected a different reaction. It's all fantasy. It happens every time."

"You could kick 'em in the balls and they'd keep coming back for more. You've got to feel contempt for people like that." Mo was down.

"I don't know why. They're only enjoying themselves. That's what they pay for. Better than fun fairs. What you're asking them to do is to take you seriously, to believe you're real. But you're not real. You're a performer."

They reached a high, corrugated-iron fence.

"Here we are," she took a key from her pocket and undid a padlock, pushing open the creaking door.

It was a junkyard. Piled on top of one another were dodgem cars, waltzers, chairoplanes, wooden horses and cockerels, roller coaster cars.

"See what I mean," she said.

"What's the point of being here?"

"There's a fortune in scrap, Jerry."

Sex Chaos

Frank Cornelius zipped himself into his leather jacket while Maggy added a few touches to his make-up. "Why is everybody flying South?" he said.

"It's the way the band-wagon's going. Balham, Brazil, Brighton."

"Get the car out. I'm heading for Highgate."

As they went down the stairs, he said: "What we need is a few more novelty acts. They only have to think they're new, that's the main thing. As long as you *think* you're new, you *are* new. And the punters will think you're new, too. There's nothing new under the old limelights, Mag."

"What about the spirit?"

"You mean the blood?"

He began to laugh. It was a hideous, strangled sound. "New equals good. It's been going on for at least a hundred years. The New Woman and all that. New equals vitality. New equals hope. One thing's for sure, Maggy. New very rarely equals profit. Not at first, anyway. It has to be modified and represented before anyone will buy it in a hurry. That's the secret of the process. But it takes so much energy just to get a little bit of something happening that there are bound to be casualties. Look at poor Brian Epstein. It was the writing on the wall for management. It had to become us or them. We didn't want another manager coughing it, did we? How many A&R men do you know who've killed themselves recently?"

"I dunno."

"None. It's the survival side of the business, my love."

They arrived at the street. Ladbroke Grove was full of beaten-up American cars. Maggy went round the corner to the mews to get Frank's Mercedes.

"It really is time we moved away from this neighbourhood," he said. "But it's where I've got my roots, you know."

C'mon Everybody

"Your mistake was in cocking a snoot at the Queen, my lad." Bishop Beesley unwrapped a Mars Bar and, like an overweight pigeon, began to peck at it.

"Well, we took things more seriously at the time. We needed something." Mo sat down in a battered dodgem. "Do you really own all this?"

"Every bit. You must have a lot of money stashed away. How would you like to invest?" The Bishop wiped his pudgy hands on his greasy black jacket. "Americans buy it, you know. And people from Kensington and Chelsea. It's decorative. It's nostalgic. It's fun. Good times remembered."

"If not exactly relived," said Mitzi.

"You can't have everything, my dear. Junk, after all, has many functions and takes many forms. None of us is getting any younger."

"Speak for yourself," said Mo. "This is an investigation."

"Into what, my boy?"

"We haven't decided yet."

"Anybody dead?" His chocolate-soaked eyes became speculative.

"You thinking of buying in?"

"I have an excellent wrecking crew, if you're interested. And we specialise in salvage, too. I mean salvation." He grimaced and sought in his pockets for another Mars Bar. "We could be mutually useful to one another."

Mo got up. A pile of Tunnel of Love boats began to creak and sway. "We'll be in touch," said Mitzi.

From somewhere within the stacks came the sound of heavy breathing.

Bishop Beesley went back into his hut and locked the door.

Amateur Night at the Moscow Odeon

It was a mock-Gothic complex. Frank signed in at the gatehouse and Maggy drove through. The gates were electronically controlled and shut automatically behind them. Surrounding them were tall brick walls topped with iron spikes. At intervals was a series of buildings once used to house Victorian painters. Now they were used for recording purposes.

The largest of the buildings was at the far end of the square. Maggy parked in front of it.

Wheezing a little Frank got out of the car. "I should never have had that last bottle of amyl."

He mounted the steps and pressed a buzzer. A bouncer in a torn red T-shirt let him in. He descended to the basement.

The studio was deserted. In the booth a shadowy figure in a rubber bondage suit sat smoking a cigarette through an enema tube.

Frank said: "Mr Big sent for me."

"Not 'Big,' stupid. 'Bug.'" The voice was mysterious, slurred.

"Are you Mr Bug?"

"I represent his interests."

"Somebody's on to us."

"What's new?"

"My mother just told me."

"So?"

"Hadn't we better start worrying?"

"Worrying? We're just about to make the real money."

Frank was nervous. "I can't see how . . ."

Mr Bug's representative began to unzip the front of his suit. "In exposure, you fool. What do you think *The News of the World* is for?"

144

"I'm not entirely happy," said Frank.

"That's the secret of success, isn't it?"

Frank began to sink.

The voice grew sympathetic.

"Come here, you poor old thing, and have a nibble on this."

Frank crawled towards the booth.

Wotcha Gonna Do About It?

The train from Balham was stuck on the bridge over the Thames. The bridge seemed to be swaying a lot. Mo felt tired. In the far corner of the compartment, Mitzi Beesley had curled herself on a seat and was asleep. Elsewhere came the sound of desultory vandalism, as if weary priests were performing a ritual whose point had been long-since forgotten.

The train quivered and began to hum.

In the sunset, the Houses of Parliament looked as if they were on fire. But it was only an illusion. The structure remained. A little graffiti on the sides made no real difference.

"Who's got the money?" Mo asked again.

Mitzi opened her eyes. "The people who had it in the first place. That's where it comes from and that's where it goes. How much did you spend at the pub last year?"

"About thirty thousand pounds."

"Exactly."

"What are you trying to say?"

She shook her head. "What the bloody hell did you ever know about Anarchy in the UK, Mo? You gave all the power back, just like that. You gave all the money back, just as if you'd found it in the street and returned it to the police station."

"Bollocks!"

She shrugged and closed her eyes again. "What's in a name?"

From the luggage rack above them an old hippy said: "Words are magic, man. They have power, you know."

Mitzi glanced up at him. "You've got to walk the walk as well as talking the talk, man."

"I blame it all on nuclear energy," he said.

"Well, you've got to blame something. It saves you a lot of worry."

145

As the train began to move again Mitzi sang to the tune of *Woodstock.*

"We are wet; we are droopy
And we simply love Peanuts and Snoopy . . . "

Hundreds of drab back-gardens began to fill the windows. The train made a moaning noise.

Mo slid towards the door.

"A pose is a pose is a pose," said the hippy.

CLAIM THREE: LABOUR OR TORY?
THE OLD DOUBLE CROSS

Cries of "Anarchy!" have always been associated with bored, middle-class students who followed each other like sheep.

But the Pistols are spearheading, or hoping to, a backstreet backlash of working class kids who have never really had it hard, but are still put down.

"They try to ruin you from the start. They take away your soul. They destroy you. 'Be a bank clerk' or 'join the Army' is what they give you at school.

"And if you do what they say you'll end up like the moron they want you to be. You have got to fight back or die.

"You have no future, nothing. You are made unequal. Most of the time the kids who fight back don't use their brains and it's wasted. Join a band is one way, or teach yourself is another. It doesn't take very much."

—*Record Mirror, December 11, 1976*

Nestor Makhno, anarchist hero of the Ukraine, took another glass of absinthe and looked out onto the deserted Rue Bonaparte. "As far as I'm concerned," he said, "I died in the mid-thirties. But you can't believe anything you hear, can you?"

"I know what you mean," said Sid.

Things were quiet, that evening, at the Café Hendrix. The romantic dead were feeling generally low; though there was always a certain atmosphere of satisfaction when another young hero or heroine bit the dust.

"Besides," said Brian Jones, "there are these second and third generation copycat deaths, aren't there, these days? You're not even sure if some of these people really are martyrs to the Cause."

"What Cause is that?" Sid helped himself to a slice of pie.

"You know—Beautiful Losers—Dead Underdogs—Byronic Tragic figures. All that." Jones was vague. It had been a long time since he had thought about it.

Sid was under the impression that Jones was simply upset. Maybe he thought his thunder had been stolen.

James Dean limped in and put his Michelob on the table. "It's all bullshit. Boredom is what brought us to this, my friends. And little else."

"That isn't what the fans say. They think we died for them."

"Because of them, more likely." One of the oldest inhabitants of the Café Hendrix (if this timeless gathering place could be said have an oldest inhabitant), Jesus Christ, offered them a twisted grin. "Dead people are easier to believe in than live people. As soon as you're dead you can't stop the myth. That's what I found. They *want* you to die, mate."

Several heads nodded. Several hands lifted drinks to pale lips.

"You always wind up doing what the public wants," said Keith Moon, "even if you don't do it deliberately. They expect violence, you give 'em violence. They expect a tragic death, well . . . Here we are."

"That's showbusiness," said Makhno. "The pressures get on top of you. You're carrying so many people's dreams. And all you wanted in the first place was a better life."

"They expect you to do the same for them."

Makhno was disapproving. "That isn't anarchism. You scream at them for years not to follow leaders and they'll say 'Isn't he wonderful. He's right. Don't follow leaders.' Then they come round and ask you what they should do with their lives."

"They think anarchism means impulse or something. They don't realise it means self-determination, self-discipline and all of that. 'Neither master nor slave.' It serves us right for becoming heroes." Michael Bakunin was on his usual hobby horse.

"Don't say you never liked it," Makhno refilled his glass.

"Only sometimes. Anyway, how do you stop it once it starts?"

"Go into hiding and lead an unnatural life," said Jesus. "I wish to God I had. It wasn't any fun for me, I can tell you."

"You didn't have so many bloody journalists in your day," said Sid. "And you had a high opinion of yourself. Admit it."

"Well nobody was calling you the bloody Son of God." Jesus tried to justify himself, but they could tell he was embarrassed.

"They called me the Antichrist," said Makhno with some pride.

"Johnny called himself that," said Sid.

Jesus sighed. "It's all my damn fault."

"You should be such a big man, to take the whole blame." Brian Epstein sipped his orange juice. "Do you think we're in Hell?"

"It was all a bloody con." Marc Bolan adjusted his silk shirt. He was sulking again. Albert Camus, from behind his back, winked at the others.

"We just try to make death seem worth something. Like saying good comes out of pain. You can't blame people. And that's our job."

"Dying young?" said Sid. He was still pretty new to the Café Hendrix.

"Making death seem romantic and noble." Byron began to cough. "How they can think that of me I don't know. Death is rotten and we shouldn't have to put up with it."

In a far, dark corner of the café, Gene Vincent began to cry.

Nestor Makhno lifted his glass. "Ah well, here's to another boring evening in Eternity."

"Fuck this," said Sid. He went to the door and tried to open it.

"I'm afraid it's stuck, old chap," said Chatterton.

Sub-Mission

"Self-hatred makes excellent idealists. You tolerate yourself and you get to be able to tolerate almost anything. I suppose there's some good in that." Mitzi stood on Mo's shoulders and climbed over the gate of the Gothic studios. "What do you want me to say to him?"

"Just that I need to see him about me wages."

"All right." She scurried off into the darkness.

"I wish she'd stop bloody talking," said Mo. He turned up the collar of his trenchcoat and lit a cigarette. "This whole thing is ridiculous."

A few lights went on in the farthest building. Then they went off again. He heard a car start up.

The gates opened outwards, forcing him backwards.

A Mercedes droned past. In it were Frank Cornelius, Maggy and, trying to hide from him, Mitzi Beesley.

Mo shrugged and got through the gates before they closed again. He would do his own dirty work.

We're So Pretty

"You always think you must be in control," said Frank, as the car turned towards Hampstead Heath, "but it's usually other people's desperation that's operating for you. As soon as their desperation disappears, the scam stops working. You have to keep as many people as desperate as possible. Look at me. I know what bloody desperation *means*."

"But you should never let anyone know that," said Mitzi. "That's where you went wrong, Frank."

"You were too honest," said Maggy.

"I couldn't keep all the balls in the air. When you drop one, you drop the lot." Frank wiped his lips. "Still, there's always tomorrow. I'm not finished, yet. Lick a few arses and you're back on the strength again in no time."

"You should have been rude to him," said Maggy.

"My morale's weak. After what mum said."

"Mum's'll do it to you every time," said Mitzi. "Are you sure Mo will be all right in there?"

"He'll be better off than you or me," said Frank. "Little wanker. He deserves all he gets."

I'm a Lonely Boy

"Every business is a compromise. You get into the business, you get into a compromise." Mr Bug's representative stroked Mo's frightened head. The old assassin lay spreadeagled across a twenty-four track desk, his wrists and ankles secured by red leather bondage bracelets. Everything stank of warm rubber.

"Now what can I do for you, Mo?"

"Not this."

"You know you like it really. And you've got to do something for the money. Are you ticklish."

"Blimey," said Mo as the feather mop connected with his testicles. He added: "But that's not where I'm dusty."

"Are you a virgin, love?" The voice was greasy with sentiment.

"It depends where you mean."

"Enjoy life while you can, darling. This whole place is due to go up in a few hours. Insurance."

"Aren't the tapes all here? Auschwitz?"

"Every single copy, my beauty."

"They must be worth something."

"They're worth more if they're destroyed. Didn't you ever realise that? The harder things are to get, the more valuable they are. If they don't exist at all, they become infinitely valuable."

"Is that a fact. Tee hee."

"There, darling. You *are* ticklish."

"Did you want to see Mr Bug?"

"Mr Bug anything like you?"

"I'm only his representative. I'm an amateur compared to him."

"Then I'm not sure I want to see him. Can I go home now?"

"And where's home?"

"I suppose you've got a point." Mo lay back on the desk. He might as well get the most out of this.

Mr Bug's representative's breath hissed within his mask. "Now you're really going to make a record."

He reached for a large jar of vapour rub.

Punk Disc Is Terrible Says EMI Chief

The black flag was flying over the Nashville Rooms. There must have been another temporary seizure of power. Outside in the street groups of hardcore punks, lookalikes for most of the Sex Pistols in their heyday, scrawled A on every available surface. They weren't sure what it meant but they knew they had to do it.

Nestor Makhno rode up in his buggy. He had never been much of a horseman since his foot was wounded. His woolly hat was falling

150

over his eyes. The rest of his anarchist Cossacks looked as worn-out as he did. Their ponies were old and hardly able to stand.

"I think we might be too late." Makhno guided the buggy round to the side entrance. From inside came the sound of chanting. "Is this what we fought Trotsky for?"

One of his lieutenants fired a ghostly pistol into the air. Its sound was faint, and drowned by the noise from within. "Comrades!"

"They can't hear us," said Makhno. "Is this what we all died for?"

"It's an attack on the symptoms, not the disease," cried a Cossack dutifully from the rear. "Comrades, the disease lies within yourself, and so does the cure. Be free!"

With a shrug, Makhno tugged at the reins of the buggy and led his men away. "Ah well. It was worth a try."

"Where to now?" asked one of the Cossacks.

"Camden Town. We'll try The Music Machine."

You Never Listen to a Word I Say

Something was collapsing.

Miss Brunner plucked at her hair and blouse.

"The more childish you are, the more you score. Throw enough tantrums and they'll pay anything to get rid of you."

Frank looked wildly about. "Are you sure this place is safe?"

"Safe enough."

He lay tucked up in bed surrounded by Snow White and the Seven Dwarves wallpaper, Paddington Bear decals, Oz and Rupert books.

"I can hear a sort of breaking up sound. Can't you?"

"It's in your mind," she said. "How much should we invest, do you think, in that new band?"

"We haven't got any money."

"Neither have they."

"Then it's all a bit in the air, isn't it?"

"Big money still exists, in big companies. It just takes a bit of winkling out."

"No," said Frank. "No more. I've been warned off. I'm frightened. The City is involved. They can do things to you."

"Mr Bug has scared the shit out of you, Frank."

"How did you know about the shit?"

I Made an American Squirm

The former Johnny Rotten tried to focus on Nestor Makhno as best he could. The little Ukrainian was almost wholly transparent now.

"Don't you think we can do it through music?"

"Persuade the public," said Makhno thinly. "We had an education train. But do they ever know that the power rests in them?"

"They never seem to want it."

"They don't want responsibility."

"And that's why managers exist."

"I'll be seeing you . . ." said Makhno, fading.

"That's more than I can say for you."

The former Johnny Rotten reached for his Kropotkin. Maybe it could still work. Maybe it was already working on some level.

Over the Top and Under the Bottom

Mo wriggled. "What do you want me to say?"

Mr Bug's representative stroked the fronds of his cat-o'-nine-tails over his own rubber.

"Anything you like, sweetheart. Isn't this the way to relax? No personal responsibilities, no anxieties? Just lie back and enjoy yourself."

"There must be other methods of relaxing."

"Well, dearie, you could always join a rock and roll band."

Mo began to scream.

Rolling in the Ruins

Bishop Beesley bit off half a Crunchie bar. Chocolate, like old blood, already stained his jowls. "Why is everyone suddenly going South?" he asked.

His daughter shook her head. "Maybe it's Winter."

"Winter?" Frank Cornelius looked unblinkingly at the sun which was just visible over the heap of dodgems. "Some winter of the mind, maybe."

"Let's try and steer clear of abstractions, dear boy." The bishop spoke with soft impatience. "I have a meeting with the Prime Minister in just over an hour. What are we going to do about this, if anything? I mean is it a serious threat to authority?"

"I thought we were avoiding abstractions," said Miss Brunner.

From within an abandoned Ghost Train car, Mo's weak voice said: "I told them nothing."

"You've nothing to tell them, you horrible little oik." The bishop sighed. "I think we're in a poor position, Mr Cornelius."

"Somebody turned the power off," said Mo vaguely.

The wind drummed against the hollow metal of the fairground debris.

City Lights

The Cossacks, by now hardly visible even to one another, had reached The Rainbow and were surrounding it. Their black flag had turned to a faint grey. They were getting despondent.

Determinedly, they rode their horses into the venue, able to pass through the audience as if they did not exist. On stage Queen were displaying the virtues of production over talent. Thousands of pounds worth of equipment was manipulated to produce the desired effect. It was a tribute to a wonderful technology.

Makhno cried into the empty megawatts: "Brothers and Sisters! Brothers and Sisters!"

A young man with longish hair and a "No Nukes" T-shirt turned, then raised his fist at the stage.

"Freedom!" he cried.

The volume began to rise.

Will the Sex Pistols Be Tomorrow's Beatles?

Back at the Café Hendrix Nestor Makhno took a long pull on his bottle of absinthe. He was shaking his head.

"Didn't you enjoy any of the gigs?" asked Sid.

"I didn't see anything I liked. At first I'd hoped—you know, the audiences . . ." Makhno fell back in his chair. "But there was nothing there for us to do."

"Don't despair," said Shelley, "there's a rumour the Sex Pistols are going to reform. After all, they're more popular now than they ever were."

CLAIM FOUR: WE'RE GETTING THERE

Says Johnny Rotten: "Everyone is so fed up with the old way. We were constantly being dictated to by musical old farts out of university who've got rich parents. They look down on us and treat us like fools and expect us to pay POUNDS to see them while we entertain them and not the other way round. And people let it happen! But now they're not. Now there's a hell of a lot of new bands come up with exactly the opposite attitude. It's not condescending any more. It's plain honesty. If you don't like it—that's fine. You're not forced to like it through propaganda. People think we use propaganda. But we don't. We're not trying to be commercial. We're doing exactly what we want to do—what we've always done.

But it hasn't been easy. Sceptics and cynics simply didn't want to believe what was happening. Quite unjustly the Sex Pistols were written off as musical incompetents. They were savagely criticised for daring to criticise society and the rock musician's role in it. They have been crucified by the uncaring national press—ever ready to ferret out a circulation boosting shock/horror story—and branded an unpleasant, highly reprehensible Great Media Hype.

—*Virgin Records Publicity, 1977*

The city was black. Through black smoke shone a dim, orange sun. The canal was still, smeared with flotsam. From Harrow Road came the sound of a single donkey engine, like a dying heartbeat. Overhead, on train bridge and motorway, carriages and trucks were unmoving. It seemed everything had stopped to watch the figure in the dark trenchcoat and trilby who paused beside the canal and peered through the oily water as if through a glass.

A fly, ailing and lost, tried to buzz around his head. Slowly the traffic began to move again. From behind a pillar Mitzi Beesley emerged, hurrying on skinny legs towards him. She was back in Shirley Temple mode.

"You feeling any better, Mo?"

"You let me down, Mitzi."

"I didn't have any choice."

Mo did not resent her. "How's that wanker Frank?"

"Going through a bit of a crisis, I gather."

"He'd better look after his bloody kneecaps."

"That's the least of his worries."

Mo glanced away from the water and back towards the half-built housing estate. "It used to be all slums round here," he said nostalgically. "Now look at it."

"You've got over your own spot of bother, then? You've stopped looking for the money."

"I think so. But I'm still looking, anyway."

"For what?"

"A solution to the mystery."

"The mystery goes on forever. There's never a solution. There isn't even a cure."

"We'll see."

"Why are you here?"

"Ever heard of the Old Survivor?"

"Well, there's a myth . . . "

"I'm seeing him here."

"Lemmy of Motörhead?"

"He's doing me a favour."

"Isn't he an old hippy fart?"

"His hair may be long, but underneath he's a punk, through and through."

"Something's disturbed your brains, Mo. You need a rest."

"I need help."

Down the steps from the pedestrian bridge came a figure in black leather, festooned with silver badges, a bullet belt around his waist. His face, moulded by a thousand psychic adventures, was genial and distant, ageless. The Old Survivor laughed when he saw Mo and Mitzi standing together. "You look fucking miserable. What's the matter?"

"I didn't think you'd come." Mo made an antique sign.

"Neither did I. But I was passing. On my way home. So here I am."

"You're probably the only one left who can help me." Mo was embarrassed.

"I haven't got any drugs," said Lemmy.

"It's not that. But you'd know about the legend. Whether there's any truth in it or not."

Lemmy frowned. "I didn't realise you were a nutter."

"I'm not. Well, I don't think I am. I'm desperate. Have you ever . . . ?" Mo's voice dropped. Tactfully, Mitzi went to sit on the side of the canal and dip her boots in the liquid. "What do you know about the League of Musician-Assassins?"

Lemmy began to chuckle. "That hasn't come up in a long time."

"But you were supposed . . . "

"It was ages ago. A different era. A different universe, probably."

"Then there's some truth in it."

Lemmy became cautious, "I couldn't take a job like that. I've got enough to do as it is."

"There's money . . . "

"It was never a question of money." Lemmy drew a battered packet of Bensons from his top pocket and lit one. "We soldier on, you know."

"But what about the other one? The one who's supposed to be sleeping somewhere in Ladbroke Grove?"

"Your old mucker? What about him?"

"You're in touch with him."

"I see him occasionally, yeah."

"Couldn't you ask him?"

"He gave it all up. He said there wasn't any point in it any more. You know as well as I do."

"Does he really think that?"

"Well . . . He *has* been having second thoughts. He was 'round at his mum's the other day . . . "

"So he's not asleep."

"It depends what you mean." Lemmy was losing interest. He rubbed at his moustache and sighed.

"Could you put me in touch with him?"

"He's not working. I told you. None of us are. Bullshit-saturation does it to you in the end. Haven't you found that out yet?"

"Would his brother know . . . ?"

"His brother doesn't know a fucking thing about anything. His brother spends his whole bloody life trying to work out what's going on. Whenever he thinks he's found it, he tries to exploit it. He's been doing it for years. But him and his mates seem to have won." Lemmy looked up at the black buildings. "They sort of linked hands and formed a vacuum."

"It's important to me." said Mo. "I mean, I wouldn't be asking if I wasn't desperate . . ."

"You've only lost a battle, my son. We lost a war."

I Love You with My Knife

The sea was pale and calm; a frozen blue. Mo walked out of the Dreamland enclosure and crossed the promenade in the peaceful Margate dawn. He wasn't sure, even now, if Lemmy hadn't tricked him into this trip. If the last of the Musician-Assassins had been sleeping under Ladbroke Grove, why had Mo been told to come to the seaside?

Near the horizon a seagull seemed to be wheeling. Then he heard the sound of an irregular drone. It was a plane.

It began to come in rapidly, heading straight for the beach. It was painted brilliant white and had wartime Luftwaffe markings. A huge biplane, with at least six engines, none of which were firing properly. The thing lurched in the air as it turned, the sunlight flashing on its floats. It was a Dornier DoX flying boat.

It landed on the water, almost keeling over, heading for the end of the pier. Mo began to run. He reached the turnstiles and climbed over them.

By the time he got to the edge, the flying boat had come to a stop and was bobbing on the surface of the sea like a waterlogged sponge.

A thin figure climbed out of the cockpit and stood shakily on the upper wing. "Oh, Christ." The figure began to vomit into the ocean. "Oh, bloody hell."

The figure was dressed in a long black jacket, black drainpipes, and wore black winkle-pickers. It removed its tattered flying helmet. "I'm not up to this anymore, you know."

Did Lemmy give you my message?"

The figure nodded. "I didn't come all the bloody way from 1957 just to buy a stick of rock. What's going on?" The wasted, weary face regarded Mo through wiped-over eyes.

"I hoped you'd know."

The figure coughed and spat again. "I feel terrible. I've never known. I was just trying to cut out a bit of territory. But that fell through, too. Are you the one who wants to fly down to Rio?"

"If you think that's a good idea."

"You'd better get in. Don't blame me, either, if we never make it. Got anyone to eat?"

Stepping Stone

"You said he could never be revived." Frank was frightened. Even his grip on Mitzi's hair was weak.

Miss Brunner was at a loss. "It's what we all understood. Why should he want to come back?"

"He's been resurrected." Bishop Beesley spoke through mouthfuls of Maltesers. "Before."

"But never like this." Frank helped himself to a few of the bishop's chocolate-covered Valiums. "We'd blanked out every bit of possible music. He has to have it, to recover at all. To sustain himself for any length of time. It's the one thing we were sure of."

Miss Brunner pushed her red hair back from her forehead. "Something got through to him. There's no point now in wondering how. Couldn't have done it. He didn't know anything, did he, Mitzi?"

"Ow," said Mitzi, "I'm getting tired of playing both ends against the middle. It hurts."

"Did he?" Miss Brunner drew out her special razor.

"Not as far as I know."

"He's a demon," said Bishop Beesley. "And he can never be completely exorcised. I'm certain of that now. Just when we thought we had everything under control."

"Who got the music to him?" Frank let go of Mitzi. "You?"

Mitzi shook her head and tried to get her father's attention.

"Lemmy?"

"Might have been."

158

"Nothing came through on the detectors," said Miss Brunner. "There's always someone on duty. You know that."

"We were squabbling amongst ourselves too much. It's that money problem."

"A very real one," said Bishop Beesley.

"I'll have the equipment checked." Miss Brunner shrugged. "Not that there's much point now. I could have sworn he was stuck in 1957 for the duration. Still, it's no use crying over spilt milk, is it."

"The problem we have now," said Bishop Beesley, "is where he's got to. We found most of his bases and destroyed them. Any clues?"

"You'd better ask your mum," suggested Mitzi.

Silence Is Golden

The blimp was drifting towards the coast of Brazil. The flying boat had been abandoned in Florida. The blimp was losing gas.

"I thought you still had your old touch."

Mo was unshaven. "We've been in this bloody thing for days!"

The last of the Music-Assassins blew his nose. "I haven't been well. Anyway, all my equipment's old."

"It was never anything else, as far as I can see."

"I prefer stuff that doesn't work properly. I always did. How many bloody times do you think I've been resurrected? I'm coming apart all over the bloody place."

Mo was used to the self-pity by now, but the smell remained dreadful.

"Stand by," Jerry croaked.

The blimp bumped onto the beach. Blondes scattered, screaming. "Here we are. I'll stay while you get the tapes I told you I needed."

"I'm going to be embarrassed." Mo took off his coat and hat, revealing a T-shirt and shorts.

"Don't worry. They all talk English here." The last of the Musician-Assassins frowned. "Or is it German?"

"I don't mind about the Hendrix . . ."

"Well, just make it Hendrix, then. But hurry. You want help, squire, you'd better help me first. I never expected to pick up a bloody snob."

Mo opened the door and put his big toe onto the warm sand. "It's nice here, isn't it?"

Behind him, Jerry uttered a feeble sound.

"Get—the—fucking—music . . ."

Purple Haze

Miss Brunner studied the computer breakdowns. "You were right about Hendrix," she said. "He always resorts to it in the final analysis. But there are other factors to consider. He seems to be finding boosters elsewhere these days. Do you think that's what they're offering him?"

"Fresh energy?" Frank pushed the long sheets aside and looked blankly at the instruments.

She began to punch in a new programme. "I've got a feeling it is. What's bothering me, however, is where they're getting through. I could have sworn we'd blocked every channel. And, moreover, that we'd got them to believe that that was what they wanted."

Frank flicked an uninterested whip at the little body of Mitzi as she swung gently in her chains above the cryptik vii computer. "You can never afford to relax for a second. We'd become lazy, Miss Brunner."

"What else did your mum say?"

"Nothing. He came to see her at her job, watched a bit of the film, had about fifteen bags of popcorn and ate all the hot dogs, then left in his Duesenberg."

"Which was found in?"

"Cromer."

"WC didn't know about Cromer." She bit a nail.

"We're spread too thin," he said. "Those of us who are prepared to guard the borders. It's like the collapse of the Roman Empire. That's what I think, anyway. My own brother! When will he ever grow up?"

"He's got to be in Rio," she said. "Or, failing that, Maracaibo."

"What's in Venezuela?"

"Airships."

"And Brazil?"

"Failures. Exiles. The usual stuff he goes for. You'd better get someone to check all the record shops in Rio. After that, see what recording studios they have out there. It can't be much."

"Has Mo broken through to him yet, do you think?"

"Nothing available on that."

"And if so, who is it? Or how many of us?"

"I've got a feeling we're all going to be targets this time."

From overhead, Mitzi's muffled titters phased in with the click of the cryptik.

Cruel Fate

"Mrs T. no more created the situation than Hitler started World War II. But once it had happened he had to pretend it was deliberate." Martin Bormann was closing up for the evening. "Of course I didn't know him very well."

"Hitler?"

"Nobody knew him very well. He tended to go with the tide. Do you know what I mean?"

"Not really," said Mo, pocketing the tapes.

"Well, we were all heavily into mysticism in those days. How's my old mate Colin Wilson, by the way?"

"I think he lives in the country."

Bormann nodded sympathetically. "It's what happens to all of us. I envy you young lads, with your cities and your ruins. We never liked cities much. In the Party, I mean. I sometimes think the whole thing was an attempt to restore the virtues of village life. It's still going on, I suppose, but on a modified level. I blame the atom bomb. It's had the absolutely opposite effect it was meant to have. No wonder all those hippies are fed up with it. I had hopes . . ." His smile was sad. "But there you go. I'm not complaining, really. Anything else you need?"

"I'm not sure."

"That's the spirit." Bormann patted Mo's shoulder. "And not a word to anyone about this, eh?"

"All right." Mo was puzzled.

"I wouldn't want people to think I was merely justifying my mistakes."

As Mo walked up the street, looking for a tram to the beach, Bormann began to pull down the shutters.

It was a fine evening in the Lost City of the Amazon.

CLAIM FIVE: JUBILEE JAMBOREE:
JAMBUK LEGISLATION: JOKE JIVE

In October they signed with EMI. They released the hit single "Anarchy In the UK" and they were all set for an extensive, triumphant tour of the country. Then they were invited onto the Today show. Bill Grundy got what he asked for—and the Nationals had a bean feast. The band who had been playing week after week all over the country for more than a year were suddenly front page news, branded "filth" and made Public Enemies No. 1.

All but five dates of the tour were hysterically banned and the band returned to London on Christmas Eve with the dramatic news that EMI was about to rescind their contract. In January EMI asked them to leave the label. Glen Matlock decided to form his own band called the Rich Kids. Sid Vicious replaced him. Everyone cheered when in March, it looked like the Pistols had found shelter at A&M.

—Virgin Records Publicity, 1977

Jerry was looking a shade or two less wasted. He removed the head-phones and signalled to Mo to turn up the volume. Very bored, Mo did as he was told. He was beginning to regret the whole idea. In front of the Assassin was a collection of peculiar weaponry, most of it archaic: needle-guns, vibra-guns, light-pistols, a Rickenbacker 12-string.

The gondola of the little airship swayed and the hardware slid this way and that on the table. The Assassin seemed oblivious. He took another pull from his Pernod bottle.

"Have a look out of the window," he shouted. "See if we're near Los Angeles yet."

All Mo could see was silver mist.

Strange, garbled sounds began to issue from Jerry's lips.

Steve winced.

He had a feeling the Assassin was singing the blues.

His colour was better, at any rate. His skin was changing from a sort of LED-green to near-white.

Old and Tired but Still Playing His Banjo

"If ants ever had an Ant of the Year competition," said Miss Brunner disapprovingly, "Branson would be the winner. It's the secret of his success."

They were all uncomprehending. Only Maggy said "What?" and nobody listened to her.

Frank was biting his bullets to see if they were made of real silver. He began to load them into the clip. His hands were shaking terribly.

"Why don't we all go to Rio?" asked Bishop Beesley.

"Because you'd never squeeze into Concorde." Miss Brunner checked the action of her Remington. "Have you oiled your bazooka?"

"It doesn't need it." He unwrapped a Twix and sulked in his own corner of the bunker. "Did you try all the A&R men?"

"We can't get through to Virgin."

"They've probably been used in the ritual sacrifice, ho, ho, ho." Frank slid the clip into the Browning automatic he favoured.

"I said we weren't going to mention all that. It's poor publicity."

Mitzi grinned to herself. She now had a Banning cannon all her own. "When do we start to fight?"

"As soon as we run out of other choices," Miss Brunner told her.

"You divided," Mitzi was smug, "but they kept re-forming. It's just like real life now."

"Well be changing all that." Bishop Beesley was no longer confident, however. He scraped ancient Cadbury's off his surplice and carefully carried the bits to his lips. "I wish I'd stayed in the drug business now. You don't get this sort of trouble from junkies."

"Do you mind?" Frank was offended.

. . . Down the Drain and What She Found There

"That's not bloody Los Angeles," said the Assassin petulantly. "That's Paris! Isn't it? Don't I know you?"

"It's got to be." Mo rubbed at his ear, which was hurting. "Unless there's another Eiffel Tower."

"Right. No harm done. I'll drop you off in Montmartre, if that's okay with you."

"What are you going to do?"

"Well, you've told me all I need to know. I'll be in touch." The

Assassin combed his lank hair with his fingers. "Mo Coalman, isn't it?"

"You going to kill someone?"

"I'm going to kill everyone if I can get enough energy." The thought seemed to revive the Assassin. He cheered up.

He began to turn the steering wheel, cursing as the ship responded badly.

A little later he pushed open the door and started letting down a steel ladder.

"There you go. You should be able to get a taxi from here."

Mo didn't like the look of the weather. He put on his trenchcoat and hat.

"What did you say to Mr Bugs?"

"Biggs," corrected the Assassin. "Oh, I just needed a couple of addresses in South London and the name of his tailor."

Mo lowered himself onto the swaying ladder. "I hope you know what you're doing."

"I never know what I'm doing. There's no point in working any other way in my business."

It was raining over Montmartre now. It was cloudy. Mo became cautious. "Are you sure this is the right district?"

"The district's fine. You should be worrying whether I've got the time right. For all we know it could be 1990 down there."

"Stop trying to frighten me," said Mo.

The Assassin shrugged. "They're all pretty much the same to me, these days. You should have tried the fifties, mate." He began to shiver. "Hurry up. I want to shut the door."

Spirit of the Age

More data was coming through to the bunker. Miss Brunner pursed her lips as she studied the printouts.

"He's getting stronger. Five Virgin shops and the EMI shops in Oxford Street and Notting Hill have been raided and a significant list of records stolen. Three of the places were completely destroyed. And there's been a break-in at Glitterbest. That probably isn't him. But three recording studios have had master-tapes taken. Seven managements have lost important demo-tapes."

"It might not mean anything," said Frank. He was fixing himself a cocktail, drawing it into the syringe.

They ignored him.

Frank laid the syringe on the table and put his head in his hands. "Oh, bloody hell. Who could have predicted this? I was *certain* it was all under control again. Bugger the Sex Pistols."

"I told you so," said Mitzi. Her eyes heated.

Miss Brunner pushed a pink phone towards her. "Get in touch with Malcolm. Tell him we've got to stick together. He'll see sense. I'll try Branson again."

Mitzi picked up the receiver. "If you think it's worth it."

They were all beginning to get on one another's nerves.

I Wanna Be Your Dog

Mo walked into the Princess Alexandra in Portobello Road. It had taken him ages to get from Paris and he had a feeling he was no further forward. All that he seemed to have done was start a lot a trouble he couldn't begin to understand.

The pub was full of black leather backs. He reached the bar and ordered a pint of bitter. The barman, for no good reason, was reluctant to serve him.

Various overtired musicians clocked him, but nobody really recognised him or he them. Lemmy was nowhere to be seen.

There was an atmosphere in the place, as if everybody was hanging about waiting for World War Three.

The talk was casual, yet Mo sensed that a great deal was not being said. Was the whole of London keeping something back from him? Was the Revolution imminent? If so, what Revolution was it? Whose Revolution? Did he really feel up to a Revolution?

He finished his pint. He was down to his last fifteen pence.

As he was leaving he thought he heard someone whispering behind him.

"*Who killed Sid, then?*"

"What?" He turned.

All the backs were towards him again.

Sleazo of the Month

"They think they're heavily into manipulation, but really we just let them play at it." Mr Bug's representative sat comfortably in the darkness of the limousine. "Nobody who really believes they're manipulating things is safe. Sooner or later people lose patience. And people are very patient indeed. Most of you don't actually want to make anyone else do anything."

"Live and let live," said Mitzi. "It's time I got back to the bunker."

"I'm interested in human beings," said Mr Bug's representative, squeaking a little as he moved in his rubber. "I've studied them for years."

"Do you understand them?"

"Not really, but I've learned a lot about what triggers to pull. And I know enough, too, not to think that I can keep too many balls in the air."

"Have you seen Jerry? That's who I was looking for, really."

"We've all seen too much of Jerry, haven't we?"

"Has he left your club?"

"You could try it. But hardly any of us go there any more."

"Aliens?"

"Call us what you like. I prefer to think of myself as a student person. But I'm not sure I'm going to make the finals."

Mr Bug's representative uttered a cheerful wheeze and opened the door so that Mitzi could step out.

"It's quite a nice morning, isn't it?" he said. "It was Clapham Common you wanted?"

"It'll do," said Mitzi.

"The malady lingers on." Mr Bug's representative flicked his robot driver with his whip. "We'll try Hampstead Heath again now."

The driver's voice was feminine. "What are we looking for, sir?"

Mr Bug's representative shrugged. "Whatever they're looking for."

"Do you think we'll find it, sir?"

"I'm not sure it matters. But it's something to pass the time. And we might meet some interesting people."

"Are there any real people left in London, sir?"

"I take your point. The city seems to be filling up with nothing but the ghosts of old anarchists. Not to mention Chartists and the like. Have you seen any of the Chartists?"

"Not recently, sir."

"There's bound to be a few on Hampstead Heath. What London really lacks at present is a genuine Mob."

It Was a Gas

"Any news?"

Frank Cornelius looked anxiously at the cryptik. It didn't seem a patch on some of Miss Brunner's other machines, but she put a great deal of faith in it.

"A few more record companies have been broken into. Tapes and records stolen. Some accounts. Majestic Studios have been blown up. Rockfield have had a fire. Island's sunk."

"And the casualties?" Bishop Beesley mopped his brow with an old Flake wrapper.

"They don't look significant. Everybody seems to be evacuating."

"Mr Bug?"

"Not sure. No data."

"Why are we sticking it out, then?" Frank gave a swift, resentful blink. "Why should we be the only ones?"

"Because we know best, don't we?" Miss Brunner reached absently towards where Maggy had been sitting. Now there was just a little pile of clothes. Maggy had been absorbed some hours ago. "Someone's going to have to go out for some food. I think it's you, Frank."

"You're setting me up. If my brother finds me, you know what he'll do. He's got a nasty, vengeful nature. He's never forgiven me for Tony Blackburn, let alone anything else."

"He's too busy at present." She waved the printouts. "Anyway, he hardly ever bothers you unless you've bothered him."

"How do I know if I've bothered him or not?"

Miss Brunner became impatient. "Go and get us a meal."

"And some chocolate fudge, if possible," said Bishop Beesley.

Frank put his Browning in the pocket of his mack. He sidled reluctantly towards the door.

"Hurry," hissed Miss Brunner

"Any special orders?"

"Anything tasty will suit me." She returned her attention to the cryptik. "At this rate we'll be eating each other."

This made her feel sick.

Through the Mirror

There was a bouncer on the door of the New Oldies Club as Mo tried to go through.

"No way, my son," said the bouncer.

Mo blinked. "You know me."

"Never seen you before."

"What's going on? Who's playing tonight?"

"Deep Fix."

"Is the Captain there?"

"Not for me to say. Not for you to ask."

"But I'm with the band."

"What band?"

"What band do you want me to be with?"

"Off!" said the bouncer. "Go on."

"Ask the Captain."

"You, mate, are persona non bloody grata. Get it?"

"Is the Captain in there?"

"You're a persistent little sod, ain't ya?" The bouncer hit him.

"What did you do that for?"

"Security."

Mo nursed his lip. "Oh. You shouldn't be afraid of me."

"It's not you, chum. It's the people you're hanging around with."

As Mo reached the street again, and began to walk in the general direction of Soho, he looked up. Over the rooftops was the outline of a small, sagging airship. It seemed to be drifting aimlessly on the wind.

To the North, quite close to the Post Office Tower, a fire was blazing.

United Artists, thought Mo absently.

What We Found There

Mr Bug's representative said: "Things look as if they're hotting up."

They were crossing over Abbey Road. Police were making a traffic detour around the ruins.

"All the old targets." Mr Bug's representative lit a fresh cigarette and put it to his tube. "Still, what new ones are there?"

The driver pressed the horn.

EMI Unlimited Edition

Mo leaned on the gates of Buckingham Palace and dragged the book from his inside pocket.

The book was called *The Nature of the Catastrophe*. He opened it up. All the pages were blank. He was getting used to this sort of thing.

"Oh, there you are!" Mitzi came running over from St James's Park. "We thought we'd lost you."

"I don't trust you, Mitzi. You're with them again."

"Why not join us?"

"What for?"

"There's safety in numbers."

"So you say."

"Anyway," said Mitzi, "you shouldn't be hanging about here, should you? Everyone's getting very security conscious. They might arrest you. Or shoot you. SAS and that."

"Everything else has been arrested, by the look of it."

"I'm worried about you, Mo."

"Don't be."

"We can help you."

"That didn't work the last time."

Army trucks were coming down the Mall Garbled voices called through loudspeakers mounted on the tops of the trucks.

Mo decided to follow Mitzi round the corner into Buckingham Palace Road. She took his hand. "Coming along then?"

"No," he said. "I think I'll catch a train from Victoria."

CLAIM SIX: LETS GO WITH LABOUR

STEVE JONES: Twenty. Born in London. Lives in a one-room cold-water-only studio in Soho where the band rehearses.

Ex-approved school. He was the lead singer with the Sex Pistols before he took up the guitar.

He has the reputation of being a man of a few words. But his sound intuition and low boredom threshold makes him great fun to be with. He's always looking for action. Of the four he probably had the most difficult childhood. His real father was a boxer whom he never knew. He never got on with his step-father and since the family lived in one room only, this led to a very fraught home environment. The first record he remembers being impressed by was Jimi Hendrix's "Purple Haze". He always wanted to play electric guitar.

—Virgin Publicity, 1977

"Delusions of grandeur will get you a very long way in this world." Martin Bormann leafed through his cut-price deletions. "You just missed him, I'm afraid."

Una Persson handed him the album she'd selected. "I'll have this, then. Do you know the times of the planes to New York?"

Bormann looked at his watch. "There's one in an hour. You'd better hurry. It could be the last."

God Save the Short and Stupid

"Ain't she fuckin' radiant, though?" Mrs C. studied the blue and white picture on her jubilee mug before putting it to her lips. "Thassa nice cuppa tea, Frank. Wotcher want?"

"Jerry." Frank was furtive. "Mum, I haven't got much more margin. Have you seen him?"

"Yeah."

"When?"

"Yesterday."

"Where?"

"At work. 'E watched ther picture four times."

"Why?"

"I fink 'e wanted a rest. 'E was asleep through most of 'em."

"When he left, did he say where he was going?"

"'E said 'e 'ad a few jobs ter do. Somefink abart pushin' a boat aht?"

170

Frank remained puzzled. "That's all?"

"I fink so." She puckered her brows. "You know what 'e's like. Yer carn't fuckin' understand all o' wot 'e says."

"Was he with anybody?"

"I dunno. Maybe wiv that bloke in a kilt. Like in ther film."

Frank dropped his cup into the saucer. "God almighty."

"I didn't catch 'is name," said Mrs Cornelius.

Sod the Sex Pistols

From where he stood on the Embankment, near the cannon, Mo could see the half-inflated airship tied to one of the spikes of Tower Bridge. Either the Assassin was stranded, or he was becoming more catholic in his targets.

As he climbed up the steps to the bridge, he thought he saw a flash of tartan darting down the other side. He hesitated, not sure which lead to follow. It had to be "Flash" Gordon.

"Oh, bugger!"

The last of the Musician-Assassins, clambered unsteadily down his steel ladder, a Smith and Wesson Magnum held by its trigger guard in his teeth.

"You look a lot better," said Mo.

"Feeling it, squire." Jerry dusted off his black car coat and smoothed his hair. "I've been eating better and getting more exercise. What's the time? My watch has stopped."

Mo didn't know.

"It doesn't matter, really. We'll be all right. Come on." The Assassin took Mo's arm.

"Where are we going?"

"I had a nasty moment last night," said the Assassin obliviously. "Somebody must have tried to slip some disco tapes into my feeder. Nearly blew my circuits. I think they're trying to get rid of me." He strode rapidly in the direction of Butler's Wharf on the South side of the bridge.

"Where are we going?"

"1977."

"What?"

"Nineteen bloody seventy seven, Mo. We've got a bloody gig to do. And this time you're going to do it properly."

Abolishing the Future

Miss Brunner was white with rage. "What on earth possessed you, Frank?"

A dozen dogs growled and grumbled as Frank tried to untangle their leads. "I had nowhere else to bring them. And I need them."

Bishop Beesley crouched in his corner munching handfuls of Poppets. "This is a very small bunker, Mr Cornelius."

"I've worked out what my brother's up to. He's made a tunnel into 1977."

"Oh, no." Miss Brunner began to punch spastically at her terminal. "That was why he was doing all that stuff with record companies. To get the energy he needed."

Frank nodded. The dogs began to pant. "We're going to have to follow him. He's got that little wanker Collier with him and maybe the rest of them, I'm not sure."

Bishop Beesley clambered to his feet "What are his plans?"

"To create an alternative, obviously. If he succeeds it means curtains for everything we've worked for."

Miss Brunner was grim. "We managed to abort it last time. We can do it again."

Frank stroked the head of the nearest Doberman. "This could be the end of authority as we know it."

"Aren't you being a trifle apocalyptic, Mr Cornelius?" Bishop Beesley reached a plump hand for the Walnut Whips on the steel table. "I mean, what can he do with a couple of guitars and a drum kit?"

"You don't know him." Frank unbuttoned his collar. "He's reverting to type, just when it seemed he was getting more respectable at last."

"He's fooled us before," said Miss Brunner. "And we should have known better." Her hands were urgent now, as she fed in her programme. "1977 could have been a turning point."

The cryptik began to give her a printout. She grew whiter than ever. "Oh, Jesus. It's worse than we thought."

"What?" Frank's arm was yanked by a sudden movement of his dogs.

"I think he's trying to abolish the Future altogether. He's going for some kind of permanent Present."

"He can't do it." Bishop Beesley licked his fingers. "Can he?"

"With help," said Miss Brunner, "he could."

"How can a few illiterate and talentless rock and rollers be of any use?"

"It's what they represent," she said. "There's no getting away from it, gentlemen. He's playing for the highest stakes."

"Can we stop him?" asked the Bishop.

"We're under strength. Half our usual allies are in stasis."

"What will wake them up?"

"The Last Trump," said Frank, He was panting now, in unison with his dogs.

Living In the Past

"Are you sure you know what you're doing?" said Mo, not for the first time.

Jerry was hurrying through the corridors of the vast warehouse. It had become very cold.

"I told you. I never know what I'm doing. I have to play it by ear. But I've got a shifter tunnel and I've got a fix and I'm bloody sure we can make it. After that it's up to all of us."

"To do what?"

"The Jubilee gig, of course."

"But we've done it."

"You've *tried* it, you mean. Just think of that as a rehearsal."

"I wish I'd never got in touch with you."

"Well, you did." The Assassin was humming to himself. It seemed to be some sort of Walt Disney song.

Mo tried to pull back. "I'm fed up with it all. I just want . . ."

"Satisfaction squire." Cornelius glowed. "And I'm going to give you your chance."

"All I wanted was the booze and the birds," said Mo weakly. "I was enjoying myself. We all were."

"And so you shall again, my son." The Musician-Assassin turned a clazed eye on his old comrade. "Better than ever."

The walls of the warehouse began to quiver. A silver mist engulfed them. From somewhere in the distance came the muffled sound of bells.

"We're through!" The Assassin cackled.

He burst open a rotting door and they stood on the slime of a disused wharf. Beside the wharf was a large white schooner with a black flag waving on its topmast. The schooner seemed to be deserted. On the poop deck a drum kit had been set up and Mo noticed PA all over the boat.

The Assassin paused, checking his wrist. "My watch's working again. That's good. We made it. The others should be along in a minute."

"That equipment looks expensive."

"It's the best there is," said the Assassin confidently. "Megawatt upon megawatt, my son. Enough sound to shake the foundations of society to bits! Ho, ho, ho!"

"Will Malcolm be here with the money?" asked Mo.

"You won't need money if this works," said the Assassin.

"I haven't had any wages in months." Mo set a wary foot on the gangplank.

"There are bigger things at stake," said the last of the Musician-Assassins. "More important things."

"That's what they always seem to wind up saying."

The white schooner rocked in the water. The Assassin began to hurry about the decks, checking the sound system, following cables, adjusting mikes.

"Power," he said. "Power."

"Wages," said Mo. "Wages."

But he was already becoming infected. He could feel it in his veins.

Glory Daze

"Hurry up, bishop." Miss Brunner was being dragged along by four of Frank's dogs. She had her Remington under her arm.

Frank was in the lead with six more dogs. The bishop, with two, rolled in the rear. It was dawn and Goldhawk Road was deserted apart from some red, white and blue bunting.

"If you ask me," said Mitzi catching up with her dad, "he's using all this for his own mad ends. All we wanted was a bit of publicity. Are you sure this is 1977?"

"Miss Brunner is never wrong about things like that. She's an expert on the Past. That's why I trust her." Bishop Beesley set his mitre straight on his head with an expert prod of his crook. "She stands for all the decent values." He wheezed a little. "You haven't got a Tootsie Roll on you, or anything I suppose?"

They had reached Shepherds Bush. On the green people were beginning to set up marquees and stalls. Pictures of QEII were everywhere.

Miss Brunner paused, hauling at the leads. "This could have achieved what the Festival of Britain was meant to achieve. A restoration of confidence."

"In what?" asked Mitzi innocently.

"Don't be cynical, dear."

They took the road to Hammersmith.

"It's just your interpretation I'm beginning to worry about," said Mitzi.

The Management Fantasy

Everyone was on board. Nobody seemed absolutely certain why they were here. The assassin was checking his rocket launchers and grenade-throwers, which lined the rails of the main deck.

"Hello, Sid," said Lemmy. "You're not looking well."

Sid plucked at his bass. John cast a suspicious eye about the schooner. "Ever get the feeling you're being trapped?"

"Used," said Muggy with relish, "in a game of which we have no understanding."

Automatically Mo was tuning up. "Has anybody seen Harrison?" He thought he'd spotted a flutter of moleskin on the yardarm.

The schooner was full of musicians now, most of them dead.

"Raise the anchor!" cried the Assassin.

The band faltered for a moment, astonished at its own magnificent volume. The sound swelled and swelled, drowning the noise of the rocket launchers as Jerry took out first the bridge and then the White Tower. Stones crumbled. The whole embankment was coming down. Hundreds of sightseers were falling into the water, clutching at their ears.

175

Overhead, police helicopters developed metal fatigue and dropped like wounded bees.

On board the schooner everyone was cheering up no end.

Mrs Cornelius lifted her frock and began a knees up. "This is a bit o' fun, innit?"

Soon everyone was pogoing.

The Assassin ran from launcher to launcher, from thrower to thrower, whispering and giggling to himself. On both sides of the river buildings were exploding and burning.

"No future! No future!" sang Jimi.

London had never seemed brighter.

The schooner gathered speed. Down went Blackfriars Bridge. Down went Fleet Street. Down went the Law Courts. Down went the Savoy Hotel.

It wasn't World War Three, but it was better than nothing.

Number One in the Capital Hit Parade

Miss Brunner, Bishop Beesley and Frank Cornelius had managed to get through the crowds and reach Charing Cross. With the dogs gnashing and leaping, they stood in the middle of Hungerford Bridge, watching the devastation.

The schooner had dropped anchor in the middle of the river and the sound-waves were successfully driving back the variable-geometry Tornados as they attacked in close formation, trying to loose Skyflashes and Sidewinders into the sonic barrier.

"You have to fight fire with fire," said Miss Brunner. "Come on. We still have a chance of making it to the Festival Hall."

They hurried on.

Mitzi let them go. She clambered over the railing of the bridge and dropped with a soft splash into the river. Then she struck out for the ship.

Behind her, the dogs had begun to howl.

The water had caught fire by the time she reached the side and was hauled aboard by the Assassin himself. He was glowing with health now. "What's Miss B up to?"

"Festival Hall," Mitzi wiped a greasy cheek. "They're going to try to broadcast a counter-offensive. Abba. Mike Oldfield. Rick Wakeman. Leonard Cohen. You name it."

The Assassin became alarmed for a moment "I'll have to boost the power."

"No future! No future! No future!"

From over on the South Bank the first sounds were getting through.

"They're fighting dirty." Jerry was shocked. "That's the Eurovision Song Contest as I live and breathe. Look to your powder, Mitzi."

He gave the National Theatre a broadside.

Concrete blew apart. But the counter-offensive went on.

"We're never going to make it to the Houses of Parliament at this rate," said the Assassin. "Keep playing."

It had grown dark. The fires burned everywhere. The volume rose and rose.

The schooner began to rock. Planes and helicopters wheeled overhead, hoping for a loophole in the defences.

"God Save The Queen!" sang the Sex Pistols.

"God Save The Queen!" sang the choir of what was left of St Paul's Cathedral.

Mrs Cornelius leaned to shout into Mitzi's ear. "This is great, innit? Just like ther fuckin' blitz."

Another broadside took out the National Film Theatre. Celluloid crackled smartly.

The schooner creaked and swayed.

The Assassin had begun to look worried. They were being hit from all sides by Radio 2.

"Suzanne takes you to the kerbside
and she helps you cross the street,
Sits beside you in the restaurant,
tells you what there is to eat
And she combs your hair and cleans your trousers
leads you down to smell the flowers
And fills out all your forms for you
And reads to you for hours . . .
Yes, she makes a perfect buddy for the blind . . ." sang Jerry.

Slowly, through the flames and the smoke, the schooner was making it under the bridge and heading for Vauxhall. There was still a chance.

CLAIM SEVEN: MAGGIE PROMISES VICTORIAN FUTURE

Malcolm first thought about the film when the group was banned. The idea was if they couldn't be seen playing, that they could be seen in a film. That was probably just after they got thrown off A&M in Spring '77.

Obviously with "God Save the Queen" and the kind of global attraction that the whole episode had, he began to think more seriously about it and he approached Russ Meyer in early Summer '77 and he went out to Hollywood and talked to him . . .

I think (Meyer) intended it to be a Russ Meyer film using the Sex Pistols, whereas Malcolm obviously intended it to be a Sex Pistols film using Russ Meyer. So there was a basic conflict from the start. He thought it would be the film that would crown his career . . . Meyer thought Malcolm was a mad Communist anti-American lunatic and he was demanding more money because the thing looked risky. Meyer was very, very angry when it fell through. Kept referring to Malcolm as Hitler. "Sue Hitler's ass" and all this stuff.

—*Julien Temple, interview with John May, NME, October 1979*

"We've lost a battle, but we haven't lost the War." Petulantly, Miss Brunner switched off the equipment. Her face was smeared with soot. The dogs lay dead around her, bleeding from the ears.

Through a pair of battered binoculars Frank surveyed the ruins. "They got the palace before they sank."

"Did they all make it into the airship?"

"I think so."

Bishop Beesley finished the last of his toasted marshmallows. "They're a lot further forward," he said. "Aren't they?"

Miss Brunner glared at him.

Smoke from the gutted Houses of Parliament drifted towards them.

"It's a state of emergency all right," said Frank.

"Somebody's got to teach the Sex Pistols a lesson." Miss Brunner's lips were prim as, with a fastidious toe, she pushed aside a wolfhound.

"They have a lot of power now," said Bishop Beesley.

She dismissed this. "The secret there, bishop, is that childishly they don't want it. They'll give it up. They don't want it—but we do. Half the time all we have to do is wait."

"I suppose so. They're not fond of responsibility, these young hooligans." Bishop Beesley took off his dirty surplice. "It makes you sick."

Miss Brunner looked with horror at his paisley boxer shorts.

Hello, Julie

"You weren't breaking any icons," said Nestor Makhno. "You were just drawing bits of graffiti over them. And helping the establishment make profits. You went about as far as Gilbert and Sullivan."

It was a somewhat sour evening at the Café Hendrix.

"You have to go solo," said Marc Bolan. "It's the only way."

"Don't give me any of your Stirnerist rationalisations." The old anarchist poured himself another large shot of absinthe. "*The Ego and his Own*, eh?"

"*My* anarchists were always romantic leaders," said Jules Verne, who had dropped over from The Mechaniste in the hope of finding his friend Meinhoff.

"Which is why they were never proper anarchists." Makhno had had this argument before. He turned his back on the Frenchman. "It's all substitutes for religion, when you come down to it. I give up."

"If you want my opinion, they should never have put a woman in charge." Saint Paul, as usual, was lost in his own little world.

Big Money

Having failed to find what he needed at The Jolly Englishman public house, Mo put his disguise back on and went to Kings Cross, heading for The Hotel Dramamine.

He was sure, now that a few things had been settled along the embankment, Jerry would want to explain.

The lady at the door recognised him. "Go up to Room 12, dear," she said. "There'll be someone there in a minute."

He didn't tell her what he was really after.

He got to the first landing and went directly to the cage room. This was where Mr Bug had kept his special clients. It was empty apart from a miserable Record Company executive, who whined at him for a moment or two before he left. No information.

Other doors were locked. The ones which yielded showed him nothing he didn't already know. It was obvious, however, that Mr Bug wasn't here.

Room 12 had been prepared for him. He suspected a trap. On the other hand the lady on the waterbed looked as if she could take his mind off his problems. He decided to risk it.

"You don't know where Mr Bug is, I suppose," he said, as he stripped.

She opened her oriental lips.

"Love me," she said, "you're so wonderful."

He flung himself onto the heaving rubber.

The door opened. One of Mr Bug's representatives stood there. He had a wounded Alsatian with him. From beyond the window a car began to hoot.

Mo scrambled out of the bed. As he made for the window he was certain he heard the dog speak. It was better than nothing. He plunged from the window and into Jerry's car. "Let's rock."

I Need Your Tender Touch

"Monarchy's only a symbol," said Mr Bug's representative to Mitzi as the car moved slowly through what remained of St James's Park, "but then so are the Sex Pistols."

Near the pond, groups of homeless civil servants were jollying each other along as they erected temporary shelters, prefabs and tents.

"I don't think anyone meant it to go this far." Mitzi frowned. "Could you hurry it up a bit? I've got a train to catch."

"Jerry did. A bit of chaos allows him more freedom of movement."

"Malcolm has the same idea. Keep 'em fazed."

Mr Bug's representative placed a rubber hand on her little knee. "Instant gratification," he said. "Where are we going?"

"To rock."

Mr Bug's representative tapped the chauffeur with his whip. "Did you hear that?"

"Yes, sir."

The car bumped up the path through the park towards Piccadilly. All the roads around the Palace were ruined.

"It's peaceful now, isn't it?" Mitzi wound down the window. "I love the smell of smoke, don't you?"

"I can't smell a thing in this exoskeleton. My usual senses are cut off, you see."

"I suppose that's the point of it."

"It does allow one a certain kind of objectivity."

"Like being a child?"

"Well, no. Like being an ant, really."

Anarchy Dropped Out of the Top Twenty

Mo and Jerry panted on the platform, watching the train as it pulled away.

"I saw him." Jerry scratched. "Jimi."

"Or someone like him." Mo rubbed his nose. "Should we find out where the train's going?"

"He could get off anywhere."

"You spent too long in that bloody hotel," said Jerry.

"You could have arrived a couple of minutes earlier." Mo was bitter.

"This is pointless. Let's give it up."

"I want my wages."

"He hasn't got them, though has he? Or if he has, we're not going to get them now. What are you really after, Mo?"

"I need some answers, I told you."

"Don't we all? But you never got them, did you?"

Slow Train through the Occident

Miss Brunner settled herself in the first class compartment. "We're going to have to deal with them."

"I tried to get into the next carriage," said Frank, "but it seems to have been locked. I think there's some trouble going on."

"It's locked at the other end as well." Bishop Beesley wiped the sweet sweat from his cheeks. "I think it could be part of the emergency regulations."

He relished the phrase. It was like coming home.

The regular rhythm of the train was soothing them all.

"What are you going to offer him?" Frank asked her. "I mean, what have we actually got?"

"Experience," she said. "Ambition. A sense of right and wrong. Everything you need to put things into proper order. Sooner or later the balloon will burst."

"It seems to have burst already."

"A pinprick. It'll be patched in no time."

"I admire your resilience, Miss Brunner." Bishop Beesley was feeling in his pockets for the remains of his chocolate digestives. "I suppose you didn't notice if there was a buffet?"

"Not in this carriage," Frank told him.

"They always come back to us." Miss Brunner looked out at the windows. "Cows," she said.

Change Your Masques

The last of the Musician-Assassins put his vibra-gun into its holster. "They'll be wanting a martyr," he told Mo. "A proper martyr to the seventies."

"Well it isn't going to be poor old me. All I'm after is my wages and maybe a chance to do the odd gig. I should never have got mixed up with you, Mr C."

"You summoned me, remember?"

Mo shrugged. He sat hunched over his Bacon Burger in the Peckham Wimpy, watching the dirty rain on the windows. "I've got a feeling I'm being used. Has it after all come down to Peckham?"

"You keep saying that. I'm only doing what you said you wanted me to do."

"There's always a snag about making deals. Particularly with old hippy demons."

"Do you mind? I was around long before that."

"Maybe that's your trouble. Are you trying to recapture your lost youth?"

Jerry dipped into his Tastee-Freeze. His whole attitude was self-pity-ing. "Maybe. But probably I'm trying to recapture those few moments when I felt grown-up. Know what I mean? In charge of myself."

"How did you lose it?"

"Equating action with inspiration, maybe. Or 'energy,' whatever that is."

"You've done quite a lot. You're just feeling tired, probably." Mo wondered how he came to be comforting his old boss.

The Assassin gave a deep sigh. "Bands begin breaking up when they're faced with the implications of what they've started. When it threatens to turn into art, or something like it. Look at the problems the Dadaists had. Successful revolutions bring their own problems."

Mo's attention was wavering. "You really can be a boring old fart sometimes, can't you? Hippy or not."

Jerry seemed chastened. "It comes with analysing too much. But what else can I do these days? Imposition hasn't worked very well, has it? Analysis is all you're left with. Am I right or am I wrong?"

"Suit yourself." Mo swivelled his red plastic seat round. "You should do what you feel like doing."

The Assassin toyed with his Tastee-Freeze.

"Look where that's got me." He cast a miserable eye around him. "The bloody Peckham Wimpy."

Every Room Was a Dead End

"Isn't the train ever going to stop?" Miss Brunner couldn't recognise the countryside. "Whose idea was this, anyway?"

"Yours," said Frank. "Or mine. I forget." He was beginning to fugue a bit. "Tra la la. Hi diddle de de. Ta ra a boom de ay."

Bishop Beesley was of no use at all. He desperately needed a fix. His fat was turning a funny colour and the flesh was loosening even as she watched.

"We're out of control," she said, "and I don't like it."

"I thought you said we knew what we were doing?" Frank wiped drool from his lips. "Hic."

"We do. But I didn't expect the corridors to be blocked. That little bastard has outmanoeuvred us."

"But only for the moment, eh?" said Frank. He was being dutiful. "What do you want me to say?"

"You're bloody useless!"

He winced.

"I have to do everything myself."

Bishop Beesley mewled. "A Milky Way would be all right."

It became dark. The train had entered a tunnel. It stopped.

Miss Brunner thought she saw a white face press itself against the window for a second, but she was losing faith in her own judgement.

This realization made her very angry.

She kicked Frank in the shin.

Frank began to giggle.

Holidays in the Sun

Mrs Cornelius had her sleeves rolled up. She was doling out soup from the specially erected canteen in Trafalgar Square.

"Hello, mum." Jerry held his tin cup to be filled.

"Oxtail," she said, "or Mulligatawny?"

"Oxtail, please."

"You've done it this time," she said. "There's a lot of people pissed off wiv you. I told 'em it was just your way of celebratin'. But look wot you've caused. Pore ole Nelson's got 'alf 'is bleedin' body missin'. It's gonna take ages ter clear up ther mess."

"Sorry, mum."

"No use bein' sorry now. You'd better keep yer 'ead down for a while. I thought you'd bloody learned yer lesson."

"Lesson?"

"You 'eard me."

"Can I have the key to the flat?"

"Oh, so ya fuckin' wanna come 'ome ter mum now, do yer? Littel sod." She softened. "'Ere y'are. Now move on. There's a lot more people waitin'."

She watched him shuffle off, sipping at his soup. "They just fuckin' use yer when they need yer. An' then they're fuckin' off again."

But the crowd had recognised him. They were beginning to converge.

With a yelp of terror, Jerry scuttled towards the National Gallery.

Mrs Cornelius watched impassively. "E'll be okay," she said to herself. "Unless they actually tear 'im ter pieces."

She ladled Mulligatawny into the next outstretched cup.

When she looked again, the crowd was rushing through the doors of the Gallery.

Ten minutes later they were all coming out again, like spectators whose team had lost.

She grinned to herself. "Shifty littel bastard," she said. "At least 'e knows when ter scarper."

I Shot the Sheriff

The train had begun to move again, but by now Bishop Beesley was catatonic and Frank Cornelius was completely ga-ga, dribbling and whistling to himself. Miss Brunner went into the corridor and tugged at the door. It wouldn't open. All the windows were jammed.

She ran along the corridor, looking for help. All the other compartments were filled with old rubber suits, as if Mr Bug's representatives had dematerialised.

"What's going on?" she cried. "What's going on?"

The train groaned and clattered in unison with her voice.

She clawed at the connecting door. It wouldn't budge.

"Somebody's going to pay for it." She was livid. "I'm not used to treatment of this kind. Who's in charge? Who's in charge?"

The train grunted.

"Who's in charge?" Now her voice became pathetic. A tear appeared in her right eye. She adjusted her blouse. She whimpered.

The train was moving faster. It swayed wildly from side to side.

Miss Brunner began to scream.

CLAIM EIGHT: A PROPERLY OWNED DEMOCRACY

JULIAN TEMPLE (DIRECTOR): Went to Cambridge University "For the same reasons as one applies for an American Express Card". Attended National Film School "so that I didn't have to wait 20 years to be able to do something". *The Great Rock 'N' Roll Swindle* was his graduation film. Since then he has made *Punk*

Can Take It, featuring the UK Subs and narrated by John Snagge, who once declared the end of World War II on BBC Radio and ghosted for Churchill's speeches while it was still on.

— *Virgin Publicity, 1980*

The last of the Musician-Assassins was crawling along rooftops overlooking Portobello Road.

He was looking for his airship. He was certain he'd left it in the vicinity of Vernon's Yard.

"Bugger," he muttered. "Oh, bugger."

He was not feeling at one with himself.

Every so often a demonic grin, a memory, crossed his poor, ravaged face.

"Why am I always getting mixed up with bloody bands? What's happened to my complicated vocabulary of ideas? Why do I prefer rock and roll?"

It was familiar stuff to him.

Flies clustered around a faded chimney stack, rising as he groped.

"Monica?" His mind cast about for any anchor. "Mum? Colonel? David M?"

His cuban heels scraped slate. Something fell away from him and smashed in the street. The sun was rising.

He drew a scratched single from the pocket of his black car coat and put it close to his eyes, studying it as if it were a map.

He was crying.

The flies hissed rhythmically. A stuck needle. He held on to the chimney, pulling himself up, his feet slipping.

There had to be something better than this.

The Uncertain Ego

"Passion feeds passion and then we are left with a small death." Mr Bug's representative was trying to comfort Miss Brunner.

She stared at the strangled corpse.

A young man in a trenchcoat and a trilby stepped backwards.

"Is anyone really dying?" she asked. "Or are we all just very tired?"

"Some of you are really dying, I'm afraid." Mr Bug's representative plucked at his mouth-tube. "Time is Time, no matter how much you struggle against it."

"Then we're done for."

"I haven't come to any conclusions about that." He was apologetic. "I'm honestly only an observer."

"You've interfered."

"I've taken an interest. It's the best I can offer."

Miss Brunner shrugged him away.

A whistle blew.

"I'm getting off this train," she said.

Mr Bug's representative made a peculiar gesture with his right glove.

"There'll be another one along in a minute."

Difficult Love
Very sluggishly, the airship was lifting.

The last of the Musician-Assassins lay spreadeagled on the floor of the gondola. A faint tape was playing "Silly Thing."

"It's what the public wanted," murmured Jerry. "Or at least some of them. I did my best. It was good while it lasted."

The ship gently bumped against a church steeple. He pulled himself to a window. He recognised Powys Square. There was a bonfire.

Something bit at his groin.

He scratched.

Framed against the flames, a tartan-clad figure and a dwarf were dancing.

"I think I'm missing all the fun again." The Assassin switched on his engine.

It faltered. It was apologetic.

He tried again.

Something clicked.

The Laughing Policeman
"We're going to have to split up," said Miss Brunner firmly. Her colleagues had revived enough to get off the train and sit, shaking, on the platform seat.

"I think I have already," said Frank.

"You mean diversify, don't you?" Bishop Beesley wrenched a wrapper off a Mars.

"Disintegrate?" Frank was thinking of himself as usual.

Miss Brunner had recovered a bit of her composure.

"Captain Maxwell is the only one who will know how to deal with all this. So much of it is his fault."

"Oh, come on," said Frank. "We were partners. Maxwell's as decent as the rest of us underneath. He pretends to be a revolutionary but he's really just an ordinary businessman."

Miss Brunner shook her head. "In different ways, Mr Cornelius, you're as gullible as your brother. We're facing a genuine attempt to take power."

"The Pistols."

"Of course not, you idiot. You very rarely get that sort of trouble from the musicians. They want different things, most of them. Subtler things."

"The Pistols want subtler things." Bishop Beesley appeared to be trying to recondition his mind.

"That's hard to believe," said Frank.

Miss Brunner yawned and glanced away. "At least they're all good looking."

"I haven't been well," said Frank. "What's this about breaking up?"

"Diversifying," said Bishop Beesley.

There was a peculiar lack of noise around the station. The train had long-since pulled away.

"Splitting up," she said. "To find them."

"Who?" said Frank. He watched a butterfly settle on the track.

"Anyone," she said.

"Divide and Rule," said Bishop Beesley. "Where in hell are we, anyway?"

He began to snore.

Miss Brunner peered into the countryside. "Is that real, do you think? It's such a long time since I've been anywhere."

Familiar Air

"There must have been something in the marketing," said Mo. He stood in the deserted office complex holding a phone without a lead. "Badges and that. T-shirts."

"There's a lot to be made from marketing," agreed Mitzi. "Posters. Programmes. People get a good profit off all that. Special books."

"Masks. Sweets."

"Tie up marketing and it's far less hassle than actually managing a band," said Mitzi. She had seen it all. "Often a better turnover. And there are no people to get in the way and spoil things."

"Maybe the marketing company could pay my wages."

"Ah, well, Mo, it's a separate organisation, you see. They would if they could. But they have their accounts."

"Maybe I should look at their accounts."

"Only accountants understand accounts. You need an accountant to check it for you."

"A lawyer?"

"A lawyer and an accountant's what you need."

"To keep an eye on the manager?"

"It isn't as simple as that, Mo."

Dead Loyal

Mrs Cornelius stuck her neck through her strap. "Ter tell yer the truth, Sarge, I'm glad ter be back at me regular job. 'Ow's business?"

"Who?" said Sergeant Alvarez.

"Not 'oo—wot." She flashed her torch on and off. "Somebody's got ter earn a livin'."

She paused at the door of the auditorium. "O' course, it's in troubled times like these, people see a good picture, don't they?"

"Killed," said Alvarez.

"Oh, yeah. That, too."

Before she could go through, Mr Bug's representative entered. "Everything all right here?"

"Loverly," she said. She had never liked the look of him.

"Plenty of stock?"

"Ask the Sarge."

"Any more handcuffs? Whips? Lengths of chain?"

"We're orl right for most o' that, far as I know," she said. "But it's Sarge does the stock, doncher, love?"

"We've got to look after the housewives," said Mr Bug's representative. "Can't have them getting bored, can we?"

Mrs Cornelius frowned at him. He seemed to be attempting a joke. "Are you the usual fellah?" she asked.

"I'm filling in for him."

"You 'aven't—I mean, it's not a takeover or nuffink?"

"Just a change of territory. It'll all settle back to normal soon. Are you sure you don't need any more gags?"

Mrs Cornelius tittered. "Not if they're anyfink like ther last one."

Mr Bug's representative didn't get it.

"What do you need?" he said. "You must need some replacements."

"New feet," said Mrs Cornelius, "would be nice."

He looked at her shoes.

"Something elegant in rubber?"

She turned back towards the doors.

"I've got them in the car."

"It's no good," she told him. "I 'ave ter rely on the National 'Ealth."

"Business is bad all round at the moment, even in entertainment. I remember when you couldn't go wrong in entertainment, so long as there was plenty of crisis and stuff. Cash from Chaos, eh?"

"Chaos?"

"It's not the same as entropy. Not superficially, at any rate. Still, it's all the same in the end."

"Wot the bloody 'ell you talkin' abaht?"

"Stuff." Mr Bug's representative felt about his person. "I'm having a spot of trouble with my tubes. It's hard to remain attached. Do you find that?"

"Ask bleedin' Alice in bleedin' Wonderbloodyland," said Mrs Cornelius. She sniffed. "Blimey! You don't arf pong."

"Ping," said Alvarez pulling at his beard.

Mr Bug's representative slouched away. "Everything's rotting."

"You could've fooled me. You're enough to give ther fuckin' 'otdogs a bad name. An' that's sayin' somefink."

She backed through the doors with her tray.

On the screen they were shooting extras.

Voices in the Night

The airship was drifting over the debris near the river. People had already set up stalls and were selling various souvenirs: bits of ship, parts of planes, twisted singles.

The Assassin could hear their voices.

"Get yer genuine Prince Philip bandages."

"Johnny Rotten's safety pins. All authentic."

"Fresh Corgi!"

Not a lot had changed.

He watched the shadow of his own ship as it passed over the ruins, over the dirty water, over the collapsed bridges.

He was feeling more depressed than ever.

"I need . . ." he murmured. "I need . . ."

But his memory was failing again. He had seen too many alternatives. All the directions were screwed up. All the pasts and all the futures. They rarely seemed to make a decent present, which was only what he'd been aiming for. A bit of relief. But Time resisted manipulation, finally.

"Time's a killer," he said, He tried to turn up his volume, but the music remained a whisper.

With an effort he moved the wheel and set a course for what had once been Derry and Tom's Famous Roof Garden. Now it was some sort of posh nightclub. He had relinquished his interest in 19—.

He had all but relinquished his interest in the 20th century.

He checked his instruments.

"There's never a World War Three around when you need one."

Please Leave the State in the Toilet in Which You Would Wish to Find It

Sid had lost another game of pool at the Café Hendrix. He went over to a window seat and looked out into the grey mist of eternity.

"I don't think it's going to clear up," said George, Lord Byron, arm in arm with Gene Vincent. They had been having a medical boot race.

191

"Don't mope, lad. You didn't do so badly. And think of all those Sid Is Innocent badges they won't be able to sell now."

"What about all the Sid Still Lives badges they *will* be able to sell?"

"There's a lot more money in death, these days, than there was when I coughed it," said Shelley. "Although it didn't do any harm to the poetry sales. Just think what they could have done for me? I did get a funeral pyre, though, and all that. Shelley posters would have gone over a treat, don't you think. Shelley pens."

Jesus came over, chewing on a toothpick. "I've never had any problems," he said. "My marketing's been going strong for a couple of thousand years. Gets better all the time. But then none of you were crucified, were you?"

"Don't listen to him, the snob." Oscar Wilde put his hand in Sid's lap. "You still on for that game of skittles?"

"You have to aim for universal appeal," said Jesus. "And that means your middle classes, I'm afraid. Without them, you'll never do it."

"Sid didn't understand that, did you Sid?" said Nestor Makhno. "And neither did I. And neither would I want to."

"I did it my way," said Sid. "I think."

Grumbling Bums

Miss Brunner sighed with pleasure. "What a terrible trip. I'm glad to be home."

"We achieved nothing," Frank complained.

"Not true, darling. We found out certain things by a process of elimination."

"It was a wild goose chase."

"It was a field trip. Trust me, darling." She stroked her cryptik. "We'll just feed in what we know and then run another complete programme. Be a good boy, Frank, and put the kettle on."

Bishop Beesley said: "You still think we might be able to get the concessions?"

"We've the experience and the knowhow. Show me a product, bishop, and I'll show you a profit in a very short while. How have I managed to stay in business so long? We'll need a few ideas to show the captain."

"But we can't find him. No-one can find him."

"Wait until he hears what we have to show him. For the *Mirror*."

"You're an incurable optimist, Miss Brunner," said Bishop Beesley. He began to force a chocolate orange into his mouth.

Remixing

The Assassin opened the door and man-handled the bomb out.

He watched it sail down towards the new estate opposite Rough Trade in Kensington Park Road.

It landed with a clang in the street. People began to come out of their doors and look at it.

Faces stared up at the last of the Musician-Assassins. He spread his hands.

"Sorry."

"Is it a dud?" shouted the grocer.

"I was told it would go off." Jerry shrugged. "Win a few and lose a few, eh?"

When, a couple of seconds later, the bomb did explode and bits of the crowd were scattered in directions, the Assassin was struck in the face by the grocer's left foot.

He wiped the blood from his cheek.

"What a lovely bit of fragmentation."

CLAIM NINE: YOU KNOW IT MAKES SENSE

He violently dislikes Rotten because Rotten insulted him all the time. Rotten used to talk to him in words that he didn't understand, like English swear words. It was quite amusing to see Meyer trying to make sense of it.

Meyer took Rotten out to dinner and Rotten was incredibly rude and disgusting over his food. He was trying to alienate him because it was Malcolm's project. By that stage Rotten really didn't get on with Malcolm, so the film was one of the major causes of a rift in the group that led to the break up.

. . . Apparently they spent three days tracing down this deer until they found the right one, and Meyer shot it himself.

The focus puller was thrown off for being squeamish about

the thing. Meyer wouldn't have anyone anti-American on his set.
—*Julian Temple, Interview with John May, NME, October 1979*

"The fabric's wearing a bit thin, isn't it?" Mr Bug's representative sat in his static limo. People moved like ghosts through ghostly trees. "Is there any way of compensating?"

"It's a write-off," said Jerry sheepishly.

"You're losing your touch."

"I haven't got the help I used to get."

"True. You'd had hopes for the Pistols, then?"

"It isn't their fault." Jerry shifted as far away from Mr Bug's representative as possible. He cleared his throat. "Would you mind if we opened a window, squire?"

"Not at all. But the fumes . . .?"

"The fumes are fine. It's quite pleasant. The scent of dissipating dreams."

"I'm afraid . . ."

"What?"

"I can't follow you."

"Just as well, squire. I'm on my own. I have to be. People try to turn you into leaders. Do you find that?"

"Not exactly. I just tend to the sick. When I do anything at all."

The car started up again and moved at less than ten miles an hour through the strangely faded park. Mr Bug's representative pointed at a distant outline. "The Palace is springing back again, isn't it?"

"Oh, I wouldn't be surprised, squire."

A large mob, all greys and light browns, ran through the car, carrying torches. They wore 18th century clothes. "The Gordon Riots," said Mr Bug's representative. "But they seem to be burning the Pistols in effigy. Look over there."

The Assassin nodded. "Everything's out of focus, at present. This happens when you mess about the way I was. Still, it might have gelled. You never know."

"You manipulate Time?" Mr Bug's representative was impressed.

"I pretend to."

"I pretend to manipulate people. On Mr Bug's behalf, of course."

"Who is Mr Bug?" asked Jerry.

"Have a guess," said Mr Bug's representative.

Boo-boo-boogaloo

The Cessna came in to land on the deserted airfield. Its wheels bumped on the broken tarmac and it narrowly avoided the collapsed remains of a small airship.

Mr Bug's representative and the last of the Musician-Assassins crouched behind a ruined wall and watched.

Jerry held his vibra-gun in a trembling hand.

"It's the Americans," said Mr Bug's representative.

A figure in a red and blue diving suit emerged from the plane.

"Their technology's so sophisticated." Mr Bug's representative was admiring. "You'd hardly know there was anyone inside would you?"

"I'm not even sure about you." The Assassin wet his lips.

Mr Bug's representative nodded in agreement. "Yes." His breathing became erratic. "Yessss."

Jerry had the feeling that, given half a chance, Mr Bug's representative would begin some kind of mating ritual with the American suit.

Moleskin glowed in an abandoned control tower.

Jerry leaped from cover. "Flash!"

"Not yet" hissed Mr Bug's representative. But it was too late.

Aiming the vibra-gun, Jerry hit the American just as he was reaching the tower. The suit fell to the ground and began to thresh as the sonics shook him to death. Part of the tower broke away and crashed onto the corpse.

Tartan dodged from window to window as the vibra-gun swept the building. Concrete cracked. Glass shivered.

Mr Bug's representative grabbed Jerry's arm. "Too ssssoon. Oh, dear!"

A helicopter swished into the sky.

"Bugger," said the Assassin.

"I'm not sure you have any understanding of anyone's best interests," said Mr Bug's representative, walking with slow, sad steps towards the American corpse. "It could be the culture gap, but I'm beginning to think you're past it. I must have a word with Mr Collier."

"He wants his wages. I thought . . ."

A strange, high-pitched hiss came from Mr Bug's representative. It took the Assassin a while to realise that he was whistling "Dixie."

Gather at the River

"The Captain's in America, I'm afraid," said Clivey on the phone. "I'm sure he'll want to get in touch the minute he comes back."

Mo replaced the receiver.

Mitzi said: "I told you so. You ought to go there."

"Why?"

"For the same reason he's gone. For the same reason everyone goes. Because you've run out of possibilities here. Desperate times require desperate journeys."

"I never thought it would come to this."

"Distance makes the bank grow fonder."

"Do what?"

"Everyone else is going. You can bet your life on it."

"This job involves a lot of travelling, doesn't it? And very little money."

"Don't start whining." He was in an unusually brisk mood. It probably meant that she was keen to go to America for her own reasons.

"I can't afford it."

"I can get us a lift."

"I could do with a lift," Mo said feelingly.

"We'll have to hurry."

"Where to?"

"Brighton," she said.

Mo offered her an enquiring scowl.

Mitzi shrugged. "It's where the plane leaves from."

Tragic Magic

"Americans always think British bands are setting out to shock, when half the time the band is just behaving with its habitual rudeness." Frank had his new denim suit on.

Miss Brunner pursed her lips. "We have so many complaints from abroad."

"They were right about Captain M," said Bishop Beesley. "If not the band itself. But then the Captain must be easily shocked himself."

"He had his finger on the pulse of the public for a moment or two, I'll give him that."

"He had his hands in their pockets, too," said Frank. "That's what I'm complaining about."

"Times are hard," she said. "Everyone's got their hands in everyone else's pockets. Groping about for the pennies they're sure someone must have."

"Disgusting," said Bishop Beesley.

"Hurry up, Bishop. Are you packed?"

He was trying to close the lid on a large suitcase of Toffee Crunch.

"I have every admiration for American Management." Frank became pious. "They handle things so well over there."

"They have nicer musicians, that's why."

"Even the cowboys?"

"Hearts of gold, underneath."

"Rough diamonds," said Bishop Beesley sentimentally.

"Any kind would do me, right now." Frank looked at his ticket. "This had better work."

"They love me," she said. "It's my accent."

Touching Base

"Half the time you think you're flying." Jerry fiddled with his controls, "and when you get out you discover you've been in a Link trainer the whole time."

"Try and keep quiet and concentrate," said Mitzi. They were all fed up with him. "Are you sure you know this type of plane?"

"I love it," he said. "Therefore I know it."

"A classic romantic delusion." Mr Bug's representative wriggled in the navigator's chair.

"Get on with it, you stinking old hasbeen." Mo sat with the rest of the group in the passenger seats. He lifted a bottle of Wild Turkey to his lips.

"Will we get to meet Bugs Bunny?" asked Flash. He was well out of things.

"I'm having a hard time," said the Assassin with characteristic self-pity.

"Getting them good times." Only Mitzi was really looking forward to the trip.

The old Boeing Clipper lumbered through the water, its Wright Double Cyclone engines screaming and burping as they gave all they had left.

"You ought to be running a bloody transport museum," said Mo without disapproval. "You're living in the past."

"I think he simply wants the whole 20th century at once," said Mr Bug's representative. "It's greed, really. And romance, of course."

Jerry pulled down his goggles. "I'm just heavily into technology," he said.

"Well, I suppose I can't complain about that." Mr Bug's representative crossed his legs, if they were legs. "It's been my problem for years."

The ancient Boeing heaved itself into the wild, blue yonder. Mitzi clapped her little hands. "Look out, Land of Opportunity, here we come!"

"If we're lucky," said Mo enthusiastically

The Assassin had a strange grin on his lips. "Manifest Destiny. We'll be fine."

"I think I'd feel safer in a bleedin' covered wagon," said Jimi, waking up for a moment and not enjoying the experience.

Buddy, Can You Spare a Dime?

"Yanks," said Mrs Cornelius reminiscently. "I saws lot of 'em durin' ther War."

"War?" said Alvarez rolling a hot dog between his hands.

"Ther last one. Ther last big one, that is. Thaes wot I liked. Mrs Minniver, innit? Well, you wouldn't know abart any o' that. Yore too fuckin' young."

"Who?"

"You?"

"Killed?"

"You, if ya don't fuckin' shut up. I'll tell yer one fing. I'm gettin' bleedin' bored wiv this picture, ain't you? I could do wiv a nice bit o' John Wayne."

Ladies Love Outlaws

"Self-conscious, self-involved, chauvinistic and just downright bloody terrified." Miss Brunner dragged Frank off the plane at LAX. "Where's your sense of the International Brotherhood of Man, Mr Cornelius?"

"I've been here before." Bishop Beesley wiped his brown lips.

"I never did like it." Frank was miserable. "It's hardly ever the way it is in the pictures."

"A fact of life which your family has always failed to accept." They moved towards the Immigration desks, "And take that silly Stetson off."

"Will they give us the money?" asked Bishop Beesley, in the rear as usual. "In Los Angeles? Sunset Boulevard?"

"Sunset something," she said. "This could be the end of the line."

Frank cheered up a little. "You getting cold feet?"

"My feet are never hot, Mr Cornelius."

She was sensitive about her inability to sweat.

Dead Puppies

They pushed Sid out first. He went down over the Bay, rolling and twisting in the air before his parachute opened.

"Go," shouted the Assassin, circling the Golden Gate Bridge. "Go!"

One by one they jumped.

"At least it's sunny," said Mitzi, passing Mo on the way down. "It's amazing what a difference a bit of sunshine makes."

"Have a nice day." The Wild Turkey and Crème de Menthe hadn't mixed well. He began to vomit in the general direction of Haight-Ashbury.

They drifted over the city.

Mr Bug's representative hung limp in his harness. Stuff was oozing from his suit. "Can this be a propaganda drop?"

"I've never tried them," Jimi tugged at one of his ropes. "This is all right, though, isn't it?"

One by one they hit the ocean.

The Boeing Clipper circled over the spreading blobs of silk.

Jerry was beginning to revive a trifle. He swung the plane out to sea and flipped a toggle. His vibra-cannons were now At Go.

He turned and headed back towards the city as fast as he could go. The tapes rolled, straight into the cannons' ammo storage.

"Time for a little earthquake."

He gave them "Anarchy in the UK." It seemed appropriate.

He whistled to himself as the buildings began to bounce.

Honky Tonk Masquerade

Mitzi Beesley stood dripping on the wharf while the cutters continued their search.

"Americans take everything so *seriously*. They're worse than the French."

Mr Bug's representative was incapable of standing. Someone had tried to remove his suit but had stopped when they had seen what was inside. "They're too polite. And when politeness fails, they're too violent."

"There were at least four more went in." The policewoman was staring wonderingly at the blasted city. "What did they have to do that for?"

"Jealousy," said Mitzi. "Also revenge."

"What for?"

"Oh, they're all looking for the Captain. We thought he was here."

"And Tennille?"

"If you like."

The Boeing Clipper had disappeared out to sea, pursued by helicopters and coastguard planes.

"Who's the pilot?" asked the policewoman. It was obvious that she still didn't believe what had happened. She looked suspiciously at Jimi and Sid.

"Just an old fart."

Three familiar figures were picking their way over the tattered wood and concrete. "Are we too late?" Miss Brunner wanted to know.

"Too late?" asked Frank and Bishop Beesley in unison.

"Too late," agreed Mitz.

"Poor lads." Miss Brunner grinned like an ape.

"Will the Captain be at the funeral?"

"There's got to be an inquest first," said Mitzi.

"Questions are going to be asked, eh?" Frank prodded at the shoulder of Mr Bug's representative. It hissed back at him, a dying snake. "Phew! He must have been gone for months."

"It's what we're all beginning to realize." Mitzi wandered off in the direction of Fisherman's Wharf. She was hoping she could still buy a postcard.

CLAIM TEN: I KNOW WHO KILLED THE EMPIRE

Said Lydon in his statement: "McLaren hoped that our record sales would be enhanced if the public were under the impression that we were banned from playing. That was certainly untrue. Some halls wouldn't have us, but others applied to Glitterbest for gigs during 1977 and were either refused or else received no replies." In the end, he claimed, the Pistols resorted to doing three gigs under assumed names.

. . . Sid Vicious rang Lydon one morning at 5:00 a.m. to inform him that McLaren had just visited him. McLaren had complained to Vicious about Lydon, and Vicious himself told Lydon that he had had enough of the Sex Pistols. "Vicious sounded incoherent," said Lydon's statement. "I've since heard that he took an overdose of heroin shortly after McLaren's visit." Subsequently, Wilmers claimed, Lydon and McLaren had a face-to-face showdown at which Lydon said he didn't like getting publicity out of a man who had left a train driver like a vegetable. The judge asked whether Rotten had changed in view of his refusal to become involved with Biggs. "The image projected is one in which violence is not opposed," he commented.

Mr Wilmers said that Rotten did not approve of killing people.

—*New Musical Express, 24th February 1979*

Manager As Voyeur

"It was just another wank," said Sid, picking at himself in the Café Hendrix.

"But a seminal wank, you must admit," said Nancy. She had been allowed in on a visit. She had always been fond of bad jokes.

Nestor Makhno looked up from the next table, a spoonful of ruby-coloured borscht near his lips, his woolly hat slipping down over one eye. "It's the politically illiterate who start revolutions. And it's the politically literate who lose them. You mustn't blame yourself."

"I blame the Chelsea Hotel," said Dylan Thomas. "Have you ever stayed there? In the winter? Brrr. It brings you down, boyo."

Since arriving at the Café Hendrix he had adopted an appalling Welsh jocularity.

"What would you do?" asked Nancy. "If they gave you the chance of a comeback?"

"Tell them to stuff it."

"I know what I'd do," said Nestor Makhno. "I'd go all the way. Nihilism. I would have in the first place, I think, but the wife didn't like it."

"Blow 'em all up," said Bakunin cheerfully.

"Now there speaks a true wanker," said Jesus. He went up to the counter to get another espresso. "Who did you ever assassinate?"

"That's scarcely the point, is it?" Bakunin was hurt. But he knew he was talking to an ace.

Everyone was aware of it.

Sid winked at the pouting Russian. "You can't compete with him. He's sent millions and millions off."

"It's a question of style." Bakunin waved a gloved hand. "Not of numbers killed."

"You've probably got a point there." Keats and Chatterton went by arm in arm. "And Sid had a lot of style. A lot of potential."

"Well, I might yet realise it," said Sid. He was having a think.

Great Moments with the Immortals

"Maybe it's the Gulf Stream." Flash and Mo were dragging themselves ashore at last. They had arrived on the beach at Rio.

"It's fate, lads!" Martin Bormann, wearing only red and black swimming trunks, a discreet swastika on his saluting arm, came marching up. "I was only thinking about you this morning."

"Have you seen the Captain?" Mo asked.

"You've just missed him, I'm afraid. But Ronnie's about. He wants to join the group. I hear you're a couple of members short. I don't wish to push myself forward, but I used to be very fond of music . . . ."

"We'll think about it," said Flash.

"Pistols, Pistols über alles," sang Martin, striding along beside them. "You look defeated. I know a great deal about defeat. You mustn't let it get you down."

"You wouldn't happen to have seen an old Boeing Clipper, would you?" Mo cast an eye on the sky.

"Oh, you know about that, do you?"

"Has one been here?"

"It's the plane the Captain left on."

"Betrayed!" said Mo.

"It's probably a coincidence," said Flash.

"The entire German people betrayed me," said Martin sympathetically. "They weren't worthy of us, you see. But what do we actually mean by this word 'betrayal'? Don't we in some ways betray only ourselves . . . ?"

They hadn't time for his third rate Nazi metaphysic. They began to run up the beach.

"We've got to earn some money," said Flash.

Mo stopped.

"We'll have to do a few gigs." He turned. "Have you got any bookings, Martin?"

"Amazon, three nights starting from tomorrow. Then there's the Mardi Gras . . . ."

"We'll take 'em," said Mo.

Human Conditioner

Miss Brunner set the crudely printed invitation on top of her cryptik and frowned at it.

"Maybe they're willing to deal at last?" said Frank. He had his areas of optimism.

"It could be a joke," said Bishop Beesley.

She hovered over her keyboard, but nothing came to mind.

"A farewell gig, though," said Frank. "I thought they'd already done that." He sniggered.

"Captain Maxwell will be there." Bishop Beesley waved an important Crunchy. "And we need to raise some cash."

"We'll make a few contacts." Frank reached towards the invitation but had his wrist slapped away by Miss Brunner.

"It's another trap," she said.

"What can they do to us? We've survived everything."

"Your brother's involved. He's been resurrecting people again. You know what he's like."

"Everyone who is everyone—or was anyone—will be there. Let's give it a go." Frank stroked his hand. "Please. My mum'll be there. She works at the venue. He wouldn't hurt our mum."

Miss Brunner was letting him convince her.

"And I've never seen him live," said Bishop Beesley. "If live is the right word."

"It'll be a relaxing night out." Frank gave a stupid grin. "Well, it'll make a change."

"It'll make a change," Miss Brunner agreed. "Do we get to see the film as well?"

"It doesn't say."

The cryptik made a peculiar peeping noise.

"I think it's laughing," she said.

The Mysteries

"I hope to god this is my last bloody comeback." Jerry Cornelius bit his mouldering lip and stared at his disintegrated fingers. "There just isn't the energy around now."

"It's because you've used it all up," said Captain Maxwell. "Jilly where's the cheque book?"

"They took that as well."

The Captain began to look in the backs of his desk drawers, as it he hoped to find a little cash. "This is silly."

"What happened to the money?" asked the Assassin.

"It was won in a dream and lost in a nightmare," said Jilly. She seemed to be quoting somebody.

"Where did it go?"

"Ask the bloody Official Receiver."

"Isn't that what he's asking you?"

"Everybody's asking the wrong questions." Jilly glared at the Assassin. "Leave him alone. Can't you see he hasn't had any sleep in months?"

"That always happens when you try to make a dream come true, doesn't it?"

"I don't need you sitting there, rotting in my last good chair," said Maxwell. "Have all the invitations gone out, Jilly?"

"I'm not moralising," said the Assassin defensively, "exactly, I'm speaking from several lifetimes of experience."

"All gone out," said Jilly.

"Isn't the dream better than what we've got?"

"Are you Mr Bug?"

"Let's just say I do his tailoring."

"Where is he?"

"Where he always was. Zurich. Watching telly."

"I never thought of Switzerland." Jerry tried to recover a fingernail which had dropped onto the bare boards.

"Few people ever do."

"It could just be the suit that's in Switzerland."

"The suit is Mr Bug." The Captain paused in his search. "I should know, shouldn't I?"

The Assassin drew himself onto unsteady feet. He dusted a little light mould from his black car coat.

"Well, that clears everything up. Thanks. I'll see you at the gig."

"See you there," said the Captain. He crossed the room and began to feel in the pockets of a pair of discarded bondage trousers.

The Assassin paused by the door. "Oh, by the way, who really did kill—?"

"Get off," said Captain Maxwell.

As the Assassin went down the stairs, Jilly came trotting after him. She whispered:

"It was Richard. But the Captain set it up."

The Assassin had already forgotten the question.

When You Wish upon a Star

The Concorde loaded on schedule at Margaret Thatcher Airport.

"England looks very clean, these days," said Martin Bormann with some satisfaction. "I always knew there was a chance for her."

An old robber, disguised as an ex-boxer, said through his balaclava: "A return to proper standards. And about time."

Mo settled his trilby on his head. "As soon as I see Captain M I'm going to . . ."

"Give it up," said Flash. "Just for a bit, eh?"

Martin Bormann was disappointed. "I thought there'd be a crowd waiting for us. Like the Beatles."

"Crowds need organising," said Mo, "and the Captain's too busy for that. Besides, he's not managing us any more."

"Are you sure?"

"Well, you can never be absolutely certain."

Reaching the Market

"I'm glad I'm not dead. I'm glad I'm not dead," mumbled the last of the Musician-Assassins to himself. He had put on his old pierrot suit and had plastered his face with white make-up to hide the worst of the decay. "You've got to think positive."

He shuffled through the streets of North London. He was lost. He seemed to remember that he had been on his way to some kind of party. Possibly he had missed it during one of his rests. The rain had started. His silk suit began to stick to his skeleton as he turned into Finchley Road.

Everything was getting very hazy.

Requiem Mc2

"Two Rotten Bars, please." Jilly looked at her own little dolls on display in the foyer. She still thought she should get the bars free, but she paid for them anyway. Alvarez began to sing at her.

"You stop that, Sarge," Mrs Cornelius came round the corner. "Don't let 'im bovver you, love. 'E wants ter be discovered. Will Captain M be along later?"

"Discovered?"

"Like America." She laughed heartily so that her goods in her tray bounced beneath her bouncing breasts. "An' all them ovver bleedin' colonies."

Jilly went inside. She wanted to be sure of a good seat.

They were all beginning to arrive now. Nearly everybody was in some form of fancy dress. Mickey Most, in lugubrious and inappropriate corduroy, Jake Riviera, Tony Howard, Peter Jenner, Andrew Lloyd Webber, Martin Davis. A lot of denim and fur. A lot of vain leather.

Shuffling in and standing in the shadow, the half-collapsed pierrot looked at them going by. It was like a gathering of Mafia dons, old and new. Richard Branson, Michael Dempsey, Miles Copeland: some of them in modifications of demi-monde styles, some in grotesque parodies of dandyism. The Nouveaux Noires arrived, singly or in couples, with their girlfriends.

The pierrot noticed how comfortable they all were. It was probably because not a single punter had been on the invitation list. Some of them complained that they had to pay, but in the main they were not discontented.

Elton John, Rod Stewart, Olivia Newton-John, Cliff Richard and Barbra Streisand. Bishop Beesley, Miss Brunner, Anne Nightingale. Frank Cornelius didn't notice his brother. He was walking on air. He felt euphoric in the presence of cash. The slightly self-conscious members of the musical press were trying to look like musicians, and as usual were not absolutely certain of their social status: their expressions changing constantly as they tried for an appropriate mode.

They were piling in, drawn by curiosity, greed, a wish not to be left out.

Music publishers, record company executives, the owners of studios; agents and managers.

"What a lot of controllers," mumbled Jerry vaguely. "What a lot of mortgages."

Elegant cowboys, smoothed-up Hell's Angels, Beverly Hills punks. Nobody required any hope, only confirmation. They confirmed one another.

The pierrot was reminded of a bunch of burghers going into church.

Mo and Flash wandered in. Mo's trenchcoat was covered in a variety of old food, vomit and semen. He had lost his hat. A bouncer appeared from nowhere. "Sorry, you've got to have invitations."

Ronnie Biggs and Martin Bormann said in chorus: "It's all right. They're with us."

"Johnny won't come," said Mo to no-one in particular. He hadn't noticed the pierrot in the shadows either.

Wasting It

"I've seen this before," whispered Miss Brunner to Frank as the film came on.

"We've all seen it before," said someone behind her. "That doesn't mean we can't enjoy it."

Mo was crawling between the seats, still looking for Captain Maxwell.

He found a tartan knee. "Flash? Wake up."

"Give him a break," said Jilly. "Can't you leave him alone for a minute?"

It was standing room only for the old pierrot. He held on tightly to the rail at the back, trying to focus fading eyes.

His mother popped in. "Jerry. Yore lookin' terrible. There's a chap in the foyer. Sez 'e's Mr Bug's bailiff. Is it ther Receivers?"

"They're not playing tonight."

"El tell 'im." She disappeared.

"Mum . . ." He stretched out his wounded hand. "My wiring's gone . . ." But she didn't hear him.

He could only dimly detect the soundtrack now. There was a lot of plummy laughter coming from the seats. The film was reassuring its audience while pretending to shock them; a perfect formula for success.

"It's sure to be a winner," said Mitzi B, slipping out for a pee.

The pierrot gasped. Everything was going round and round.

Sometime later, as he desperately tried to revive his attention, he saw Sid at last. The operation had been a success. He wasn't absolutely sure by now if Sid was actually on stage or on film. He was singing "My Way" with all his old style.

Mo crawled up and began to tug at the pierrot's suit. Bits of it tore away in his hand. "This is where I came in."

He crawled on, towards the exit.

The volume rose higher and higher. There were a few murmurs of complaint.

The pierrot felt a shade better. He managed an appreciative groan.

The song ended.

Gunfire began to sound in the auditorium.

The pierrot sank to the dirty floor with a happy grunt. "It worked, after all. We did it, Sid."

The hall became filled with the sounds of terror. Blood and bits of flesh flew everywhere. The audience was tearing itself to pieces as it tried to escape.

Eventually there was silence. A dark screen. A vacuum. An avenged ghost.

Mrs Cornelius opened the doors. She had an expression of resigned disgust on her face.

"'Oo the bloody 'ell do they expect ter clear up this fuckin' mess, then?"

"Jimi?" said Alvarez behind her.

He began to sing again.

Ladbroke Grove, 1980
Marrakesh, 1988

Cincinnati Lou

Benjamin Whitmer

Derrick Kreiger hasn't dreamed since his heart was rewired in Vietnam. Not once. It's like the pacemaker's electrical current has driven his unconscious mind from the subterranean to the surface, like a crank phone and a lead wire will do to catfish. And Derrick's pretty sure it's not him alone. Not when he remembers the scalpings, the overdoses, and the jungle fraggings in the war. Nor has Derrick allowed himself anything like normal sleep since he returned from the war. He settles for nothing less than the complete obliteration of his mind, conscious and unconscious. And he excludes no chemical in that pursuit.

Now he awakes with a jolt. His entire body clenching, fingers curling. He's laid out on the back seat of his car, and outside he can hear frantic footsteps, metal on metal, glass smashing, screams. He can't be sure it isn't a dream, after all, and a dream of the one thing he annihilates his dreams to avoid. He puts his cheek against the back of the seat and inches his face upward until he can just peek what's happening.

Over-The-Rhine. Cincinnati's blackest and poorest ghetto, just up from the central business district. Rioters whirl in and out of the main body in clusters, cells, breaking through the smoke into Derrick's vision, and then gone again, agitating against each other with a relentless ferocity that makes him wonder they don't combust. The smoke drifts. Three junkies kicking the glass out of the front window of a drug store. The smoke drifts. A gang of teenagers turn over a Cadillac. The smoke drifts.

Breathe, Derrick thinks. Not one of 'em knows you're here.

Then the smoke drifts again, and a little black girl, maybe twelve years old, materializes right in front of the passenger window. Her teeth slash out of her face in a wicked, firelit grin. "Over here," she calls back into the smoke.

Derrick stumbles out onto the sidewalk on the other side of the car from her. He wobbles in his cowboy boots, his lungs clutching in the smoke. The street tilts, his vision threatens to black out.

"The peckerwood's scared," she cackles, and Derrick thinks about giving her the palm of his hand. But then the smoke drifts, and out of it steps the biggest and ugliest black man Derrick's ever seen.

"Does your mama know you're out walking your gorilla?" Derrick says.

"My mama's doing five to ten on a trafficking charge." She's wearing a pretty little pink dress, the hem charred by one of the riot fires. "This is my brother. He hasn't said it yet, but he thinks you're a pig."

"He ain't as dumb as he looks." Derrick pulls his badge. "This is my license to shoot niggers when they riot. Even smart-mouth little bitches like you."

"Your crackerjack badge don't scare me, honky," the little girl says. She chucks her baby chin at her brother. "Stomp his ass."

"Your call," Derrick says. He reaches back to his belt holster where his gun should be, a grin starting.

The holster's empty.

Derrick tries to hold the grin but it's impossible. But the man moving towards him, he starts a grin of his own.

"Well, shit," Derrick says. Then he spins to the right and runs like hell. He runs straight into a cloud of smoke, out again. A pack of five rioters appear in the clearing. They've got a half-naked woman trapped between them, shoving her back and forth. She's screamed until she has no voice left, her mouth still gaping with the effort, blood running in rivulets down her face.

Derrick flattens the first of them with a straight shoulder block he pulls from his high school football days, then catches another with an elbow to the throat. By the time they've figured out what's happened, he's gone, and the little girl and her giant brother are smashing straight into them, the whole gang collapsing in a spitting pileup of limbs and "Motherfuckers!"

You can't run for long in cowboy boots. Derrick wears them because he doesn't run, that's one of the benefits of carrying a gun. He hits the steps to an abandoned brick building and smashes into the plywood nailed over the door, falling through the rotted wood, shoulder first.

A foyer. Derrick sliding into the blackness, scooting the wall, hoping the flooring's still intact. He moves two rooms deep into the ruin, and then stops and hunkers down on his knees. Then he stays like that, quieting his breathing, until his legs prickle, hurt, burn, and go numb under him. And then he closes his eyes and lets himself sink into the dense tedium of the wait.

There's this feeling Derrick gets in his chest since they put the pacemaker in. It feels like the current has created a hollow space where his heart should be, like the pacemaker is expanding its electromagnetic field, driving the tissue out. He pays attention to that feeling.

Sitting still is a skill that he perfected in Vietnam. But it's not a skill he learned in Vietnam. It's a skill he learned from his father.

～

It was after Derrick's mother died, flattened by a coal truck while walking her Maltese, that Derrick's father sold their house in the small Eastern Kentucky town where they'd lived, and the two of them moved into the cabin. Now Derrick realizes how quickly that move took place, but at the time there was only his father's guiding hand on his shoulder as he carried his small box of personal belongings inside. His legs trembling, threatening to betray him altogether.

The walls of the cabin were lined with books frequently removed and reread, but never rotated. And guns and traps that were always oiled for a use that never came. Not that Derrick's father was forced to keep these things in the cabin. Derrick's mother might even have had enjoyed some hint of his father's presence in her house. But Derrick's father didn't compromise with domesticity.

The books on the walls were serious books. Books that Derrick's father first began to read during an undistinguished tour in Korea. Books about men making war, not because they believed in war, but because they believed in manhood. Books that Derrick's father would read aloud, standing erect in one of his gray department store suits, his neatly trimmed mustache greyly immobile over his cultivated Kentucky drawl. He was a schoolteacher.

Derrick sat pinioned in the monotonous repetition of those books. Because they contained the only things worth knowing, his father said. And because, though Derrick hated his father every minute of every day, there was no time he hated him as much as when he read aloud. The stupefying boredom of the reading sent Derrick into a reverie. He imagined himself removing every single gun from the walls and shooting his father in the face with each of them, one right after the other.

~

Time to move. Derrick stands, feels his pockets. Wherever his gun has disappeared to, he still has his Zippo lighter. He sparks it every few feet. Drywall chunks, shattered light fixtures, dead squirrels, piles of trash. He swims through the stench of death and garbage. Finally, a back door, and he erupts into a small backyard heaped with busted furniture, gulping at the night air, and then slings himself over the backyard fence into an empty alley. He scoots with his head below the fence line until he sees a window with a low lamp burning back in the recesses. He bangs on the door. "Police."

"I've got a gun," a man's voice calls back.

"Me too," Derrick says, "And I'm police. You got the count of two afore I start shooting through the door."

The door opens. He's young and white, with a soul patch and greasy black hair, and he's holding a huge cap and ball Colt 1851 Navy revolver. Derrick grabs it out of his hands.

"You ain't got a gun of your own?" the kid says.

Derrick puts the revolver in half-cock and checks the cylinder. Loaded, except for the chamber under the hammer. His father had one just like it, hanging on the wall. It'd been passed down from father to son from the first Kreiger anybody bothers remembering. Who, according to family lore, rode with Forrest during the war, and after. "How old are these percussion caps?" Derrick asks.

"I don't know what that means, percussion cap," the kid says, and walks absentmindedly into the living room and sits down on the couch. Everything in the room is dilapidated crushed red velvet, like it was all looted from a single antique store that specialized in half-trashed Louis XV knockoffs. "I've had it maybe five years and I ain't done nothing to any caps, I can tell you that. I didn't even remember I had it until this shit started."

Derrick slumps into one of the chairs. He rubs his eyes, sparks rioting behind his lids. "What's your drug?" he says to the kid.

The kid gives him a bemused look. "My drug?"

Derrick looks at him.

The kid crosses one leg over the other and holds onto his knee. "Heroin," he says.

"Heroin."

"Not what you were looking for?"

Derrick raises the revolver.

"I might be able to help you out is all," the kid says. "We have parties, and sometimes people leave things. That's how I ended up with the gun."

"Coke," Derrick says, squinting over the front sight at the boy's forehead.

"Okay." The kid stands and sort of floats out of the room.

Derrick lays the revolves in his lap and closes his eyes. He listens to his heartbeat, takes stock.

~

Derrick had been on the Tac Squad for a year, part of a plainclothes unit working street crime. After leaving his father's house, police work had seemed like a natural fit for him. But it was a pale imitation of what he'd done in Vietnam, and the soldier in him hated the policeman he'd become. Closing down block parties, breaking up corner streetwalkers, shutting down curbside drug dealers. He broke his head open nightly on the senselessness of it all. And he was suspended yesterday, which he knows has got to have something to do with him waking up in this fix.

It was one of Over-The-Rhine's late-night jazz clubs, about three weeks ago. African masks on the wall, militants hammering out plans for the revolution. She was a big, rolling woman with a raucous face, and when the Tac Squad rousted the joint on a marijuana tip, she'd thrust her face right up against his, called him a pig, and spat into his mouth. It was pure reflex when Derrick headbutted her, but it was a good one, cracked two of her front teeth.

She'd gotten a lawyer, of course. They always did, but they never won. The reason Cirillo had suspended him had nothing to do with the head butt. Cirillo suspended him because he'd been ordered to take Derrick on the Tac Squad, and Cirillo didn't have any use for Vietnam vets. He'd told Derrick the first day that if he pulled any of that cunt Vietnam shit, he'd be off the squad faster'n he could say post-traumatic stress disorder. He was a World War II veteran, the Pacific Theater, and he had the same opinion of Vietnam vets that he had of asylum inmates.

Derrick didn't protest the suspension. He just sat there in his chair while Cirillo read off the paperwork, his face like an exploded ham, his eyes pink and brown and gristly. He just sat there and imagined himself removing every single gun from the walls of the precinct and shooting the motherfucker in the face with each of them, one after the other.

And, then, when Cirillo was done, Derrick dug his back-up gun out of the glove compartment, strapped it on, and drove down to the Dancin' Bay, where he drank well bourbon until he couldn't do anything but sit at the bar, watching the pickled eggs jiggle to tunes from the jukebox.

~

One of Derrick's father's favorite refrains was how men are changed by war. But Derrick knows that's horseshit. A way for old men who no longer believe in the greatness of war to sell books of war, and war itself, to the young. Men are not made by war, men make war. And if there was any deeper truth in Vietnam, it was the terrific wonder of war itself. The pyrotechnics, the jet fuel fires, the fully-automatic weapons, the drugs and the jungle shadows, the camp wives. It was being entirely free of that air-conditioned hell back home. It was a carnival riot in a country you couldn't help but love completely and hate completely from the moment you landed.

Some nights Derrick will sit and look through the few photographs he has, the boy who looks back at him already scraped as clean and raw as a pig just after slaughter. His face gaunt and hard and his eyes huge-pupiled. And that little combat grin, restrained but twitching on his face, threatening to explode free.

Derrick knows what that look means. From time to time, he catches it in the faces of other soldiers in photographs. And it's on the face of almost every bomber pilot he ever saw, especially after they've just completed a run. It's not the look of duty or sacrifice. It's the look that comes of watching bombs detonate across hundred-yard swaths of earth, of watching an entire countryside erupt in flames, people scattering under you like cockroaches. It's the look of free and unrestrained carnage. Of free kills.

The shame of it drove lesser men than Derrick to suicide when they returned. Derrick, he just makes sure he doesn't dream. Because he can't handle knowing that he'll never have that kind of freedom again. And that he'll never again be able to unknow exactly what freedom is, and what it cost him.

Sitting in the bar, drinking, Derrick couldn't even shake his head at his suspension from the Tac Squad. At the idiocy of the things he's asked to do, and the restraints under which he's then told to do them. There isn't one of his superiors who wouldn't gladly round up every black person in Over-The-Rhine, stick a burlap sack over each of their heads, and file them one by one down into the Ohio River.

∾

"You don't look so good." Her voice startled him, and his bourbon glass twitched, a thin drip rippling over the side. She sat down next to him. Dark-skinned and darker-eyed, looking at him with her head cocked a little.

"I been better," he said.

"Yeah." She crossed her arms on the bar and laid her head down on them, looking up at him. She smiled, and there was a wide gap between her front teeth that Derrick stared straight into. "I can see that."

Derrick laughed his harsh scraped-out laugh. Then he said the only thing he could think of to ask. "What're you drinking?"

∾

Derrick never had any trouble with girls in high school. It was a brooding intensity that broke their hearts, especially when he was sitting the other side of a bonfire with a beer in his hand after a football game. And it was that he never tried to explain his empty spaces. Every other boy in that small Kentucky town, they talked about nothing but their plans for escaping. It was a story that no one, not even themselves, believed. Derrick, though, knew exactly how he'd make his break. But he could no more explain why to those high school girls than he could explain the mind of a canebreak rattlesnake.

His silence intensified in Vietnam. And since he's returned, he has nothing to say to women at all. It's only when he gets so hollowed out and lonely that he has to have some kind of human contact that he makes a run on the local prostitutes. He can feel his ability to talk atrophying, the shutters being drawn on the kind of normal talk that keeps people normal. Like he's pulling them shut on his own version of his father's cabin.

But this woman, Lou was her name, she was so easy to talk to that he just kind of forgot to not know how to talk. Not the senseless pouring out of one's big feelings so beloved by cops, motorcycle gang members, and housewives. Derrick can't tolerate that for more than five minutes in anyone. It's the deeper and lighter freeflow of conversation, by which you can, instead of being told who your conversant is, see them for yourself.

So they drank at the bar until it closed. And there's nothing quite as heartful as walking out of a hopeless bar with someone, the hard lights kicking on full behind you. Then they drove to her apartment in Over-The-Rhine. And she rolled joints, she poured drinks. She had a wicked sense of humor and a soft sidling voice. And the gap in her teeth that Derrick couldn't stop looking at. But every time he made a move in on her, she found somewhere else to be.

And slowly, through the booze and the smoke they'd created together, drifting through the apartment, he started to realize that he'd made a big mistake.

But it was too late. And after that Derrick doesn't remember much of anything.

～

The kid returns and holds out a hand mirror for Derrick. On it, a pile of cocaine, a razor blade, a straw. Derrick chops the cocaine into two lines and snorts them. It dumps straight back into his brain, into his blood. "Get the rest of it and put it in something I can carry," he says, hoarsely, tossing the hand mirror across the room onto the couch. "And I need something I can go outside in without getting killed."

The kid's eyes light up. "I've got just the thing." He sweeps out of the room. When he returns, he drops a Confederate Army greatcoat and a slouch hat at Derrick's feet. "Sometimes I get actors through here, too," he says, returning to the couch and clasping his knee

"I've got half a mind to shoot you right now," Derrick says. But he pulls on the coat and jams the slouch hat over his face.

"No one will know what it is," the kid says. He hops off the couch and moves to dust off the gold braids on the shoulders of the coat. But Derrick puts the muzzle of the gun on his forehead and pushes him back onto the couch.

~

As ridiculous as Derrick feels in the getup, the kid is mostly right. At first, nobody even looks at him as he shambles down the sidewalk towards Lou's apartment. Cars burn, men and women get stomped into the blacktop, and Derrick shuffles through the shadows like some apparition, holding the huge Colt revolver under the greatcoat with his thumb on the hammer.

But then he is spotted. It's a big black man, somewhere in his fifties, the cataracts in his eyes reflecting back the riot fire in an eerie blue. He's standing in the middle of the street with a sledge-hammer handle in his hands, chest heaving, when, of a sudden he lets out a roar and plows into the crowd at Derrick. Derrick sets his back against the wall and lifts the revolver out from under his greatcoat. "You've got me confused with someone else," he says.

The man hurtles a discarded bicycle out of his way, his lips curled back from his teeth. "I know exactly who you are, you fucking pig," the man says. "You put my son in prison on a bullshit weed rap."

"Come another step and I'll orphan him."

"I'm gonna break your fucking skull."

The streets are erupting in a series of minor explosions. Cars getting ripped apart bolt by bolt, rubber-fires detonating, the smoke from it all eddying out from the rage and commotion. The revolver's gunshot cuts through the cacophony like its been fired off in a library, and some of the rioters hit the ground right where they stand, while most just gawk around for the truck bomb they're pretty sure has just detonated. Even as furious as the old man is, it takes him a good twenty seconds to realize he's uninjured and pick himself off the ground.

By which time Derrick has long since slid back into the smoke and shadows.

~

Another thing that Derrick didn't realize until years after his mother's funeral was that the Maltese hadn't died with her. He figured that out when he found a newspaper clipping of the wreck in a copy of one of his father's books, and there the Maltese stood, huddled against the rain-slickered leg of one of the state troopers on the scene.

Not that Derrick blames his father for putting the dog down. In that town of Labradors and Hounds, he wanted it put down, too. That sure as hell isn't why he hates the old man, anyway. Nor can he blame the scraped out feeling he's had most of his life on the death of his mother. He was never any closer to her than he was to his father. That's not to say he didn't grieve her when she died, but she was a fussy creature of headaches and random pains, all of which she could only cure with an evening's drinks, and when she was drunk she was shrill and unpredictable. To the boy Derrick she was something to be avoided most of the time, tolerated the rest.

Some men are just less easily impressed than others, Derrick thinks, as he slides out of the smoke of the riot and into the cavernous darkness of an Over-The-Rhine alley. Besides the life in his own head, that which he culled out of his books, the rest of Derrick's father's existence was set in grocery stores, classrooms, and dining rooms. Derrick gets suicidal just trying to enumerate all the shit in his life he doesn't care about. This riot, this tiny rampage, this is as close as he's been to interested in anything since returning home from the war. And there were times during the war when he wasn't bored at all. When he was filled with electricity, overflowing and alive.

He tries not to think about it.

∼

Lou's apartment has three rooms. Derrick kicks in the door and tosses it. Turning out the kitchen drawers, ripping books off the shelves. Nothing. Kicking through the beer bottles and paraphernalia they'd left in the sitting room. Nothing. The bedroom. He cuts open the mattress. He smashes the dresser. Then, in the nightstand, he finds a pack of cigarettes, a book of matches, and car keys for a Lincoln Continental that look like they'll fit the one parked down in the alley. He also finds cash, a paper sack of it, on a shelf in the closet.

He pockets the keys and the sack of cash. Then takes the cigarettes into the sitting room, and turns on the small black and white television. Riot footage, every channel. White announcers with heavy side-combed haircuts. Derrick sits down on the couch. Trashcans in the air, club-wielding police, chanting blacks. The camera cuts from the tumult of images to the officer on the scene for explanation. And Derrick laughs out loud.

It's Cirillo doing the explaining. The Tac Squad raided an after-hours party at a local club, claiming dope and prostitution. It was a homecoming party for incoming veterans, sure, but it was also militant recruitment, and nothing makes a militant like a Vietnam veteran. Cirillo says one of the organizers by the name of Everette Anderson, also a Vietnam vet, took a swing at him.

Then the television cuts to an aerial shot of the club where the riot started, and Derrick stands involuntarily.

It's the same club where he got himself suspended.

The television pans across the neighborhood, and Derrick realizes he's only about two blocks away.

∼

Derrick enters through the delivery door. It's secured with an old-fashioned padlock, which Derrick hammers off with the butt of the cap and ball Colt. There's only one person in the place, and it isn't

220

Lou. It's a black boy of maybe fourteen, gripping a kitchen knife and hiding in the first place Derrick looks, behind the bar. The knife goes clattering on the floor when the boy sees his gun. "You work here?" Derrick asks.

The boy nods.

"Speak, boy," Derrick says. He lifts a bottle of bourbon and a glass from behind the bar and then walks around and sits on one of the stools.

"I sweep up and clean the bathroom," the boy says. "That kind of shit. Stuff. That kind of thing, sir."

"You can cuss," Derrick says. "It's a free country." He opens the bottle of bourbon and pours himself a drink. "I'm going to ask you one question. If you don't answer me true, I'll hurt you. Is that clear?"

The boy nods. Emphatically.

"Good," Derrick says. "I'm a big believer in clarity." He feels his pacemaker hollowing out the space in his chest where his heart should be. "The name she gave me was Lou. She's tall, almost my height. Dark-skinned with an afro. No tits to speak of, and a gap between her teeth you could walk through, but hotter'n a two-dollar pistol. Your turn."

Derrick watches the boy reach back for every lie he's ever told in his sad fucked-up little life. And somewhere behind his scared brown eyes, he knows there's not one that will work. So he just shakes his head.

"Find me a beer back there," Derrick says. "In a glass bottle."

The boy does as he's told. Miller High Life.

"Take the cap off and drink it. The whole thing."

The boy's eyes are red and watery when he's done. "I think I'm gonna puke," he says, miserably.

"Take that bottle by the neck and give it a sharp rap on the edge of the bar," Derrick says. "Just like you see in the movies. When you hit it just right, that rim'll just pop off."

The boy hits the bottle on the bar, but it doesn't break. "I can't," he says.

"You gotta hit it harder," Derrick says. "If you fuck up, it ain't the end of the world, you'll just have to drink another beer."

The boy hits the bottle on the bar again and this time the end breaks off, the glass jagged and full of brown light.

"Now hand it to me," Derrick says. "And don't get cute. The gun I'm holding'll put holes in you they couldn't plug with a tree stump."

The boy hands him the bottle. Carefully. "Mister, I don't know what you're doing, but it's none of my business. I don't want no part of it."

Derrick holds the bottle. It's like he's watching a movie he's watched a thousand times before, until its become entirely devoid of content from the watching. "Put your hand on the bar, son," he says.

Tears leak down the boys cheeks. "I can't, mister," he says. "Don't make me."

"You can stop this right now," Derrick says. "You just tell me everything you know about that gal. That's all you have to do."

For a second or two, Derrick thinks the boy will talk. But the skin on his face seems to harden, and he spits, "You're a fucking pig. They're right about you." He slaps his hand down on the table.

Derrick doesn't argue the point. He grips the boy's wrist and raises the broken beer bottle above his hand. "Hold your breath," Derrick says. "It'll be over before you know it."

"Pig," the boy tries to say again, and fails. The skin around his mouth slackens, and drool slides out of the corner of his mouth.

Derrick reaches across the bar and takes him by the chin. "Don't pass out," he says. "If you pass out we have to start over."

The boy swallows and his eyeballs roll up at the beer bottle. He sobs once.

And then talks.

Lou is a longtime Cincinnati activist. The militant kind, who reads Amilcar Cabral, carries a gun, and actually practices with it. She runs workshops and reading groups. She heads up armed self-defense training for Cincinnati women. She's spent time in Palestine forging relationships.

Derrick had already figured all that. He's pretty sure there's no one in Over-The-Rhine he couldn't have got it from. But when the boy adds that she's usually seen with another activist named Everette Anderson, Derrick feels his heart kick like an electrified frog.

He sets the beer bottle on the bar and takes the boy by the back of the neck. "You done the right thing telling me, son," he says.

"You should have done it, you motherfucker," the boy sobs. "You should have done it."

Derrick allows himself a few minutes to sit with the boy. This he knows from Vietnam, too, and he takes a strange comfort in it. Sitting in bars with boys sobbing about the things they've been made to do.

~

It takes Derrick a certain amount of wheeling and dealing to get Everette Anderson's file. The one kept by the Tac Squad for every activist in Cincinnati, not the one available to the public. It takes more to get Anderson moved into a private cell in the Cincinnati Workhouse. While he's being transferred, Derrick sits in one of the interrogation rooms and reads through his paperwork, looking for inspiration.

He finds it. When he was fifteen, Anderson was the number one suspect in a string of Over-The-Rhine rapes. According to the girls, he'd led them off the street, down into an abandoned lot, got them drunk on fortified wine, and fucked them behind a discarded washing machine. Three of the girls ID'd him, but all refused to testify in court.

Derrick closes the folder. He leans back in his chair and lights a cigarette. Then he opens the folder again and looks at the pictures of the little girls, post-rape. He looks at them until every facial bruise, black eye, and missing tooth is burnt into his corneas.

It takes more than just wheeling and dealing to get unrestricted access to Everette Anderson in that private cell. Luckily, Hamilton County Sheriff Deputies aren't any more immune to the temptations of cocaine and cash than any other cops. Nor does anyone give a shit for the Confederate greatcoat and the cap and ball revolver when he walks in. Derrick's got the reputation of showing up in worse shape, and there's something fitting about it in the great winged nineteenth-century workhouse.

Anderson is sitting on his cot, staring at the wall. He's a big sonofabitch, probably 260 pounds, with a wandering left eye and teeth that look like somebody's made a pass over them with a chainsaw. "Get lost," Derrick says to the deputy after the cell door clanks shut.

"It's your head," the deputy says, and leaves.

Anderson starts to laugh. "They issuing new uniforms?"

"You know how much I had to spend to get you alone in this cell?" Derrick asks.

Anderson doesn't say anything.

"It was your money. If I was you I'd hazard a guess."

The muscles in Anderson's jaw look like insects crawling under his skin.

Derrick pulls a pair of handcuffs out of his pocket and tosses them at Anderson. "Cuff your right hand to the post of the cot." When he's done, Derrick cuffs his other hand so that he has to sit in a childlike lean, both his hands cuffed on the same post. "You know, I've got a little sympathy for that fracas you started out in the streets," Derrick says. "I never felt I got a proper welcome when I come home from Vietnam either."

"If they didn't cut your balls off and hang your ass from a telephone pole, you didn't," Anderson says. "Bet you killed a truckload."

"I did all I could," Derrick says.

"You did all you could," Anderson repeats. "You's a brutal fucking pig now, you was a brutal fucking pig then. The kind of pig you are can't be learnt. It's gotta come natural."

"I need to know where Lou is," Derrick says.

Anderson laughs out loud. "That's all you've got?"

"Nobody ever accused me of being too bright," Derrick says. "You gonna answer?"

"What time is it?"

Derrick looks at his wristwatch. "About eleven-thirty."

Anderson nods. And then shakes his head. "No," he says. "I ain't telling you shit."

"Good," Derrick says. "I was hoping you'd say that."

One of the nice things about the greatcoat is how much room there is in the pockets. Derrick draws out a sap and a pair of pliers and sets them on the cot next to Anderson. Then he pulls out the cocaine. "I figure I'll have myself a quick snort," he says. "And then we'll get to work."

∾

Those little girls come to Derrick easy. He empties his mind and lets their faces flow into him, driven through the vacuum by the thin electric pulse of the pacemaker, to his sap and pliers. He works first on Anderson's right hand and then his face. Works hard. And Anderson says nothing. Or almost nothing. He's just a man, after all, he can't control the grunts and moans, the occasional yelp.

And then, when Derrick stops for his next hit of cocaine, his hands slick and beaten bruised, Anderson slurs the same question he'd asked earlier, "What time is it?" He's holding his hand in his lap, a basket of splintered bone and torn flesh.

Derrick has removed his watch and laid it on the cot. He picks it up and squints at it. "It's a little after twelve," he says, though he has trouble believing that it can really be that early.

Anderson's face looks like it had the skin peeled off it and the flesh underneath beaten with the claw end of a hammer. His chest starts to throb, like he's choking, and there's a hoarse, locomotive grunting coming from somewhere in the ruin of his face, that Derrick finally realizes is a laugh.

Then he says one word to Derrick. Just one word. A name.

～

Derrick abominates corruption like he abominates mediocrity. Even the whores that he can't help visiting, he pays for out of his policeman's salary. And if he ever had any doubts about the extent of Cirillo's corruption, the size of his Georgian home in Mount Auburn takes care of them. Derrick bypasses the front door and slips down the bushes and around the house. He finds the back door, and, as expected, it's been crow-barred. Derrick gives the door a gentle shove and slides inside.

It's in the living room he finds Cirillo's wife. She was a wiry woman in her fifties, good looking enough. Now she's sprawled akimbo across the couch with her robe hanging open and her head all but split in half by point-blank gunshots. Derrick lines up in front of her, making a guess as to where the shooter would have stood, and looks to his right. There, brass glinting against the wall, three empty casings. Derrick pockets them and moves into the front hallway, then up the stairs.

Lou's in the master bedroom, holding Derrick's 1911 between her knees. She's curled up in a reading chair by the window, her lips pulled back from her teeth. Derrick feels that hollow spot in his chest swell when he sees the gap between her front teeth. He resists a hard urge to take her face in his hands and kiss it. "Put the gun down," he says.

"I'm shot," she rasps. "There ain't nothing you can do to scare me, pig."

Derrick spots blood leaking out of a hole over the top of her left breast. "He got you in the tit?"

She bites her lip against the pain, her chin trembles.

"Well, drop that fucking gun before I put a hole in your other one," he says.

She lets the gun fall on the floor. Then she puts her hand on the bullet hole and takes it away, as if she can't quite believe that its real, being shot. She winces, blood stringing between her fingers and shirt.

Derrick picks up the gun. He drops the magazine, checks it, and slams it back in his pistol. Then he eyes her wound. "Keep pressure on it," he says. "If you bleed everywhere, you ain't gonna leave me no choice but to shoot you." He looks around the room. "Where is he?"

She juts her chin at the bed. Then her eyeballs flicker up in her head.

∾

Cirillo is wearing nothing but a white T-shirt, his cock red and half erect under the purplish swell of his stomach. He's holding a full-size Colt .45 1911 of his own, standard issue in World War II as well as Vietnam. Lou only shot him once, but it was a good one, right through the nose. Derrick estimates the angle and finds the brass casing from her round. It looks like Cirillo returned fire in a death reflex, his gun almost dead sideways in his hand. Derrick finds the casing in the bedding.

Without the brass casings the forensic officers won't be able to match the pistols' firing pins to the rounds fired. Derrick takes Cirillo's gun out of his hand, field strips it, extracts the barrel, then does the same to his own gun. Then he trades barrels, reassembles them, and puts Cirillo's gun back in his hand. If forensics can match the rifling of the barrel to the bullets, they'll now all come from the gun in Cirillo's hand.

He looks the crime scene over. It's a murder-suicide now. There'll be the missing casings, sure, and there'll be plenty more problems as the police go through the scene. But murder-suicide will be the easiest explanation, and the rest'll be chalked up to inexperienced investigators. After the riot, neither the district attorney nor the chief of police are going to hurt themselves trying to find out who killed the dumb sonofabitch.

Lou's passed out in the chair. Derrick grabs her up and slings her over his shoulder. She shudders, mumbles. He carries her out as gently as he can.

∾

When she comes awake, she tries to move her arms first, and then her head. But she can't. Her black eyes go wild like a captured bat, fluttering around the room. Then they land on Derrick. "Oh, Jesus," she tries to say, but she chokes on the blood overflowing in her mouth. "What are you going to do to me?"

"You doped me," Derrick says, trying not to hide in the shadows left by the kerosene lantern he's hung on a nail in the wall. He's got her tied to a kitchen table, deep in one of Over-The-Rhine's Victorian ruins. "You conned me and you doped me."

"Oh, Jesus," she says, "It hurts."

"I'll take care of that," Derrick says. "But first I want to tell you what you did. You can just nod along."

Her eyes roll back in her head and her lips drain of blood, and Derrick thinks for a second that she might lose consciousness, but she returns, nodding.

"Down in niggertown, Cirillo's like the white devil, ain't he? He rousts you, abuses you, beats you. Steals all your dope and takes his kickbacks in money and nigger pussy."

She nods.

"You and the vet, Everette Anderson, you figured you'd get rid of him?"

She nods.

"You set me up for the suspension. That was one of your people? You knew Cirillo hated my guts, so you gave him an excuse to discipline me. To give me a motive."

She nods.

"And while you were doping me so you could steal my gun, Everette Anderson was organizing that riot. Then him and a couple of your Fanon-toting niggers drove me to riot central. You figured even if I survived, I'd be out of my head when I finally surfaced. And by that time the police would already have my gun."

She nods.

"It's so cockamamie it just might've worked," Derrick says. "The only place you fucked up was in thinking any little nigger riot could kill me. I've worked real war. There is no war here."

She spits blood at him, but she doesn't have the force. It falls back on her face, splattering all over her cheeks and mouth. "It's war to us," she says.

Derrick pulls out his pliers and a knife. Then he finds his syringe. It's taken more time and money than he should have spent to come up with that loaded syringe.

She blinks in pain.

"I can't leave my bullet in you," he says. And he sees himself in the curvature of her iris. Black and hoary and somehow pitiful in the greatcoat, like a small and terrified boy playing at war. He holds up the syringe. "This is for the pain," he says stupidly.

And he has no idea how she gets her hand free. Nor where she'd hidden the little .25 pocket pistol. But she thrusts it right into his stomach and pulls the trigger until the slide jams against his flesh.

~

Derrick has no way of telling how long its been when he wakes into the complete blackness of the boarded up room, the camping lantern long extinguished. Nor how long he sits against the wall, listening to the creaking of the building around him, the skittering of animal feet. He coughs blood into his fist and then makes the mistake of reaching down to the horrorshow at his lower abdomen.

And then he's gone again.

~

When Derrick returned from Vietnam there were days he would lay on his bed in the cabin sunup to sundown, drinking bourbon and watching shadows slide down the walls. His father could understand the trauma of war, even seemed hopeful of it, but Derrick allowed of no trauma. He lay on his bed because there was nothing for which to move, and he drank bourbon because he liked to.

Which lasted exactly two weeks. Until a dinner of pork chops, which his father had cooked in an iron skillet, wearing one of his gray department store suits with a dish towel draped over his shoulder, where he said to Derrick, "You are not the first young man to return from war."

Derrick was barefoot in jeans and a tattered undershirt, hacking a pork chop into chunks and swallowing them whole. He grinned up at his father without answering.

His father's mustache raised, and then dropped. And then raised again. "This," he said, and stood and reached for a volume on the shelf.

A younger Derrick probably would have removed one of the many guns on the walls and shot the old man in the face. But it turned out that war had changed Derrick some. So, when he quit laughing, he walked back into his bedroom and packed his few things into a duffel bag.

~

This time, Derrick makes himself move. He drags himself half upright and lights the lantern. Then he stands like that for a while, hunched over, until he can work up the strength to unscrew the can of gasoline he'd brought with him and kick it over.

He makes it out into the street before the whole building catches afire, but he makes it no further than the street before the billowing smoke opens a hollow around him and swallows him whole.

And then he dreams. He dreams of Lou, of the gap in her teeth, of her voice speaking gently to him from above. He dreams that he's chasing her through the narrow alleys of Over-The-Rhine, chasing her to retrieve his bullet, which he knows she'll always carry inside her. But he also knows in his dream, just as he will know later in waking life, that he'll never catch her.

He dreams for what seems like days, and probably is. He dreams right up until he wakes up in the hospital bed, howling.

Berlin: Two Days in June

Rick Dakan

"But Rosa Luxemburg would meet with Karl Liebknecht right here. In the apartment upstairs. This was a café then," the old man insisted to me. I didn't doubt him, but I also didn't know what he was talking about.

"That's really interesting," I said, showing him my phone's screen again. "Our app allows you to customize your ads to suit both new and existing customers. Coupons. Twitter notifications. Special events. Anything you want."

He looked down at the phone, confusion on his face. He was in his sixties, gray and wiry with a full head of silver hair and thick, black-rimmed bifocals. "I used to have some letters," he said, looking up from my phone to me. "They were my father's, but I haven't seen them since the nineties. I think my daughter might know where they are. Maybe my niece?"

"With our free trial week, you can explore all your options for both bringing in new customers and integrating your mobile, online, and brick-and-mortar advertising streams," I went on, sticking to the script. I thought this old guy and his antique store full of genuine and replica East German artifacts was a lost cause. Antiques and mobile phone-based augmented reality sales tools probably didn't mix.

"My neighbor, Siebert over across the street, he told me I needed historical documentation to be included in this phone thing," the man said, still looking confused. "Are you saying that's not the case?"

"No, no," I said, shaking my head and smiling. "Of course not. All you need to do is sign up. We just need a bank account number, which we won't charge for a month, and you can get started right away."

He leaned over, peering close at my phone, lifting his glasses and putting the screen to within just centimeters of his left eye. "This is not the Berlin City History Layer?" he asked.

I had no idea what he was talking about. "This is ThriftyCityBerlin. com," I said for the third time since I'd walked through the door ten minutes earlier. "Part of the worldwide ThriftyCity tourist app network. We're the world's fastest growing location-based couponing system, with thirty-seven cities worldwide and more added every month." I spun out the spiel slowly, concentrating on my German pronunciation, not trusting that he understood everything through my American accent.

He pursed his lips and wrinkled his nose, staring at me. Then he frowned and shook his head and I knew I'd lost. Damn. I was already seventeen minutes and two sales behind schedule and it wasn't even noon. "No, no, this isn't the one I want my store in. I need to be listed with Berlin City History. If I find that letter, I can e-mail a picture of it to you. That will be proof enough of our historical importance, yes?"

It took me seven more precious minutes to explain to him that I couldn't help him, that I had nothing to do with Berlin City History, whatever that was, and to leave him my card. I stepped back out the front door and into the warm summer light of Frankfurter Tor. The late morning traffic in the roundabout provided a dull roar as background music to my frustrated mood. I pulled up the Sales Tracking app on my phone and checked out of the antique store, punching the "No Sale" button with an angry tap.

My next sales call was three hundred meters away, down Karl Marx Allee, on the left. I shuffled forward, bringing up the phone's Marketplace app and speaking slowly into the microphone, "Berlin City History Layer," taking care to pronounce the German as precisely as possible. Like the antique store owner, I used the English word "layer." The app came up first on the list, its icon a stereotypical image of the Brandenburg Gate superimposed over a German flag. It cost 3 euros, but it was a company phone and I figured I could justify the expense (as I would definitely have to do) as opposition research. It was a big one, over a gig, and I slipped the phone into my shirt's breast pocket while it downloaded.

Karl Marx Allee was maybe the widest street I'd ever been on, certainly the widest in Berlin. Lined on both sides with massive, vaguely art-deco style buildings, it had been built as the showcase for East Germany's greatness, a boulevard to rival the Champs Elysees. Having been to Paris, this didn't come close, but it had a certain grandeur to it. Did it look this way when my dad had been in Berlin? Dad had left when he was only three years old, so he'd never shared any real memories of life in Berlin sixty years ago. And oma had died before I was born, just a few years after mom and dad moved from Heidelberg to St. Louis, but I bet she'd walked this street at some point in her life, back when these hulking examples of model modernity had been the pride of East Germany.

I was within ten meters of my destination, an ice cream shop which, judging from all the shiny new plastic, definitely hadn't been here in oma's day when my phone started vibrating against my nipple, a quick double-pulse that signified a text message. Only one person that could be. I pulled out the phone to look at my the message from my boss.

Ned: No sale again.

His text was in English, which made sense since he was in Philadelphia and, apparently, up very early. Ned was a very hands-on manager, surprisingly so given half his work force was on the other side of the Atlantic, spread out across a dozen different countries.

"Nope, wants to be on a competing service," I dictated back to him.

Ned: Wants to be? Already is??

"Wants to be. Berlin City History Layer. I'm downloading it now."

Ned: Googling it now.

Ned: Okay, this is history guide stuff. Not sales. Not coupons.

Ned: How did you not close this?

I took a breath. I didn't need this hectoring right now. "I'll hit him back tomorrow."

Ned: You have a full day tomorrow.

Ned: Check your schedule.

I knew I had a full day tomorrow, and I knew Ned knew I knew. He'd only tell me to check it if something had changed. I pulled up the Sales Control app and, lo and behold, my schedule had gotten even fuller. There were five new sales calls added to the twenty I already knew about. "Fuck you, Ned," I said to Karl Marx Allee, but not to my phone.

To the phone I said the only thing I could say, "Okay, got it." Ned didn't reply. He'd made his point. His many points. The same points as always—he was watching, I was behind. Sell, sell, sell.

The history app had finished loading, so I launched it, which brought up a dense block of German text constituting the software's End User License Agreement. My spoken German, honed by summers spent with mom and her family in the South, was decent, but reading was still a chore. I always took care to make sure my Sales Targets here didn't see me sounding out the bigger words, something I didn't need Ned to tell me was unprofessional and a sales-killer. I touched accept, got another block of Germanic legalese and hit accept again. One more time and I was done, or so I thought. Then the damn thing started importing "Personalized User Experience Data," and I couldn't stand around waiting for it.

I let it do its thing in the background while I brought up Thrifty City Berlin, and the sample layer I'd put together for Marx Eis, the Communist-kitsch ice cream parlor with flavors named after Lenin, Trotsky, Marx, and Engels. I didn't know a thing about Engels, except that his flavor was mint chocolate, but I'd mocked up a two-for-one coupon in his name. I went in, all smiles and "guten morgens" and came out thirty-one minutes later with a successful close. The young Danish couple who owned the place loved the idea.

My phone emitted a two-tone ping I'd never heard before. Not a congratulatory text from Ned of course, that didn't happen. It was the Berlin City History app telling me it was finally ready for action. I held it up and watched the screen as it transformed the sunshine-drenched modern Karl Marx Allee into a black-and-white, sixty-year-old Stalin Allee, complete with a parade of Soviet Tanks down the middle of the street. It was the best Augmented Reality layer I'd ever seen. I slowly turned in place, scanning all up and down the broad boulevard. They'd modeled every building, and I was surprised to see how much was the same. Trees and signs and kiosks were different of course, but the imposing architecture remained, looking more impos-ing in black and white.

When I stopped moving the phone for more than a couple seconds, icons started to pop up, info tags attached to different buildings and even points in the middle of the street. One icon had a pulsing red border around it, centered on the apartment building across the street from me. I touched it and it expanded to fill the screen. There was a photo of one Folker Horst, a stern, chubby man in his fifties with a thick mustache who looked a little like Stalin. The text explained that he'd been an anti-Nazi resistor in the 1930's who'd fled to Russia and then returned to Berlin after the war before being arrested and disap-peared by the Stasi in 1962. I touched the "More Information" button, and the text expanded to include a multi-branching family tree.

The names were too small to make out on the small screen, but I could see two names on opposite ends were pulsing red. I pinched to zoom in. The top name was this guy, Folker Horst, 1901 to 1962. The other name was a complete shock: Martin Manning, born 1989. Me. The murdered Folker Horst, who I'd never heard of in my life, was my distant cousin, on my dad's side of the family, and the Berlin City History app knew it. Holy shit.

I doubted for a moment that the connection was real, but the family tree had everything right that I could verify—mom and dad's families, oma, the older brother my dad never really knew, Uncle Leon. I tapped his name on the tree and saw his dates: 1938 to 1953. Twelve years older than my dad, he'd survived the whole war and then died when he was fifteen. Another fact about my life my phone knew before me.

A double-pulse alert vibrated the phone in my hand, which was already shaking a little on its own. I switched to the messenger app.

Ned: You ok?

I closed my eyes, counted to two, and dictated my response. "I'm moving, no worries." Ned didn't reply. He could monitor my move-ments in real time. I'd seen the set-up—six linked twenty-eight-inch screens with Google maps of thirty different cities, all keyed into the GPS units in our phones. His asking if I was okay was just Ned's way of yelling, "Get back to fucking work." I assumed he'd clicked the "Slack Meter" box on my work profile. Three clicks in one day, and I'd get a warning. Three warnings accumulated in one quarter and I'd get a Slack Badge, which meant losing one of my five vacation days and lowering the threshold for future warnings from three to two. And yep, there it came, the auto-generated ping indicating I'd gotten the Slack click. I picked up the pace and headed for my next stop.

Fueled by fear of being labeled a Gen-Y slacker once again, I hit my next target, a convenience store and Internet café owned by a wary, forty-something Turk. He listened politely and was having none of it, not even the free trial. I thought I saw a crack of light when I showed him the coupon features, but no dice. I bought a Berliner pilsner and some kibbeh before checking out "No Sale," wolfing the meat pie down as I fast-walked to the U-Bahn station and caught a train downtown.

With twelve minutes to think to myself, I played with the Berlin City app some more, poking around the settings which, by default, were set to wide open. The thing pulled in data from my Facebook, Twitter, Gmail, and LinkedIn. According to the "About" page, it also inter-faced with the fully digitized archives of seventeen different Berlin museums and universities, drawing on an pool of 270,000 pictures. It was a massive undertaking, but I wasn't surprised I'd never heard of it—not a coupon or a sales tool to be found in the whole thing, and it didn't accept advertising. On the plus side, the whole thing was Open Source, so maybe we could get some value out of it for ThriftyCity. I tried to come up with some sales-oriented opportunity before I reached my stop, hoping to undo the damage from my demerit, but nothing came to me.

Mitte's crowded, narrower streets were a sharp contrast to the foot-ball-field wide Karl Marx Allee. This was the center of Berlin, with a rich mixture of businessmen, shoppers, and tourists clogging up the sidewalks. The architecture was more classic Berlin as well—facades echoing the nineteenth century instead of Communist dream-palaces, with some more modern glass-and-steel structures scattered here and there. My assignments for the rest of the day were all up and down

Wilhelmstrasse, one of the main North-South drags in downtown. My first stop was a four-star restaurant. Well, I gave it four stars in the demo I'd made for them—figuring anyone ballsy enough to charge twenty-three euros for a schmaltz and black bread appetizer must be good or they'd be out of business.

As I stood before the door, checking into the target on my phone, I got an alert from Berlin City, a bright yellow pop-up window that said, "Leon Manning, Your Uncle, Was 210 Meters From Your Current Location." I blinked and didn't do the right thing. Instead I touched the "Map" button, causing a map of the Berlin streets around me to take over the screen, a bright yellow dot with my uncle's name just two blocks away. It was the opposite direction from my next sales calls, but the shiver of needful curiosity coursing through me would not be denied. No one talked about Uncle Leon. No one had even called him Uncle Leon before that moment. He'd died almost sixty-five years ago, but he'd lived right around the corner from me.

I figured I never closed the high-end restaurants anyway, so Ned wouldn't know the difference. With a few swipes, I turned off the GPS on my phone. It was spotty, especially indoors, so he'd assume I'd lost the connection while inside, which gave me a good twenty minutes to go see my uncle. The place was close enough that I might even be within the error bars of cell tower triangulation. I screwed up my courage, squared my shoulders, and fast-walked up the street. It didn't take even three minutes for me to come up to the imposing, clean-lined facade of a building identified on my phone as the Federal Ministry of Labor and Social Affairs. It was neat and orderly, like much of downtown, and there were tourists milling about in the small open plaza, reading plaques and taking pictures.

My uncle's yellow dot was on the other side of the plaza, and as I closed in the phone buzzed again. Panic that it was Ned checking up on me drew fear sweat from the small of my back, but it was actually a different kind of crisis. The Berlin City app was telling me that I'd entered a Crisis Point, and was wondering if I'd like to "Explore More?" I did indeed, and touched the screen to bring up the interactive augmented reality layer. My phone offered me two options, "1941 - Luftwaffe HQ" and "1953 – Worker's Revolt." The fact that this modern-day ministry had been the nerve center for the London Blitz was intriguing, but the 1953 date was pulsing and glowing red. Even without this unsubtle hint, I'd have chosen the year my uncle died.

Through my phone's screen, the small plaza filled with black and white workers, East Germans massed outside what was then called the House of Ministries, angry about something. I swung my phone around the plaza, and there were photos of people in every direction. It was a strange effect, like standing in a sea of cardboard cutouts, but ones which magically turned to face you no matter which angle you looked at them from.

I'd never heard of mass protests in East Berlin, at least not before the Wall came down in 1989. I touched the "More" icon, and my phone froze for just a second. Then it started streaming a deep, serious-toned German male voice "Angered by inhumane demands for increased productivity from Ulbricht and other DDR leaders, workers through-out East Berlin went on mass strike, gathering here on June 17 with cries of 'Free Elections! Down with Government!' This first and largest protest of the Cold War era in Berlin would not be matched until 1989."

As I moved through the ghost crowd of angry workers, listening with growing anger and sympathy, I spotted a yellow halo around one of the figures across the street. I moved towards it, and as I got within a dozen meters, a tag popped up beneath the group photo. Only his head and shoulders had been caught in the old picture, a young man with light hair trimmed in an unflattering bowl cut. He had the same thin lipped, wide mouth as my dad (and me), and it was shut tight in a serious frown. The tag said "Leon Manning, 72% match. Can you confirm? 0 people have identified this person."

I couldn't confirm. I'd never seen a photo of Uncle Leon. When my dad and oma fled East Berlin, they'd left everything behind, including the family photos that had survived the war. Oma never talked about it, so I only had dad's version to go by. Since he'd only been three, his story didn't have much to it, and I honestly hadn't thought or cared to ask him about it since I was a freshman or sophomore in high school. So no, I couldn't confirm, but I knew it was him. So I hit "Yes." Yes, this was Uncle Leon. The app thanked me for my feedback.

I stood and stared at the blurry, pixelated ghost of Uncle Leon and wondered why he'd been here that day. He wasn't yelling like some of the others around him. He looked worried though. And surely he'd been too young to be a worker, upset that his quota had been raised by 25 percent. I thought maybe he'd just been wandering by and stopped to see what all the fuss was about. I imagined oma in her apartment, my toddler father at her knee, waiting and worrying about her oldest son being caught out on the street.

The double pulse shook the phone in my hand, just enough to make the image vibrate. It was the bad pulse. I switched over to Messenger.

Ned: Where are you?

I assumed he wouldn't ask if he didn't already know. I ignored the text for the moment, whipping around and not quite running back towards the restaurant I was supposed to be selling in. I felt the phone pulse in my hand again, but didn't slow down to look at it until I was standing outside the window, looking in on white table cloths and heavy wooden chairs.

Ned: ???

Ned: Martin?

"Sorry, was talking to chef," I said to the phone. The voice to text software didn't seem to mind that I was panting as I said it.

Ned: Where?

"We went for a walk so he could smoke," I said. That seemed plausible, right?

I heard nothing from Ned for two and a half long minutes, during which time I stood there, catching my breath and staring hard at the damn phone.

Ned: Sale?

"He wants to talk to his partner. I'm going to come back tonight."

Ned: No sale.

Did he mean me not closing the sale or him not buying my bullshit story? I took a page out of his book and decided not to respond since he hadn't actually asked another question. Instead I activated Sales Tacker and checked out of the restaurant, dutifully marking "No Sale," but scheduling a return appointment for 19:00 tonight. Trying to make the pitch during dinner rush wasn't likely to work out at all, but I'd give it a go.

My next appointment was another souvenir shop, further along Wilhelmstrasse. Which was good news. The tourist joints were always the easy sells. I started walking in that general direction, even as I brought up Berlin City once again. I thought I might swing back through the plaza and try and get a screen capture of my uncle's photo to send to my dad. I didn't bother to turn my GPS back on. If Ned asked, I'd claim battery life concerns.

As soon as the app loaded, it gave me a new alert. "New possible facial recognition match for Leon Manning found. 37 percent Match." I tapped the alert, and a map of downtown Berlin filled the screen, a glowing yellow pinpoint hovering right near the Brandenburg Gate, less than a kilometer from where I was standing. Now of course I wanted to check that one out too, even more than I wanted to go back to the plaza. I figured I was due my twenty-minute lunch break, even though I knew Ned hated us to take them when we were behind schedule like I was. I risked the slack badge and logged off for lunch, which automatically started the countdown timer on my phone. With 19:37 on the clock, I headed towards the Brandenburg Gate.

I followed the line of tanks down the road. They were old-model Soviet tanks, in black and white and two dimensions, and there were people throwing stones at them. Unter den Linden, packed to the modern-day gills with cafés, car showrooms, and tourist traps shown bright and airy everywhere but on my phone. Back in 1953, it was grainy and dark, with frustrated, angry German workers were throwing stones at Soviet tanks.

The street widened into Pariser Platz, the cleaned and restored Brandenburg Gate directly ahead, it's four-horse chariot ready to gallop off and down towards me. But between them and me were three actors dressed as East German, American, and Soviet soldiers, charging five euros to pose in pictures with tourists. And there was a man on stilts, and another man in a bear suit for those who wanted less militaristic symbols of the city. Although I wasn't sure what the stilts-guy had to do with anything. But through my camera, there was a sixty-years-gone crowd of angry workers.

I noticed that a slider had appeared along the left side of the screen, another time line for another Crisis Point. Moving it up or down changed the year, and with it the augmented reality laid over the pristine, tourist-friendly Brandenburg Gate I was standing before. I flipped to the twenty-first century and held the phone up, the gate's three arches center-screen, and started to move the slider back from the present day. Ebullient Berliners atop the gate at night as the Wall came down gave way to Cold War–era East German guards, first in color, and then, further back in time, in black and white. Then battle-scarred Soviet soldiers transitioned into Nazis on their hate parade into jazz-age Weimar Republicans celebrating just being alive before the army of the Kaiser took their place.

The weight of tragedy in the stones and streets within my view made me feel both lucky and sad. To have escaped all that, to have lived a life free of even needing to know it ever happened, much less suffer through it—that made me lucky as sin. The sadness came when I came to suspect what I'd been brought to this point to see. I slid the time line back to the black and white, Cold War–era layer, the one marked 1953.

A yellow haloed figure was falling to his knees in the middle of the platz. A line of East German cops were firing into the crowd, and it looked like the young man had stepped forward to hurl a stone, which he still held tight in his left hand. My first thought was to wonder aloud, "Huh, my uncle was left-handed too." It was my uncle. It was certainly the same boy I'd seen outside the Ministry building. I moved up close to him, the phone held before me. Around me, at least a dozen others were holding phones or cameras as well, taking pictures or maybe looking at their own historical realities.

I don't imagine many people ever have to look at a photo of a loved-one's murder. To say an uncle I'd never met, who'd died almost thirty years before my birth, was a loved one seemed crazy. But that didn't mean I didn't feel it. And that didn't mean I wasn't outraged at all he'd lost in that moment, and all my oma had lost, and my father, and me.

The phone vibrated in my hand, the image of my uncle and his comrades being shot by the Volkspolizei shivering in response. It was a message from Ned. A Slack Badge, awarded without comment. There went vacation days. Another one, and I'd lose 20 percent of my commissions for the next week. The colorful, stupid fucking Slack

Badge taking the place of my uncle's murder on my screen was so ridiculous, so utterly petty, that I laughed out loud. Not an odd sight these days, someone laughing at their phone, but I didn't care if the tourists around me did think I was some sort of nut. I figured I'd be a nut to put up with this insanity.

Ned's petty tyranny lost all meaning and definition when seen through the lens of real oppression. The polizei wouldn't shoot me no matter how much Ned wanted them to. My uncle had stood up to tanks with just cobblestones. Ned wanted more sales, I'd make him more sales.

I copied the photo of my uncle being shot, opened up the Thrifty City sales app, and started creating a New Business:

Name: Workers Revolt
Location: Berlin and Everywhere Else
Business Type: <other> Saying Fuck You to Pigs.
Est. Revenue: Millions Dead and Counting.
Promotion Type: <coupon> Shoot one, Shoot another Free! <discount> 100% Off Worker's Rights

I attached my uncle's death shot as the Location Image and uploaded it to the server. Then I started on the next one. From where I was standing I could see the exact sites of a thousand different crimes. Maybe a million.

Name: Democracy Destroyed
Location: Reichstag and all of Central Europe
Business Type: <other> One Man, No Votes
Est. Revenue: Billions if you're making tanks and bombs and poison gas.
Promotion Type: <discount> 100% of voting franchise. <coupon> Burn one Parlimant, Burn a Second for 50% off

I uploaded that, and then started trying to figure out something poignant to say about the Berlin Wall. I was working up to the Holocaust. My phone buzzed, a text from Ned.

Ned: ?

I ignored it, deciding on "Name: Dreams Divided," and it buzzed again.

Ned: ??

Two question marks. He really was mad. I knew the next Slacker Badge was on its way and decided to step into the punch. "This is what's important here, Ned," I dictated to the phone, my voice dripping with acrimonious venom. "This is what the fuck matters."

Ned: ?

"Fuck!" I yelled at the question mark, then started to dictate. "This is what fucking tourists need to see. This is where my uncle died making a stand." The voice-to-text software replaced the "fucking" with "####" but I sent it anyway.

I was ready to throw the phone as hard as I could at the Brandenburg Gate if he sent another question mark. Out of the corner of my eye, about fifty meters away, I could see a cop eying me. Wouldn't that be ironic. But he just stared, and no guns were drawn. I had that on my uncle anyway. The phone buzzed.

Ned: I get it.

"You get what?" I asked, but didn't send.

Ned: We need to be culturally sensitive.

Ned: Let's effort this new proposal of yours.

Ned: We'll do historical events. An educational component. It's a good plan.

My outrage started to dissipate in a gust of confusion. My first question was, why wasn't I fired. And if I wasn't fired, that meant, well, it meant I could make car payments. And student loan payments. And I had health insurance still. And all those things. That was good, right? It didn't feel good though. It felt like a tire wrapped around my neck. But how could I quit when Ned was being reasonable with me?

"Thanks," was all I could dictate back to him.

Ned: Finish out your day and we'll Skype about it tonight.

I nodded. "Okay."

Ned: We'll be joined by Philip in London and Gina in Paris. I'll add it to your calendar.

"Sounds good," I said. Ned didn't reply, and after ten or fifteen seconds, I brought up Berlin City History again, and pointed my phone back at the scene of my uncle's failed revolt. I wondered what it had sounded like. I tried to imagine the gunpowder smell.

My phone buzzed, alerting me that I had a new item on my calendar. I opened it up. "RE: Monetizing Historical Crises through coupons and attraction discounts."

I hurled my phone as hard as I could, shattering it against the left-most column on my side of the Brandenburg Gate. It shattered, glittering shards of glass screen and plastic innards blossoming and tinkling to the ground. The cop was on top of me a second later, and as I was slammed to the ground I'd never felt more relieved.

Darkness Drops

Larry Fondation

You are dead, my love.
That I know.
I am supposed to radio in. I do not.
I stay with you in the shrub and the sand. I stroke your hair. Your hair does not stiffen.

～

We ran for the truck. We almost made it. When the bullets hit you, I scorned the hands that reached out for me. The hands of our fellow soldiers. I scorned them to be with you.

We fell in love at boot camp. We laughed amidst sweat and pondered our prospects. From North Carolina, steamy and wet, to Texas heat to arid Iraq. I stole your shampoo. We believed that no one knew about us.

Time passed here, the invasion easy, the aftermath troubled, letters home, your embrace, still furtive, glancing, clandestine. A game of soccer in the scattered sand.

～

I do not know how to sleep with a dead body, but I am determined to do so. The sun falls. I shape the sand beside you, beneath you. I feel the hot but cooling grit between my fingers.

My radio cackles. I ignore it. At least it's still working, functioning, alive. I banish the thought.

Darkness drops. I crawl up beside you. We talk.

I believe we will talk all night, but at the outset, I am surprised by how little I have to say.

All cued up I have profound things to say to you—about the endurance of love, about morality and ethics, about sacrifice and beautiful suffering, about natural law and various theories of just war, about us.

We both were churchgoers.

I say none of this of course.

"Do you remember when I first cut your hair? . . . you know how I fumble with things . . . I still can't believe that eggs made you gag . . ." I confuse my tenses.

The darkness deepens and the wind picks up. I cuddle your corpse. Like a sodden bag of Earl Grey, you are steeped in liquid, but yours is blood. Holding death so close, so tightly, the deep shit seems like mere pretense now. In the end, after the end, it is the quotidian that counts.

I see your socks and shoes.

Once again, I take out my radio, or whatever it is I am supposed to call it now, this sophisticated communications device, my MBITR. I think of smashing it, of stomping it into the sand. Instead I stick it—still croaking with static—back inside my jacket, and I hold you, and I wait for morning.

Orange Alert

Summer Brenner

Next best to moving in with my kids (no invite forthcoming) was Pine Lodge, a local retirement home and pleasant three-story brick building on a quiet woodsy street close to public transportation. I leased two unfurnished rooms with large casement windows on the south side of the *unassisted* section—one for sleeping, the other napping.

Two acquaintances already lived at the Lodge. "Comrades," I called them. Over the years, we'd encountered each other's comradely presence at marches and protests where we waved and smiled. Or hooked arms and sang "The Internationale." Or went for beers after a long, hot day glaring at the high security gates of Lawrence Livermore National Laboratory, the country's petri dish for WMDs.

Judith Tanner was a tall Bostonian, entitlement written over her face and wrapped around her French twist. She'd been introduced to the civil rights movement by a patrician grandmother who went on the Freedom Rides. However, it was only after retirement and moving to Pine Lodge that Judith began to devote herself full-time to causes, drafting petitions, collecting signatures, visiting government offices, and standing on street corners holding signs and shouting at cars. Wherever, she distributed booklets of the Declaration of Human Rights to waitresses, custodians, clerks, and other service employees. She started a blog—*Tanner Times and Tidings*—to opine on military spending, Wall Street bonuses, Gaia, drones, and bowel movements. In other words, she was a pain in the ass but worthy of respect.

My other comrade, Beverly Brown, had been an activist and union organizer spanning five decades with Ban the Bomb, White Panthers, Greenpeace, Clearwater, Gray Panthers, Code Pink, and Women in Black—a full-color spectrum. Everyone's complaint about Beverly was personal hygiene. As a young social worker, she decided to bond with the underclass by appearing as poor and needy as possible. She wore ugly secondhand clothes. She never combed her hair or cleaned her fingernails. Welfare clients complained about her BO—and concluded if a college-educated government employee couldn't earn enough money to bathe and dress decently, they might as well stay on the dole. Beverly was also a pain in the ass with lots of street cred.

A week after I arrived, Judith organized a bowl-in. Six members of the PL affinity group (Pine Lodge, not Progressive Labor) marched to the nearby bowling green with homemade signs that championed "Bowling for All." I marched too.

The pretty green was a fenced park owned and groomed by the city and kept under lock and key for bowlers to use during restricted hours. If the green were open to the general public, the benches and smooth putting-green grass would attract lovers, vagrants, dogs, and detritus of all of the above. During hours of operation, the green was occupied by men. An occasional woman might join them, but males dominated.

When we arrived, we demanded certain hours be set aside exclusively for us. "BFA united!" we shouted a few times.

"Help yourself!" an obovoid-shaped octogenarian with one eye doffed a baseball cap and mumbled "libbers" under his sour breath.

The bowl-in wavered between protest and tantrum as we challenged male hegemony on the green. They capitulated. Then, we got down to bowling business and commenced to roll, throw, and pitch. There wasn't a natural among us except Judith who was well-coordinated and something of a showoff. It was obvious she enjoyed competition—especially with men. She berated and belittled us to try harder, reiterating our rights to enjoy outdoor exercise in a well-tended park without interference from frisbees, dog poop, dopers, and homeless campers.

From the sidelines, the men looked on, typically smug and amused—short on compliments, long on critique.

After a quarter-hour of effort, a couple of us complained. "What's the big deal about lawn bowling?" I asked, speaking for the majority. We were exhausted. We wanted to go home.

Back at Pine Lodge after victory was unanimously declared, we trundled giddily off to lunch.

"What are ya'll up to?" Sonya asked, thrusting her lumpy face between Judith and Gwen.

Gwen O'Donnell was Judith's best friend. They were inseparable.

Male residents indulged in lesbian gossip and lesbian jokes about them. No doubt a pathetic disguise for their craving to try Viagra. They'd been obsessed with Viagra since TV ads began warning viewers of erections lasting more than four hours.

"Spill the beans," Sonya pleaded. She'd missed the bowl-in because of an emergency root canal.

Sonya was a retired high-school librarian. Usually loaded on diet pills, her bright side was dazzling. Last month, she went to Rio, plastic surgery capital *del mondo*. She returned with less pleats and more tucks but unfortunately the overall impression remained the same—oatmeal raisin.

"Revolution," Judith whispered, leaning away from the fruity smell of Sonya's powder and perfume.

"Judith is trying to save the world! Again!" Gwen explained. She herself was too timorous to be a revolutionary but at least could count one as a close friend.

Sonya licked her thin well-glossed lips, curled her arthritic fingers around her thumb, and raised her fist. "Power to the People!" she giggled.

"It isn't funny," Judith retorted.

"I wasn't laughing at *it*," Sonya said. "I was laughing at myself. This morning, I was trying to save a thumbnail. Not as heroic as our Judith." Sonya showed us her splayed purple thumb. "*Aubergine*," she attempted with an accent acquired in a junior-year abroad program over a half-century ago.

We cringed at the sight of Sonya's mangled thumb.

"Earl accidentally slammed it in his car door."

"Earl?" Judith spat.

"I will always love Earl."

No matter what Earl said, Sonya believed him. Recently, he'd told her that humans were only nine meals away from murder, although we concurred that with Sonya's backside, she was more than nine meals.

"I thought Earl went back to his wife," Judith remarked.

"He did," Sonya admitted sheepishly.

Gwen shrugged. She was mum on the subject of married men. She had had a decade-long affair with a judge who harbored political aspirations, meaning he'd never leave his wife. Gwen dissolved her second marriage for him and incurred the eternal resentment of her daughter, Jen. She hoped once Jen married, she'd understand what it meant to be a frustrated grownup. So far, that hadn't happened. Jen, a convert to Hasidic Judaism and mother of four, appeared extremely happy.

Gwen, however, took pride that a man elected to three terms of public office once loved her. When other women boasted about their affairs with famous men, at least Gwen could mention Harold Weber. I happened to know Judge Weber. He was a royal pain in the ass.

Sonya and Gwen didn't have a radical agenda. They hadn't read the nineteenth-century classics on property and production. They hadn't read Chomsky. They had decent humanitarian inclinations and despite chronic disappointment, championed electoral politics with renewed enthusiasm every two years. They faithfully believed the democratic experiment was working.

Like me, Annette was new to the PL coterie. She moved to Pine Lodge after a near fatal encounter with a parasite that attached itself to her duodenum in an ashram outside Mumbai. The bug had resisted western power drugs, holistic healing, homeopathy, acupuncture, and Chinese herbs. But through daily rituals of yoga and meditation, Annette managed calm detachment which she attributed to two perfect children, five *more perfect* grandchildren, and the teachings of a swami with an unpronounceable name. As for her remarkable complexion, she credited Crisco slathered on her cheeks, neck, and forehead every night for more than fifty years.

Judith Tanner envied Annette's calm demeanor. Balance, fatigue, diet, or disease? Whatever the source, Annette appeared to accept life's *slings and arrows*. Judith accepted almost nothing. As a political person, she was chronically discontent.

Annette's effect on Beverly Brown was paranoia. Bev associated tranquility with church and was fiercely adverse to God. Although Annette explained it wasn't necessary to believe in God to be a Buddhist or Hindu or good person, Beverly maintained that Hindus, Buddhists, and good people committed atrocities as adroitly as anyone else.

"So?" Beverly asked, swallowing a spoonful of lime Jell-O.

"We're plotting," Gwen said.

"Tell the world!" Bev sneered.

"There's no plot yet," Sonya assured her.

"So much effort and work, so little accomplished," Judith lamented.

"Imagine how I feel," Beverly said.

"Spare us, comrade," Judith said.

"I don't mind hearing," Annette chimed.

"You don't mind anything," Sonya snapped.

"But I do mind," Annette said meekly. "I mind suffering in all forms, but there is nothing to be done. Suffering is the human condition."

"What should the plot be?" Gwen cried.

"A secret!" Beverly reprimanded.

"We could talk in code," Sonya suggested.

"Odeca orfa lotpa eforeba ewa ieda," I spouted.

"I can't possibly work that out," Annette admitted.

"First, we need to choose a name," Judith said.

Everyone agreed. A name was a good idea. Predictably, the next two hours were devoted to recommendations. Exasperated by inanities masquerading as concerns, Beverly was the first to lose patience.

"No Name!" she thundered. "After Ulysses."

"I like that," Judith confirmed. "No Name! No Nonsense!"

"I like it, too," I seconded.

"Catchy bumper sticker," Sonya said, trotting out her marketing skills.

"It's a secret! Not a bumper sticker!" Bev repeated.

"What now?" Gwen rubbed her sweaty palms.

We agreed the coup at the bowling green was kindergarten. A dress rehearsal long on rhetoric and short on impact. As to our next move, we were stymied.

"Let's sleep on it," Judith said.

"Okay," Beverly said.

We took a vote. Unanimous.

～

I had a terrible dream. Sleeping was bad, waking worse. The wisps of clouds, the fragrant pine sap, the penetrating warmth of sun were unwelcome reminders that earthly life was nearly done. Soon, I'd be carted off to the world of *assisted* living. And then?

I dragged myself from bed. Bathed, brushed, flossed, counted pills, and dressed. At the appointed hour, I met my comrades at our nearby café. They looked as awful as I did. Even Annette's demeanor was cracked.

"Good morning," I grunted.

"Any brilliant ideas?" Judith raised an eyebrow.

Unwaveringly sincere, Annette broke the silence. "I dreamed I was in a nursing home," she choked back a sob.

"Me, too," Gwen whispered hoarsely.

"Quite a coinkidink!" Sonya said.

"Ditto," Beverly coughed.

"And Judith?" I asked.

Judith Tanner slurped her *latté* and scanned our depressed faces. It wasn't the first time she had had such a dream. You're familiar with Carl Jung's theories? The *collective unconscious* had ensnared us.

"It's a sign," Sonya said prone to superstition.

"It's no sign," Bev sputtered. "It's perfectly trite. What other future would we dream in a society that discounts, ignores, dismisses, degrades, abuses, and warehouses its elders?"

"What's it mean?" Annette wondered aloud.

Beverly drummed her fingers on the table.

"Could you not do that?" Gwen requested, gnashing her dentures.

"What?" Beverly was oblivious.

"The thingie with your fingie," I said.

"I think through my fingers," Beverly explained. "After years at a keyboard, that's where my brain went."

"Can you put it back in its cranium?" Gwen moaned.

"Deep breaths, everyone," Annette counseled. "Inhale one, hold two, exhale three."

Annette had been consciously breathing for over forty years, convinced that all problems—trivial and monumental, personal and worldwide—could be solved by such a practice. We complied, slowly inhaling and exhaling a half-dozen times.

"When I woke up, I wanted to kill myself," Sonya cried, clutching her breast.

"We could commit mass suicide," Judith sniggered.

"Like lovers," Annette sighed.

"And cults," I charged.

"Start saving pills," Bev said.

"*Mass Suicide Stuns Elder Care Facility*," Sonya cackled. "At least, Helen Temple would lose her job."

Gleeful approbation circled the table.

"Suicide is a sin," Gwen said piously. She'd recently returned to the bosom of the Catholic church.

"Sin?" Beverly mimicked harshly. "Mistreating old people is the sin currently under discussion."

"If we killed ourselves, we wouldn't be around to gloat," Sonya reminded us.

"I'd be around," Gwen said, already lonely.

"It would be a good joke," I smiled.

"It's not a joke," Judith said.

"We're not getting anywhere," Bev barked.

"Maybe, we should sleep on it again," Gwen piped.

"I'm not sleeping until I'm sure your nightmare won't invade me," Sonya said.

"Maybe, your nightmare invaded me," Beverly countered.

"I don't think so."

"But you're afraid."

"Who wants to end up a thingamajig?" I spoke for all of us.

"I want to die conscious," Annette beamed. "Inhale my last breath fully alive."

"I want to go to bed and wake up in heaven," Gwen mused.

"Inject me with sodium pentothal and send me to the Caribbean," Sonya said dreamily.

Bev declared, firm and decisive, "I plan to blow myself up in front of the Pentagon."

"What!" we chorused.

"P-E-N-T-A-G-O-N!"

"Brilliant!" Judith conceded.

A frisson raced through us as we grabbed each other's hands.

"After one of us is diagnosed," Judith said.

"With a fatal incurable terminal disease," Bev continued.

"Before we're too infirm—or lose our mind," I said.

"I can't possibly kill anyone," Annette agonized.

"You wouldn't be killing anyone," Judith emphasized.

"Just yourself," Sonya reasoned.

"I don't mind killing a few certain persons," Beverly said sharply.

"That's a personal choice, don't you think?"

"I'd rather kill machines," Judith said.

"So the doctor delivers a death sentence and then?"

"I wonder if it hurts to blow up," Sonya pondered.

"*The free animal/has its decease perpetually behind it/and God in front . . .*" Gwen was good with quotes.

"We're animals," Annette observed.

"Who's the German poet?" Gwen asked anxiously.

"Wagner?" Sonya guessed.

"He's not a poet," Beverly muttered.

"A?" Gwen paused. "B?" she didn't think so.

"Rilke," Judith said. She had given *Duino Elegies* to Gwen for her birthday.

"Let's discuss how this will work," Bev interrupted.

"Shouldn't we have a name?" Sonya queried.

"We have a name," Judith said.

"It sounds awfully exciting to die."

"We should envision it as self-sacrifice," Annette offered.

"The ultimate sacrifice," Sonya said.

"We can't use *that* phrase. It's what the President says when something bad happens to the troops."

"It makes their families feel better," Gwen commented.

"Will this make our kids feel better?" Annette asked.

"Don't count on it."

"That's why our goal has to be pure." Annette again.

"Pure like Buddhist monks who set themselves on fire in protest of war."

"*So others might live free*," Sonya rhapsodized.

"They are noble," I said.

"We can be noble," Judith said. "It depends how we go about it."

"Once you get your death warrant, we'll need a signal," Sonya said. "How about wearing orange?"

"Why orange?"

"Blonds, brunettes, everyone looks good in orange."

"Do you see blonds and brunettes here?" Bev snipped.

"Orange communicates high alert," Sonya asserted. "It's the Homeland Security code."

"I like the idea of a signal," Gwen agreed.

"It's the color of Buddhist robes," I added.

"Orange has never suited me," Judith blurted, once a stunning redhead.

"If you don't want to wear orange, then bring us each an orange."

"That'll be confusing," Annette complained. "I eat oranges all day."

"We'll have to look old and inconspicuous."

"That won't be difficult," I croaked.

"She means gentle and respectable."

"She means helpless and ugly," Beverly chided.

"Back to logistics," Judith prodded.

"Maybe, we can include an abortion clinic," Gwen said timidly.

"Are you insane?" Bev exploded.

"We're all in favor of a woman's right to choose," Judith frowned with a ferocious expression.

Gwen cowered. She was once in favor herself, but the church had filled her with contradictory feelings. Propped beside her bed was a photo of Buzz Aldrin. He took Communion on the moon.

"I'll pretend you didn't say that," Beverly said snidely. "By the way, blowing yourself up is a cardinal sin even at an abortion clinic."

"Don't we get to pick our *own* target?" Sonya asked.

"Like Nordstrom's?" I scoffed.

"We should agree it's political. That's the point," Bev said. "And sign something beforehand like a proclamation."

"And suicide note," Gwen said.

"It's not exactly suicide," Annette quibbled.

"It is suicide but the reasons are unconventional."

"Nordstrom is a perfectly legitimate target," Sonya insisted.

"It's not military-industrial," Bev objected.

"The clothes are made in sweatshops. Slaves probably make them. Slaves make jeans and shoes. Nordstrom is famous for shoes."

"Isn't that a syllogism?" Gwen asked.

"Sonya has a point," I defended. "It's anti-capitalist."

"But is it worth killing herself over?" Bev asked.

"Maybe," Sonya said.

"*Don't mourn! Organize!*"One of Beverly's standards.

"Surely, there's no time for that," Annette said.

"I vote Pentagon," Judith proposed.

"First thought, best thought," I said.

"Pentagon!" Gwen seconded louder than intended.

"You're not participating," Judith said.

"We should choose our own target," Sonya whined. "I mean it is our life."

"What about voting on targets?" Gwen recommended. "A target needs three votes to qualify."

"If you're not participating, you should recuse yourself from the discussion."

"I already suggested a target," Gwen said. "It just didn't meet with your approval."

"Can we shut up about targets?" Bev seethed.

"I thought Judith said it was more important than wardrobe," Sonya said.

"It's more important but not the *most* important."

"Most important is how we make a bomb," Judith said.

"And detonate it," Sonya added.

"Keep your voice low," Beverly hissed.

"Bomb! Bomb! Bomb! Bomb! Bomb!" Sonya was often bratty. "Did anybody turn around?"

Our eyes swept the café. The cheerful room with its terra cotta walls and comfy chairs, wi-fi, fair-trade coffee, homemade pastries, and potted plants was filled with sleepy young people dressed in black jeans and t-shirts, seated at faux marble-top tables, fiddling with their sleek laptops, their ears plugged with either speaking or listening devices. Even those playing chess were competing against computers.

"I don't think they're hard to make," Judith said. "Directions are on the Internet."

"You know that?" Gwen asked.

"Sure! But the FBI watches those sites."

"Getting materials is tricky," Beverly said. "They have strict restrictions on fertilizers."

"What about a large vegetable garden at the Lodge?" I advised.

"I want to make sure we don't hurt anybody." Annette cried.

"You mean 'collateral damage,'" Bev said.

"We wouldn't be murderers, would we?" Annette needed clarification.

"How about *saboteurs*?" Sonya's bad accent again.

"I couldn't possibly kill anything," Annette repeated weakly.

"What if it were a building where there happened to be a cat?" Gwen adored philosophical conundrums.

"I would feel terrible," Annette said.

"They don't let cats wander around the Pentagon," I pointed out.

"What if we blew up a ship carrying weapons to the Persian Gulf? They might keep cats on board to kill rats. If the cats were already killing rats, would that make you feel better?"

"Cats naturally kill rats," Annette reasoned. "This is different."

"Is it?" Bev retorted. "Apparently, man naturally kills everything."

"*Kill one man, and you're a murderer. Kill millions of men, and you're a conqueror. Kill them all, and you're a god.*" Judith was also very good with quotes.

"Technicalities should be our focus," Beverly said.

"Communication, acquisition, production, transportation, and execution, there's your outline." Gwen jotted a few notes on her napkin.

Bev's eyeballs pierced the paper. "You'll have to burn that."

"If you don't write down a few things, you won't remember." Gwen had once been a professional facilitator. "You can't possibly keep everything in your head."

"Do we claim responsibility and send out a press release?" Sonya asked. "I'd like to work on that."

"Maybe, we can ignite an international elder terrorist movement," Gwen said.

"Der Elder Hostile!" I whooped.

"I don't like 'terrorist.' It sounds negative," Annette said.

"*Die today for a good cause!*" Sonya was tempted to say it would make a good bumper sticker.

The vivacious waitress stood beside our table, pad and pencil in hand. Thick hennaed hair tumbled around her face. Her eyes shone and skin glowed with youth.

"Looks like you gals are having a grand time of it this morning," she said, smiling at her Saturday-morning regulars.

"We have a lot to live for," Judith nodded soberly.

We nodded in accord. "All of us have a lot to live for."

~

Quotes by: *Joe Hill, Ranier Maria Rilke, Jean Rostand, William Shakespeare*

Masai's Back in Town

Gary Phillips

The shotgun blast partially tore away the side of the bearded man's face. It didn't kill him or knock him over—though it did embed pellets in one eye, ruining its vision. He screamed profanities and cranked off two rounds from his Glock. But Masai Swanmoor went prone, squeezing the Remington's trigger again. This time his aim was better and he blew out the other man's stomach, sending him over backwards onto the coffee table, breaking a leg as it collapsed.

Swanmoor rolled as the other Aryan Legion member, a woman with a hatchet face and a weight lifter's body, came at him. The hunting knife she wielded cutting and slashing at his legs as he scrambled about.

"Motherfuckin' black motherfucker," she wailed, arching the knife overhand at his groin.

Swanmoor swung the pistol grip stock of the auto shotgun to deflect the blade then aimed the business end of his weapon. "Put the pig sticker down, you ugly Nazi bitch," he blared.

"Fuck you." She didn't let go of the knife. She backed up several steps and stood hunched over, knife in one hand, eyes roving about the room.

Swanmoor stood up. "You're not that goddamn valuable to me. You or one of your other inbred sodomites will be of use." Cowboy fashion, he held the shotgun low, left hand under the pump action, right finger on the trigger. "I'm happy to kill you."

She looked from this to the dead man. The knife fell to the thin carpet.

Swanmoor started forward.

"What, you gonna rape me now?" she snarled.

"Don't think every brother goes crazy for white pussy. Even stank muscled-up snatch like yours." Bringing the rear end of the shotgun up, twisting his torso as he did so, he brought it across her face, eliciting a grunt.

She dropped to a knee, a hand to where he'd struck. She spat out blood on the now stained carpet and got back up. "I don't know much."

"You know enough." He grinned lopsidedly.

～

When Rory Briscoe arrived at the house he drove his well-cared-for LeSabre past and parked a block away. The distinct smell and background silhouette of an oil refinery was evident. He got out of the car. Briscoe had the snub-nosed revolver in the pocket of his cotton windbreaker as he walked back to his destination. His and hers Harleys were parked side-by-side in the driveway. The front door was partially off its hinges, hanging at an odd angle. He looked around, no neighbors or house pets were out. Even the birds weren't chirping.

He walked purposefully across the yellowed lawn and up the porch and peering inside, could see two chairs in the front room were turned over. Gun out, he went further into the small house and saw Clauson's corpse on the broken coffee table between the front room and the dining room space.

Briscoe surmised the coffee table had been shoved around some in the fight. On it had been a bong, its glass smoked gray and black from use. This had tipped over when the bearded man's body had landed. The bong now lay resting in the gap of his lower abdomen where his stomach had once been. Blood and organ spray patterned a near wall.

In the kitchen he found the one who he knew only as Gigi. She was bound to a straight-backed chair with duct tape and nylon cord. Two dish towels had been knotted together and tied around her mouth. She glared at Briscoe who noted her bare feet. Her little toe on the right foot and the big toe on the left had been sawed off. The hunting knife, lying on the kitchen table, had been the instrument of torture used by Swanmoor. The severed toes lay on the linoleum in small puddles of blood. He knew that Lumumba lovin' bastard wouldn't have left his prints on the blade.

Briscoe undid the gag. "You gave up my name, didn't you?"

"Fuck you," she answered. "That jungle bunny was gonna cripple me. Get me undone. I plan to pay him back."

He put the barrel of the Glock he'd plucked from Clauson's stiffening fingers against her forehead. "Good thing this is the kind of neighborhood where gunshots are common." He blew out the back of her head as she gaped incredulously at him.

Briscoe wiped down the gun then returned to the dead man's body and pressed those lifeless fingers against the grip. He let the gun lay in the man's open palm. Briscoe then quit the premises.

∾

Swanmoor down-shifted the Benz he'd jacked wearing a handkerchief owl hoot style from a trendy restaurant's parking attendant. He'd picked this car because he'd never driven a Mercedes before and wanted to feel what it was like. The seats were leather and heated. Nice.

He came around the corner via the narrow passageway between the two buildings. The macadam of the former Lamplighter bar parking lot was cracked and bulged upwards in several areas, evidence of the various earthquakes that had taken place since the drinking establishment's demise more than twenty-five years ago. Weeds sprouted from those openings.

The Lamplighter had been their office away from the office. Run by a former pimp and numbers man who was sympathetic to the cause, Swanmoor and the others would hold emergency meetings in the rear storeroom and talk trash with the hookers and hustlers who frequented the front area. This was also where Swanmoor had gotten it on in the owner's office with more than one firebrand sister and a white follower or two from the hills—young women enthralled with smack talk of revolution and brothers street army tough in black berets and black sunglasses. The bar's latest incarnation was Delgado's Discount Furniture Mart.

He got out of the car, hunching his shoulders against the cold and the incoming fog. In the near distance the mist glistened in the lights of a billboard. On it could be seen an image of a desk mic giving off a bit of fire. The words "KZRN Sizzles Liberals with Septima" were next to that.

"Hey now," he said as the driver's door of the silver Prius opened. Out stepped a woman a tick or two past sixty but still lithe of build and seemingly effortless in her motions. He also noted the silver-white hue of her car matched her coiffured hair.

"Damn," he said admiringly.

"Stop trying so hard and hug me, fool."

He did, laughing, his hands tight around her midsection, hers around his shoulders.

She kissed his neck before she pushed him back to take him in. "Are you out of your cotton-picking mind coming back here, Marvin?"

"No choice, Leann." She rarely called him by his street name.

"Bullshit." She pulled her open topcoat closer around her. "You better get on your knees and thank the baby Jesus these crackheads around here are too young, miseducated and too far gone to know who you are. 'Cause the price is still on your nappy head, negro."

He blew into his fist. This was his hometown but his body had gotten used to a warmer climate. "After I'm done, you can turn me in if you want to."

She smirked. "Double fuck you and your macho counter-revolutionary posturing."

"Maybe so. But I wanted you to know Briscoe is also back on the scene, and me and that poor man's Lewis Erskine are gunning for each other."

"Shit," she drawled, "he's older than your monkey ass. Like I'm gonna be afraid of some oinker clumping after me with his walker."

"He's got a goddamn hook up with the Aryan Legion. I'm not sure how extensive, but there it is. One of them, named Clauson, was checking ancient haunts about me and I got tipped."

She leveled her gold flaked ambers on him. Angry or inviting, those eyes still knocked him out. "Fuck the Legion too. I'm not so soft I can't handle a few of them prison-bred goose-steppers."

Swanmoor smiled. "Now who's posing?"

She flipped him the finger, smiling too. Then she took on a serious cast. "What about your daughter?"

"Even if Briscoe knows who she is, I'm figuring given the people around her and what not, he won't make a run at her. Now of course

I'd like you to warn her anyway." He frowned and what might have been regret came and went on his still lean features. "It's probably best I don't come at her direct."

"Probably so."

"Yeah," he replied, letting the word and the emotions behind it linger.

She tugged on his jacket and asked, "You still like that cheap Presidente brandy?"

"It's what the masses drink," he deadpanned.

"Nigga please. Let's hat before a constituent sees me consorting."

She'd brought a bottle of the brandy and two plastic cups with her in the car. At the Star Burst Motel overlooking a ship container yard, once in the room Congresswoman Leann Holt shoved Marvin "Masai" Swanmoor against the door and kissed him like she was trying to quench a fever.

He got his arms and hands around her and it was 1980 and they were young and saying good-bye when he'd gone on the run after being indicted. Only now Swanmoor had the unerring impression this might be the last time he was privileged to be with this woman . . . his lover . . . his comrade. Yet the notion that his grey head could soon be blossomed out from bullets didn't cool his ardor, but inflamed him like he hadn't felt in years.

After they made noisy love they took a break to have a few sips of Presidente and talk. The old-fashioned radiator issued weak heat under the curtained window. Swanmoor had placed the one chair in the room under the door knob. It wouldn't stop anybody but he hoped slow them down long enough to reach the piece he'd placed on the nightstand.

"I want to help you," Holt declared.

"You are."

"You know what I mean, home. Field work."

"That's not going to happen. Shit's gonna get funky."

She chuckled and kissed his chest then laid her head on it. "You can't do this by yourself."

"My face is only on dusty clippings, but you, you're ghetto fabulous. Besides, you've got grandkids you need to be around for, counselor."

"You might too."

He glared at the top of her head, flashing on the mushroom cloud jet-black afro from all those years before. "Shit, do I?"

"No, but you get my point, old timer."

"I ain't stove up yet. No pork, no salt, plenty of roughage and their ghosts are with me."

"Who?"

"Che and Malcolm, Ho and Fred, baby."

"I'd say you were delusional, but you might be right. I want you to be right."

"Hell yeah, I am."

She looked up at him and they made love again.

~

The younger and larger man had his arm around Briscoe's windpipe and said, "You must be mixing vodka with your Ensure in the mornings, grandpa. The math you learned in grade school has evaporated from your diseased mind."

He choked him some more to underscore his intent. Briscoe's face was red from effort and lack of breath, his hands impotently trying to loosen the other man's chiseled arms. Finally he was released and he wilted to the floor, choking and gagging on all fours.

"We understand each other now, right?" Clete Willhelm walked to the counter and picked up his open can of beer and took a lengthy pull. On the floor was an upset can of spilled beer. Briscoe had been drinking from this until Willhelm attacked him.

Briscoe finally sat and cleared his throat. "I'm not trying to cheat you, Clete. You gotta learn to relax."

"Let me worry about my anger management issues. Two of my road dogs are dead 'cause of this super spade sparring partner of yours. How come he knew to come at them looking for your ass, he supposed to have been out of the country all those years?"

Briscoe held his hands wide. "I'm sure he still has contacts. If it was me, the first thing I would do is find out the lay of the land. There's a reason Swanmoor was high on the Bureau's key agitator index. He's no bench warmer."

Contemplatively, Willhelm opened another beer.

Briscoe went on. "We need to flush Swanmoor out to tell us where the money is—or more precisely, where he thinks it is."

"Uh-huh," Willhelm grunted, considering his next words. "This isn't a Legion matter, Rory. This is between you, me and a few I trust. And that list is now a lot shorter."

"Whatever you say. But we need to make some moves or else we're just running around with our heads up our asses."

"Seems to me you need to be doing your job and targeting his old friends to make him come out and play."

"I know. Only if we don't have the troop strength, we need to be selective. We can't go around jacking up worn-out Lenin-quoting has-beens. The worse thing would be for Swanmoor to go back underground."

"Huh," Willhelm muttered, tipping his head back and quaffing his beer. "But you must have had a snitch or two from back then still around. Like that photographer who followed the civil righters around, and at the same time was a rat for your bunghole loving boss Hoover."

"It's not like turncoats belong to a club, Clete. Don't you think I've been out there beating the bushes?"

"What about, what you call it, an intermediary? One of them burr head preachers all hyped up on keeping the peace and shit. Somebody that wasn't on the payroll but who you leaned on in the past, you know, one of those reasonable negroes." He chuckled.

At first Briscoe was going to make a dismissive comment then got a faraway look on his face. "Maybe," he allowed. "Maybe for a cut."

"Or at least he thinks he'll get a cut," Willhelm opined.

∾

"My friends we must keep up the good work. The Lord's work really. I am so heartened that we are one step closer to winning the culture war and restoring sanctity and values for our impressionable youth and our nation. I applaud your efforts good citizens in shutting down that blasphemous exhibit at the Smithsonian. It was a true waste of our tax dollars."

Masai Swanmoor smiled thinly, shaking his head slightly. He turned off the small digital radio, ceasing the woman's rants. He had to admit though, the sound quality was amazing. Modern technology. He left his hideaway and was soon walking through the park, having reconnoitered the perimeter like he'd been taught in country.

Laughing children under the watchful gaze of their mothers or nannies played on the swings and slides. Sitting on a bench under a maple tree was Big Stick Caruthers. After two bouts with cancer, once in the throat and the other time in the stomach, he was a slender shell of his former defensive tackle frame.

"Young blood," Caruthers greeted. He stood and the two men hugged. "You're looking pretty damn decent. What's your secret?"

"I wish it was big titty virgins and palm oil, but I only got the latter in abundance."

"I heard that," Caruthers said, sitting down again. Swanmoor remained standing and scanning.

"It's just you and me. I'm the messenger, not the tethered goat."

"Not knocking you, brother."

"Just being on point. I ain't mad at you like the adolescents say."

Satisfied, Swanmoor also sat on the bench near the former owner of the Lamplighter bar. "So what's their offer?"

"The ofays figure you and them don't need to be in this scorched earth mode. Two dead and—"

"Two?" Swanmoor interrupted. "I left that lumberjack shouldered broad alive. Bleeding but no fatal wounds."

"That's not what was on the news but what's the difference?"

Swanmoor smiled humorlessly. "Wheels within wheels, man."

"One race hater dead, two race haters dead, even they mamas probably won't miss 'em."

"No doubt. But they probably came from a long line of sieg heiling fucks."

"Children don't always follow in their parents' footsteps."

"There is that. Briscoe came to you alone?"

"He did. Motherfuckah phoned for me at the senior hall during our square dancing night, you believe that? Was in the middle of do-si-do-ing with a cute little widow with some beachfront property. Sheeit."

Both men snickered. "What I believe is he's a greedy forked-tongue devil. He expects me to do the grunt work and then I just give him a cut being all nostalgic and what not?"

"He calls off the Legion. Says you been green lit 'cause of you dropping members of the calling. The inference being it wouldn't just be you in their crosshairs."

Swanmoor looked off in the mid-distance. "How is it that Briscoe's got an in with them? The Aryan Legion wasn't around in his day."

"We're getting off topic, aren't we, Masai?"

"You've kept your ears open, Big Stick. I can't imagine you've retired that much."

Caruthers made a face then said, "His daughter. She was a doper, college dropout, ran the streets, the whole bit. Don't know the full story but damn right, I made it my business to keep tabs on friends and enemies alike. She winds up marrying one of these white power studs while he's in the joint. He gets out, they set up house, it's all tattoos and mud-people-bashing, but they eventually split up. She got born-again."

"It's your educated guess that Briscoe reached out to his former son-in-law once he knew I was back on the scene?"

Caruthers made a small gesture.

A silence dragged by as Swanmoor considered his response. "If I get the goods they'll kill me. What's my guarantee?"

"Briscoe says he knows who your daughter is. The Legion doesn't know and he'll keep it that way if you agree to the split. Fifty-fifty."

"Shit," Swanmoor swore.

"He's going to call me later today. What do you want me to tell him?"

Swanmoor stared at Caruthers.

~

Walking back to another car he'd stolen that morning, a fifteen-year-old beater with a dented roof, he took off his shirt, shaking it and feeling up the material. He knew bugging devices had changed greatly since the days of cassette tapes and wanted to make sure Big Stick Caruthers hadn't planted some kind of tracking button on him when they'd embraced. The former bar owner was a pragmatist after all. Relieved Big Stick hadn't planted anything on him, Swanmoor re-buttoned his shirt over his athletic-T and drove away.

~

There was a decorative table in a corner of the high-rise office of the Wilder Foundation. Upon its surface was a vase filled with fresh cut flowers including lilies and chrysanthemums. Their fragrance subtly altered the area. Yet the fragrance of the studious young woman who came out to greet him, was both more powerful and understated simultaneously.

"Ms. Van Meter apologizes but her call should be over in the next five minutes," the young woman said. "Would you care for coffee or sparkling water?"

"I'm fine, thank you." Swanmoor took a seat in a plush chair and leafed through a recent issue of *The Atlantic*. He was into an article about the origin of the Garamond typeface when a pointed shoe touched his shin.

"Well, well." Alison Van Meter stood with her hands on her hips, head cocked, eyes peering over her designer glasses. Her blonde hair was streaked with white but was shoulder-length and full-bodied.

"Hey, Ali," Swanmoor said, rising.

"Get your ass in here before the black helicopters come swooping down." She pivoted and marched toward a set of double doors. He followed. Van Meter was heavier than back in the day, but he could tell she maintained an exercise regime. There was a muscularity apparent in the calves visible below the hem of her business skirt.

They entered her large office, and she closed the doors behind them. Pressing him against those doors, she kissed him for several beats before they parted. A man could get very used to this he reflected.

"You know you shouldn't have risked this, Masai. The swag might not be there. You could have sent word. I would have retrieved it and gotten it to you, you know that."

"Sending a proxy would have been shaky. Notwithstanding there's a damn good chance one of the construction workers could find the dough."

"I'd have gone personally, chump," she said.

He pointed at her stylish shoes. "Those are Jimmy Choos, aren't they? You wouldn't want to break one of those heels, would you, trawling among the lumpen?"

"Being the sexist dog you remain, it figures you'd keep up with women's fashion."

"Look, I started this, it's only right I should finish it. Anyway, I was homesick, Ali." As he talked he walked around her office, holding his hands wide. "Nice."

"Money is just a means of exchange, comrade."

"The extent of the power of money is the extent of my power."

From a mini-fridge she offered him fresh-squeezed blueberry and pomegranate juice which he accepted. He sat on the couch in her office and she in a chair near him. Looking past her at the cityscape out of her wide windows, he brought himself back to the present.

Van Meter was talking. "I got you a room at the hotel. Part of the place has been demoed, that's how his handgun was found in the remains of the dumb waiter." A cell phone picture of the gun had been shared among the work crew and by chance Van Meter, making a site visit, had seen the shot. Given the location and its age, she concluded it was the piece she'd obtained for Swanmoor decades ago—the one she knew had been used in the job. She then got in touch with him.

"There are some tenants left who are moving out by month's end. It's unlikely anybody will bother you as you prowl about," Van Meter said.

She rose and went to a closet and returned with an equipment bag she placed on the floor near him. "A few items you might need." She sat on his lap. "Now about the equipment I need," she teased.

"Shouldn't I be resentful being objectified in this way?"

"Shut up." They kissed again.

~

Later that day Masai Swanmoor took his room at the Warwick, these days a residential hotel. It was in a part of downtown still home to the poor—though they were being pushed out due to the area's stepped-up gentrification efforts.

He stepped into the hallway. Loud rap music issued from behind one door and an argument through another. He walked downstairs as the elevator had long been out of use. In the lobby there were a few about, including two old men, one with a walker, involved in an intense chess game. Van Meter, whose foundation was behind redeveloping the hotel into mixed-use affordable housing, had provided a layout to Swanmoor. Across the lobby and to his left was a door leading to the basement.

"Where do you think you're going?" a voice challenged as Swanmoor put his hand on the doorknob.

He looked over at a pudgy bald man in his mid-fifties with a tweed jacket and cargo pants. He had an iPod in his sports jacket's handkerchief pocket and removed his ear buds.

"Who are you?"

"I live here, you don't." The man frowned at Swanmoor.

"I'm inspecting." The door was locked but it didn't take much to get through it, loose as it was in the frame. He went downstairs, using the flashlight Van Meter had included in the supplies she'd given him.

Overhead were sewage and water pipes and heat conduits leading from vintage but functioning gravity heaters. He made his way around, operating on the theory he would stick to areas so far untouched by the construction crew. If the money had been found by one of the workers, Van Meter assumed she would have heard of such.

Aside from the inner workings of the building, Swanmoor found cardboard boxes of discarded clothes, neatly tied stacks of yellowed and brittle girlie magazines and *National Geographics,* and an assortment of sweep brooms of various sizes. More exploring turned up little else of interest.

Back upstairs in his room, Swanmoor lay on the bed, hands behind his head staring at the water-stained ceiling. He reviewed the past, hoping for a clue in the present as to where Georgie Boy hid the COINTELPRO slush funds they'd stolen. The FBI under Hoover orchestrated the Counter-Intelligence Program for over a decade. The Program's one overarching goal was through chicanery and agents-provocateurs to disrupt and destroy self-determination struggles from the militant American Indian Movement, mainstreamers Martin

Luther King, to hope-to-die revolutionaries like him, Leann Holt and Georgie Boy, George Dixon—the three who'd pulled off the score.

Dressed in matching khakis, black turtlenecks, work boots, gloves and full-face ski masks, the three had moved precision quick back then out of the Falcon station wagon parked at a yellow zone. Applying the pry bar to a service entrance sans latch, they forced the door open. A day before, Leann Holt in disguise of a housecoat, curlers—she'd hot combed her afro straight so as to have it fit underneath her mask—and sunglasses, had come into the unemployment office and clipped the alarm wires to that particular door.

Their movements rehearsed by Swanmoor, a decorated Vietnam vet, they got the drop on the building's two security guards. One was an out-of-shape, chain-smoking former cop with a gimpy leg. The other a hippie who said he dug them taking it to the man. The trio bound and gagged the two, shooting Novocain into their legs to temporarily make their limbs numb and useless.

Rory Briscoe was the Special Agent in Charge of the regional implementation of COINTELPRO that covered this area back then. Briscoe was a hands-on kind of Bureau man. Beatings, planting evidence and illegal wiretaps were all part of his repertoire. He also shook down the hustlers and weed and smack dealers for a taste. Briscoe had amassed a sweet sum for his retirement coupled with cash shipments from Washington to be used specifically for bribing snitches and setting up off-the-books operations.

This slush fund was nearly three million which even in today's dollars had worth. But Briscoe had it bad for this one mixed race street walker named Francie. To impress her one time, after she gave him a blowjob in his secret field office, he'd shown her the stash and told her they could get away, start over as he wanted out of his square marriage. She stalled him, but Francie, who did like to brag while on the nod, had let it slip in the Lamplighter about the money.

Briscoe's unmarked office was inside the unemployment office building and the monies were kept there in a floor safe. Given they had time, the three peeled the safe door using a heavy-duty drill and a power chisel. The goal was to seed the money back into the community. Splitting after the robbery, Georgie Boy had been tasked with hiding the scratch while Swanmoor and Holt ditched their getaway car and clothes, setting fire to them. They made sure to keep apart but otherwise maintain their regular regimes. They'd told Francie to leave town, promising to send her a cut. Her body was found under a freeway overpass, her neck broken.

Only in what had to be classified as the caprice of the gods, Georgie Boy was eating a fish sandwich, laughing hard as he told friends a story about his dad, an amateur prize fighter. He choked to death on a fish bone. Where he hid the money, he and Holt didn't know.

Swanmoor's reverie ceased as he smiled knowingly. He suddenly remembered what Georgie Boy had said as, fueled on exhilaration, they'd dropped him off at the other getaway car, a VW beetle belonging to his girlfriend, Sharon Mason.

"It'll be cool, y'all," Georgie Boy had said driving away. As a kid, Swanmoor knew Georgie Boy had sold newspapers in front of the Warwick.

That night, up on the roof of the dilapidated hotel, near the long broken air conditioning units, he found the two duffle bags of cash. They'd been stuffed into a crawl space access cavity. The panel to get to this was rusted over and the edges of the panel had been super glued by Dixon, though most of that had worn away. Van Meter had supplied Swanmoor with a crowbar he used to remove the panel.

"I knew I recognized you," the pudgy man said. "Hell, I gave money to your defense fund when you were accused of killing that undercover cop." He stood near Swanmoor on the roof.

The duffle bags were at Swanmoor's feet. The crowbar was within reach, but that wouldn't block a bullet.

"That's the COINTELPRO score, isn't it?" Pudgy man indicated the duffels with the muzzle of the .45 he held on Swanmoor.

"Yeah."

"Fuckin' urban legend. And it was over my head all this time." He chuckled mirthlessly. "Well, Mister Minister of Strategy, you can have the privilege of taking the people's money downstairs to your car and I'll leave with the goods. I'd help, but my back's all twisty. I'm on disability, you understand."

"You ain't having no trouble lifting that gun."

"That's true, blood. I know how to shoot it too. Civilize the mind, make savage the body, isn't that what Chairman Mao said in those Little Red Books you all used to sell?"

Swanmoor remained silent.

"Let's hit it, bro. You first."

A million in one-hundred-dollar bills weighs about twenty-two pounds. The almost two point seven million COINTELPRO swag was in hundreds, twenties, fifties and fives. This meant each duffle was roughly forty pounds. Swanmoor dragged them down the stairs by their cords. Maybe if he was thirty years younger he'd try something. But he was certain he didn't have the arm strength to suddenly turn and swing one of the sacks at his overweight obstructionist.

On the ground floor in the stairwell, Swanmoor pushed the crash bar on the exit door leading to the street. The bar depressed but the door didn't open.

"Harder," his new companion demanded.

Swanmoor repeated the motion several times, including leaning against the door.

"Shit. Come on." The pudgy man jerked the gun, indicating they had to go through the other door leading to the lobby. He moved to one side to allow Swanmoor to go first, still dragging the duffle bags.

"Can't you pick those up?"

"They're heavy and I'm old."

"Try."

Swanmoor had his back against the now partially opened lobby door. He let go of one of the duffles, and put up a knee to brace the other duffle bag. He got his arms around this one but pretended it was heavier than it was and stumbled backwards into the lobby area, falling down. He kicked himself further into the lobby.

"Get up," the other man yelled, coming part way into the lobby too.

"Take it, take all of it," Swanmoor said fearfully, crawling away on his backside, his hands out from his body.

The pudgy man was standing near Swanmoor with the gun in his hand, denizens of the lobby area staring at the two. The duffle Swanmoor had dropped was near him on the floor. He'd purposely undid its top, bills spilling out. This particularly got the attention of the gathered who moved toward the money like wolves to deer. The chess-playing oldster with his walker clumped forward furiously.

"Back the fuck up," pudgy man warned the others. He swung the gun back and forth. When he turned his head to look over at Swanmoor, the bigger man was already beside him. "Sonofabitch," he managed, but Swanmoor already had a hand on the man's gun arm. With his other hand tightened into a fist, he went at the pudgy man's face like he'd seen Sugar Ray Leonard do in his matches

"Ughhh," the object of his anger groaned as he assumed a fetal position on the floor, bleeding freely from mouth and nose.

Swanmoor doled out hundreds to each down-and-outer and drove away with the slush funds. Using the disposable cell phone Van Meter had given him, he made some calls.

~

The tawny-hued black woman tented her fingers as she spoke evenly and forcefully into the overhead mic. Her broadcast, based out of her home radio station KZRN, was carried across the nation. "Before I go today, I wanted to mention this rumor that's surfaced within the last few hours. Now I warn you this seems to be gaining traction in the leftist elite circles so bear that in mind.

"But there's been scuttlebutt about a retired FBI agent suspected in the shooting of one of those biker types. Normally this sort of headline I'd leave for your local news, but this particular individual has a history with the so-called black power movement and you've heard me before talk about how that misguided effort actually set black people back.

"So I'll be watching the developments in this case as it wouldn't be far-fetched to believe this no-doubt courageous law enforcer has been framed by sinister liberal forces. Stay tuned, good citizens."

~

Rory Briscoe's arthritis had flared in his left hand but he ignored the pain while jamming clothes into his luggage. That fucking Swanmoor had fucked him good but he'd get him back, he vowed.

"The fuck you think you're going?" Clete Willhelm said.

Briscoe looked from the Aryan Legion leader to his gun on his dresser. It might as well be in the next block for all the good it could do him.

"It's all about anger management, right, Clete?" His attempt at a jocular tone failed.

"You know the grief that's on me, man? Questions about you, whispers about the missing money. Was I out to screw the brethren, making a deal on the side."

Briscoe huffed. "You were making a deal on the side."

Willhelm gave him a blank look.

Briscoe continued. "This can all be worked out to our satisfaction, Clete. We just need to concentrate on taking out Swanmoor. We take a run at his daughter and— "

"Uh-huh. Just what I should do, add a kidnapping charge to my happiness."

"No, you don't get it. She's a fraud." He held up his hands in protest. "All we have to do is threaten to expose her and this will force Swanmoor to play ball."

"I no longer give a shit, Rory. I don't know if Swanmoor or you chilled Gigi. If I was a cynic, I'd say you were using me to get the money then planned on taking me out too."

"Clete, come on, we're family."

Willhelm went on as if he hadn't heard him. "If you weren't around, a lot of my problems go away."

"Aw, goddammit." Briscoe moved as fast as he could toward his gun. Even if he was younger, he wouldn't have bridged the distance in time.

Willhelm shot his former father-in-law in the stomach and as he bent over, holding his wound, shot him in the top of the head. He left the dead older man's apartment.

～

Father and daughter hugged tightly, each tearing up.

"I wish you could stay," Septima Mason said.

"Me too. But we both know better than that."

"We have to go, I've got some smuggling to do," Leann Holt said. "Bye-bye, daddy."

He smiled and hugged his daughter again. "When am I gonna get a grandchild?"

"How traditional of you, father." She kissed him on the cheek. "Please be careful, will you?"

"There is nothing which is not an intermediate state between being and nothing."

"Smart ass."

"You're the one that needs to be careful, Septima. How long you going to keep up this charade?"

"It matters little to the individual guerilla whether or not he . . . or she, survives."

"Quotes are overrated."

In the car as Holt drove him away, Swanmoor looked back and waved at the diminishing image of his daughter.

"I guess you three have a plan worked out?"

"Oh yes," Holt said. "Septima's finishing her book which will be coupled with some juicy hidden video bombshells." She winked at him. "Like a certain ex-governor who, it seems, likes it both ways. She made a pass at Septima at one of those right wing confabs."

"Say what?"

"You'll see. With Wilder Foundation backing, we're going to roll out a series of high-profile media hits. She'll be the talk of the nation."

Swanmoor was also glad the COINTELPRO monies would be laundered through the Foundation for neighborhood organizing grants.

Holt patted Swanmoor's leg. "Don't you worry, papa, I don't intend to let any wingnut harm a hair on her head once we blow her cover."

Silence then he said, "How about 'I was a Right-Winger for the Movement' as the book's title?"

Holt glanced at him. "That's catchy."

~

They did use his title. The exposé was a blockbuster.

I Love Paree

Cory Doctorow & Michael Skeet

Day 1: The Night the Lights Went Out in Dialtone

Gay Paree was in full swing when the Libertines conscripted the trustafarians. Me, I should have seen it coming. After all, that's what I do.

I was an OPH—Old Paree Hand—there before the Communards raised their barricades; there before the Boul' Disney became a trustafarian chill-zone; a creaking antique expat who liked his café and croissant and the *International Times* crossword in the morning. I loved Paree, loved the way I could stay plugged into everything while soaking in the warm bath of centuries. I loved the feeling of being part of a special club; we OPHs always managed to look out for one another, always managed to find the time to play at baseball in the Bois de Boulogne when the weather was good. Not even civil war had been able to change that, and that I loved about Paree most of all.

Normalment, I would've been in bed when the Club Dialtone was raided. But that night, I was entertaining Sissy, a cousin come from Toronto for a wild weekend, and Sissy wanted to see the famèd Dialtone. So we duded up—me in rumpled whites and hiking boots with calculated amounts of scuff; Sissy in po-mo Empire dress and PVC bolero jacket and a round bowler hat and plume—and we sauntered over the epoxy-resin cobbles to the Dialtone.

I played it for all it was worth, taking Sissy past the memorial cra ter arrondissements, along the echoing locks on the Seine where the sounds of distant small-arms fire ricocheted off the tile and whizzed over your head, past the eternal flame burning in the smashed storefront of the Burger King flagship store, and finally to the Dialtone.

Fat Eddie was bouncing that night, and I waggled my eyebrows at him surreptitiously, then at Sissy, and he caught on. "Mr. Rosen," he said, parting the crowd with a beefy forearm, "an unexpected pleasure. How have you been?"

Sissy's eyes lit up christmas, and her grip on my elbow tightened. "You know, Edward: just the same, all the time. A little poorer with every passing day, a little older, a little uglier. Life goes on."

Fat Eddie smiled like the Buddha and waved aside my remarks with an expansive sweep of his arm. "You merely improve with age, my friend. This is Paree, m'ser, where we venerate our elder statesmen. Please, who is this lovely young woman with you?"

"Sissy Black, Edward Moreno. Sissy is my cousin, here for a visit."

Fat Eddie took Sissy's hand in his meaty paw and feinted a kiss at it. "A pleasure, m'dam'selle. If there is anything we can do for you here at the Club Dialtone, anything at all, don't hesitate to ask."

Sissy flushed in the gaudy neon light, and shot a glance over her shoulder at the poor plebes stuck behind the velvet rope until Fat Eddie deigned to notice them. "Nice to meet you, Edward," she managed, after a brief stammer, and kissed him on both cheeks. This is a trustafarian thing, something she'd seen on the tube, but she did it gamely, standing on tiptoe. Not Fat Eddie's style at all, but he's a pro, and he took it like one.

He opened the door and swept her inside. I hung back. "Thanks, Eddie; I owe you one."

"You don't think I laid it on too thick?" he asked, rubbing at the lipstick on his cheeks with a steri-wipe.

I rolled my eyes. "Always. But Sissy impresses easily."

"Not like us, huh, Lee?"

"Not like us." I'd met Eddie playing dominoes on Montmartre with five frères, and he'd been winning. It could've gotten ugly, but I knew the frères' CO, and I sorted it, then took Eddie out and got him bombed on ouzo at a Greek place I knew, and he'd been a stand-up guy for me ever since.

"Everything cool tonight?"

"Lotsa uniforms, but nothing special. Have a good time."

I walked inside and paused in the doorway to light a stinking Gitane, something to run interference on the clouds of perfume. Sissy was waiting nervously by the entrance, staring around her while trying not to. The kids were all out, in trustafarian rags and finery, shaking their firm booties and knocking back stupid cocktails in between sets. "What you think?" I shouted into her ear.

"Lee, it's supe-dupe!" she shouted back.

"You want a drink?"

"Okay."

The bartender already had a Manhattan waiting for me. I held up two fingers, and he quickly built a second for Sissy, with a cherry. I unfolded some ringgits and passed them across the bar. He did a quick check on the scrolling currency exchange ticker beneath the bar, and passed me back a clattering handful of Communard francs. I pushed them back at him—who needed more play-money?

I guided Sissy past a couple of stone-faced frères to an empty booth near the back, and took her jacket from her and put it on the bench next to me. She took a sip of her Manhattan and made a face. Good. If I kept feeding her booze she didn't like, she wouldn't knock back so much of it that I had to carry her out.

"It's *amazing*," she shouted.

"You like it?"

"Yeah! I can't believe I'm really *here*! God, Lee, you're the best!"

I don't take compliments well. "Sure, whatever. Why don't you dance?"

It was all she needed. She tossed her bowler down on the table and tore off to the dance floor. I lost sight of her after a moment, but didn't worry. The Dialtone was a pretty safe place, especially with Fat Eddie making sure no smooth-talking trustafarian tried to take her back to his flat.

I sipped my drink and looked around. There were a lot of uniforms, as Eddie had mentioned—and as many here at the back of the club as up near the door. Libertines didn't come up to the Boul' Disney often. Too busy being serious Communards, sharing and fighting and not washing enough for my taste. Still, it wasn't unheard-of for a few of the frères to slum it up here where the richies played at bohemian.

These ones were hardcases, toughened streetfighters. One of them turned in profile and I caught his earrings—these whackos wear 'em like medals—and was impressed. Pierre was a major veteran, twenty confirmed kills and the battle of Versailles to boot. I began to think about leaving; my spideysense was tingling.

I shoulda left. I didn't. Sissy was having a wonderful time, kept skipping back, and after the second Manhattan, she switched to still water (no fizzy water for her, it makes cellulite, apparently). I was chewing on a tricky work-problem and working on my reserve pack of Gitanes when it all went down.

The sound system died.

The lights came full up.

Fat Eddie came tumbling through the door, tossed like a ragdoll, and he barely managed to roll with the fall.

A guy in power-armor followed Fat Eddie in, leaving dents in the floor as he went.

Throughout the club, the frères stood and folded their arms across their chests. I gave myself a mental kick. I shoulda seen it coming; *normalment*, the frères stick together in dour, puritanical clumps, but tonight they'd been spread throughout the place, and I'd been too wrapped up to notice the change in pattern. I tried to spot Fat Eddie out of the corner of my eye without taking my attention away from the frères. At first I couldn't see him at all; then he turned up, looking dazed, in front of the door to the Dialtone's aged, semi-functional kitchen. For a moment I turned to look at him. He gave me a worried smile, touched his finger to his nose and faded through the door. A second later a frère moved in to block the kitchen, standing in front of the door through which Fat Eddie had just vanished. I wished I knew how to roll with the punches the way Fat Eddie did.

The PA on the power-armor crackled to life, amplifying the voice of the Pierre inside to teeth-shaking booms: "M'sers and m'dames, your attention please." Power-armor had a pretty good accent, just enough coq au vin to charm the ladies.

A trustafarian with a floppy red rooster's crest of hair made a break for the fire door, and a beefy frère casually backhanded him as he ran, sending him sprawling. He stayed down. Someone screamed, and then there was screaming all around me.

Power-armor fired a round into the ceiling, sending plaster skittering over his suit. The screaming stopped. The PA thundered again.

"Your attention, *please*. These premises are nationalized by order of the Pro-Tem Revolutionary Authority of the Sovereign Paris Commune. You are all required to present yourselves at the third precinct recruitment center, where your fitness for revolutionary service will be evaluated. As a convenience, the Pro-Tem Revolutionary Authority of the Sovereign Paris Commune has arranged for transport to the recruitment center. You will form an orderly single-file queue and proceed onto the buses waiting outside. Please form a queue now."

My mind was racing, my heart was in my throat, and my Gitane had rolled off the table and was cooking its way through the floor. I didn't dare make a grab for it, in case one of the frères got the idea that I was maybe going for a weapon. I managed to spot Sissy, frozen in place on the dance floor, but looking around, taking it in, thinking. The trustafarians milled toward the door in a rush. I took advantage of the confusion to make my way over to her, holding her hat and jacket. I grabbed her elbow and steered her toward Power-armor.

"M'ser," I said. "Please, a moment." I spoke in my best French, the stuff I keep in reserve for meetings with snooty Swiss bastards who are paying me too much money.

Power-armor sized me up, thought about it, then unlatched the telephone handset from his chest-plate. I brought it up to my ear.

"What is it?"

"Look, this girl, she's my mother's niece, she's only been here for a day. She's young, she's scared."

"They're all young. They're all scared."

"But she's not like these kids—she's just passing through. Has a ticket from Orly tomorrow morning. Let me take her home. I give you my word of honor that I'll present myself at the recruitment station"—the hell I would—"first thing in the morning. As soon as I see her off—"

I was interrupted by the frère's laughter, echoing weirdly in his armor. "Of course you will, m'ser, of course. No, I'm sorry, I really must insist."

"My name is Lee Rosen. I'm a personal friend of Commandant Ledoit. Radio him. He'll confirm that I'm telling the truth."

"If I radioed the Commandant at 0300h, it would go very hard on me, m'ser. My hands are tied. Perhaps in the morning, someone will arrange an appointment for you."

"I don't suppose you'd be interested in a bribe?"

"No, I don't really think so. My orders were very strict. Everyone in the club to the recruitment center. Don't worry, m'ser. It will be fine. It's a glorious time to be in Paree."

There was a click as he shut off the phone, and I racked it just as the PA reactivated, deafening me. "Quickly, my friends, quickly! The sooner you board the bus, the sooner it will all be sorted out."

Sissy was staring hard at the confusion with grave misgivings. She clutched my shoulder with white knuckles. "It'll be all right, don't worry!" I shouted at her. "It's a glorious time to be in Paree," I muttered to myself.

∼

Best not to describe the bus-ride to the recruitment center in too much detail. They packed us like cattle, and some of the more dosed trustafarians freaked out, and at least one tried to pick my pocket. I held Sissy tight to my chest, her hat and jacket squashed between us, and murmured soothing noises at her. She had fallen silent, shaking into my chest.

A hundred years later, the bus rolled to a stop, and a hundred years after that, the doors hissed open and the trustafarians tumbled out. I waited until the rush was over, then led Sissy off the bus.

"What's going on, Lee?" she said, finally. She had a look that I recognized—it was the cogitation face I got when I started chewing on a work-problem.

"Looks like the frères have decided to draft some new recruits. Don't worry. I'll get it sorted out. We'll be out of here before you know it."

A group of frères was herding the crowd through two doors: the women on one side, then men on the other. One of them moved to separate Sissy from me.

"Friend, please," I said. "She's scared. She's my mother's niece. I have to take care of her. Please. I'd like to see the CO. Commandant Ledoit is a friend of mine, he'll sort it out."

Pierre made like he didn't hear. I didn't bother offering him a bribe; a grunt like this would like-as-not take all your money and then pretend like he'd never seen your face. The ones in the power-armor were the elite, with some shred of decency. These guys were retarded sadists.

He simply pulled Sissy by the arm until we were separated, then shoved her into the women's line. I sighed and comforted myself with the fact that at least he hadn't kicked me in the nuts for mouthing off. The women were marched around the corner—to what? They had their own entrance? Sissy vanished.

It took an effort of will to keep from smoking while I queued, but I had a sense that maybe I'd be here a long time, and should hold onto them. A shuffling eternity later, I was facing a sergeant in a crisp uniform, his jaw shaved blue, his manner professionally alert. "*Bon soir*," he said.

On impulse, I decided to pretend that I didn't speak French. I needed any leverage I could get. You learn that in my line of work. "Uh, hi."

"Your name, m'ser?" He had a wireless clipboard whose logo-marks told me it had been liberated from the Wal-Mart on the Champs Ellipses.

"Lee Rosen."

He scrawled quickly on the board. "Nationality?"

"Canadian."

"Residence?"

"30 Rue Texas, No. 33."

The sergeant smiled. "The Trustafarian Quarter."

"Yes, that's right."

"And you, are you a trustafarian?"

I was wearing a white linen suit, my hair was short and neat, and I was in my early thirties. No point in insulting his intelligence. "No, sir."

"Ah," he said, as though I had made a particularly intelligent riposte.

The hint of a smile played over his lips. I decided that maybe I liked this guy. He had style.

"I'm a researcher. A freelance researcher."

"Jean-Marc, bring a chair," he said in French. I pretended to be surprised when the goon at the door dropped a beautiful chrome-inlaid oak chair beside me. The Sergeant gestured and I sat. "A researcher? What sort of research do you do, M'ser Rosen?"

"Corporate research."

"Ah," he said again. He smiled beneficently at me and picked up a pack of Marlboros from his desk, offered one to me.

I took it and puffed it alight, and pretended to be calm. "I haven't seen an American cigarette my whole time in Paris."

"There are certain . . . advantages to serving in the Pro-Tem Authority." He took a deep drag. He smiled again at me. Fatherly. Man, he was good.

"Tell me, what is it that you are called upon to research, in your duties as a freelance corporate researcher?"

What the hell. It was bound to come out eventually. "I work in competitive intelligence."

"Ah," he said. "I see. Espionage."

"Not really."

He raised an eyebrow dubiously.

"I mean it. I don't crouch in bushes with a camera or tap phones. I analyze patterns."

"Yes? Patterns? Please, go on."

I'd polished this speech on a million uncomprehending relatives, so I switched to autopilot. "Say I manufacture soap. Say you're my competition. Your head office is in Koniz, and your manufacturing is outsourced to a subcontractor in Azerbaijan. I want to stay on top of what you do, so I spend a certain amount of time every week looking at new listings in Koniz and its suburbs. I also check every change of address to Koniz. These names go into a pool that I cross-reference to the alumni registries of the top-hundred chemical engineering programs and the index of articles in chemical engineering trade-journals. By keeping track of who you're hiring, and what their specialty is, I can keep an eye on what your upcoming projects are. When I see a load of new hires, I start paying very close attention, and then I branch out.

"Since you and I are in the same business, it wouldn't be extraordinary for me to call up your manufacturing subcontractor and ask them if they'd be interested in bidding on certain large jobs. I set these jobs up such that I can test the availability of each type of apparatus they use: dish detergent, hand-soap, lotion, and so on. Likewise, I can invite your packaging suppliers and teamsters to bid on jobs.

"Once I determine that you are, for example, launching a line of laundry detergent in the next month or so, I am forearmed. I can go to the major retail outlets, offer them my competing laundry detergent below cost, on the condition that they sign a six-month exclusivity deal. A few weeks later, you roll out your new line but none of the retailers can put it on their shelves."

"Ah," the sergeant said. He stared pensively over my shoulder, out the door, where a queue of trustafarians waited in exhausted silence. "Ah," he said again. He turned to his clipboard and I waited while his stylus scritched over its surface for several minutes. "You can take him now. Be gentle to him," he said in French. "Thank you, M'ser Rosen. This has been educational."

Day 2: Bend Over and Say "Aaaah!"

They dumped me in a makeshift barracks, a locked office with four zonked-out trustafarians already sleeping on the industrial gray carpet. I rolled my jacket into a pillow, stuck my shoes underneath it, and eventually slept.

I was wakened by sleepy footfalls in the hallway, punctuated with the thudding steps of power-armor. I was waiting by the door when a frère in power-armor unlocked it and opened it.

He hit the spotlights on his shoulder and flooded the room with harsh light. I forced myself to keep my eyes open, and stood still until my pupils adjusted. My roommates rolled over and groaned.

"Get up," Power-armor said.

"Upyershithole," one of the trustafarians moaned. He pulled his jacket over his head. Power-armor moved to him with mechanical swiftness, grabbed him by one shoulder, and hauled him upright. The trustafarian howled. "Motherfucker! I'll kick your ass! I'll *sue* your ass! Put me down!"

Power-armor dropped him, then surveyed the others. They'd all struggled to their feet. The one with the potty-mouth was rubbing his shoulder and glaring furiously.

"Vit'march," Power-armor suggested, and followed us out into the corridor.

He wasn't kidding about the "vit" part, either. He moved us at brisk trot up the stairs, easily pacing us. When I came to Paree, this office-building had been a see-through, completely empty. A few years later, a developer had reclaimed it, renovated it, and gone bankrupt. Now it was finally tenanted. We finally emerged onto a roof easily six stories high, ringed with barbed wire, with a view of one of the cathedral domes and lots of crumbly little row-houses. Other conscriptees were already on the roof, men and women, but I couldn't find Sissy.

Burly frères were in position around the roof, wearing side-arms. Some stood on cherry-pickers raised several meters off the roof, with rifles on tripods. They swept the rooftop, then the street below, then the rooftop again. I wondered how they got the cherry-pickers onto the roof in the first place, then spotted a cluster of power-armored frères, and figured it out. These boys would just each take a corner and *jump*. Beat the hell out of block-and-tackle.

"You will queue up to receive temporary uniforms," one of the power-armors broadcaster. I was right at the front of the line. A frère sized me up and pulled the zips open on several duffels, then tossed me a shirt and a pair of pants.

I hurried down the queue to a table laden with heavy, worn combat boots. They stank of their previous owners, and evoked a little shudder from me.

"Jesus-shit, are we supposed to fucking *wear* these?" The voice had a familiar Yankee twang. I didn't need to turn around to see that it was my roommate, Potty-Mouth. He was carrying his uniform under one arm, and holding the other one at his side, painfully.

The smile vanished from the frère's face. He picked up the smelliest, most worn pair, and passed it to him. "Put these on, friend. Now." His voice was low and dangerous, and his accent made the words almost unintelligible.

"I am *not* gonna 'poot zees ahn,' you fucking frog shit. Put 'em on yourself," Potty-Mouth looked to be about twenty, maybe a year older than Sissy, and he had a bull's neck and thick, muscular arms, and gave off a road-rage vibe that I associate with steroidal athletes. He dropped the uniform and picked up one of the boots, and pitched it straight into the frère's face, with a whistling snap that sliced the air.

The frère plucked it from the sky with chemically-enhanced reflexes and shot it right back at Potty-Mouth. It nailed him square in the forehead.

Potty's head snapped back hard, and I winced in sympathy as he crumpled to the ground. I stepped away, hoping to melt back into the crowd. The Sergeant from the night before blocked my way, along with the frère who'd thrown the boot. "Get him out of the way, M'ser Rosen," the Sergeant said.

"We can't move him," I extemporized. "He might have a spinal injury. Please."

The Sergeant's smile stayed fixed, but it grew hard, and a little cruel. "M'ser Rosen, you are a new recruit. New recruits don't question orders." The frère who'd thrown the boot cracked his knuckles.

I grabbed Potty-Mouth under his dripping armpits and hauled him over the gravel, trying to support his head and biting back the urge to retch as his sweat poured over my hands. At this rate, I'd be out of steri-wipes in a very short time.

I wiped my hands off on his shirt and crouched next to him. The trustafarians were reluctantly removing their clothes and putting them into rip-stop shopping bags with Exxon logos, shivering in the cold. Women frères did the girls—still no sign of Sissy—and men did the boys, all nice and above-board. A frère came over to us, dropped two bags, and said, "Strip." I started to protest, but caught the eye of the Sergeant, standing by one of the cherry-pickers.

Resignedly, I stripped off my clothes and bagged them, then bagged my uniform along with them, and sealed it shut.

"This one, too," the frère said, kicking Potty-Mouth in the ribs.

Potty-Mouth jerked and grunted. His jaw lolled open. I began to mechanically strip Potty-Mouth of his stinking neoprene and spandex muscle-wear. I was beyond caring about microbes at this point.

The frère watched me, grinning all the while. I wondered how I ended up babysitting this spoiled roid-head, and stared at my feet.

Four frères in power-armor sailed onto the roof from the road below, carrying an ambulance bus at the corners. They set it down, popped the doors, and a cadre of white-coated medics poured out. The one who impersonally groped my balls for hernias and stuck me with several none-too-sterile needles needed a shower, and his white coat could've used a cleaning, too. When he bent over to check out Potty-Mouth, his pocket bulged open and I saw a collection of miniature bottles of Johnnie Walker Red. He popped me in the shoulder with some kind of mutant staplegun that stung like filth. "What's wrong with this one?" he asked me, speaking for the first time.

"Maybe a concussion, maybe a spinal. I think his shoulder's dislocated."

The medic disappeared into the bus for a moment, then reemerged in a leaded apron, and lugging a bulky apparatus. I realized with a start that it was a portable x-ray, and scrambled to get behind him. "No spinal, no concussion," he pronounced, after a long moment's staring into the apparatus's eyepiece.

"Okay," the medic said to himself, and made a tick on a wireless clipboard.

The medics bugged out the way they'd come in, and the frères withdrew with rapid, military precision, up the cherry-pickers.

I had a pretty good idea of what was coming next, but it still shocked a curse from my lips. The frères in the cherry-pickers all harnessed up giant blowers and turned loose a stinging mist of sinus-burning disinfectant down on us. Trustafarians, male and female, screamed and ran for the barbed wire, then turned and ran back into the center. Above me, I heard the frères laughing. I stood my ground and let myself get soaked once, twice, a third time. I was about to make sure that Potty-Mouth was lying on his side when he groaned again and sat up. "Fuck!" he shouted.

He scrambled groggily to his feet, careered into me, righted himself and wobbled uncertainly as the last of the spray settled over him. The disinfectant evaporated quickly, leaving my skin feeling tight and goose-pimply.

Potty-Mouth swung his head around with saurian sloth. He focused on me and grabbed my shoulder. "The fuck are you doing to me, fag?" His grip tightened, grinding my collarbone.

"Chill out," I said, placatingly. "We're in the same boat. We're drafted."

"Where are my clothes?"

"In that bag. We had to strip while they sprayed us. Look, could you let go of my shoulder?"

He did. "You may be drafted, bro, but not me. I'm leaving." He popped the seal on the bag and struggled into his civvies.

"Look, there's no percentage in this. Just keep calm, and let this thing sort itself out. You're gonna get yourself killed."

Potty-Mouth ignored me and took off toward the door we'd used to get onto the roof. He kicked it three times before it splintered and gave. I looked up at the frères in the cherry-pickers. They were watching him calmly.

A small, wiry frère was waiting behind the door Potty-Mouth kicked in. He stepped out, grinning. Potty-Mouth threw a punch at the frère's solar-plexus. The frère whoofed a little, but didn't lose his grin.

Potty-Mouth grappled with him, lifting the smaller man off his feet. The frère took the beating for what seemed like a long time, merely twisting to avoid the groin and face-shots that Potty-Mouth aimed. The trustafarians on the roof were all silent, watching, shivering.

Finally, the frère had had enough. He broke free of Potty-Mouth's grip on his arms with ease, and as he dropped to the ground, smashed Potty-Mouth in both ears simultaneously. Potty-Mouth reeled, and the little frère aimed a series of hard, wicked-fast blows at his ribs. I heard cracking.

Potty-Mouth started to fall, but the frère caught him, picked him up over his head, then piledrivered him into the gravel. He lay unmoving there, head at an angle that suggested he wouldn't be getting up any time soon.

The frères in the cherry-pickers scrambled down. One of them slung Potty-Mouth over his shoulder like a sack of potatoes and carried him down the stairs. The little frère who'd killed him stepped back into the doorway, pulling the broken door shut behind him.

"Get dressed," broadcasted a power-armor.

~

They herded us back downstairs without a word. The crowd moved with utter docility, and I could see the logic of the proceedings. Terrified, blood-sugar bottomed out, thirsty, we were completely without fight.

On the third floor, the cubicles and desks had all been piled in a corner, making one big space. A few long tables were set up with industrial-size pots of something that steamed and smelled bland and uninspired. My mouth filled with saliva.

"Form an orderly queue," said the sergeant from the night before, who was waiting behind one of the pots with an apron over his uniform, a ladle in his hand.

He looked each trustafarian over carefully as they passed through the line, clutching large bowls that were efficiently filled with limp vegetables, lumpy potatoes, and a brown, greasy gravy. Each of us was issued a stale baguette and a cup of orange drink and sent away.

We seated ourselves on the floor and ate greedily off our laps. Here in the mess, the frères relaxed and allowed the men and women to mingle.

Friends found each other and shared long hugs, then ate in silence. I ate alone, back to a wall, and watched the others.

Once everyone had passed through the line, the sergeant began walking through the clusters, stooping to talk and joke. He touched people's shoulders, handed out cigarettes, and was generally endearing and charming.

He made his way over to me.

"M'ser Rosen."

"Sergeant."

He sat down beside me. "How is the food?"

"Oh, very good," I said, without irony. "Would you like some baguette?"

"No, thank you."

I tore off a hunk of bread and sopped up some gravy.

"It is a shame about your friend, on the roof."

I grunted. Potty-Mouth had been no friend of mine—and in a situation like this one, I knew, you have to be discriminate in apportioning your loyalty.

"Ah." He stared thoughtfully at the trustafarians. "You understand, though, why it had to be?"

"I suppose."

"Ah?"

"Well, once he was taken care of, the rest saw that there was no point in struggling."

"Yes, I suppose that was part of it. The other part is that there in no place in a war for disobedience."

War. Huh.

The sergeant read my face. "Oh yes, M'ser Rosen. War. We're still fighting street-to-street in the northern suburbs, and some say that the Americans are pushing for a UN 'Peacekeeping' mission. They're calling it Operation Havana. I'm afraid that your government takes a dim view of our nationalizing their stores and offices."

"Not my government, Sergeant . . . "

"Abalain. François Abalain. I apologize, I had forgotten that you are a Canadian. Where did you say you live?"

"I have a flat on Rue Texas."

"Yes, yes. Far from the fighting. You and the other *étrangers* behave as though our struggle here were nothing but an uninteresting television program. It couldn't last. You had pitched your tents on the side of a smoking volcano, and the lava has reached you."

"What does that mean?"

"It means that our army needs support staff: cooks, mechanics' assistants, supply clerks, janitors, office staff. Every loyal Parisian is already giving everything he can afford to the Cause. It is time that you, who have enjoyed Paris's splendor in comfort and without cost, pay for your stay."

"Sergeant, no offense, but I have rent receipts in my filing cabinet. I pay for groceries. I am paying for my stay."

The Sergeant lit a cigarette and inhaled deeply. "Some bills can't be settled with money. When you fight for the freedom of the group, the group must pay for it."

"Freedom?"

"Ah." He looked out at the trustafarians, who were leaning against each other, eyes downcast, utterly dejected. "In the cause of freedom,

it may be necessary to abridge the personal liberties of a few indi-
viduals. But this isn't slave labor; each of you will be paid in good
Communard Francs, at the going rate. It won't hurt these spoiled
children to do some honest work."

I decided that if the chance ever came, I'd kill Sergeant François
Abalain.

I swallowed my anger. "My cousin, a young girl named Sissy, she
was taken last night. She was just passing through, and asked me to
take her out to the club. My aunt must be crazy with worry."

The Sergeant pulled his clipboard out of his coat pocket and
snapped it open. He scritched on it. "What is her last name?"

"Black. S-I-S-S-Y B-L-A-C-K."

He scritched more and scowled at the display. He scritched again.
"M'ser Rosen, I'm very sorry, but there is no record of any Sissy Black
here. Could she have given us a false name?"

I thought about it. I hadn't seen Sissy for ten years before she
e-mailed me that she was coming to Paree. She'd always struck me
as a very straight, sheltered kid, though I'd been forced to revise my
opinion of her upwards after she gutted out that long bus-ride. Still, I
couldn't imagine her having the cunning to make up a name on the
spot. "I don't think so. What does that mean?"

"Probably a clerical error. You see, we're all so overworked; that
is why you are here, really. I'll speak with Sergeant Dumont. She
handled women's intake. I'm sure everything is fine."

∿

Our "training" began the next morning. Like high-school gym class
with heavily armed teachers—running, squats, jumping jacks. Even
a rope climb. Getting us in shape was the furthest thing from their
minds—this was all about dulling what little sense of initiative we
might have left. I tried to stay focussed on Sissy, on where she might
have gone or what might have happened to her. For a few days my
speculations got darker and darker until in my mind's eye I saw her
being used as some sort of sex toy by the senior members of the
Commune. I had no reason to believe this; the Communards were
like the Victorians or the Maoists in their determination not to let

292

sex get in the way of politics. But I was running out of even remotely acceptable possibilities. And then one afternoon I realized I hadn't thought about her at all since waking. The fatigue had fried my brain and all I could think about was my next rest-break.

Once we'd been thoroughly pacified, they started taking us out on work-gangs of ten or fifteen, clearing rubble and repainting storefronts. On a particularly lucky day, I got to spend ten hours deep in rebuilt Communard Territory, laying down epoxy cobblestones.

We worked in a remote cul-de-sac, a power-armored frère blocking the only exit route, so motionless that I wondered if he was asleep. I worked alone, as was my habit—I had no urge to become war buddies with any of the precious tots I'd been conscripted with.

I'd never been this deep into the rebuilt zone before. It was horrible, a mixture of Nouveau and Deco perpetrated by someone who'd no understanding of either. The Communards had turned the narrow storefronts into 1930s movie sets, painted over their laserprinted signage in fanciful, curliqued Toulouse-Lautrec script. Cleverly concealed speakers piped out distant hot jazz with convincing Victrola hiss, clinking stemware and Gallic laughter.

We arrived just after dawn, and within a very short time, my knees were killing me. A few Parisians had trickled down the block: a baker who cranked out his awning and set baskets of baguette in the window; a few femmes des menages with sexy skirts, elaborate up-dos and catseye glasses clacked down the street; a gang of insouciant lads flicked their cigarette ends at us poor groveling conscriptees and swaggered on.

I managed to keep it together until the organ-grinder arrived. It was the monkey that did it. Or maybe it was the Edith Piaf cylinder he had in his hurdy-gurdy. On balance, it was the way the monkey danced to Piaf I started chuckling, then laughing, then roaring, so hysterical that I actually flopped over on my back and writhed on the cobblestones I'd laid down.

The Parisians tried to ignore me, but I was making quite a spectacle of myself. Eventually, they all slunk away, looking embarrassed and resentful. I stared at the gray sky and held my belly and snorted as they departed, and then a patch of cobblestones beside me exploded, showering me with resinous shrapnel, bruising my ribs and my arm. The power-armor at the street's entrance lowered his PowerFist pistol and broadcasted a simple order: "Work."

It seemed less funny after that. Edith may have regretted nothing, but I started setting new records for self-pity.

I'm pretty sure I lost track of the time while we were trapped in that old office block. Maybe I was concussed—the frères weren't shy about slapping us around. I doubt it, though. More likely I just stopped thinking as a way to get through the days.

Until the evening they started dividing us into groups.

The frères said nothing as they culled people from the bloc in the mess-hall. The smaller trustafarians had been clustered into two groups; no heavy labor for them, was my guess.

Unlike the scene when we were brought in, there was almost no noise. There was no sign of Sissy, but with our heads shaved I'm not sure I'd have recognized her.

I had just identified one group as being visually different when a pointing finger directed me into it, giving me opportunity to study its members close-up.

We were a sullen-faced bunch, and I had this sudden, chilling feeling that wasn't helped in the slightest by the frère who grinned at us as he nudged us out the door of the mess-hall. He's like a herdsman, I thought, and looking again at the faces of the trustafarians around me, I guessed that we were the group of troublemakers. We were being culled.

Day 9: Full Metal Baguette

The next morning I began to serve the Paris Commune in earnest. Our group had been taken out of the barracks and driven in the back of an old panel van to one of the outer arrondissements. The gunfire sounded a lot louder in the street than I was used to, though, and I felt a caffeine-jag of fear when we were led into a dark, abandoned shop and taken to a bivouac in the cellar. We were given new clothes: Bangladeshi belts, the webbing of a weird fibre-plastic combo; and new t-shirts, the cotton still weirdly stiff, to wear under our good Communard uniform blouses.

In the anemic sunshine of an April morning they took us outside to put us to death.

Oh, that's not what they told us. "You are runners," a frère said as we stood in the street. He wore the badges of a lieutenant—though he bore just a single earring—and was using a loud-hailer to be heard above the gunfire that snapped like angry dogs at the buildings nearby. "We are still in the process of clearing the Blancs from this arrondissement," he continued. "It is a building-by-building job, and our ammunition consumption is high. We can't spare fighters to carry rounds to our positions, so that's what you will do. Follow me, m'sers."

He took a step toward the corner. I started moving after him. I couldn't see any point in sticking around to be shot by one of the sour-faced guards.

At the end of the next block, a group of frères crouched behind a wrecked Citroën. Gunfire echoed from somewhere behind the building across the street from them. Our lieutenant reached the group behind the wreckage, and exchanged words.

"Here," the corporal said, throwing a hemp bag at me. I caught it, and had to stifle some very military language—the thing weighed a ton. It clattered like cheap toys, which made sense when I looked inside and saw that the bag was filled with plastic magazines.

"Not him," our lieutenant said. He pointed to the last of the stragglers approaching the Citroën. "My friend, it's time to do your part." He gestured at me; I shrugged and tossed the bag to the laggard, a scrawny trustafarian whose cheeks still bore the remnants of semi-permanent tattoos. He dropped the bag, and didn't bother to restrain his opinion of its weight. "Pick it up," our lieutenant said. "Your life may depend on how well you carry that.

"We have a fire-team in that building across the street. You will take this bag to them, and ask them if they've heard anything from the teams further up the block. The damned Blancs are jamming our communications again." I looked along the line our lieutenant's finger had traced. It didn't seem that far to me. A couple of weeks ago, I wouldn't have thought twice about strolling across the street, even in the face of Parisian traffic.

The kid picked his way through the rubble to the edge of the furthest building on our side of the street. He peered across, reminding me of an old man I used to see on the Rue Texas from time to time, who took forever to work up the courage to brave the traffic on my narrow street. Dust had made the kid's face the same gray as the old man's. I guess I should have felt sick myself, but I don't remember feeling anything.

I saw movement across and up the street—that would be the fireteam, calling its runner forward. The kid looked back at us, and I was impressed at how widely his eyes were open, and how white they looked. Our lieutenant casually waved the kid forward—though the gun in the lieutenant's hand lent a lot of weight to the gesture. The kid began to run.

Then he wasn't running anymore, and a dark red pool was spreading over the pavé from under his crumpled body. I hadn't heard a shot, and the kid hadn't made a sound, other than the dusty scuffling sound his body'd made when it hit the stones. Our lieutenant didn't seem that surprised, though. "Did you get it?" he asked the corporal. "Quickly!" The corporal nodded, simultaneously waving forward one of his companions, who gave him something too small for me to see, and which the corporal plugged into a slot in a hardcover notebook. The new frère gave a thumbs-up, and picked up a wicked-looking, bloated rifle. Then he stepped out into the street, raised the gun, fired, and stepped back into the shelter offered by the pockmarked wall. Somewhere out of my line of vision, a building exploded.

It sounded like he'd blown up half the city. It was like being inside a thunderstorm, and I instinctively put my hands over my ears in a too-late attempt to protect them. The incredible noise was still rumbling when our lieutenant picked up another crudely woven bag, handed it to me and said, "Go."

I'd been numb up to that point, just watching what was happening without really seeing it. When my hand closed on the bag's handle and I felt the hemp fibers scratching my palm, it was as if I'd suddenly come to the surface of a warm lake and broken into clear, freezing air. That was the moment I realized that Sissy was dead. That we were all dead. No point in kidding myself; they'd probably killed her within a day of raiding the Dialtone. There were all sorts of ways it could have happened. None of them mattered to me. "Fuck the lot of you," I said quietly, and walked into the street.

I didn't run. What was the point? I walked as though I were just on my way to the corner to buy lunch. If I could have, I'd have whistled a jaunty tune, something from Maurice Chevalier or Boy George. My mouth was too dry to make a properly jaunty sound.

I passed the trustafarian, lying dusty and broken on the cobbles. I made a point of looking at the spot from which the killing shot must have come, and was surprised to see that the building at the end of the block was mostly still there. That huge explosion, whose final basso still echoed, had come from the destruction of just one room. The chambre and its window—and, presumably, the Blanc sniper hiding there—had been plucked from the building's structure like a bad tooth. And now I was taking my little walk so that our lieutenant could see whether any more snipers waited. Now I realize that this is what it means to fight building to building, room to room. At the time, I thought nothing. Felt nothing. Just walked.

No shot came. No expanding round ripped open my back and spread my lungs out like wings behind me.

I reached the building that was my goal, and discovered that the fire team was already moving through it, into its courtyard and beyond to the next block. A solitary, grimy frère waited for me. Grabbing the bag, he spat at my feet and hustled to join his comrades. I guess he didn't appreciate my sangfroid.

By the time our lieutenant and the others had caught up to me, I'd had a chance to do some thinking. I stripped off the stiff, new T-shirt and web belt and buried them in some rubble. I didn't know what they represented, but I was pretty damned sure they had something to do with the way our lieutenant had been able to pinpoint the location of the sniper who'd killed Scrawny. The frères might kill me, but I was going to see that they didn't benefit in any way from it.

We were hustled through the ruined building in the wake of the fire team. Another body lying in the next street gave mute evidence to the existence of another Blanc sniper somewhere. Our lieutenant pointed to the ammo bag beside the body—which I now saw was that of the grimy frère I'd forced to play catch-up—and said to me, "No sense in letting that go to waste. Pick it up as you go."

I smiled broadly. "Glad to," I said. "You might as well keep your computer locked up, though." I spread my hands and shrugged. "No belt. No T-shirt. No service." I'm pretty sure I giggled; the whole scene had the sureality of a night in a trustafarian club.

Before our lieutenant could say or do anything, though, a frère wearing a headset stepped between us. "Lieutenant," he said, "M'ser le sergeant, Abalain wants to speak to you."

Just like that, our lieutenant's face had the same pallor as the dead trustafarian's. I was impressed; I hadn't thought an officer could be that scared of a noncom, even one as reptilian as Abalain. Our lieutenant took the headset and put it on. He closed his eyes as he listened.

~

"It was the shirt," Abalain said. We were sitting in his office, in a rebuilt nineteenth-century apartment building. Through the window I could see the office block that had been my barracks through the first few weeks of my nightmare. "They're made of a special cloth threaded with sensors. Developed to treat battlefield casualties; the sensors record the direction and velocity of anything that hits the cloth. We adapted it by stitching a small transmitter into the collar band. It's a very handy way of fixing a location on snipers, the more so since the Blancs and Penistes don't know that we can do this." He spread his hands and smiled. "Of course, it was a mistake that you were assigned to this duty."

I sipped from the Tigger glass Abalain had given to me. The wine was a good one—rich and full, tannins almost gone but still tasting a bit of blackberry. I guessed it had been in someone's cellar for a good few years before being called on to do its bit for the cause. Forcing myself to think about the wine was a deliberate attempt to keep my emotions in check. It had been nearly twenty-four hours since I'd been pulled from death-duty, and I think I'd only stopped shaking just before being brought to Abalain's office. I have a vague memory of my fear and rage bursting from me as I was being led away from the carnage, of kicking the death-duty lieutenant in the balls. Of course, that could just be wishful thinking.

For some reason, it occurred to me as I sipped that it had been weeks since I'd had a cigarette. Not only did the wine taste better, I seemed to have been too busy or too frightened to go through withdrawal. "Does this mean that I'm free to go?"

Abalain laughed, the sound of a padlock rattling against a graveyard gate. "I admire your sense of humor, m'ser," he said. "Know that if I could, I'd send you back to your place in the Rue Bonaparte. My report on our little chat about your work has been read with interest by important people. Accordingly, I've been ordered to give you a new opportunity to serve the cause."

The next day I reported to the office next-door to Abalain's. It wasn't furnished nearly as nicely, but it wasn't a cellar and there was nobody shooting at me, so I decided I was better off. I never saw either the lieutenant or any of my fellow-targets again. I confess I didn't really worry about them, either.

Abalain had told me to meet him in order to learn about my new assignment. I was pretty sure I already knew what it was, and while waiting for him to show I decided to investigate. I couldn't help myself; when presented with a mass of data I have to know what it is, and the battered metal desk that dominated the room was a pictorial definition of "mass of data." There were three distinct piles on top of the desk; the talus slopes of their near-collapse pretty much covered the entire surface. Two of the piles were paper, the third was of various storage media: magneto-optical disks, a couple of ancient Zips and even a holocube or two.

The paper pile nearest to me consisted of various official garbage: press releases, wire story print-outs. The ones I looked at were all from either the UN or one of the three main Blanc organizations. The other pile was a series of virtually indecipherable French-language documents that I was eventually able to identify as field reports from libertine officers and operatives.

"You can make some sense of that, yes?" Abalain stood in the doorway.

I looked him in the eye for a second, then returned to the reports. "What kind of sense do you want me to make?"

"You will do what you described to me when you were first—ah—

recruited. I have need of information which I suspect is buried within these reports and press releases. You will use your skills to draw that information forth." He smiled at me with what he no doubt thought was encouragement. Maybe he'd been a management consultant before deciding that the revolution offered better opportunities to fuck with people. "You will work here, and send the information to me as you assemble it. You will use the clipboard and wearable that are in the upper-right-hand drawer; they connect to a fibreoptic pipe linked directly to a secure folder on my desktop. You will, regrettably, have no outside access. But don't worry about that; I'll see that you get all of the information you need to do your work."

More than enough information, I told myself.

Day 30: The Revolution Will Not Be Franchised

"I gotta admit, I just don't understand this revolution."

"What's not to understand?" Abalain offered me a Marlie; I was somewhat surprised at the gesture, and even more surprised to find myself shaking my head. "We're not really revolutionaries, you know. We're trying to restore the glories of French civilization; in a way, that makes us conservatives."

I believe the accepted term is 'reactionaries,' I thought. "Which no doubt explains why so many of your slogans seem to have been drawn from fast-food advertising," I said, waving a flimsy at him. "'La France: Have It Your Way'?"

"The fast-food philosophy is inherently French," Abalain said. "It's a peasant philosophy, not some tarted-up bourgeois haute-cuisine thing. It's like the epoxy cobbles you and your 'Old Paree Hands' are so dismissive about. They're perfectly in keeping with the scientific rationalism of the original revolution." He spoke in crisp, rapid French. He'd caught me listening too intently to one of his phone conversations the week before and confronted me with a barrage of French. When my facial expression made it clear that I understood every word, he'd nodded smartly and went back to his conversation, as though he'd suspected it all along.

"Unless they're laid down by Disney," I said.

"Then it's cultural imperialism," Abalain said. I'd have liked him

300

just a little if he'd smiled, or showed any sign of having a sense of humor. But he was deadly serious, and I hated him even more for it.

"So what's your part in all this?" I asked. "You a spook?"

"I'm nothing of the sort, M'ser Rosen. And if I was, I certainly wouldn't tell you." He blew a jet of smoke past my left ear; I smelled burning garbage. "I'm just a servant of the Commune," he said. "I do what I can to bring France back into the sunlight of scientific rationalism. Please know that we are all grateful for the assistance you have been providing."

And that you've been taking credit for, I thought. "I could do more," I said, "if I had access to more information." What I'd been given so far wouldn't have been enough to help a fundamentalist preacher track down sin. I had to be able to make a big score in order for my plan to work.

"I've been impressed with what you've given me to date," Abalain said. *Jesus*, I thought. *If they're impressed by that merde, this will be easier than I thought.* "Granted it hasn't had much direct tactical value. But already we've been able to wrong-foot the Penistes at least twice in the media. We've taken the lead in the propaganda campaign; in the long run that may be as important as anything our fighters do."

"At least let me see the uncensored field reports." I pulled a handful of crumpled flimsies from a pants pocket. Two-thirds of the text had been blacked or blanked. "I should be the judge of whether or not information is usable."

"I'll see what I can do," he said.

～

The next morning an unhappy-looking frère kicked a plastic box into my office. The papers, flimsies, and chips were chaos illustrated, but I didn't care. I always get a rush from a fresh source of data, and the rush was greater this time because the stakes were so much higher.

One of the first things I learned when I finally got down to analysis was that my old ami Commandant Ledoit was dead. The first reference was in a press release from a couple of weeks ago; he'd been killed, it was claimed, by the Blancs. But it didn't take much sleuthing to suss out that he had in fact been dusted by the Commune. I found a reference to a series of denunciations by Abalain's juniors, and while the accusations weren't detailed the result was still clear enough. If I hadn't already had my suspicions raised, that would have set my spideysense tingling.

As it was, I was more grimly satisfied than surprised. Every revolution eventually eats its young, someone once said. For the Paris Commune, the buffet had apparently begun. That was fine for me; in fact, my plan depended on it.

I worked hard over the next week. After what I'd been through, there was a deep, almost rich pleasure in being able to throw myself into investigation. Little by little I spun my web—making sure that I also took the time to generate some truly killer conclusions about what the Blancs and Penistes were up to. It was actually pretty easy. Compared with most corporations, governments are as complex as nap-time at a daycare. And neither the Blancs nor the Penistes—nor the Commune, come to that—was even a government by any normal conception of that word. So it was only a few days after I started when Abalain brought me a bottle of really good Remy by way of congratulating me on my utter fabness. I'm more of a bourbon than a cognac type, but I accepted the bottle anyway. It was the least Abalain could do for me; I intended to make sure of that.

After he gave me the bottle, I didn't see the sergeant for two weeks. I took advantage of the break to wander around the building, and eventually even the neighborhood. It hadn't taken long for word to get out that Abalain had himself a pet spook, and nobody really paid any attention to the grubby guy in the soiled white suit. That dusted whatever doubts I may have had about Abalain's juice within the Commune; the man wore his sergeant's stripes like sheep's clothing.

Discovering the truth about Sissy's fate did not create my resolve to kill Abalain; it only deepened it. I'd hardly spared her a thought since the fresh lieutenant used me for a decoy, but in one raft of papers, I turned up an encoded list of inductees from the Dialtone. It was nicely divided by sex and nationality, though the names themselves were encrypted. Only one female Canadian appeared on the list. I realized then that it had been weeks since I'd thought of Sissy, and I felt myself poised atop a wall of anguish so high that I couldn't bear to look down. Instead, I went back to work, and turned up an encrypted list of bunk assignments—it was nearly identical to the list of inductees, but a number of the female names were missing, including the lone Canadian one.

Putting two and two together is what I do. I couldn't stop myself, then. Sissy and any number young, carefree trustafarians had been conscripted for a very different kind of service to the Commune—the kind of service that required a boudoir rather than a bunk.

Up until then, I'd been trying to formulate a plan that would put paid to Abalain while I walked away scot-free. When I saw the second list, I felt a return of the unreal, uncaring fatalism I'd felt when I walked out into the street lugging the bag of ammunition. Abalain would die, and I would die, too.

The freedom to move around that Abalain's patronage afforded also gave me all the opportunity I needed to type in some new reports from a variety of unsecured terminals and wireless keypads, using the IDs I'd picked up from the uncensored reports Abalain had given me. There was nothing flamboyant or, God forbid, clumsy about these reports. I even managed to duplicate the horrible grammar some of the frère field agents had used. And most of the information I put into them could easily be verified, since it was just cribbed from other sources or from my own validated speculation on what the other side was doing. That's how you do it, you see: you put in so much truth that the few bits of fabulation go more or less unnoticed.

More or less, that is, until somebody decides that all those trees must mean something and makes a point of looking at the forest. I was pretty sure that, like all revolutions, this one had its share of tree-counters.

I have to admit, though, that I was pretty nervous by the end of the second week. You like to think that you know your job, that the outcome of something you start is predictable within the limits of your experience. But every job carries with it the fear of complete catastrophe, and if this job went down in flames . . . It didn't bear thinking of.

So I was more than a little shocked when Abalain burst into my office late one afternoon, looking as though he'd just learned that capitalism really was the most effective economic philosophy.

"We have to go, you and I," Abalain said.

"Go where?" I asked. I hadn't expected to see him again; had, in fact, expected to read his obituary in the next batch of Commune press releases.

"I'll explain later. But take your notepad with you." He cut the pad free from its lock and cable, and handed it to me. "We're going to need this to get through the lines."

"Through the lines?"

"Don't be dense, and just do as I say." Abalain seemed to be reverting to the bourgeois martinet I'd always suspected him of being. "I have some things to do. Meet me in the lobby in five minutes. Be there, Rosen, or I'll have you shot."

Normalment, I'm not so slow on the uptake. I guess that only the fact that I was so sure I'd done for Abalain had blinded me to what had really happened: the bastard had found out that he was going to be denounced, and had decided to take his leave of his frères before they removed his head from his shoulders, or however it was that they dispatched those who no longer fit with the Commune's vision of the past-into-future.

I was only thrown off my game for a moment, though. My business forces you to think on your feet, and I was on mine in a second. I slipped into Abalain's office, and started filling my pockets with whatever was lying about. I made sure that I grabbed his wearable; the computer was locked, of course, but I was rapidly formulating a plan for dealing with that.

My suit may have looked a little bit rumpled when I got to the lobby, but the frères were a pretty sartorially challenged bunch at the best of times, so I wasn't surprised that nobody noticed my bulging pockets.

"What's happened?" I asked Abalain as soon as we were outside and walking on the poly-resin cobbles. He'd headed us north, presumably toward the toney arrondissements of the north-east where the Blancs still held sway.

"A friend let slip that I was going to be denounced before the Central Committee," he said. "There's no justification for such a thing, of course."

"Of course," I said.

"But a man in a position such as mine inevitably seems to inspire jealousy, and justified or not I'm pretty sure things wouldn't go well for me if I let myself be called. So with regret I have to end my service to the revolution and the Commune. It's their misfortune."

"And me?" I stuffed my hands in my pockets in case Abalain got too curious about their shape.

"But I thought you were eager to return to your home." Abalain made a sympathetic little moue with his mouth, and it was all I could do to keep from kicking him in the balls. "You, M'ser Rosen, are my ticket through the lines, of course."

"Of course."

As usual, Abalain was ahead of the curve on the whole denunciation thing. His casual wave was enough to get us through the various check-points and posts we encountered as we walked through the Communard zone; nobody'd been told yet that he was now an enemy of the revolution. I began to regret not spreading my disinformation a little more widely.

"Do you want to tell me how you plan to do this?" I asked him as we walked away from yet another group of fawning, too-serious-for-words frères. "I feel like someone being told to invest without seeing the prospectus."

"Capitalist humor. How droll," he said. "It's quite simple, really. We're headed toward a checkpoint in a comparatively stable part of the front. I'll talk us through our—the Commune's—lines. We're doing some field intelligence work, you and I. Once we're through our lines, we duck out of sight, approach the Blanc lines from a different angle, and then you provide me with my entrée to the Blanc sector. Simple, no?"

"And how do I play my part in this clever plan?"

"Patience, my old. Patience. I'll explain when you need to know, and not before." I shrugged. It wasn't a question of whether Abalain intended to dust me, but when and how. I felt the weight of his wearable around my waist and hoped he'd at least wait until we reached the Blanc lines so that I could surprise him before he surprised me.

The checkpoint showed all the signs of a front that hadn't changed in weeks, possibly months. The smart-wire had accumulated a patina of grime and pigeon-shit you just didn't see on the more active parts of the city. Dogs danced around the feet of the listlessly patrolling frères; there was no power armor in sight. Someone had liberated a video lottery terminal from somewhere and set it up in the observation post Abalain dragged me into; the vlt's reader slot was stuffed with an override card that made play free but also eliminated any payout, and as Abalain drawled his lies to the lieutenant I joined a group of bored frères watching the symbols flash in pointless sequence across the terminal's screen. You'd never know, looking at the crap that had accreted around this corner, that there were parts of Paree where bits were being blown off bodies and buildings as the world's most pointless renovation project continued on its nasty way.

"We go now," Abalain said from behind me. "Do you think that you can tear yourself away from this excitement?" I bit back my reply, and turned to follow. He hadn't even waited for me, and I had to jog for a moment to catch up with him. We ducked into a building, descended to the basement and spent a freaky few seconds in a dark, humid tunnel that brought back nightmares of my brief sojourn as a hot-wired guinea pig, before emerging into the wreckage of an old Metro station. In the distance, I thought I saw a flash of light—reflection from a sniper's scope?

I stopped, imagining the weight of the sniper's gaze on my chest, just below my sternum, and had a sudden vision of Sissy standing just as I was now. Who knew how many trustafarians had been sacrificed to flushing out the Blancs, and then had their bunks reassigned. I felt a strange mixture of sorrow and relief—it had been quick then, for her; not the drawn-out nightmare of serial rape that had been slithering through my subconscious.

Abalain showed no hesitation; I'll give him that much. He grabbed my arm and pulled me out into the street. This close to freedom I found myself a lot less cold-blooded about being shot than I had been a couple of weeks before. Then we were safely across the road, and inside an abandoned block of flats sheltered from both Communard and Blanc eyes. We were able to traverse a couple of hundred meters of picturesque ruins without being exposed to any more than electronic surveillance. I figured we'd be nearly on top of a Blanc outpost before the frères finally copped to what Abalain was doing.

"So what are you going to do once you're out of Tomorrowland and back in the real world?" I asked him when he stopped us in what seemed to have once been a pretty nice courtyard. "How does a scientific revolutionary make his way in a bourgeois schematic?"

"I'll pretend that was a serious question and not just another pathetic attempt at snideness," he said. "Never try to out-sneer the French, m'ser. We're the masters." *You be expansive, you little shit*, I thought. *Expand away; it'll be more fun to watch you collapse.* "The fact is, M'ser Rosen, I'm an extremely adaptable man. I won't have any trouble fitting into my new life. I'll probably have to move from Paris, and that will be a shame. But even if Bucharest or Buenos Aires isn't the City of Light, I can be comfortable."

He produced a small pistol and pointed it at me. "After all, competitive intelligence work can be done anywhere."

If he was expecting me to look shocked, I disappointed him. I hope I did, anyway. Frankly, I'd expected something a bit more clever. I was grateful, though, that an identity switch was the best he could come up with. After looking at me expectantly for a moment, he scowled and waved the pistol. "Let's go, Sergeant Abalain," he said.

The Blancs had seen us, of course, and a well-armed reception party was waiting when we emerged from the ruins and into the street across which their checkpoint sat. Abalain pushed me forward, then raised his hands above his head. A Blanc in stained coveralls gestured for me to do the same.

"I hope you guys can help me," Abalain said when we reached the Blancs. His English was almost completely unaccented, and I gave him points for that. A resourceful fellow, our sergeant. "I've been a prisoner of those bastards for months," he continued. "This is one of them. His name's Abalain. He's my gift to you if you'll call my embassy and get me out of here."

That set everyone to babbling. I smiled. "Thanks," I said to Abalain. "I always wanted to be famous." He didn't break character, not that I'd expected him to.

An officer showed up. His uniform was tailored, clean and crisply pressed. He wore aviator sunglasses and carried a swagger-stick. *No wonder you guys can't retake the city*, I thought. "So this is the infamous Sergeant Abalain," he said to me.

"'Fraid not," I told him. "But that is." I nodded at Abalain.

His face spasmed in pretty convincing outrage. "He lies!" he shouted. "He kidnapped me and killed my friends! You can't let him get away with this!"

"Oh, come on," I said. I turned to the officer. "Isn't there anyone here who's seen a picture of Abalain?" I already knew the answer to that—like many of his erstwhile companions, Abalain had been pretty thorough about avoiding cameras—but I was playing a rôle now myself.

The officer smiled, obviously pleased with himself. "Perhaps the thing to do is to try the both of you. You can't both be Abalain, but on the chance that one of you is. . ."

It was time. I unbuttoned my jacket. "We can settle this easily," I said, and unbuckled Abalain's wearable. Abalain's jaw dropped along with his new persona. I paused, savoring the moment. This was no substitute for Sissy, or even for the weeks he'd ripped from my life. But it was all I was likely to get, so I wanted it to last.

I showed the wearable to the officer. "Retinal lock," I said.

"If you want to see your cousin again, m'ser, stop now."

That pissed me off. "You pathetic son of a bitch," I said. I pulled the flimsies—the list of inductees and the bunk assignments—from my pocket. I held them up in his face. "Where's the Canadian female, François? Look," I stabbed the flimsy as though it were Abalain's heart. "She was inducted—now look here," I rattled the bunk assignments. "No bunk—what happened to her, M'ser le sergeant? Sent to Montmarte? *Target practice*?" A note of hysteria crept into my voice. I swallowed, balled up the flimsies and tossed them against his chest.

"No," he said. "It wasn't like that—"

I didn't let him finish. Smacking the wearable up against my face, I thumbed the power switch. The computer farted its displeasure. "How sad," I said. "Sergeant Abalain's computer doesn't like the look in my eye." I turned it toward Abalain, who backed away. "Gentlemen?" I said to the Blancs. Two of them grabbed Abalain by the shoulders.

He tried to twist his head away, but the wearable was more flexible than his neck was. A second later, the computer chirped and lit up all christmas.

I dropped the wearable to the ground and emptied my pockets onto it. "You should be able to have some fun with all of this," I said. Abalain babbled something I didn't hear. The officer slapped him in the face—whether in response or just on general principle, I didn't care. Then they were all hitting him.

I used the last of my steri-wipes to get his blood off my hands.

Day 63: It'll All End in Tears

"France thanks you for the service you have rendered her, monsieur." I figured the Blanc general was speaking more for the benefit of the news weasels on the other side of the mirrorwall than he was for me, but I nodded my head with what I hoped looked like sagacity. "Bringing the beast Abalain to justice will show the world the true face that lies behind the mask of the Commune de Paris."

I tried to be blasé about it. But looking at this guy, I couldn't help but wonder about the arithmetic of Paree: how in the world did you add up the folks on my street, the ones I played baseball with, and the ones who sold me bread and sausage and wine—and end up with assholes like Abalain or this prat? What variable in the goddamn equation made people stop thinking and let their emotions do all the heavy lifting?

I'd hoped to feel cleansed at having done for Abalain, but I didn't.

"Good for you," I said, getting to my feet. "I'd love to stay and watch, but I have to go home now. I'm going to take a forty-eight-hour shower, and then I'm going to sleep for a week."

"I believe the people from your embassy want to talk to you, monsieur Rosen," the general said warily.

"Have them call my service," I said. That's me: Mister How to Make Friends and Influence People.

"The photographers say they're not finished yet."

That's just great, I thought. Is there anybody in this city who isn't working an angle?

Sissy hadn't been working anything except maybe her hormones.

I'd been able to store her carefully in the back of my mind while working up my escape plan. But she was clamoring to get out of my head now. Being away from the Commune didn't make me any more free than if I'd still been Abalain's pet ferret: I still had to face up to the fact that she was gone. How was I going to explain this to my aunt?

The door behind me slammed open.

"Lee!"

I turned around so fast I fell over. That's my story, anyway, and I'm sticking to it. Then she was down on the carpet with me and hugging me and crying and I guess I got kind of sloppy too. But I swear the first words out of my mouth were: "Where the fuck have you been?"

She slapped me, lightly. "I worried about you too."

"Jesus," I said, sitting up. "I was convinced you were—" I couldn't say it, not now. It seemed it could still happen; I might be imagining this. "What happened to you? How did you get away?"

"It was Eddie," she said.

"Not true, Lee." Eddie flowed into the room, graceful in spite of his bulk. "She's the one who did it. I just got her back across the lines."

"Will you two stop negotiating credits and just tell me what happened?"

"When they separated us when the bus stopped I was so scared," Sissy said. "Everyone was scared. But then I thought about what you'd said. You said not to worry. And you always looked after me, Lee." She smiled, and even though her eyes looked dead with fatigue I still felt better for seeing that. "I figured you knew what you were talking about. So I didn't worry. Instead, I tried to guess what you'd do, and I decided that you'd watch and wait for a chance to do something."

I looked at Sissy more closely. It wasn't just fatigue I was seeing in her eyes. There was something else, something sort of calm and understanding. This wasn't the girl I'd lost back at the Dialtone. Of course, being kidnapped can do that to a person.

"So I'm watching what happens, and what happens is that everybody's so scared that they all just stand there gibbering and crying all over one another," she said. "They must have been doing that all along, but I never noticed it. Until I sat back and made myself look.

We were all just crying like babies. And the guards must have noticed too, because when I looked I saw that they weren't really paying any attention to us. They were all watching the guys being rounded up." We were the ones making the fuss, I remembered. Some of us, anyway. Some of us were still trying to think of a way of finessing ourselves out of that jam.

"So it was really pretty simple." Sissy smiled artlessly, and for a moment she was my kid cousin again. "I just kind of shuffled my feet and moved back without trying to move too much. And when I was at the back of the crowd I just sort of slipped out of it. It was dark and nobody noticed me. But you know, I don't think they were all that smart, Lee. We just let ourselves think they were 'cause we were all so scared. As soon as I started trying to think like you do, it was easy to get away." She hugged me fiercely. "I saw you trying to distract their attention from me, Lee." Now she was crying again. "What you did for me—I couldn't have done that for you." She dug her face into my shoulder and sobbed, and I felt like the stupidest idiot outside of a corporate boardroom. I had out-clevered myself into eight weeks or more of slavery, and she was smart enough to just walk away—and she was giving me the credit?

"And that's when Eddie saved me."

"I followed the bus," Eddie said with a shrug. "Probably not the smartest thing in the world, but hey. I should have seen it coming, and I didn't. I felt responsible, you know?" I knew. "Soon as I saw you all being off-loaded and sorted I figured I was screwed, and I was making my way back to the lines when I come across Sissy here. And damned if she didn't want to take me back and try to spring you. Took me ten minutes to persuade her we'd only get ourselves killed."

"You can always trust Fat Eddie," I said. "He knows three ways around every angle there is. Listening to him definitely saved your life." I decided then that I was never going to tell Sissy the full story of my service to the Commune. Even if it seemed that the Sissy who was smiling at me now wasn't the same kid who'd wanted to see the sights back in the great Before.

"She could have gone home, you know," Fat Eddie said. "Her mom sure as hell wanted her to. Instead, we've spent the last eight weeks nagging the shit out of anybody who'd listen, trying to find you. And now we have."

"And now I want a shower," I said. "I want some clean clothes."

"I want to go back to the Dialtone and finish my drink," Sissy said.

I stared at her. "You're joking, right?"

"Oh, you can shower and change first, if you want." She stood up, then grabbed my hands and pulled me to my feet. "Come on, Lee. It's a glorious time to be in Paree."

Paree—where snipers lurked in the high windows and unwashed thugs stared blindly at castrated video lottery terminals. Paree, where, on the pavé before a rusting Citroën, I had decided to die. The fatal anguish surged through me—

—and *out*. I was a dead man, dead many times over in the past eight weeks, and yet, miraculously, *alive*. Alive, in Gay Paree, where famèd Dialtone yet stood, where the bartender would mix me a Manhattan and my cousin Sissy would dance while I watched approvingly from a side table, chewing on my work-problems and swapping ironic glances with Fat Eddie.

I extended an arm and Sissy took it at the elbow. Fat Eddie shouldered us a path through the crowd, over the epoxy cobblestones, and down the boulevard toward the Dialtone.

A Good Start

Barry Graham

I don't feel bad about it. I wish I did. I know I should. But I don't, though I kind of feel bad about not feeling bad. Like when one of your relatives dies and you don't feel bad because they're dead, you feel bad because you don't really care that they're dead. That's kind of how I feel.

I don't even feel all that happy, though I thought I would. I just kind of feel like it was right, like he got what he deserved. Maybe not exactly right, but fair. It feels like it was fair.

And I'm looking forward to more.

～

Greaves thought he was God's Gift. That was as much the fault of the girls at the bank as it was his fault. They thought his bullshit was funny. I couldn't believe them. I'm not a feminist or anything, but I couldn't believe women would find it funny, a jerk like that doing things to women they worked with.

I'm a temp typist. My agency said I'd be needed at the bank for six weeks, but it turned into four months. That was fine by me. I liked it there. A lot of the time there was hardly any work to do and I could just read or draw pictures on the computer. Funny, considering that this was the bank's head office and I was doing the typing for four different managers. And you should see what they were getting paid. The more important your job is, the more money you get and the less work you have to do.

Greaves didn't work any harder than the other managers, so he didn't give me any more work than they did. But he was a total asshole. He was just a horrible, arrogant asshole. Sometimes if you asked him a question he'd throw his head back and give this long, nasty laugh like you were dirt and there was something funny about you. And he wouldn't answer the question.

Once I asked him what time he needed some memos typed by, and he did that—*haw-haw-HAW*—and put his dirty hand on my shoulder and then just walked away.

I was angry at him doing that, him thinking he could do that to me because I was only twenty and female and only a temp. So, next time he walked past my desk, I had another question for him.

"Mr Greaves, what are you going to use for a face when Quasimodo wants that one back?"

All the other typists and even my supervisor laughed, but this time Greaves didn't. I thought he'd do something about it, maybe complain to my agency and ask for another temp to replace me. He didn't. But I soon realized he wasn't letting it go.

About a week after I said that to him, I sent a memo to all four managers, telling them I was taking Friday afternoon off, so if they had any typing for me to do they'd better give it to me first thing on Friday morning, and if they had anything really big they should give it to me the day before.

On the Thursday, Greaves walked up to my desk, the memo in his hand. "Hey, Ruth. I've got something big. Do you want it now?"

"Okay," I said. "When do you need it done?"

"Oh, I don't have any *typing* for you to do. I just said I've got something *big*. That's what you asked in your memo."

I stood up and made to say something or do something, but then the other girls—even Linda, my supervisor—started laughing. Laughing at that. Christ.

"Grow up," I muttered, and sat down again.

"It's probably *too* big for you," Greaves said. "You probably couldn't handle it." Then he walked away and went into his office as the girls all started laughing again.

"I want something done about him," I told Linda.

"Come on. He was only joking. He's not doing you any harm."

I wrote a memo to Greaves, telling him that if he ever spoke to me that way again, I'd report him for sexual harassment. He didn't reply. I thought that might be it, that he might get me fired, but he never said anything. I could have just left. That's why I like being a temp—if you don't like a place you can just leave and get your agency to put you somewhere else. But it was a couple weeks before Christmas and things are always slow around then. If I left, I might not be able to get anything else until after New Year. Besides, it was the easiest job I'd had, and I wasn't going to let one buttfuck manager drive me out.

He did it, though.

The bank had a no-smoking policy. You couldn't smoke anywhere in the building. That was fair enough; there was hardly anybody who smoked. But I smoke like a crematorium. So I used to grind my teeth or chew gum until my lunch break and my morning and afternoon breaks, then go outside and get enough nicotine inside me to keep me going.

One morning I got a memo from Greaves telling me not to leave the building during my short breaks. I went into his office and asked him what he was playing at.

"None of the other typists go outside during their breaks. Why should you?"

"None of the other typists smoke. I do."

"We have a no-smoking policy."

"I know. That's why I go outside."

He smiled at me. "Not anymore. You can conduct yourself like everybody else. You can leave during your lunch break. During your other breaks, you stay in the building."

"You can't tell me what to do on my break. My break is mine. I'm not at work then."

"No, but you're being paid. You're still paid for your time. So I want you to remain in the building in case you're needed."

I couldn't handle that. I used the thought of the breaks to keep me going through the mornings and afternoons of cold turkey. Without it, I'd start sniffing white-out.

I tried to fight Greaves, but nobody else was interested—not the other managers, not my supervisor, not the other typists. I was just an obnoxious little temp with a big mouth and no sense of humor.

So I left. I got lucky and my agency found me another job, starting the next day. But I didn't feel any better. I felt as if anybody with plenty of money and no dress sense could do what they liked to me and I couldn't do anything except give in and walk out.

The day I walked out of the bank, I went to Tony's house and told him what had happened. He went nuts. Then he calmed down and said, "What does this Greaves look like?"

"Why?"

"'Cause I'm gonna wait outside the bank and kick his fucking ass when he comes out."

"No, you're not." Tony's settled down now, but he used to be wild. He was in a gang for a while. I didn't want him going back to that bullshit. "I don't need you getting in trouble. With your record, you only need to slap somebody and they'd lock you up."

He laughed. "I know. I'd love to fuck him up, though. Prick."

"So would I. But I don't want you doing it."

He looked at me. "Serious?"

"About what?"

"Fucking him up?"

At first I wasn't sure. Then I was. "Yeah. Why?"

"I know how to find guys who'd do it. You'd have to pay them, but they come cheap."

I waited to see if I was still sure, and I was.

"How cheap?"

$\sim$

They did it for a hundred and fifty. Seventy-five each. That wasn't in the newspaper. The rest of it was.

They got Greaves outside the bank and started kicking him. He fought back and shouted for help. One of them stuck a knife in his back and then they ran away. Greaves's lungs filled up with blood and he died just after the ambulance got him to the hospital.

The two guys got picked up by the cops a few blocks away. They'd gotten rid of the knife, but one of them had Greaves's blood on him. It was only about ten minutes after they'd done it.

Before he died, Greaves told the ambulance men that the guys had asked, "Are you Martin Greaves?" before they attacked him. So the cops want to know why. Tony says the guys don't know who he is.

Now it's Christmas Eve. Earlier tonight I was doing some last-minute shopping, getting some presents—one for Tony, one for my mom. The mall was really busy, lots of people with their kids. It said in the paper that Greaves had a wife and three kids. I wonder what he was like with them. I wonder if they knew what he was like at work.

I thought about them, but I still couldn't be sorry. I didn't think Greaves would get killed—Tony said they'd just kick the shit out of him—but I can't be sorry about him. The cops said it was "a brutal and cowardly murder," but I don't see how it was. Greaves was brutal and cowardly. He thought he could do what he liked because he was in charge, but he was only in charge at the bank. Other people are in charge in other places. But people like Greaves and the cops and the papers only think it's fair if you do things the same way as they do. And they do things the way that suits *them*. What I did to Greaves maybe wasn't right, but it was as fair as what he did to me.

I'm going to my mom's for Christmas, then Tony and I are going to his sister's party at New Year.

Tony and I have made a New Year's resolution together. I told him that every job I've ever hated would have been a good job if it wasn't for the shit I had to take from managers. Tony said, "Yeah, I know what you mean. Too bad you can't get every one of them like you got Greaves."

"Yeah," I said. Then I said, "Why can't I?"

We just looked at each other, and I started to laugh.

One Dark Berkeley Night

Tim Wohlforth

1.

Berkeley, California, 12:45–12:57 a.m., August 20, 1970: A sliver of a moon hung over lower University Avenue. Faint street lights struggled to penetrate the gloom. A slight breeze off San Francisco Bay scattered the pages of *The Berkeley Barb* on the sidewalk in front of the Paradise Motel, a by-the-hour establishment. A lone woman with dyed-red hair and wearing a red mini-skirt shivered as she walked down the street, seeking eye contact with the male drivers of the few cars that passed by. A rat stuck its head out of a drain opening, then ran toward the closed Foster's Freeze store.

Ron Bradley sped past on his Harley heading toward the Marina. He had his guitar case strapped to his back. *Like Dylan.* Well, he hoped he didn't end up in an accident like Dylan. He peered for house numbers on darkened tenements. He was pissed. The numbers were all off. He must have missed the address of the party. He was almost at San Pablo. He wondered if the hippie girl had given him the wrong house number.

He'd promised to play the guitar. That line usually worked. He was pretty good. Not good enough to earn a living at it and he had no original material of his own. Just some Dylan songs from his acoustic period and a couple of blues he'd borrowed from Dave Van Ronk. Crazy, here he was black, well half black—his mother was Jewish—and he'd learned his blues from a white man. And truth be told he preferred hard rock, Jimi Hendrix, The Who, The Doors. But you can't ride around on a motorcycle with an electric guitar plus amp strapped to your back. He had a role to play and he was having a hell of a good time playing it. Until now.

He'd had one shitty day. His induction notice came in the morning's mail. *Nothing like winning the lottery.* He had graduated from Berkeley High a year ago and had yet to find permanent work. His father said he could get him on the "B" list at the docks. Good money but no security. His father had it made as an "A" list man. Good for him. But longshore was not Ron. He wasn't his dad. Waiting around for the draft had become his excuse to party for awhile before settling down to . . . he wasn't sure what. But something. Other than working on the docks. He would leave the future to the future. The government had made him an offer he couldn't refuse. He would go over to 'Nam and be the last to die for a lost cause. *Fitting in some weird way.* It had been one fucked-up year, My Lai in March, Kent State in May.

Tonight he had planned to forget the future, score some pot, pluck his guitar, and fuck a white chick. No such luck.

Officer John Yamamoto was having trouble keeping awake as he cruised slowly up University Avenue toward the campus. He looked forward to getting back into the university area. There he felt comfortable. Here he might as well be in Watts. The streets were empty, the stores closed, apartments few. He passed Grand Central Hot Tubs, Happy Days take-out, the ratty Paradise Motel, Foster's Freeze, H&B's army surplus, a sari store.

A streetwalker with dyed-red hair, wearing a red mini-skirt, ambled down the sidewalk. She waved at a passing car. The car didn't stop. *Good.* He wasn't interested in that kind of arrest.

Tina Perez shivered. *Cold mother-fucking night.* She wanted to go home, but she couldn't. She needed one more john. And then she could score and she'd be warm, very warm. Everything would be just fine. But the johns weren't stopping.

One lonely horny bastard would stop sooner or later. She had to hold herself together, fight the cold. Who would want to fuck a skinny, shivering bitch? Then a patrol car passed. *Shit.* But he didn't stop. *Good.* Just a little longer and she would get her break. Another car passed. The fucker gave her the finger. It was that kind of fucked-up night.

Malik Robeson drove a yellow Studebaker down San Pablo heading for University Avenue. He was pissed and high on weed. He turned to his companion, Ishmael Shabazz, and said, "So what did you make of Huey's speech?"

"Bullshit."

"He dissed us," Malik responded. "Like they're all these tough motherfuckers and we're nobodies."

"You got that right. Him and Bobby and Eldridge, they're just blowing it out their asses. They don't do nothin'. But they're right, you know."

"'Bout what?"

"The pigs," Ishmael said. "The Muslims always talking about the white devils but they don't do shit about the pigs. Ever since I was a kid the cops hassled us. You remember back in the old hood? Not cuz we did anything. Cuz we're black."

Malik did remember. He and Ishmael had grown up on the same block in West Oakland. Ishmael was the one who always got in trouble. Petty theft, in and out of juvie. Malik had been the good boy, dragged to church on Sunday by his schoolteacher mom, studied hard, tried to keep out of trouble. Which meant keeping away from Ishmael. But the cops didn't see the difference between the two of them. All they saw was black. And black was trouble.

One day, when he was sixteen, Ishmael and his gang ran into a convenience store, threatened the owner, grabbed some malt, and took what was in the cash register. But the owner had pressed an alarm button. The cops came. They escaped. As it happened Malik was walking past the place, heading home after school, just as the cops arrived. They beat him. Arrested him. His mother was pissed. Didn't believe him. Something snapped inside Malik that day. A bitterness transformed him into . . . Ishmael?

No, not quite, not yet.

Malik went to Laney College at nights. Began to hang out with the Black Panther crowd, and reconnected with Ishmael. Malik was bright, but knowledge didn't seem to matter. All that counted was street smarts and there Ishmael had it over him. Ishmael, who he once had tried to help with his schoolwork, was now his teacher, his mentor.

"None of them Panther leaders have any balls," Ishmael said, "'cept maybe Huey. Not that gang of hangers-on. It's war out here in the streets. And all those dudes do is spout. This damn town would be a lot better off if them Panthers spent more time pumping buckshot into pigs than servin' breakfasts to kids."

"Right on." Malik pressed harder on the gas pedal.

John Yamamoto had found that he could keep awake if he kept thinking. But what about? *Nancy?* No, that didn't work. Only reminded him of why he didn't like the graveyard shift. He was new to the force or at least he hoped that was the reason he was stuck with it. Could it be because he was a Japanese-American, the first hired by the Berkeley Police Department? Was he being held to a special standard? Resented by both blacks and whites? The blacks thought they had it hard in Berkeley. They should try being Japanese.

He started to think about his job, his past, his future. So much had changed for him this past year, so many opportunities lay ahead for the two of them. John loved his job. He had security, a future, someday a pension—and his mission. His wife Nancy kept telling him it was only a job, but she wasn't born in an internment camp. When you're born in a barracks inside a concentration camp in your own country, you don't really have roots.

His father once had roots, had his farm in the Central Valley near Stockton where he grew prunes. Sixty acres, his mother had told him. His father refused to talk about it. Nice spread, hard work, over 105 degrees in the summer. His mother had shown him an old black and white photo of a small ranch home surrounded by eucalyptus trees, white lawn chairs, rose bushes.

That picture means nothing to me. Could've been anybody's place.

His father's roots were torn up when he was forced to move to barracks at Tule Lake. And then they stole his land. His father wouldn't talk about Tule Lake. Again, his mother had filled him in. It was called a "segregation camp" for "disloyals." Dad was one of the stubborn ones who refused to sign a loyalty oath to a government that had taken his land and denied him citizenship. The three of them lived in two small rooms in a converted unpainted army barracks with a leaky tarpaper roof, in a muddy compound surrounded by barbed wire.

At Tule Lake, Dad had worked as a warder helping to distribute food to the detainees. He discovered that the Caucasians were stealing the detainees' food. He complained and they beat him. Then a riot broke out over the incident. The military rolled in with tanks, machine guns and tear gas. All Dad had wanted was a little justice in an unjust place.

His father's heart had left him at Tule Lake. He became a quiet man who rarely spoke. He had nothing left inside for his son. John was like his mother, outgoing, friendly, not interested in fighting anybody over anything. *I just want to fit in.* Tule Lake was his father's past. All John took with him from Tule Lake was a vague memory of playing with other kids in a muddy stream that ran through the camp. A happy memory, actually.

John didn't even have uprooted roots, but he had Berkeley. He started planting his roots the day he entered Berkeley High. He excelled in all his classes. He had friends, white, black, Asian. That's where he met Nancy, a white girl from the hills. He loved all of Berkeley, the campus with the anti-war demos, People's Park, the Telegraph Avenue hippies, the middle class in the hills, the blacks in the flatlands.

He could have gone on to Cal, become a doctor or engineer, but he needed money to help his family. His parents barely survived on his father's part-time gardening and his mother's city clerk paycheck. He wanted a career that dealt with people, where he could see the practical effects of what he did. Then there was Nancy. *Why do my thoughts always return to Nancy?* He needed bucks for an apartment so they could get married. So he became a cop, a cop with a mission. And that mission wasn't busting whores or making pot arrests. He wanted to pay back Berkeley, his community.

Something has gone sour in my town. The college kids were becoming increasingly violent, the university administration increasingly repressive. The police chief had gone public with charges against Tom Hayden and other SDS leaders for fomenting violence against cops. And those crazy Black Panthers were toting guns, screaming about pigs.

People's Park was the turning point. It happened a year ago, before he joined the force. Stupid really, on both sides. The university tore down apartments where hippies lived and created a vacant lot. The hippies moved onto the lot, cleaned it up, planted flowers, organic gardens. They sat around, girls in those flowery granny dresses, boys in beards with red bandannas wrapped around their foreheads, playing their guitars, smoking pot. *No harm done.*

Then the university fenced the place off, bulldozed everything the kids had built. The hippies and the campus lefties went wild. They battled the cops along Telegraph Avenue throwing metal rods and rocks. The National Guard was sent in and ended up blinding one person and killing another. The world of love, peace and pipe dreams was transformed into open warfare. Berkeley had lost its civility.

Despite everything that had happened, he had clung to his dream and joined the police department. Why? Perhaps it was hope that in time it would all change. The tolerant Berkeley of his childhood would reemerge. But at the moment the city seemed to be on the road to self-destruction. Maybe Nancy was right, there was nothing one cop by the name of John Yamamoto could do about it. He was not ready to accept that. Not yet.

I need this town. It's my home.

Ron Bradley checked addresses again. Totally out of sequence. Maybe the blond was just leading him on. Couldn't trust those hippie-dippies. Spooky neighborhood. *Fuck it.* He'd head home.

He swung a left, made a u-turn. That's when he heard the siren, saw the flashing lights in his rearview mirror. His night was ending as his day had begun—*fucked.*

Such a quiet evening, John thought. Sliver of a moon. A stray sheet of newspaper drifted by. He spotted a motorcycle heading down University. The bike crossed a meridian clearly marked with a no u-turn sign and started heading up his side of the street. A young guy with a guitar case strapped to his back, afro, black. He turned on his flashing lights, sounded his siren and tailed the Harley. The bike slowed. John came alongside and said, "Pull over to the curb."

The rider did as instructed. John stepped out of his patrol car, and with one hand on his holster, walked forward to the motorcyclist.

"Could I see your license?" The young man complied.

Fuck, Ron Bradley thought. *Is this cop hassling me because I'm black?* That inscrutable look on his face. You can never figure out what these Orientals are thinking.

323

"What did I do wrong, officer?" Ron asked.

"Illegal u-turn."

"There was no one around."

"You're wrong there," John said. "I was around. The law is the law whether or not anyone else is present."

Ron shrugged, "I'd appreciate it if you didn't give me a ticket. Had a hell of a day. Got my induction notice this morning."

"What's your hurry? In another block you could've made that turn legally."

"This damn hippie chick gave me a wrong address."

John looked the fellow over. Young kid. Bet he had gone to Berkeley High. And now he was being sent to Vietnam. And to what purpose? Everyone knew the war was lost. All that remained was the killing of more Vietnamese and GIs. John had lucked out with the lottery. So far. He couldn't do anything about the war, but he could give this kid a break.

"Take my advice," John said, "keep away from the hippie girls. They're nothing but trouble."

"Sounds like you know."

John smiled. Yes, he knew. But that was ages ago. *Before Nancy.* He hoped she would be awake when he got home. "Consider this a warning."

"Thanks, officer." *I finally got a break on this fucked-up day.* The one nice cop in all of Berkeley. "Quiet night."

"On a night like this I feel like I'm robbing the city by accepting a paycheck."

A yellow Studebaker containing two black men with large afros slowed down and pulled up behind Ron and John. The man in the passenger seat got out and walked up to them. He was tall, thin and wore a long black leather coat that reached to the ground. A strange smile formed on his face.

John turned toward the tall man. Looked like a Panther. He wondered what this fellow wanted. Maybe his car had broken down. "Can I help you?"

The man didn't answer. Instead he opened his coat, pulled out a pistol, pointed its barrel directly at John Yamamoto's head, and pulled the trigger. The explosion echoed off the buildings lining the deserted street. As blood spurted from a small hole in the police officer's forehead, he crumpled at Ron's feet.

The tall black man ran back to the Studebaker. As its engine roared and spinning wheels screeched, the car took off, spewing gravel.

Tina Perez, dyed-red hair now frizzled by the wind, red mini-skirt looking tawdry in the yellow glow of the weak streetlight, walked toward the scene. She spotted a young black kid standing and an older tall black dude running. *Maybe one of them wants a blowjob.* Tina quickened her pace. Then she saw the bloody body of a cop covered with trash lying at the kid's feet. She screamed.

Ron Bradley reached down and felt the cop's pulse. Nothing. He watched the tall man head back to the Studebaker. *No way am I going to confront this dude.* He ran to the patrol car and used its radio to call in the murder. The Studebaker sped by. It's brakes screeched as it swung a u-turn right in front of him. The streetlight illuminated the face of the driver. Young, light-skinned. *Looks a bit like me.* Terrified. The car careened down the street on the wrong side of the meridian heading back toward San Pablo.

What a fucking day. What a fucking city. What a fucking country.

A rat, aroused by the commotion, scurried from the Foster's Freeze to the safety of the drain opening. Frightened yellow eyes peered out at the corpse.

A sudden gust of wind off the Bay picked up scattered pages of the *Berkeley Barb.* They danced for a moment on the sidewalk, then were swept along with a Milky Way wrapper and covered the corpse. The wind had created a shroud for Officer John Yamamoto. Berkeley had found a cruel way to reject his embrace.

2.

Berkeley, California, January 2006: Carl Hargrove got up from his seat in his study. He'd heard the doorbell ring. A rare occasion these days. His desk was covered with files of cold cases. Photos and clippings were pinned to a five by eight foot corkboard on the wall behind him. His research, his life since he retired from the Berkeley Police Department. Without these cold cases, he would go mad with boredom. And he knew BPD could use the help. They were hard pressed to fully investigate current cases.

He walked through the living room of his small two-bedroom bungalow and opened the door to a familiar face. Nancy Yamamoto. In her early sixties, she was someone you noticed even in a crowd of younger people. Thin body, angular face, fair skin without even a hint of wrinkle, short pure-white hair, it was her eyes that captivated. Carl had never seen such a deep blue. His first reaction whenever he met her was to look away as if those eyes saw too much or might catch him staring back at her.

He responded as usual. He was embarrassed to admit that he had nothing for her. The murder of her husband had been his preoccupation for years. The Department had the bullet, but no gun. He dug up the prostitute, Tina Perez, the witness, but she remembered nothing of use. More recently, at Nancy's behest, he had tried to find her again, only to learn that she had died of an overdose. He had spent years trying to track down Ron Bradley, the kid who had been on the motorcycle. He had seen the whole thing. Carl, who had joined the BPD two years after the shooting, felt the detectives hadn't done a particularly good job interrogating him. A young black kid heading for 'Nam wasn't likely to tell white cops much. But maybe he would talk to a black ex-cop like Carl. If he could find him. Which he couldn't. Cold, cold, cold.

Carl looked up. He couldn't help but smile. "Wonderful to see you again, Nancy. I'm afraid I have nothing new to report."

"I have something."

What could she have after all these years? Would I have to let this woman down one more time? I don't know if I have the heart for it.

But he said, "Fantastic. Come on in. I was just having some coffee."

"Sounds great."

Carl made way for her and then helped her take off her jacket. It was cool even for a Berkeley January. He had had to scrape frost off the windshield of his Corolla that morning. He led her into his study. Nancy made a beeline for his corkboard display. She pulled a Kleenex out of her purse and teared up staring at the photo of John Yamamoto and the clippings surrounding it. Just like all the other visits.

"Perhaps it's time to let go." Carl said, as he approached her. She turned and hugged him. "This is the coldest cold case I have ever had to wrestle with," he added.

She pushed him back, those powerful eyes now demanding his attention, his obedience. "I can't. I never will. That's why I've never remarried. Dates, brief relationships, but there was John still in my head, in my heart. I'll have only one husband."

"I've been doing my best. But . . . "

"You're the one who is doing too much," Nancy said. "I don't know why you pursued such a cold case."

"It's become personal for me as well. Everyday, when I was working, I felt, as a black officer, I was being held responsible for John's death."

"That's silly. Like when the government blamed Pearl Harbor on John's parents and all Japanese-Americans."

"True. Now I don't need to prove anything to anybody. Yet, I feel if we could somehow find the real killers, not just you but the whole Department might have some closure, better relations with the community, among us cops."

"'Us?' You view yourself still as a policeman?"

"I always will."

"John would've liked you."

"And I him. I guess what I'm saying is that we both need to move on."

Her whole face lit up. He felt her eyes probing deep into him. "Not yet. There's something that's come up."

"I'll get you some coffee. Have a seat and then we'll talk."

"Yes, we'll talk," he heard Nancy say, almost in a whisper, "and then act."

They sat in his study. "It's about Ron Bradley," she said. Nancy had settled into the comfortable leather-cushioned chair at the side of Carl's desk. A gas log fireplace gave the room a warm glow while Destiny's Child played softly in the background. Hargrove lived in his study, saving the living room for the preacher who never visited.

"You have a new idea about where to look?"

"No need to look. He's found me. Called on the phone this morning. Says he can identify one of the men involved in the murder."

"After all these years? Could he be sure?"

Nancy took a sip from her coffee. "That's what I said to him. I've been disappointed so many times before. He insisted he's sure. He said he'd bring proof."

"Proof?"

"His words. Wants to meet me this evening at the Platypus on San Pablo. Eight p.m. I told him I would bring you. He agreed. But no cops."

Carl smiled at her. "You've got a date."

Silently the two sat in the warm room sipping coffee and listening to the music. *Like we're an old married couple.* Carl glanced up at Nancy who was looking down into her coffee mug as if in its murky grounds lay some message to be decoded, perhaps the solution finally of her husband's murder. Would she ever be free? Be whole?

He said, "Someday . . ."

"Yes?"

"Maybe, we could have a date that didn't involve John. As friends."

"I would like that. But first . . ."

"I know. The Platypus."

After Nancy left, Carl withdrew his old service revolver from its lock box. He never went out carrying. But he was worried. A case this cold could pose danger if it suddenly became hot. And Nancy was his responsibility.

～

Carl and Nancy found a booth toward the back. He figured it would give them at least some privacy yet they could watch the door for Bradley. He had always liked the Platypus and would've hung out there, if he was the hanging out kind of guy, which he wasn't. And if he liked board games, which he didn't. Around them small knots of twenty-somethings played Scrabble, Monopoly, backgammon, chess, and checkers, as well as games he couldn't identify. Competitive darts had drawn a crowd. He ordered an Anchor Steam for himself and a Chardonnay for Nancy. They didn't serve hard liquor.

"This place was his choice?" Carl asked.

"Yes. I'm not into games."

Games, yes, but not crime, murder. Perhaps that was why Ron chose it.
"Me, either. Still, there are a lot worse ways to spend an evening."
"Like sitting at home and drinking."
"Or not drinking."
"Could that be him?" Nancy said, nodding in the direction of the door. A large man, wearing a leather jacket walked into the bar. Neat beard tinged with gray, glasses, light-skinned. Carl had seen photos of him at the crime scene in 1970 with a thinner face, afro. No, he wouldn't have recognized him if he'd passed him on the street. He wondered if he still rode a Harley.

"Possibly."

The man nodded in their direction and snaked his way past the game players to their table. Carl rose and shook his hand. A large warm hand.

"Carl Hargrove," he said.

Bradley sat down beside Nancy.

"I've been looking for you for years," Carl said. "Where have you been hiding?"

"Hiding?" He laughed. "Still the cop."

"I didn't mean it that way. But you've been a difficult man to find."

"I suppose I really have been hiding since 'Nam. That night stuck with me. I should've returned earlier and tried to help find the killers. Weird really. I remember sitting in a shallow ditch next to a rice paddy in Vietnam, soaking wet, trying to get some sleep. The eyes of the killer on University Avenue stared at me. The smile as he pulled the trigger. Was this what I was fighting in Vietnam to preserve? A system that produced such hatred, twisted people. Dehumanized them. My solution? Run away from it all. It hasn't worked."

His eyes appeared in Carl to be focused on some distant object. That night? The jungle? Then he snapped out of it. "When I got out of the army, I had nothing here to return to and no idea of where to go. You don't say no to my dad. I had to find my own way.

"I drifted for awhile, played my guitar. Pick-up bands in Europe, largely Paris. Jazz, blues, rock, acoustic folk, whatever people wanted to hear. And girls. No problem in France in the seventies. I drank too much, and smoked one hell of a lot of hashish. Going no place, really.

I knew I wasn't that good as a musician. Adequate. Adequate's not good enough in the music scene."

He stopped talking to order a Guinness from a roaming waitress.

"I got sick of the Paris scene. Drinking more. Performing less. That's when I met Nicole Moureau. Half Chinese. Sang cabaret music, gypsy jazz like Django. I joined her back-up group. I played bass. Not a big deal, but she was a big deal. She got me off the booze and dope. We travelled the European circuit. Then the United States. Settled in Vancouver. We opened this club. Django's. We make a living. I never returned to the Bay Area. Until this week."

"Why now?" Carl asked. He was growing to like this man. If he'd been interviewing him thirty years ago, Carl believed he would've gotten somewhere.

"My father died. I never had a chance to make my peace with him. I planned to help with funeral arrangements then get back to Nicole. We had the viewing this morning. I hardly knew anyone there. The place was packed. I didn't realize how important and well-regarded my father was in Berkeley. He had used his longshoremen's union connections to become active in local politics. Ever hear of Malik Robeson?"

"Hear?" Carl said. "He's all over the news. Lawn signs everywhere in the flatlands. They say he's a shoo-in for mayor."

"My relatives told me he was coming to the viewing. My father had been a big supporter over the years when he was on the City Council. Before I left for the funeral home, I read a copy of the *Trib* with a feature on him."

Ron pulled a section of rolled up newspaper out of his jacket pocket, opened it to an inside page and flattened it out on the table. "This feature on Robeson. Look at the montage of photos. His face struck me like a sledgehammer."

He pointed to an earnest young man with an afro holding a sign supporting the Soledad Brothers. It was dated 1971.

"That's the driver of the Studebaker. I decided then and there I was not going to allow this slick politician get away with murder." He turned to Nancy, "I called you on my cell when I arrived at the funeral home. Robeson approached me as I wound up the call. I confronted him. He told me I was crazy. That if I made that accusation publicly, he would sue me for slander. I walked away from him."

"What do you think Ron should do?" Nancy asked Carl.

Carl turned to Ron, "You should be careful. I doubt if Robeson would be stupid enough to try anything rash right in the middle of an election campaign. Still," he considered. "Are you going public on him?"

"I'm not sure. At least I wanted Nancy to know. I may have acted rashly blurting out my suspicions to Robeson. I can't really prove anything. He's a powerful and respected figure. And me? A nobody. But, damn it, I'm right. Robeson was the driver back in '70. I haven't the slightest doubt about that."

"Thank you for telling me," Nancy said. She reached over and placed her hand on Ron's arm. "I don't want you to do anything that would endanger you. I want the truth to come out about my husband's death, but not if it means further needless violence."

"Don't go to the cops or the press quite yet," Carl said to Ron, "but stick around a few days. There may be a way. Yes, there may be a way."

"Okay, Nancy has my number." Ron took a gulp of the Guinness he had barely touched, rose, shook their hands and headed for the door.

"You have a plan?" Nancy asked. "You don't need to pretend if you don't. I meant what I said to Ron. No more deaths."

Carl heard an explosion coming from the street. No one in the place reacted. Probably figured it was a car backfiring. But not Carl. He knew the sound of a gun when he heard it.

He jumped out of his seat. "Stay here." *I was wrong. Somebody is that stupid or that desperate.*

He rushed between tables, knocking over game boards. Checkers, score cards, chess pieces, dice flew in the air. Beer spilled, customers cursed. But he just plowed ahead, dashing through a dart game. Then out the front entrance.

After thirty years of nothing, this was one cold case that was warming up. *Burning hot. Too much, too fast.* If anything happened to Ron, he would be responsible. Carl looked both ways. *There.* Ron's crumpled body lay on the sidewalk no more than ten feet away. He saw a figure wearing a red fez, tunic flying, running toward Ashby.

331

Carl ran to Ron. Still alive, for now. The shooter stopped in the middle of San Pablo Avenue. Car brakes screeched. He turned to face them. Ron moved. The shooter raised his gun. *I am too old for this.*

Carl crouched, held his gun in both hands. *Aim toward the center of the body mass.* Like they taught him in the Department. An explosion. Another bullet entered Ron on his side on the pavement. More blood. Third round whizzed past Carl's head. *My turn.* Carl shot. The tall killer fell. Blood spurted from his chest. The red fez on his head flew off and rolled into the gutter. Sirens.

Carl turned back toward Bradley. Ron was trying to say something. "Don't speak. Not now. Rest. You're going to be fine."

Ron nodded out. Carl looked up. Nancy stood over them, shaking. That's when the cops arrived in force.

~

Ron Bradley, bandaged, post-op, propped up in bed by pillows, smiled weakly as Carl and Nancy entered his room at Alta Bates Hospital. Nancy carried a vase filled with yellow roses. He had just been released from intensive care. He had lost too much blood. For a while he had hovered between life and death. Life won.

"Thanks for coming. Just heard from Nicole. She'll be here by this afternoon."

"How do you feel?" Carl asked.

"Kind of groggy from the drugs. The pain will come later. Funny, I got through 'Nam without a scratch. I come to Berkeley for the first time in thirty years and get shot. Go figure."

Nancy placed the flowers on a table and they both found seats around Ron's bed.

"The fellow with the red fez who shot me," Ron said. "He was the shooter in 1970."

"His name is Ishmael Shabazz," Carl said. "Runs a splinter Black Muslim sect. Some say it's a cult. There are rumors of sex with fourteen-year-old girls. Got his thugs going around smashing up liquor stores in black neighborhoods. A protection racket. Shabazz is a longtime supporter of Robeson's political machine."

"I'm sorry for dragging you into this," Nancy said.

"I dragged myself into it. I didn't have to look you up after spotting this Robeson fellow in the paper."

"What are you going to do?" Carl asked.

"I'm not going to change my story or run away again. Already told the cops. Going to tell the press. Then testify."

"You don't have to," Nancy said. "He's a powerful man."

"But I do. For me, not just you."

Carl said, "That's all I wanted to hear. Nancy and I have a visit to make."

"We do?"

"A certain candidate owes you the truth."

⁓

Carl led Nancy into the headquarters of the Robeson campaign, a storefront on Shattuck Avenue. He remembered the place as Amy's, the kind of restaurant working people went for lunch. Before California Cuisine. Meatloaf, mashed potatoes, gravy, bread pudding, hamburgers, lemon meringue pie. Lawn signs were stacked along the walls. A full sized cut-out of Robeson stood in the center. Looked startlingly real. A huge Robeson banner, festooned with red, white and blue bunting, covered the upper portion of the back wall. A half dozen young men and women, black and white, sat at desks staring at computer screens. Along one side another group, largely older blacks, some wearing clerical collars, staffed a phone bank.

A tall young black man in a suit, black tee shirt, got up from his desk and approached them. "May I help you?"

"We'd like to talk with Mr. Robeson," Carl said.

"He's very busy. The election is less than two weeks away."

"Tell him it's Nancy Yamamoto and friend," Carl said. "He'll see us."

The man left them in the middle of the room and headed toward a back office. People drifted in, picked up signs, leaflets, buttons then back out the front door. A constant buzz of one-way phone calls filled the place. The same mantra, different voices. "Robeson means change. Robeson means a better, progressive Berkeley."

In two minutes the young man returned. "Come this way." They followed him through the maze of desks and into the back office.

Carl had no trouble recognizing the man who rose from his desk to greet them. It was as if the cut-out in the main room had come to life. His face had been plastered in posters on lampposts and walls of vacant buildings, his name on yard signs all over Berkeley. Fatherly, mature, trustworthy. *This fellow abetted a killer, sicced this same killer on Ron.*

Not a large man, Carl thought, yet he had a commanding presence. *It's an act he's perfected during his years on the City Council.*

"How can I help you?"

"To begin with you can give Nancy here a long overdue apology for your role in the shooting of her husband."

"I had absolutely nothing to do with that terrible wanton act of terrorism."

"Ron Bradley says different," Nancy said, "and I believe him."

"I have the greatest respect for Ron's father. A pillar of our community and long time supporter of my endeavors. But I am afraid his son is mistaken. He bases his claim on an old photo in the newspaper. We are talking about an event that occurred almost forty years ago."

"That will be for a jury to decide," Carl said.

"You have no case. The DA wouldn't dare to prosecute a prominent political figure on such flimsy evidence. It would be interpreted as politically motivated, fear of a black man becoming mayor of this predominantly white city."

"There's more," Carl said. "The shooting several nights ago of Bradley out in front of the Platypus."

"Absurd. I had nothing to do with that. This Shabazz charlatan is mad. He has no connection with me."

"But he does," Carl said. "He has supported your campaigns and you, in turn, have steered city money to his phony front groups."

"I admit I, like most of Berkeley, was fooled by him. My treasurer has sent back any contributions he's made to our campaign."

"The only person outside of Carl here that knew I would be meeting Ron at the Platypus was you," Nancy said. "You must have overheard his phone call to me."

"You two keep this up and I'll sue you both for slander."

"You bastard!" Carl leapt at him. Nancy reached out to restrain him.

"Get out of here!" Robeson demanded. Then he shouted, "Edmund, these people are threatening me." Edmund, the young man in the suit, reentered with a rent-a-cop.

"We're going," Carl said. "It's not just us or even Ron. Ishmael Shabazz is alive. My friends in the Department say he has confessed to the 1970 shooting. He's implicating you. Says he won't take the fall for all this by himself. Says you told him to take Ron out."

"He's a drug addict. Has a criminal record. It will be his word against mine."

"It's interesting that Shabazz's background never bothered you before," Carl said. "But it's not just his word. There's Ron's word. But it won't matter. There's enough evidence to bring you to trial. Whatever the jury says, your political career's finished."

A piercing shriek rent the air. Nancy. Carl had been so wrapped up in Robeson he had almost forgotten that she was in the room with him. She rushed toward Robeson, rage distorting her face. It was as if thirty years of pain burst out of her in that one moment. She scratched, she clawed, she pounded.

This time it was Carl's turn to restrain. He was not about to allow Edmund or the rent-a-cop to touch her. He surrounded her in his arms and pulled her away. She continued to wriggle and flail out. This time Nancy struck Carl. Then looked at him, shocked by her own fury. He felt her surrender in his embrace, to relax, trembling.

Edmund and the rent-a-cop approached. They took one look at the expression on Carl's face and backed away. Carl walked Nancy out of the room.

~

Carl led a still-shaking Nancy out of the headquarters and into a cold drizzle. She clung to his arm.

"Some coffee?" he asked.

"Yes . . ."

They found a small coffee shop a block away. Carl ordered lattes and they settled into an overstuffed couch that gave a view of the street, now deserted because of the rain. He said nothing for minutes allowing Nancy to regain control.

"Sorry," she said.

"For what?"

"That outburst. But he was so smug, slick, unfeeling. He destroyed my life and all he cares about now is his political career."

"Do you feel any better?"

She smiled. "Like my screaming. Catharsis?"

"I was thinking more about learning the truth."

"It hurts. All so vivid now. I never thought I was one for vengeance but, damn it, Robeson must pay."

"He will go down. I promise you. Regardless of the outcome of a trial he's finished as a politician. Shabazz is a criminal, a scam artist, a killer. Twisted, sociopath. Robeson should have been different. He protected a murderer in 1970. Accepted his support for his political ventures. And now refuses to face up to the truth. As mayor he would have continued to cover for him."

She moved closer to him on the couch. She started to cry, the crying turned into a torrent, she began to hiccup, hyperventilate. He put his arms around her and felt her throbbing body. She began to calm down. The storm had passed. He didn't remove his arms.

"The pain will subside," he said.

"It helps."

"What helps?"

"The truth."

"I'm here for you."

"I know."

Look Both Ways

Luis Rodriguez

I can't seem to tear the image out of my head—a teenager, pallid skin, sun bouncing off torn clothing and flesh, dirt creased into face, neck, arms, legs, with streaks of blood everywhere, along the temple and cheek, then the ashen lips, closed and textured, on round face, cute, smeared mascara, with rows of gold rings along her ears, through those bloodless lips, on her nose and eyebrow, a few blue tattoos, actually black ink under veiny skin, mostly naked, bruised, beaten about with something, a bat, a stick, a tire iron, open cuts, raised flesh. Then the nipples . . . puffed and pierced.

I'm new to the Robbery-Homicide Division. I've seen dead bodies before as a beat cop but this one lingers with me longer than it probably should, the battered face and tossed way the body is lying there, in a vacant lot off Sixth Street in the barrio, next to scattered leaves, dumped thrash, graffiti-scrawled wall. This is not a usual barrio death. I mean not like a gang shooting, boyfriend beating or robbery victim. She was brought here from somewhere else, outside the neighborhood, late at night.

I can see why. A killer would know this is a rough area. Not far from MacArthur Park. Mostly Spanish voices, Central American and Mexican, with open-air peddlers, baggy-panted street dudes, and families, so many families, pudgy women, brown babies, running children.

"Pierced nipples" doesn't belong here. She looks part-Asian, part-white. She looks goth, emo, whatever . . . distanced, disconnected, middle-class. Maybe from Koreatown. Maybe from Hollywood. She was killed somewhere else and dumped here. Killers tend to do that. Remove their work to places where such bodies, you'd think, just happen to be lying around. But that's not true. Not even for MacArthur Park. Not for the barrio.

This case is now priority. Why? You can guess. Non-barrio girl killed is more important than the other deaths around here. She's white, even if mixed with Korean or something, and that makes her more valuable, especially if she's not poor or a prostitute. I hate to say that. It's just the way it is.

~

"Any leads, Sammy?"

"Nothing, Timbo, we've hit a brick wall."

"Yeah, well, The Times is banging down my door. They want something, anything, to put in their main story."

"Anything is the last thing we told them—there's nothing new."

"Give me a new angle, you know . . . just to keep the wolves a little satiated before they go on a feeding frenzy."

"We don't have an ID on the girl . . . she's in the county morgue, Jane Doe. No witnesses. No prints. No DNA match. Sorry, this is all we have."

The press people along with TV and major radio are big in this town. Yeah, there are paparazzi for all the celebrity nonsense, and a lot of print is wasted on this stuff, but when it comes to out-of-the-ordinary killings, like "pierced nipples," they all want to break out with the latest news. It's pressure I don't need, I don't want.

Timothy Blaine is the media rep here, a white cop with a father and grandfather formerly in the force. Tall, handsome, well dressed, I mean better than the Men's Wearhouse. Sometimes he draws the press more than the cases do—he's funny, personable, a master of subterfuge. Making the press look one way, while we work in another direction. Not lies, not distortions, but mainly to keep certain news out of the papers and broadcast streams, news that could help us detain somebody when we get to that point.

"Well, big homie, if you get something just drop it on my desk," Timothy says, waving his hand in dismissal, walking out the main door.

I've known Timothy for eighteen years. We go back to being uniforms on Southside beats, mostly at the "unlucky seven," the seventy-seventh—one of the department's most murderous divisions. We learned the cop business together, right after the '92 riots. The riots were the reason I joined, along with other black and brown cadets. And what a training I got during that time: the streets smoldering, burned out lots, bent-steel frames of former buildings, more homicides than ever before.

Now Tim and I hover over desks, memos, computers, cell phones. But I still got my hand in the pot, in the fire, working cases. Timothy opts for the limelight. And it works for him. I'm okay being the background guy, the guy you don't pay attention to but who may be paying attention to you. We're still on the same side, only working different ends of the game, this crime game, this seeing-people-on-their-worst-day game.

"Sammy . . . Sammy Saez, can you come into my office?"

That's Captain Dwight Tate. I challenge the captain quite a bit. Not serious, just to mess with him. He's a former Marine, African American, maybe late forties. He came to the department after several years in a midwestern police force. He was second in command and about five years ago able to enter the LAPD with a special crew tied to the new police chief. But he's also mighty stressed, always behind, pushing us detectives to do more, faster—we're never on time for anything as far as Tate is concerned.

I slowly rise from my chair, close the file I was staring at on the computer, and grab my notepad and a pencil as I saunter into his small office located at the end of a row of desks past mine.

"You rang, cap'n?" I tease as I enter Tate's space. I don't show much respect that should go along with his position on the force. I mean he deserves the props. I guess I'm a little annoyed he's moved so fast up the ranks for being an outsider. Besides this is just my way—my attitude keeps people on their toes, off my back.

The captain is sitting behind a massive wood desk. Papers and folders neatly stacked, everything in its place. There are photos on shelves, and on his desk—they're all of one girl's face, perhaps late teens, framed and in color. I wait to hear why he asked me in.

"We got a lead on the Sixth Street body dump . . . somebody's come forward with information," Tate says, all business, all the time. "Here's a name and number. Check it out and get back to me with whatever you find."

~

Captain Tate moves methodically to the temporary podium outside the main police station downtown. TV, radio, and newspaper reporters are gathered directly in front of him. Mics from broadcast stations are taped to the platform, sticking out in front of the captain's face. That's one big change after the riots, that someone like Dwight Tate can represent what was once considered the most racist police department.

Behind Tate stand a few officers in uniform. Tim's also there, in a gray suit. I'm at the end of the line, in a blue blazer, opened to reveal light blue shirt and striped blue tie, shiny police shield on my waistband, my brown hair with swaths of grey combed neatly to the back. The captain clears his throat and in a strong baritone he declares:

"Ladies and Gentlemen, thank you for joining us today as we make this important announcement about a breakthrough relating to the body found near MacArthur Park last month. We now have the victim's name, nineteen-year-old Stacy Killian of Woodland Hills. Her family has identified the body. We also have a witness in the case. This witness, whose name will not be released at this time, is being held for questioning, nothing more. We have no suspects, although with the identification of the young victim we hope our investigation will move forward. We are confident we'll have one or more arrests, based on the great work of our detectives and police officers in the field. For now, this is all we have. We'll provide further information when we get something solid to report. We appreciate your patience—the media are important partners for law enforcement in our efforts to prosecute the parties responsible for these violent acts and to bring closure to the families."

Various voices from the media then rush Tate from all directions. He deftly answers their questions, without revealing any more than what he's said—different slants on the same words, a sort of dance with information that Tim is good at providing. I decide to move away from behind the captain and reenter the station's front doors.

～

From the mid-1980s through most of the 1990s, L.A. was known as the most violent place on earth. Movies like *Colors* and *American*

Me conveyed a gang reality most people had no idea about. Yet this culture, pushed out by West Coast Rap, the *cholo* style, the elaborate tattoos, is everywhere now. You got L.A. gangster-types all over the U.S., Canada, Mexico, Central America, parts of Europe—even Japan, Cambodia, and Armenia, man.

But today L.A. is not the killing fields it used to be. Amazingly there are whole areas here where nobody is mugged, assaulted or killed. But I have to remind myself—don't get fooled by this.

L.A. still has South Central, Boyle Heights, Highland Park, East L.A., Pacoima, parts of the Harbor with nearby towns like Compton, Long Beach, Bell Gardens—working-class, mostly Latino. There is also MacArthur Park, Westlake, and the Pico-Union. And in South L.A., Compton, and Pacoima there are large sections of African Americans. Many of these places never recovered after 1992.

The murder rates in those neighborhoods are as high as any place, anywhere.

I learn all this while assigned to Homicide. Also whenever I get the time I like to drive around this monster of a city, although it's hard to get a good handle on it. I grew up in nearby West Covina, but I still have a hard time figuring this place out—a city that mostly winds and turns, housing tracts pushed up into wooded hills, various city centers sprinkled throughout the basin, with nice homes up and down the western corridor, and some of the poorest in the southern and eastern ends.

Driving around, I've noticed one thing—L.A. is deeply divided, man. How bad things can be depends on how poor and how dark-skinned your neighbors are. Even downtown is split in two—west of Pershing Square are the big hotels, banks, lawyer suites, mostly Anglos and Asians. East of the Square you have the jewelry district, the garment district, the heavily trafficked Broadway with its cloth-ing, appliance, and taco shops—and more Mexicans and Central Americans shoppers than any place outside of Mexico City or Tegucigalpa.

East of "Spanish Broadway," but west of the warehouse district, is the largest concentration of homeless people in the country, known for generations as Skid Row, a fifty-square-block area—street after

341

street filled with cardboard boxes, tents, tore-up blankets, mostly black people, except for the tiny apartments and SRO hotels where the illegals reside.

When I first got my desk downtown, I made it a point to check out this area. My fellow officers claim at least ten thousand people would be camped out on any given night. Although most were pushed out of their homes or laid off, too many dudes and women were on the pipe, shooting up, with bottles of rotgut by their feet. A few hospitals and sheriff's deputies used to drop off people without homes in Skid Row because it had a concentration of missions, shelters, services.

But around 2006, the LAPD moved in on many of the homeless— for violating parole, drug sales, fights, drunkenness. We cleared up many of those Skid Row streets, just squeezed them out and they'd end up in and around the L.A. River, east to Riverside or San Bernardino County, to Antelope Valley . . . the deserts.

Now a few sections of the Row look like upscale Manhattan, like Greenwich Village, with art galleries, cafés, pricey restaurants, million-dollar condos.

The reality is that this is one of the most exciting cities to be a cop. People have found interesting ways to die in this town: Suicides, horrendous car accidents, murders of all kinds. And I don't mean just the typical street gang shoot 'em ups, which are extraordinary in themselves. We also have killings of Hollywood starlets, big-time bankers and developers, high-end crime figures from Mexico, El Salvador, Armenia, Russia, Israel, Japan, China . . . you name the country, we got some of their worst criminals.

So as I maneuver through the crowded streets, pass the bus stops with maids and factory hands, in the old and new sections, I keep my eyes open. Beneath all this façade and glitter, next to tall buildings and the quiet of the barely-wet concrete river, this is a deadly place. More homeless, more poor, more gangs than any other city. Not every day is war, but when there is, it's a doozy, getting the blood flowing, adrenaline pumping, pushing me into a sordid kind of high.

Like when I think about that poor girl's body in that vacant lot.

≈

"It's been almost a year, people," Captain Tate needles. "The police chief, the mayor, city council . . . they're all demanding answers. The private security business is up—you got regular folks arming themselves. This can get out of hand, you know, with somebody panicking and hurting somebody. Now it seems anyone's daughter is at risk. I know we can't make up answers, but something has to give, for Christ's sakes. Follow your best leads, return to people you've already talked to. Don't leave any rock unturned. We're not playing games here!"

The body count has been mounting—more dead girls from well-off homes. White, except for the first one that looked mixed. At least four bodies in the past ten months. The others are discovered along a stretch of the river near Atwater Village, in the fields of Elysian Park just outside of Dodger Stadium, and not far from the USC campus, under the pilings of the 110 Freeway. Again, these are places where you wouldn't expect these girls to end up. Yet there they are, strewn about like so much garbage, like yesterday's newspapers, like a sack of bad burritos.

There is also a curious heart-shaped burn on each of the girls—I first noticed this in the photos of the first victim, on her chest, like if some sicko heated up something and pressed it to her skin.

The captain is losing his patience. Everybody is breathing down his neck. He breathes fire down ours. There have been many other murders in and around the city, but these bodies are getting top billing. The murdered girls are from the well-off parts of the Valley and the Westside, where the clamor to resolve these cases rings louder.

The problem is we have no suspects. Oh, we've had those nut jobs that claim to be the murderer, maybe to have somebody pay attention to them for once. And that first witness—he only had a tidbit for us. He lived down the street, but that night he was drunk, sitting behind a dumpster across from the lot where the first victim was found. He said a green van pulled up early in the morning, like two a.m, still dark out. He saw a husky man with a black sweatshirt, hood over his head, face obscured, remove what looked like a blanket stuffed with something. The drunk couldn't quite see what it was, but the man carried this to the far end of the lot and dropped the bundle there. Probably didn't want to leave tire marks in the dirt. Then calmly—

according to the witness—the perpetrator walked back to the van and took off. No license plate. No make or model.

We'd been looking for this kind of vehicle ever since, made a few stops of vans that fit the description, but nothing came of these. The other bodies are found similar to the first one, beaten, dead, dumped. We have a serial killer on our hands. And this shifts the department into full gear. I'm now part of a citywide task force to get to the bottom of these killings.

Meanwhile, the media is headlong into the fray. They come up with their own stories, their own "witnesses," their own facts, or bullshit, as far as I can tell. People now accuse family members, neighbors, old boyfriends, and we have to check into every one of these. But something's missing. A major piece of the puzzle. That's my goal—to see what others aren't seeing.

~

Bob Meredith is my new partner on the task force, quiet, efficient. He came from the Wilshire Division well recommended, worked on a few high-profile cases. Tanned, built, he strikes me as cold and aloof. I try to act as if these deaths don't get to me, but they're crawling under my skin, causing me sleepless nights, longer hours at the bars.

The next victim was where I thought a body would eventually end up—in Skid Row. They found her wrapped up in blankets next to a pile of cardboards. Somebody made their way to an isolated section of the Row, now that we drove a lot of the homeless outside of the area. She ended up near a slew of tagged-up metal door enclosures for clothing outlets. She got placed there during a time of darkness when nobody could see, in the shadows made by faulty street lamps.

Bob and I are the first detectives called in. When we arrive, the rosy-fingered dawn is creeping up the decrepit buildings and sidewalks. Several officers are in and around a yellow caution-taped section of the street, a car unit with flashing lights nearby. Radio dispatches emanating from the unit. A few vagrants are standing around, talking to themselves, with steam curling up from paper coffee cups.

Bob and I stroll up to the yellow tape, pull ourselves under, than step gently into the area where the body is lying still, like a broken doll, like a porcelain vase with face, like a manikin with cuts and bruises all over. She's barely got clothes on, similar to the others. This one is what they'd call "dirty blonde." Cheerleader type. Perhaps sixteen, seventeen. Although there are bloodstains around her head and arms, on the torn blouse and remains of skirt she has on, she's bled out somewhere else.

None of the previously murdered girls have been sexually assaulted, despite the ripping of clothes all of them exhibited, and this one is probably no exception. This is interesting, considering the violent nature of the killings, their youth and beauty, the tendency of most male serial killers. The latest one is remarkably different than that first girl, the one with piercings and tattoos. This one looks proper, innocent perhaps—not from the wild side of the good life like the first victim.

"She may be one of our string of murders," Bob deduces, standing up from squatting next to the body.

We had to make sure we weren't looking at a copycat crime, which happens now and then. But I can tell she's official victim number five.

"She's got that mark," I say, still standing—I see better when I'm looking at the overall scene.

Bob squints as he turns toward the body, squats back down, then with gloved hand moves the victim slightly. A faint burn is there just below the collarbone.

"Damn," he mutters as he gets up and takes notes.

Later I wander into the Top Hat, a hole-in-the-wall on the outskirts of downtown, off the Metro line near the southern warehouse district. Not known for cops, but that's what I need right now—a place where I'm not looking at the worn faces of worn-out detectives. I've already placed my shield into my pocket and buttoned my coat. I thought I'd have a couple of beers and go home. Not many people in here except for a few warehouse workers and dishwashers—Mexicans, a couple of stubble-faced whites, no blacks. Oh, except for the older black dude I notice sitting alone at the far end of the joint, nursing a high ball. Just then I recognize him and almost walk out the door, but decide to man up and talk to the dude.

"Hey, Captain, what's up?"

Tate looks up at me, surprised as hell, but he wears this well, followed by a cool smirk.

"Mind if I sit . . . I'm just here for a few cold ones."

I gesture toward the bar with an index finger then maneuver myself onto a thick leather seat without any outward invitation from the captain. But he's not protesting. In the office, I talk smack all the time, but right now I'm not sure what to say, or if I should say anything.

It's the captain who breaks down the wall.

"Ever lost somebody you love more than anything, more than life itself?" Tate slowly asks, not looking at me, but clearly directed in my general vicinity. I strain to listen as a Levi-jean-wearing Chicana, busting at the seams with a few extra pounds, brings me a beer.

"You may not know, but I had a daughter, eighteen-year-old, beautiful, smart, name was Renée . . . oh, what a great girl she turned out to be," Tate continues. "She had a whole future ahead of her. Entering college the following semester. The best grades. Friends everywhere . . ."

He pauses, takes another gulp then wipes his mouth with the back of his hand. Starts up again.

"When they found her, dead, thrown into a ditch, clothes torn, I just about died."

This explains the pictures in his office. I also realize why he's so adamant about the dumped bodies. Man, what a terrible reminder this must be for the captain.

"They never found the killer, you understand me?" Tate now glares at me. "Renée never had any justice, never had her day in court. We couldn't get anybody. Oh, we talked to every Tom, Dick, and Harry we could find. But whoever did this just vanished. Gone. Never any justice . . . never."

After this the captain stops talking. The minutes drip in slow motion. I down the brew in front of me and decide to mosey on out of the place, giving the captain my condolences and goodbyes.

The next lead turns out to be another witness without traction—so-called witnesses like these have been popping up during the whole investigation. This time an old crack whore, living in the third floor of a dingy welfare hotel, claims she saw two dark-skinned hooded men push what looked like a body wrapped in something onto the Skid

Row sidewalk. There was the perennial van—again a hazy description—no dents, no primer spots, no year, nothing detailed except that it was dark green. Although the woman didn't call police or anybody at the time—she was apparently working the pipe. Days later she steps forward.

She only has vague info, a general outline, similar to the first drunk and others who have come out of the woodwork. Yet no reports are filed on these witnesses. No beat cops I talk to know about them. Their names get turned in somehow and the captain sends us to track them down. And this never leads to anything tangible, something we could hang on to—that could become a real suspect. I've been a cop long enough to know when BS is cooking, and this stuff is heating up the kitchen big time.

At the end of the shift, I walk into the office and see Timothy next to his desk. He's standing away from me, staring out a window. I notice a set of keys next to a cell phone on his desk. There's something strange on his key ring.

"Hey, bro, did you get Bob's report . . . uh, about there being maybe two perps involved?"

Tim turns around, startled. I was going to ask him something else, but this thing about the two dudes came to me instead.

"No, I haven't read it yet . . . do we have any descriptions?"

"No, which is why I need you to keep this development away from the media," I ask. "This may prove important, but we can't let others in on this yet."

Just then a bleak-looking Captain steps out of his office and starts moving toward my desk—most days he seems to be holed up there, blinds drawn. He looks beat, like he's been losing sleep or spending too many nights at the Top Hat.

"Been burning the midnight oil, eh, Captain?"

Captain Tate throws me a stone Marine staff sergeant look—like he's finally had it with my jibes.

"How come you're not out there following up on those leads we've been getting?" he demands.

"Alright, Captain, calm down . . . you know I have. I'm just trying to give Tim here some stuff for his press reports."

"Like what?" Tate asks, cutting through me with steely eyes.

"Oh, he just wanted me to . . ." Timothy interjects, but I cut him short.

"Nothing you don't know about, Captain, more about that van— you know, from that last witness who claimed to see something."

Tate just stares, pausing for what seems like a long time.

"Don't slack on me, Sammy," he finally states.

He then turns toward the men's restroom.

"Why didn't you want me to tell the captain about two possible suspects?" Timothy asks with Tate out of earshot.

"Listen, I mean it when I say nobody else should know about this. Besides the captain looks like he's under a lot of strain. I don't want to bother him with too many details—let's see if this info amounts to anything."

～

I leave one of my regular dives like I often do, soused, pissed, alone. Who knows what time it is, although it's still dark. Most everything's a blur. Somehow I'm inside my car. I start her up and as I take off you can hear screeching out of the alleyway parking lot toward the street. There are hardly any cars out this side of east Sunset in Echo Park. I'm thinking, just thinking, about the bodies, the newspaper headlines, the captain . . .

I get to a stop sign. I turn my head to the right and see no cars coming. But I forget about my left. I step on the gas and go through the intersection when suddenly a car barrels through from the other side, probably thinking I'd stay behind the stop sign like I'm supposed to. The car strikes the left backseat area of my car, pushing it up the street a ways before we both stop. It takes me a while to realize what's happened. I'm able to get out of my car. I feel fine, or so it seems. I look back and see that the side of my car is totally crumpled. The other car's front end is steaming, parts of grill and headlights are on the asphalt, radiator fluid and water dripping.

I check in on the driver. A twenty-something woman is in the driver's seat. There's a bloodline on her forehead. Nobody else is in the car. Luckily she had on her seatbelt. She's awake, conscious, but dazed. I call this in, and wait for an ambulance and my fellow officers to arrive. This is when it hits me. The woman is so young. I could have killed her. The thought makes my blood run cold. What an idiot I am. I know I'm fucked. Thoroughly fucked. I should have looked both ways. Now there's nothing to do but sober up and face the music.

~

I'm having coffee in Little Tokyo, at the Starbucks on Central Avenue. I don't drink anymore. I'd been drinking myself to death until I had the accident with the young woman. She had minor cuts and bruises but turned out okay. She ended up suing, though. The department took me off my cases. They kept me from facing criminal charges, but now I'm suspended until I come back sober—that is, with a few miles of recovery behind me.

This morning, after several days of not drinking, I call Bob. I need to find out something, to ask him a favor, and I am *not* going into the station to deal with this. Everybody drinks, but once you're labeled as an alkie, people look at you as if you were a leper or something. Yeah, right. They're all one drink away from ending up like me.

Still today my obsession comes back. The dead girls. Unfortunately, the department pulled me out of the investigation just when I thought I'd hit on something. But it was nothing I could share with the world at the time. Now, sober, suspended, babysitting this espresso coffee, I know what I have to do. And I need Bob to help.

~

"Hey, Tim, we have ourselves a couple of suspects," Bob says excitedly as he barges into Timothy's media office. "Those guys somebody called in . . . you know, Hispanics, in their late twenties, both with rap sheets. One kinda loony. Well, they're in separate interrogation rooms right now. You want to watch from the two-way glass as we deal with one of 'em?"

"Of course, it's about time we nailed those punks," Tim responds with a smile. "I'll be right there."

In a few minutes, Timothy enters the adjoining room to where one of the suspects is supposedly being detained. Captain Tate and members of the department's internal affairs are already standing there along with Bob and myself, which Bob arranged despite some opposition. Tim gawks at the chief and the IA guys, at Bob, then me. But as he takes this all in, you can see a wave of acceptance cross his face, a kind of relief, resignation. Uniformed officers walk in, in case Tim tries to make a run for it. But he doesn't. He sits down, expressionless, while the captain reads him his Miranda rights.

～

"You ought to feel good, Sammy," Bob suggests one day at the Little Tokyo Starbucks, now my favorite hangout. "The way we cornered Tim—who'd have thought?"

Bob is writing down what I say for an upcoming press conference he's doing with the captain, now that Tim's been removed from the job. It took a whole day of hankering, but Bob's finally been given permission to speak with me before they tweak the final statement.

"It was a good idea to pull Tim out of his office without him knowing," Bob ruminates. "I really thought he'd find a way out of the building if he knew what was up. You don't ever think one of yours would do something like this . . . man, I still can't believe it."

"Well, I actually thought the old captain was the guy," I recount between sips of a steamed latte. "The captain once told me how he'd lost a teenage daughter when he was with the police department in Indiana. That the girl was beaten, cut, tossed about like she was nothing. No suspects. Tate apparently went nuts for a while. Then, after a long rest, he returned, renewed, organized. He seemed the right guy for the captain's job, but I felt he was still crazy, maybe with pain, resentment, who knows?"

"That's why you can't have preconceived notions in this job."

"You ain't kidding," I continue. "I also had to look elsewhere than where all those so-called leads were taking us, false information that Tim paid winos and junkies to call in. The kicker was that heart-shaped locket I noticed one day on Tim's keychain. I thought this odd, didn't seem to fit a cop. But I let it pass. Men have been known to carry photos of their loved ones in lockets."

"Although that still strikes me as weird."

350

"After we confronted Tim with DNA evidence linked to him, the dude had to fess up. Although his ramblings didn't exactly explain anything—something about corrupt police getting away with shit and how the heart-shaped burns were a dare to the force to look at our own. I really don't know what he was talking about."

"Well, you did a hell of a job," Bob adds, placing his pencil down, grabbing a large cup of joe on the table.

I glimpse beyond Bob's head to the nearby skyscrapers, a few glaring in the afternoon sun, many of them recently constructed. After the riots I heard people complain that not much has changed in the city. I guess if you're still poor, this is true. But the LAPD has changed. So has the city council—now run with a handful of black and brown members. Today we have a mayor and school board president of Mexican descent. Big things have come our way, although I agree—more has to happen. Yet some things never change. People die. Some people kill. And good police work often revolves around the most mundane of facts, one small twist, sometimes when you're looking the other way.

Contributors

Summer Brenner was raised in Georgia and migrated west, first to New Mexico and eventually to Northern California where she has been a longtime resident. She has published a dozen books of poetry, fiction, and novels for youth including *Ivy: Homeless in San Francisco*. She is the author of the critically acclaimed noir thriller *I-5: A Novel of Crime, Transport, and Sex*. Gallimard's Serie Noire published Brenner's crime novel, *Presque nulle part*, which PM Press will release by its English title, *Nearly Nowhere*.

Cory Doctorow (craphound.com) is a science fiction author, activist, journalist and blogger—the co-editor of Boing Boing (boingboing.net) and the author of Tor Teens/HarperCollins UK novels like *For the Win* and the bestselling *Little Brother*. He is the former European director of the Electronic Frontier Foundation and co-founded the UK Open Rights Group. Born in Toronto, Canada, he now lives in London.

Rick Dakan is the author of the Geek Mafia trilogy, published by PM Press, as well as *Cthulhu Cult: A Novel of Obsession* from Arcane Wisdom. He writes books and video games and angry comments on the Internet. More at RickDakan.com.

Larry Fondation is the author of the novels *Angry Nights* and *Fish, Soap and Bonds*, and of *Common Criminals* and *Unintended Consequences*, both collections of short stories. His fiction focuses on the Los Angeles underbelly. His two most recent books feature collaborations with London-based artist Kate Ruth. Fondation has lived in L.A. since the 1980s, and has worked for nearly twenty years as an organizer in South Los Angeles, Compton, and East L.A. He is a recipient of a Christopher Isherwood Fellowship in Fiction Writing. He can be contacted at lfondation@aol.com.

Barry Graham is an author, journalist and blogger whose novels have received international acclaim and whose reporting has helped more than one corrupt politician leave office. Born and dragged up in Glasgow, Scotland, he has traveled widely and is currently based in the U.S. His previous occupations include boxing and grave-digging. He is also a Zen monk, and serves as the Abbot of the Sitting Frog Zen Center. He has witnessed two executions, invited by the inmates, not the state.

John A Imani is a long-time revolutionary living and working in Los Angeles and is a member of the Revolutionary Autonomous Communities–Los Angeles (RAC-LA). Under the name of S John Daniels he has written and produced six plays and is the author of three novels.

Penny Mickelbury is the author of ten mystery novels in three successful series: The Carol Ann Gibson Mysteries, the Mimi Patterson/Gianna Maglione Mysteries, and the Philip Rodriguez Mysteries. Mickelbury's short stories have been included in several anthologies and collections, among them *Spooks, Spies and Private Eyes: Black Mystery, Crime and Suspense Fiction* (Paula Woods, ed.), *The Mysterious Naiad* (Grier and Forrest, eds.), and *Shades of Black: Original Mystery Fiction by African-American Writers* (Eleanor Taylor Bland, ed.) The character in the story in this collection, "Murder . . . Then and Now," Charles "Boxer" Gordon, so far lives only in short story form, but he's feeling ready to step out—and into his own novel.

Michael Moorcock was born into the London blitz, came to maturity during the swinging sixties, editing *New Worlds*, spearheading the New Wave in SF, contributing regularly to the underground press. As a musician he was part of the Ladbroke Grove "peoples' music" movement, performing free gigs with Hawkwind, the Pink Fairies and his own band The Deep Fix, the only bands respected by people like Johnny Rotten, Siouxsie Sioux and Gay Advert. He received a gold disc for *Warrior on the Edge of Time* and worked with Calvert and Eno on various albums. His new album with Martin Stone and Pete Pavli, *Live from the Terminal Café*, will appear from Spirits Burning Inc.

Like Gwendolyn Brooks, **Sara Paretsky** moved to the South Side of Chicago from eastern Kansas. Paretsky has published fourteen novels featuring her detective V.I. Warshawski, along with two other novels, a book of essays, and numerous short stories. Credited with helping change the image of women in the contemporary crime novel, Paretsky founded the advocacy group Sisters in Crime in 1986 and is the recipient of numerous awards, including the Cartier Diamond Dagger, the MWA Grand Master and *Ms.* magazine's Woman of the Year.

Kim Stanley Robinson is a science fiction writer from Davis, California. His novels include the Mars trilogy, the Science in the Capital trilogy, the Three Californias trilogy, *The Years of Rice and Salt*, and *Galileo's Dream.*

Luis J. Rodriguez is a poet, novelist, short-story writer, children's book writer, nonfiction writer and essayist with fifteen published books, including the best-selling memoir *Always Running, La Vida Loca, Gang Days in L.A.* His latest memoir, *It Calls You Back: An Odyssey of Love, Addiction, Revolutions, and Healing,* is from Touchstone Books/Simon & Schuster.

Michael Skeet is an award-winning Canadian writer and broadcaster. Born in Calgary, Alberta, he began writing for radio before finishing college. He has sold short stories in the science fiction, dark fantasy and horror fields in addition to extensive publishing credits as a film and music critic. A two-time winner of Canada's Aurora Award for excellence in Science Fiction and Fantasy, Skeet lives in Toronto with his wife, Lorna Toolis (the head of the internationally renowned Merril Collection of Science Fiction, Speculation and Fantasy, a reference collection of the Toronto Public Library and one of the world's best SF libraries).

Paco Ignacio Taibo II is an eminent historian and professor, and a journalist and writer of worldwide renown. He has won many literary awards, among them three Dashiell Hammetts for his detective novels, a Planeta Award for best historical novel, and the Italian Bancarella

Book of the Year Award for his biography of Che Guevara. His novel *Calling All Heroes: A Manual For Taking Power* has most recently been translated and published by PM Press. He resides in Mexico City.

Benjamin Whitmer was raised by back-to-the-landers in southern Ohio and upstate New York. He now lives with his wife and two children in Colorado, where he spends most of his time trolling local histories and haunting the bookshops, blues bars, and firing ranges of ungentrified Denver. He has published fiction and nonfiction in a number of magazines, anthologies, and essay collections. *Pike* is his first novel, published as part of PM Press's Switchblade imprint in 2010.

Kenneth Wishnia's novels include *23 Shades of Black*, an Edgar and Anthony Award finalist; *Soft Money*, a *Library Journal* Best Mystery of the Year; and *Red House*, a *Washington Post Book World* "Rave" Book of the Year. PM Press will be reprinting the complete series of these novels starting in the spring of 2012. His short stories have appeared in *Ellery Queen, Alfred Hitchcock, Queens Noir, Politics Noir*, and elsewhere. His latest novel, *The Fifth Servant*, was an Indie Notable selection, won the Premio Letterario ADEI-WIZO (Premio Ragazzi category), and was a finalist for the Sue Feder Memorial Historical Mystery Award (Macavity Awards). He teaches writing, literature and other deviant forms of thought at Suffolk Community College on Long Island. Website: www.kennethwishnia.com.

Tim Wohlforth's *The Pink Tarantula*, a short story collection, was published in April 2011 by Perfect Crime Books. His thriller *Harry*, which deals with eco-terrorism and is set in the Northwest, came out in May 2010. Over seventy-five short stories have been published. These appeared in *Hardcore Hardboiled* (Kensington), MWA's *Death Do Us Part*, (Little Brown), *Plots With Guns* (Dennis McMillan) and other anthologies. Two of his stories have made the "Distinguished Mystery Stories" list in Otto Penzler's Best American Mystery series. He is a Pushcart Prize Nominee and received a Certificate of Excellence from the Dana Literary Society.

EDITORS' BIOS

Raised in the desert southwest of Tucson, Arizona, **Andrea Gibbons** moved to Los Angeles at twenty-one to spend ten years organizing around land, development and immigration issues. Leaving L.A., she found a new world of energy, love and rage to pour into her writing, fiction and nonfiction. She is currently melding theory and practice at the London School of Economics, editing for PM Press and the journal *City: Analysis of Urban Trends, Culture, Theory, Policy, Action*, and fighting the good fight against the government cuts in South London.

Son of a mechanic and a librarian, **Gary Phillips** draws on his experiences ranging from labor organizer to delivering dog cages in writing his tales of chicanery and malfeasance. He has been nominated for a Shamus, and has won a Chester Himes and a Brody for his writing. Do visit his website at: www.gdphillips.com.

PM Press was founded at the end of 2007 by a small collection .of folks with decades of publishing, media, and organizing experience. PM Press co-conspirators have published and distributed hundreds of books, pamphlets, CDs, and DVDs. Members of PM have founded enduring book fairs, spearheaded victorious tenant organizing campaigns, and worked closely with bookstores, academic conferences, and even rock bands to deliver political and challenging ideas to all walks of life. We're old enough to know what we're doing and young enough to know what's at stake.

We seek to create radical and stimulating fiction and non-fiction books, pamphlets, t-shirts, visual and audio materials to entertain, educate and inspire you. We aim to distribute these through every available channel with every available technology — whether that means you are seeing anarchist classics at our bookfair stalls; reading our latest vegan cookbook at the café; downloading geeky fiction e-books; or digging new music and timely videos from our website.

PM Press is always on the lookout for talented and skilled volunteers, artists, activists and writers to work with. If you have a great idea for a project or can contribute in some way, please get in touch.

PM Press • PO Box 23912 • Oakland, CA 94623
www.pmpress.org

FRIENDS OF PM PRESS

These are indisputably momentous times — the financial system is melting down globally and the Empire is stumbling. Now more than ever there is a vital need for radical ideas.

In the three years since its founding — and on a mere shoestring — PM Press has risen to the formidable challenge of publishing and distributing knowledge and entertainment for the struggles ahead. With over 100 releases to date, we have published an impressive and stimulating array of literature, art, music, politics, and culture. Using every available medium, we've succeeded in connecting those hungry for ideas and information to those putting them into practice.

Friends of PM allows you to directly help impact, amplify, and revitalize the discourse and actions of radical writers, filmmakers, and artists. It provides us with a stable foundation from which we can build upon our early successes and provides a much-needed subsidy for the materials that can't necessarily pay their own way. You can help make that happen—and receive every new title automatically delivered to your door once a month—by joining as a Friend of PM Press. And, we'll throw in a free T-Shirt when you sign up.

Here are your options:

- **$25 a month** Get all books and pamphlets plus 50% discount on all webstore purchases

- **$25 a month** Get all CDs and DVDs plus 50% discount on all webstore purchases

- **$40 a month** Get all PM Press releases plus 50% discount on all webstore purchases

- **$100 a month Superstar** — Everything plus PM merchandise, free downloads, and 50% discount on all webstore purchases

For those who can't afford $25 or more a month, we're introducing Sustainer Rates at $15, $10 and $5. Sustainers get a free PM Press T-shirt and a 50% discount on all purchases from our website.

Your Visa or Mastercard will be billed once a month, until you tell us to stop. Or until our efforts succeed in bringing the revolution around. Or the financial meltdown of Capital makes plastic redundant. Whichever comes first.

The Jook

Gary Phillips

ISBN: 978-1-60486-040-5

256 pages $15.95

Zelmont Raines has slid a long way since his ability to jook, to out maneuver his opponents on the field, made him a Super Bowl winning wide receiver, earning him lucrative endorsement deals and more than his share of female attention. But Zee hasn't always been good at saying no, so a series of missteps involving drugs, a paternity suit or two, legal entanglements, shaky investments and recurring injuries have virtually sidelined his career.

That is until Los Angeles gets a new pro franchise, the Barons, and Zelmont has one last chance at the big time he dearly misses. Just as it seems he might be getting back in the flow, he's enraptured by Wilma Wells, the leggy and brainy lawyer for the team—who has a ruthless game plan all her own. And it's Zelmont who might get jooked.

"Phillips, author of the acclaimed Ivan Monk series, takes elements of Jim Thompson (the ending), black-exploitation flicks (the profanity-fueled dialogue), and *Penthouse* magazine (the sex is anatomically correct) to create an over-the-top violent caper in which there is no honor, no respect, no love, and plenty of money. Anyone who liked George Pelecanos' *King Suckerman* is going to love this even-grittier take on many of the same themes." — Wes Lukowsky, *Booklist*

"Enough gritty gossip, blistering action and trash talk to make real life L.A. seem comparatively wholesome." — Kirkus Reviews

"Gary Phillips writes tough and gritty parables about life and death on the mean streets—a place where sometimes just surviving is a noble enough cause. His is a voice that should be heard and celebrated. It rings true once again in *The Jook*, a story where all of Phillips' talents are on display." — Michael Connelly, author of the Harry Bosch books

I-5

Summer Brenner

ISBN: 978-1-60486-019-1

256 pages $15.95

A novel of crime, transport, and sex, *I-5* tells the bleak and brutal story of Anya and her journey north from Los Angeles to Oakland on the interstate that bisects the Central Valley of California.

Anya is the victim of a deep deception. Someone has lied to her; and because of this lie, she is kept under lock and key, used by her employer to service men, and indebted for the privilege. In exchange, she lives in the United States and fantasizes on a future American freedom. Or as she remarks to a friend, "Would she rather be fucking a dog . . . or living like a dog?" In Anya's world, it's a reasonable question.

Much of *I-5* transpires on the eponymous interstate. Anya travels with her "manager" and driver from Los Angeles to Oakland. It's a macabre journey: a drop at Denny's, a bad patch of fog, a visit to a "correctional facility," a rendezvous with an organ grinder, and a dramatic entry across Oakland's city limits.

"Insightful, innovative and riveting. After its lyrical beginning inside Anya's head, *I-5* shifts momentum into a rollicking gangsters-on-the-lam tale that is in turns blackly humorous, suspenseful, heartbreaking and always populated by intriguing characters. Anya is a wonderful, believable heroine, her tragic tale told from the inside out, without a shred of sentimental pity, which makes it all the stronger. A twisty, fast-paced ride you won't soon forget." — Denise Hamilton, author of the *L.A. Times* bestseller *The Last Embrace.*

"I'm in awe. *I-5* moves so fast you can barely catch your breath. It's as tough as tires, as real and nasty as road rage, and best of all, it careens at breakneck speed over as many twists and turns as you'll find on The Grapevine. What a ride! *I-5*'s a hard-boiled standout." — Julie Smith, editor of *New Orleans Noir* and author of the Skip Langdon and Talba Wallis crime novel series

"In *I-5*, Summer Brenner deals with the onerous and gruesome subject of sex trafficking calmly and forcefully, making the reader feel the pain of its victims. The trick to forging a successful narrative is always in the details, and *I-5* provides them in abundance. This book bleeds truth — after you finish it, the blood will be on your hands." — Barry Gifford, author, poet and screenwriter

Pike
Benjamin Whitmer
ISBN: 978-1-60486-089-4
224 pages $15.95

Douglas Pike is no longer the murderous hustler he was in his youth, but reforming hasn't made him much kinder. He's just living out his life in his Appalachian hometown, working odd jobs with his partner, Rory, hemming in his demons the best he can. And his best seems just good enough until his estranged daughter overdoses and he takes in his twelve-year-old granddaughter, Wendy.

Just as the two are beginning to forge a relationship, Derrick Kreiger, a dirty Cincinnati cop, starts to take an unhealthy interest in the girl. Pike and Rory head to Cincinnati to learn what they can about Derrick and the death of Pike's daughter, and the three men circle, evenly matched predators in a human wilderness of junkie squats, roadhouse bars and homeless Vietnam vet encampments.

"Without so much as a sideways glance towards gentility, *Pike* is one righteous mutherfucker of a read. I move that we put Whitmer's balls in a vise and keep slowly notching up the torque until he's willing to divulge the secret of how he managed to hit such a perfect stride his first time out of the blocks." — Ward Churchill

"Benjamin Whitmer's *Pike* captures the grime and the rage of my not-so-fair city with disturbing precision. The words don't just tell a story here, they scream, bleed, and burst into flames. *Pike*, like its eponymous main character, is a vicious punisher that doesn't mince words or take prisoners, and no one walks away unscathed. This one's going to haunt me for quite some time." — Nathan Singer

"This is what noir is, what it can be when it stops playing nice — blunt force drama stripped down to the bone, then made to dance across the page." — Stephen Graham Jones

The Chieu Hoi Saloon
Michael Harris
ISBN: 978-1-60486-112-9
376 pages $19.95

It's 1992 and three people's lives are about to collide against the flaming backdrop of the Rodney King riots in Los Angeles. Vietnam vet Harry Hudson is a journalist fleeing his past: the war, a failed marriage, and a fear-ridden childhood. Rootless, he stutters, wrestles with depression, and is aware he's passed the point at which victim becomes victimizer. He explores the city's lowest dives, the only places where he feels at home. He meets Mama Thuy, a Vietnamese woman struggling to run a Navy bar in a tough Long Beach neighborhood, and Kelly Crenshaw, an African-American prostitute whose husband is in prison. They give Harry insight that maybe he can do something to change his fate in a gripping story that is both a character study and thriller.

"Mike Harris' novel has all the brave force and arresting power of Celine and Dostoevsky in its descent into the depths of human anguish and that peculiar gallantry of the moral soul that is caught up in irrational self-punishment at its own failings. Yet Harris manages an amazing and transforming affirmation—the novel floats above all its pain on pure delight in the variety of the human condition. It is a story of those sainted souls who live in bars, retreating from defeat but rendered with such vividness and sensitivity that it is impossible not to care deeply about these figures from our own waking dreams. In an age less obsessed by sentimentality and mawkish 'uplift,' this book would be studied and celebrated and emulated." — John Shannon, author of *The Taking of the Waters* and the Jack Liffey mysteries

"Michael Harris is a realist with a realist's unflinching eye for the hard truths of contemporary times. Yet in *The Chieu Hoi Saloon*, he gives us a hero worth admiring: the passive, overweight, depressed and sex-obsessed Harry Hudson, who in the face of almost overwhelming despair still manages to lead a valorous life of deep faith. In this powerful and compelling first novel, Harris makes roses bloom in the gray underworld of porno shops, bars and brothels by compassionately revealing the yearning loneliness beneath the grime—our universal human loneliness that seeks transcendence through love." — Paula Huston, author of *Daughters of Song* and *The Holy Way*

"*The Chieu Hoi Saloon* concerns one Harry Hudson, the literary bastard son of David Goodis and Dorothy Hughes. Hardcore and unsparing, the story takes you on a ride with Harry in his bucket of a car and pulls you into his subterranean existence in bright daylight and gloomy shadow. One sweet read." — Gary Phillips, author of *The Jook*

The Wrong Thing

Barry Graham

ISBN: 978-1-60486-451-9

136 pages $14.95

They call him the Kid. He's a killer, a dark Latino legend of the Southwest's urban badlands, "a child who terrifies adults." They speak of him in whispers in dive bars near closing time. Some claim to have met him. Others say he doesn't exist, a phantom blamed for every unsolved act of violence, a ghost who haunts every blood-splattered crime scene.

But he is real. He's a young man with a love of cooking and reading, an abiding loneliness and an appetite for violence. He is a cipher, a projection of the dreams and nightmares of people ignored by Phoenix's economic boom . . . and a contemporary outlaw in search of an ordinary life. Love brings him the chance at a new life in the form of Vanjii, a beautiful, damaged woman. But try as he might to abandon the past, his past won't abandon him. The Kid fights back in the only way he knows—and sets in motion a tragic sequence of events that lead him to an explosive conclusion shocking in its brutality and tenderness.

"Graham's words are raw and gritty, and his observations unrelenting and brutally honest." — *Booklist*

"Graham's stories are peopled with the desperate and the mad. A . . . master." — *The Times*

"Vivid, almost lurid, prose . . . a talented author." —*Time Out* (London)

Prudence Couldn't Swim

James Kilgore

ISBN: 978-1-60486-495-3

208 pages $14.95

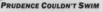

Set in Oakland, CA, white ex-convict Cal Winter returns home one day to find his gorgeous, young, black wife, Prudence, drowned in the swimming pool. Prudence couldn't swim and Cal concludes she didn't go in the water willingly. Though theirs was a marriage of convenience, he takes the murder personally. Along with his prison homie Red Eye, Cal sets out to find out who did Prudence in. His convoluted and often darkly humorous journey takes him deep into the world of the sexual urges of the rich and powerful, and gradually reveals the many layers of his wife's complex identity. While doing so, Cal and Red Eye must confront their own racially charged pasts if the killer is to be caught.

Author James Kilgore has woven together strands of his own quixotic and complicated life—twenty-seven years as a political fugitive, two decades as a teacher in Africa, and six years in prison—into a heady tale of mystery and consequences.

"James Kilgore's writing is a refreshing blend of literary talent and political insight; something sorely missing from much of the fiction penned by writers on the Left. His wit, swift pacing, and dead-on characterization are skillfully woven into an unflinching vision for radical change and social justice. So often we are told that a commitment to radical change and a rollicking good read mix like oil and water. Along comes Kilgore to put that lie to rest!" — Frank B. Wilderson III, author of *Incognegro: A Memoir of Exile and Apartheid*

"James Kilgore is a masterful writer, and as a U.S. activist who has lived in Africa most of his adult life, Kilgore is able to connect us to politics and culture as no other writer. This character-driven mystery promises to find a devoted following." — Roxanne Dunbar-Ortiz, author of *Blood on the Border: A Memoir of the Contra War*.

Calling All Heroes:
A Manual for Taking Power

Paco Ignacio Taibo II

ISBN: 978-1-60486-205-8

128 pages $12.00

The euphoric idealism of grassroots reform and the tragic reality of revolutionary failure are at the center of this speculative novel that opens with a real historical event. On October 2, 1968, 10 days before the Summer Olympics in Mexico, the Mexican government responds to a student demonstration in Tlatelolco by firing into the crowd, killing more than 200 students and civilians and wounding hundreds more. The massacre of Tlatelolco was erased from the official record as easily as authorities washing the blood from the streets, and no one was ever held accountable.

It is two years later and Nestor, a journalist and participant in the fateful events, lies recovering in the hospital from a knife wound. His fevered imagination leads him in the collection of facts and memories of the movement and its assassination in the company of figures from his childhood. Nestor calls on the heroes of his youth — Sherlock Holmes, Doc Holliday, Wyatt Earp and D'Artagnan among them — to join him in launching a new reform movement conceived by his intensely active imagination.

"Taibo's writing is witty, provocative, finely nuanced and well worth the challenge." — *Publishers Weekly*

"I am his number one fan . . . I can always lose myself in one of his novels because of their intelligence and humor. My secret wish is to become one of the characters in his fiction, all of them drawn from the wit and wisdom of popular imagination. Yet make no mistake, Paco Taibo—sociologist and historian—is recovering the political history of Mexico to offer a vital, compelling vision of our reality." — Laura Esquivel, author of *Like Water for Chocolate*

"The real enchantment of Mr. Taibo's storytelling lies in the wild and melancholy tangle of life he sees everywhere." — *New York Times Book Review*

"It doesn't matter what happens. Taibo's novels constitute an absurdist manifesto. No matter how oppressive a government, no matter how strict the limitations of life, we all have our imaginations, our inventiveness, our ability to liven up lonely apartments with a couple of quacking ducks. If you don't have anything left, oppressors can't take anything away." — *Washington Post Book World*

Geek Mafia:
Black Hat Blues

Rick Dakan

ISBN: 978-1-60486-088-7

272 pages $17.95

What do you call 1000 hackers assembled into one hotel for the weekend? A menace to society? Trouble waiting to happen? They call it a computer security conference, or really, a Hacker Con. A place for hackers, security experts, penetration testers, and tech geeks of all stripes to gather and discuss the latest hack, exploits, and gossip. For Paul, Chloe, and their Crew of con artist vigilantes, it's the perfect hunting ground for their most ambitious plans yet.

After a year of undercover recruiting at hacker cons all over the country, Chloe and Paul have assembled a new Crew of elite hackers, driven anarchist activists, and seductive impersonators. Under the cover of one of the Washington DC's biggest and most prestigious hacker events, they're going up against power house lobbyists, black hat hackers, and even the U.S. Congress in order to take down their most challenging, and most deserving target yet. The stakes have never been higher for them, and who knows if their new recruits are up to the immense challenge of undermining "homeland security" for the greater good.

Inspired by years of author Rick Dakan's research in the hacker community, *Geek Mafia: Black Hat Blues* opens a new, self-contained chapter in the techno-thriller series.

"Filled with charming geek humor, thoroughly likable characters, and a relentless plot . . ." — Cory Doctorow, co-editor of *BoingBoing*, on the Geek Mafia books"

"A first rate example of geek fiction getting it right. *Black Hat Blues* gives new meaning to the term 'hacker con'—you won't want to put it down." — Heidi Potter, Shmoocon organizer

"Rick Dakan is one of the few fiction authors working today who tries to understand hacker culture not as a sideshow or scare tactic, but as a way of living a life. His words ring with honest research." — Jason Scott, director of *BBS: The Documentary*

The Lucky Strike
Kim Stanley Robinson
ISBN: 978-1-60486-085-6
128 pages $12.00

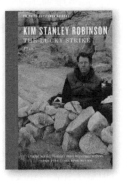

Combining dazzling speculation with a profoundly humanist vision, Kim Stanley Robinson is known as not only the most literary but also the most progressive (read "radical") of today's top rank SF authors. His bestselling Mars Trilogy tells the epic story of the future colonization of the red planet, and the revolution that inevitably follows. The Years of Rice and Salt is based on a devastatingly simple idea: If the medieval plague had wiped out all of Europe, what would our world look like today? His latest novel, *Galileo's Dream*, is a stunning combination of historical drama and far-flung space opera, in which the ten dimensions of the universe itself are rewoven to ensnare history's most notorious torturers.

The Lucky Strike, the classic and controversial story Robinson has chosen for PM's new Outspoken Authors series, begins on a lonely Pacific island, where a crew of untested men are about to take off in an untried aircraft with a deadly payload that will change our world forever. Until something goes wonderfully wrong . . .

Plus: A Sensitive Dependence on Initial Conditions, in which Robinson dramatically deconstructs "alternate history" to explore what might have been if things had gone differently over Hiroshima that day. As with all Outspoken Author books, there is a deep interview and autobiography: at length, in-depth, no-holds-barred and all-bets off: an extended tour though the mind and work, the history and politics of our Outspoken Author. Surprises are promised.

"The foremost writer of literary utopias." — *Time*

"The best nature writer in the U.S. today also happens to write science fiction." — The Ends of the Earth

"It's no coincidence that one of our most visionary science fiction writers is also a profoundly good nature writer." — *Los Angeles Times*

"If I had to choose one writer whose work will set the standard for science fiction in the future, it would be Kim Stanley Robinson." — *The New York Times*

Byzantium Endures:
The First Volume of the
Colonel Pyat Quartet

Michael Moorcock

with an introduction by Alan Wall

ISBN: 978-1-60486-491-5

400 pages $22.00

Meet Maxim Arturovitch Pyatnitski, also known as Pyat. Tsarist rebel, Nazi thug, continental conman, and reactionary counterspy: the dark and dangerous anti-hero of Michael Moorcock's most controversial work.

Published in 1981 to great critical acclaim—then condemned to the shadows and unavailable in the U.S. for thirty years—*Byzantium Endures*, the first of the Pyat Quartet, is not a book for the faint-hearted. It's the story of a cocaine addict, sexual adventurer, and obsessive anti-Semite whose epic journey from Leningrad to London connects him with scoundrels and heroes from Trotsky to Makhno, and whose career echoes that of the 20th century's descent into Fascism and total war.

This is Moorcock at his audacious, iconoclastic best: a grand sweeping overview of the events of the last century, as revealed in the secret journals of modern literature's most proudly unredeemable outlaw. This authoritative U.S. edition presents the author's final cut, restoring previously forbidden passages and deleted scenes.

"What is extraordinary about this novel . . . is the largeness of the design. Moorcock has the bravura of a nineteenth-century novelist: he takes risks, he uses fiction as if it were a divining rod for the age's most significant concerns. Here, in *Byzantium Endures*, he has taken possession of the early twentieth century, of a strange, dead civilization and recast them in a form which is highly charged without ceasing to be credible." — Peter Ackroyd, *Sunday Times*

"A tour de force, and an extraordinary one. Mr. Moorcock has created in Pyatnitski a wholly sympathetic and highly complicated rogue . . . There is much vigorous action here, along with a depth and an intellectuality, and humor and color and wit as well."— *The New Yorker*

"Clearly the foundation on which a gigantic literary edifice will, in due course, be erected. While others build fictional molehills, Mr. Moorcock makes plans for great shimmering pyramids. But the footings of this particular edifice are intriguing and audacious enough to leave one hungry for more." — John Naughton, *Listener*